HUNGRY GHOST

A HOWARD MOON DEER MYSTERY

Books by Robert Westbrook

Howard Moon Deer Mysteries
Ghost Dancer
Warrior Circle
Red Moon
Ancient Enemy
Turquoise Lady
Blue Moon
Hungry Ghost

Coming Soon!
Walking Rain
A Howard Moon Deer Mystery

An Almost Perfect Ending
A Torch Singer Trilogy

The Torch Singer Trilogy
An Overnight Sensation
The Saint of Make-Believe

Left-Handed Policeman *series*
The Left-Handed Policeman
Nostalgia Kills
Lady Left

Other Books
Intimate Lies:
F. Scott Fitzgerald and Sheilah Graham – Her Son's Story
Journey Behind the Iron Curtain
The Magic Garden of Stanley Sweetheart

HUNGRY GHOST

A HOWARD MOON DEER MYSTERY

Robert Westbrook

SPEAKING VOLUMES, LLC
NAPLES, FLORIDA
2021

Hungry Ghost

ISBN 978-1-64540-411-8

For Gail, always, whose love, laughter,
and wise editorial help makes these books possible.

This is a work of fiction. There is no town in northern New Mexico called San Geronimo, and I have altered geography to suit my narrative needs. Any similarity in these pages to actual people, places, or events is entirely coincidental.

Prologue

November, 1970

They took away his name.

They took away his language.

They sent him to an Indian School in New Mexico far from home. They called him Ralph White. They said from now on he was supposed to be a White Man. But he couldn't even pronounce the name Ralph. He had a small speech impediment and it came out "Waph."

He was 12-years-old, small for his age, delicately built, still on the childhood side of puberty.

At the Indian School, he lived in fear. The teachers punished him because he was dreamy and paid little attention in class. The older boys picked on him because he was shy and small and he wasn't good at baseball. Often at night he cried himself to sleep. Sometimes he wet his bed and he was punished for this as well.

He had arrived here at the age of ten with his big sister, who was two years older. This might have been a comfort, to have his sister nearby, but the school had been founded by Christian missionaries and the boys and girls were kept strictly apart. At night, the girls were locked inside their dormitory so that they couldn't backslide into savagery and sneak out to mingle with the boys. The mission of the school was expressed in a famous motto that was hung in a frame in the headmaster's office: KILL THE INDIAN, SAVE THE MAN.

Despite his small size and speech impediment, the boy wasn't stupid. He knew he wasn't Ralph White, the name the White Man had given him. But beyond that, all he knew about himself was that he was the most unhappy creature who ever walked the earth. He was The Boy with No Name.

When he was twelve, a Navajo who worked in the kitchen slipped him a colored 30-page pamphlet. Its cover was torn, it had been passed around many times. It had been published by a group that called itself IOAT, Indians of All Tribes, and it told a story that was so fantastical it was hard to believe. With photographs and text, it told how in 1969, 89 Native Americans and a handful of non-Indian supporters had occupied a small island in California called Alcatraz, once a federal prison. The occupiers claimed that under the Treaty of Fort Laramie between the U.S. and the Lakota tribe, "all retired, abandoned, or out-of-use federal land" must be returned to the Indians who once occupied it.

Alcatraz prison fit this description to a T. It had been closed and abandoned in 1963, so Indians of All Tribes claimed the island for themselves. It was all perfectly legal, though the Nixon administration—which had great regard for the law—did not agree.

The boy didn't understand everything the pamphlet said, in fact he understood very little. But what he did understand excited him, how Indians of All Tribes had taken over Alcatraz Island in San Francisco Bay. He loved the photographs of teepees on the island bluff overlooking blue water with the great white city in the distance.

He thought it very funny, how they had offered to sell it back to the U.S. government for 47 cents per acre, which came to $9.40 for the entire island. 47 cents per acre was the price the U.S. had paid the Sioux for the land they had taken in the Great Plains, so this seemed a reasonable offer. Nevertheless, the Nixon administration refused. Sometimes he daydreamed that he was on the island, too, the youngest chief ever chosen to lead Indians of All Tribes, the great gathering of his people. In his fantasy, he dreamed he had power and nobody would ever again be able to bully or abuse him.

But then one day he was caught reading the IOAT pamphlet.

"Ralph! What is that?" a master demanded, coming into the bathroom where he was sitting on the toilet after the 8:30 PM lights out, hoping to be alone. "Are you looking at dirty pictures? Are you committing a sin?"

The master snatched the pamphlet and his eyes narrowed in anger when he saw what it was. As far as he was concerned, this was far worse than dirty pictures. This was Communism!

The master took the boy by the ear and led him across the compound to the headmaster's office.

The headmaster was a very large man with glasses, more than twice the size of the boy. He was dressed in khaki pants and a plaid shirt that was enormous. To the boy, he looked like an elephant without a trunk.

"I see," said the headmaster as he browsed through the brochure. He sat behind a huge desk in a huge chair as the boy stood before him. "Where did you get this filth?"

The Boy with No Name didn't answer.

"Ralph, I'm going to ask you again. Where did you get these lies?"

Still, the boy refused to answer.

The headmaster sighed. "You know, Ralph, it's very disturbing to find you reading such trash. Your Father in Washington has given you a tremendous opportunity to enjoy the benefits of civilization. He's paying for your education so that you can become a useful American. When you leave here, you'll be able to live in a nice home with a television and a refrigerator. Now, I'm going to ask you again. Who gave you this pamphlet?"

But still the boy refused to answer.

The headmaster stood from behind his huge desk.

"I'm going to have to punish you. You've been a bad boy and I'm going to give you a good whipping, and then you're never going to do anything this bad again. Do you understand me?"

The boy did understand and he was terrified. Nevertheless, he stood without flinching, determined to be brave like the Indians who had taken over Alcatraz Island where a prison once stood.

"Pull down your pants," said the man. "Bend over the desk."

The boy didn't cry. He pulled down his pants, he bent over the desk.

The headmaster locked the door. He came up behind the boy with a riding whip.

SMACK! The whip slashed against his bare buttocks. The whip came down again and again. The pain was terrible, a hot agony that caused his eyes to tear. He gasped each time the whip slashed against his skin, but still he refused to cry.

The headmaster kept whipping him, caught up in a frenzy.

And then something else happened, something worse. The headmaster pulled down his own pants and came at him from behind with something huge and hard that penetrated his very being.

At first, the boy didn't know what was being done to him because it seemed so strange. It was like a piston piercing his rear end, in and out, coming at him with remorseless power.

The pain was unbearable and now the boy did cry. He screamed in agony.

"Shut up, you bad boy!" said the man. His huge hand came down on the back of the boy's head, pushing his face hard into the desk so that the boy could barely breathe.

It went on for a long time, pain without end. It felt like his body was being torn apart.

Until at last there came a pulsing throb from the thing that was inside of him and he felt a hot liquid shooting up into his innards. It was the final desecration.

The headmaster pulled up his pants. He was breathing hard. "You see what you made me do!" he said. "You sinful boy!"

Blood ran down his leg. The headmaster put his mouth close to the boy's ear. His breath was hot and smelled of whiskey and meat.

"If you tell anyone about this, no one will believe you. And I will make you regret it, I swear!"

At last, he let the boy go.

***

Boy with No Name spent three days in the infirmary. The school nurse was a nun. She treated him in silence and never once asked what had happened to him.

When the boy could walk again, he returned to his dormitory but he couldn't sleep. He stayed awake full of hatred, thinking of what he would do. Thoughts of revenge swirled in his mind, night after night.

Two weeks after he had been raped, the boy convinced his older sister, who worked in the kitchen, to steal a knife for him. He told her that he wanted it to protect himself from the boys who were tormenting him. But that wasn't what he had in mind.

On a dark night, when the moon was void and everyone was asleep, he crept out of his dorm and crossed the playing field to the headmaster's house on the far side of the compound, barely making a sound.

The front door wasn't locked. The boy slipped inside and found the bedroom where the headmaster was sleeping, snoring loudly. The headmaster was a bachelor and he was alone.

"Headmaster, oh, headmaster!" whispered the boy.

The snoring stopped. The headmaster opened his eyes. His look of incomprehension quickly changed to terror.

The boy was quick. He grabbed the large man by his hair and held him fast while he cut his throat. The cut made a thin line that filled with blood, at first only a hint of red, but then the blood gushed out. The headmaster thrashed on the bed with a wet, gurgling sound coming from his throat. It took only a few moments before he was still.

The boy used the tip of the knife to cut a line in a circle around the top of the headmaster's head. He grabbed the tuft of hair and pulled the scalp free.

He carried the scalp in his belt as he left the house and climbed over the adobe wall to the open desert on the other side. It was a cold, clear November night and the moon was almost full.

He ran into the desert, through the sagebrush, up and over the uneven ground. The moon made everything silvery and bright.

At last he stopped, out of breath, and raised his arms to the night.

"I am Boy Who Fights Back!" he cried exultantly to the moon.

He had found his true name at last.

Chapter One

"Moon Deer!"

A voice whispered his name in the dark. The voice was half-familiar but he couldn't place it. It came from the depths of the forest where no voice should be.

It was after midnight on a cold November night and Howie had believed himself to be alone. He had left his car at the edge of his land and was walking up the narrow trail through the woods to his home. His land abutted the national forest and his nearest neighbor was a half mile away. At this time of night, there shouldn't be a half-familiar voice calling his name.

"Moon Deer, it's me!"

He stopped and saw a ghostly figure standing deep in the shadow of the trees. Howie wasn't entirely sober. He'd been celebrating with Jack and Emma, a blow-out dinner at the Blue Mesa Café complete with two good bottles of wine, wrapping up a long, difficult case that they were glad to see the end of.

The woods were lit softly in silver light from the waning moon. Howie wished he had a weapon. A knife. A rock. A gun. When you were a private detective there were people you had crossed that you didn't want to meet late at night in a lonely place.

"Don't you know me?" said the voice.

The figure stepped from the shadows of the forest and came closer. It was a man in dark clothing, barely visible in the moonlight.

"Nick?" Howie said after a moment, not really sure.

"*C'est moi, amigo*," he answered. "Aren't you going to invite me inside?"

Howie felt his shoulders relax, but only slightly. Nicolas Stanton had been his roommate at Dartmouth and there was a long history between them. It had been at least ten years since they had met last.

"What are you doing here, Nick?" Howie asked.

"That's not a friendly way to greet an old pal. Aren't you pleased to see me?"

"Are you on the run?"

"Sure, just like old times. The Feds don't give up just because a few years pass. They have one-track minds."

"That's because you're on their most wanted list, Nick."

"Look, Moon Deer, I'm hungry, I'm cold, I haven't slept for two days. I could use a warm place to put up my feet. What do you say?"

What could he say? Nicolas Stanton had once been Howie's best friend and it was hard to turn him away.

"Well," Howie said reluctantly, "you'd better come in."

***

Howie made a pot of coffee and a turkey sandwich with whole wheat bread, tomato, pickle, red onion, Jarlsberg cheese, no mayo. Howie had given up mayonnaise as part of his new regime for healthy living, so Nick wasn't going to get it either.

Nick didn't seem to mind. Howie sat back and watched his old roommate devour the sandwich with greedy concentration. He didn't bother to talk.

"You have anything else in that fridge of yours?" Nick asked when the sandwich was gone.

"There are two slices of pizza left over from yesterday's dinner."

"I'll take them."

Howie stood and found the pizza slices wrapped in aluminum foil in his small refrigerator. "I can heat them for you."

"Don't bother. Cold pizza's fine . . . Jesus, what's on these things?" he asked when Howie set the two slices in front of him on a plate.

"Shiitake mushrooms, sun-dried tomatoes, smoked duck, capers, provolone cheese."

"You're kidding!"

"It's from Michelangelo's, a new Italian place. Pizza's been evolving, Nick. To open a restaurant these days, you've got to astonish modern taste buds with unexpected thrills."

"Decadence, you mean!" said Nick. "Half the planet is starving while the privileged few pamper themselves with excess!"

"I don't have any gruel, Nick. But I can get you a few crusts of stale bread if you like."

Nick took a huge bite of pizza and shook his head. "Got any beer to wash this down?"

Howie stood and opened a bottle from the fridge.

Nick laughed when he read the label. "Third Eye Organic Stout . . . Brewed mindfully in San Geronimo, New Mexico. For chrissake, Howie, what happened to the shy Indian kid I knew fresh off the rez?"

"He grew up, Nick. How about you?"

"Grow up? Naw! I just got old and weary."

Nick Stanton, in fact, had aged considerably in the ten years since Howie had seen him last. His face was gaunt, his cheeks hollow, his dark blond hair long and gritty. He had always been handsome, and he was handsome still. But now it was the half-starved poetic dying-in-the-garret kind of handsome. His face was sharp and wan where once it had been pleasant and soft.

He was dressed in shapeless dark brown corduroy pants that were smudged with dirt. He wore a heavy black turtleneck sweater and a grey ski parka that had seen better days. His boots looked as though they had walked a thousand miles. His face and hands were deeply tanned, but it wasn't the sort of tan you got on the beach in Florida. It was an outdoor tan from living rough.

It was hard to believe this was the same Nicolas Stanton he had known at Dartmouth, a rich kid from one of the oldest families in New Mexico.

The Stantons went back to the Territorial days before New Mexico was a state. Nick's grandfather had been Adam Stanton, the Bureau of Indian Affairs Commissioner in Washington, D.C. His father was U.S. Senator Harlan Stanton, now retired, a pillar of the conservative wing of the Republican party. You wouldn't imagine any of this by looking at Nick now.

"Summing me up, are you?" Nick asked, looking up from his empty plate.

"Looks like you've had a few adventures since I saw you last."

Nick laughed soundlessly. "Life is an adventure, Howie. You've changed, too, my friend. You've gained weight."

Howie could only shrug. It was true, he liked food too much. He was a large man with a round, moonish face and broad shoulders. His hair was black and he wore it in a ponytail that fell halfway down his back. At least his stomach was flat and most of his bulk was muscle.

"Aren't you going to have a beer with me?" Nick asked.

Howie shook his head. "I had too much to drink earlier."

When he was finished eating, Nick took out a pouch of Drum tobacco from his coat and rolled a cigarette. Howie didn't smoke these days and normally he didn't allow anyone to smoke in his pod. But that seemed picky tonight so he let it go.

He watched as Nick lit his cigarette with a Zippo lighter and exhaled a leisurely cloud of smoke. He made a show of looking around at

Howie's unusual home, top to bottom. It wasn't standard housing. Howie had put his money into the land, ten wooded acres in the foothills of the Sangre de Cristo mountains, forty minutes from town. He hadn't had much money left over, so instead of putting up a real house, he had bought a kit.

"What do you call this high-tech wigwam of yours?" Nick asked.

"It's an eco pod. It was designed by two architects I met in Berlin. I bought it as a kit and had it shipped."

"I'm surprised at you, Moon Deer. I've always thought of you as more traditional."

"There's plenty of experimental architecture happening in New Mexico, Nick. More and more people are living off the grid in structures like this."

"Yuppies with money. Building themselves their little paradise!"

Howie's girlfriend, Claire, liked to describe his eco pod as a large metallic egg standing on four chicken legs. Howie saw it more as a Mars lander that had set down on his ten acres.

The pod was small, but it had all the essentials cleverly built in, including a shower that was the size of a telephone booth. The German architects had found ways to utilize nearly every cubic inch of space. The kit had cost Howie over a hundred thousand dollars and somehow another thirty thousand had gone into it before it was entirely set up. Still, that was a deal when you considered the average price of a home in San Geronimo had crept up to $325,000.

"I have solar power, a composting toilet, a satellite connection to the Internet, I'm totally self-contained," Howie said. "Plus, you can disassemble the pod in a day and move it someplace else."

"And you think this makes you some kind of eco warrior?"

Howie shrugged. Nick was the eco warrior. That's why he was on the run. He had been one of the founders of Earth Strikes Back, ESB, one of the environmental groups that had appeared at the end of the last century. What began modestly with peaceful sit-ins, blocking bulldozers from entering building sites, had become gradually more radical until ESP had set fire to a group of expensive townhouses that were being built in sensitive wetlands in northern California. Two security guards had died in the blaze and Nick and the remaining members of his group had been forced underground. Now, ten years later, all the others had been captured. Only Nicolas Stanton was still at large.

"So, what can I do for you?" Howie asked. "You didn't look me up to talk about architecture. Are you looking for a place to hide? Do you need money?"

Nick grinned. "Trying to get rid of me?"

Howie shook his head. "Look, I'm tired. I've had a long day. But I'll help you if I can."

"For old time's sake?"

"Nick, I'm not going to judge you. We were good friends once and I'll always remember that. But I don't like what you did. Killing those security guards just made everything worse."

"It was an accident, Howie. You know that. I didn't mean for anyone to die."

Howie sighed. "Well, you sure gave the oil companies a gift! You gave environmentalism a bad name."

"And you're in the Martin Luther King camp, are you? Peaceful sit-ins. Holding hands and singing 'We Shall Overcome.' But that approach doesn't change anything, Howie. The people who run things only laugh at you!"

Howie had a good many thoughts about these issues, but not at two o'clock in the morning after a blowout dinner with Jack and Emma.

"What can I do for you, Nick?" he asked again.

"Well, I can use a place to sleep tonight. And money. How much cash do you have on you?"

"A few hundred dollars. I can get more in the morning, if you'd like."

"No, a few hundred bucks will see me through. I don't have time to stick around. But that's not why I'm here. I want you to do something for me."

Howie waited without enthusiasm to learn what this something was. "What?" he said after a moment.

"I want you to get a message to my sister."

"Grace?" He said the name reluctantly. It sent a tremor through his body, head to toe.

"You remember my sister Grace, Howie."

He did. He remembered Nick's sister, Grace.

***

Howie let the name wash over him. Grace Stanton. He was surprised how little it affected him. No trumpets sounded, his pulse didn't race, the sky didn't come crashing down. He remained pretty much normal.

"Here's the deal," Nick explained. "My grandfather left me some money in a trust fund and I'm trying to get my hands on it."

"Your grandfather the Indian Commissioner? The one you despised?"

"Yes, Howie. The one whose manifest destiny was to be a jerk. But he was wealthy. And some of that wealth is now mine."

"I thought you didn't like money, Nick."

"I don't. I hate the stuff. But I need it anyway. Are you going to listen or what?"

"I'm listening."

"Okay. When Adam Stanton died back in the eighties, he left all his money to his grandchildren—me, Grace, and my brother, Justin. He put it in a trust for us. He made my parents joint executors of the trust with the power to decide when each of us grandkids would receive our share. We had to prove ourselves worthy, you see. We had to show we were mature enough to be responsible for 'great wealth,' as he put it in his will. Unfortunately, he left it up to my parents to decide when this magic moment arrived. Which in effect, means my father, since my mother always does what Dad says.

"Well, you can imagine how this has played out. My asshole brother, Justin, got his share when he was twenty-five—he was mature by then, you see. Like ripe cheese. And Grace will get her share when she's forty."

"Grace is what . . . thirty-six now?" Howie said in wonderment. In his memory, she remained forever twenty-one years old. "Why does she have to wait that long?"

"She's thirty-eight, Howie. The reason she has to wait until forty is she's a girl. In my father's universe, girls are flighty creatures who need to be guided by big strong men. But at least she'll get her dough eventually. I'm not so sure about me."

"Because you're on the FBI's wanted list, I imagine."

"Right. And with my father in charge of that trust, I'm never going to see a penny. He hasn't even said my name aloud for ten years. He's crossed my name off the family Bible. Literally. I kid you not."

"How much money are you talking about?"

"Well, the trust was just over three million when grandpa died in '89. But it's grown over the years. I figure today, the way the stock market has been going, there's maybe $13 million with my name on it. And I need it, Howie. I need it bad. It's my money and he doesn't have any right to keep it from me just because he doesn't like what I've done."

"May I ask what you're planning to do with all that dough?"

Nick laughed. "Howie, I've been on the run for ten long years, living rough, always looking over my shoulder. I can't do it anymore. I'm tired. I'm used up."

"And money will help?"

"You bet! With that kind of bread, I'll be able to buy myself a new identity. A passport, a new face—I'll be able to get myself to some friendly South Pacific island, maybe buy myself a nice little boat that I can charter out. I'll be able to start over again."

Howie shook his head.

"Listen to me, Howie. I'm sorry for what happened. All I wanted was to stop those townhouses from getting built. I didn't mean for those guards to die. But I've paid for it, believe me. All I'm asking is for you to deliver a letter to Grace. I can't get near her, but you can. We were close once, Grace and me. Tell her you've seen me and I'm desperate. She's the only person I know who might be able to convince Dad to relent. All I'm asking is you give her my letter and let her decide. Okay? Will you do that?"

"That's it? Deliver a letter to Grace?"

"That's it," Nick said. His eyes shone with sincerity. "I swear to God!"

***

They talked for another hour, as Nick polished off what remained of Howie's four-pack of Third Eye Stout. Mindfully brewed in San Geronimo, New Mexico, it was so expensive it didn't come in the usual six-pack quantities. At some point around three in the morning, Howie agreed to take a message to Nick's sister, Grace. He wasn't happy about it, but it was hard to turn down a request from his best friend at college who was on the run from the law.

When the talk ran out, he made up a futon for Nick on his floor, climbed up wearily into his sleeping loft, and fell into an uneasy sleep. When he woke in the morning, he found his old roommate gone.

He didn't see the sealed white envelope on his kitchen table until after he had made himself a pot of coffee. His over-indulged cat, Orange, had been stretched out on the envelope, hiding it from view. He moved her gently, careful not to ruffle her dignity. The name Grace Stanton was written on the front with an address in Santa Fe.

Howie regarded the envelope as though it were a bomb that might explode.

Santa Fe! He'd had no idea that Grace was so nearby, an hour and a half from San Geronimo by car. The last he had heard, she was living in Spain, having herself an arty time in Barcelona. But that was ten years ago and he hadn't actually seen her for more years than that. Thirteen years by his reckoning. There had come a time when Howie had deliberately lost touch with the Stantons.

It was a cold November morning, 27 degrees according to the screen on the wall of his computer nook, but he bundled up and took his coffee outside. He sat on the bench by the withered remains of his vegetable garden and wondered what he was going to do.

He didn't owe Nick anything, not really. It was a long time now since they had been friends. He had done his best, giving him a place to sleep for the night, as well as $237 in cash and a meal. There was no reason he absolutely had to go see Grace Stanton. He could put a stamp on the envelope and put it in the mail.

Last night before leaving the Blue Moon Café, he and Jack had agreed that they would take the day off. Ruth, the agency's secretary, would come in today to type up some invoices and notes connected to the case they had just wrapped up, but other than that, the agency was closed. There was no need for Howie to go into town.

He could stay home, read a book, watch a movie, have a leisurely lunch, maybe a nice siesta.

Or he could drive to Santa Fe and see Grace Stanton.

You never really get over your first affair, that was the problem. You grow up, move on, but something lingers, some part of yourself that will always remember that first plunge into adulthood.

Howie played his options back and forth, a kind of mental ping-pong. He was a licensed private investigator and he knew the law. The phrase *aiding and abetting a fugitive* flickered through his mind. But that had little power compared to the pull of nostalgia.

He took a shower, put on his cleanest jeans, and set out for Santa Fe to revisit the past.

Chapter Two

The address on the envelope led Howie to a wealthy residential neighborhood, a street of houses that were partially hidden behind high adobe walls on a few acres of land.

Grace Stanton had been born rich, and she had made more money still due to the fact that she had become a bestselling author. Writing was her most recent accomplishment, added to all her other accomplishments. Wealth, talent, beauty, Grace had it all.

The novels she wrote belonged to a category Howie thought of as Chick Lit Thrillers. All the titles had "the girl who" in them. *The Girl Who Said No, The Girl Who Laughed Last, The Girl Who Ran Away.* The protagonists were attractive upper middle-class women, generally married to successful men who had unpleasant secrets that the women only discovered once the honeymoon was over. Much of the narrative consisted of shopping for clothes, dieting, having sex, going to yoga classes, and being stalked by psychopathic killers.

They were awful books, really. Shallow. Formulaic. Nevertheless, Howie had read every one of them compulsively. According to the covers, they had sold millions of copies worldwide. How Grace had managed this, he couldn't say. She had done very well for herself. But that had been in her stars from the start. *The Girl Who Had Everything.*

Driving south from San Geronimo, Howie hadn't considered the possibility that she might not be home. He had hurried here on the wings of memory, and memory didn't allow for an old lover not being home. He parked outside the electric gate on the driveway that led to her house. Peering through the decorative wrought-iron bars, he could see a modern two-story Southwestern home that was tastefully built of adobe, natural wood, and large sections of glass. The house was surrounded by huge old cottonwood trees that were bare of leaves this time of year, as well as a number of large evergreens. He could just make out a tennis court and the edge of a swimming pool, empty now of water. A dark green Bentley stood in the parking area in front of the house.

A Bentley!

Howie sat in his beat-up Subaru with the window down staring at the squawk box at the side of the gate. Now that he was here, he was tempted to sneak off without pressing the buzzer. But there was a security camera pointed his way from the far side of the wall and he didn't want to look indecisive if someone was watching. He reached out his window and pressed the buzzer.

"Yes?" said a voice. It was a woman with a Spanish accent. A maid, he presumed.

"Hello, my name is Howard Moon Deer and I'm here to see Grace Stanton. I'm an old friend," he added optimistically.

"Is Ms. Stanton expecting you?"

"No, she's not," Howie admitted. "Would you tell her I have a message for her from her brother."

In fact, there were two Stanton brothers: Justin, the white sheep of the flock, and Nicolas, the black. Howie thought it best for the moment to keep it vague, which brother his message was from.

"If you will wait, please."

Howie smiled inanely at the security camera. A few minutes passed and then a man's voice came through the small speaker.

"Hey, you're here to see Grace? She's not here right now. This is Lorenzo—can I help you?"

Lorenzo? Her boyfriend, perhaps? The name was slithery. It slipped off the tongue. Howie remained calm.

"I'm Howard Moon Deer, an old friend," he said. "Her brother gave me a message for her, so I thought I'd stop by. I should have called first."

"Howard Moon Deer? Good God, *the* Howie Moon Deer?"

"Well—"

"Let me find the damn buzzer . . . oh, here it is . . . look, drive on in. I'm just on my way out, but we can go to the book party together. We'll surprise her!"

Howie knew nothing about a book party, and still less about a surprise. But the wrought-iron gate swung open with a soft electric whirr and there was nothing for him to do but drive in and see what adventures awaited in Graceland. He passed the tennis court on his left, the swimming pool on his right. He parked by the Bentley.

A jaunty, good-looking man in his late thirties came bouncing out from the front door. He had dark, wavy hair that was slightly long, but not overly so. He radiated health and good humor. He wore tan pants, a dark blue polo shirt, and a dark blue blazer with gold buttons. There was a pair of sunglasses riding on the top of his head. His teeth were white and flashed sharkishly as he came forward to Howie's ancient Subaru.

"Howard Moon Deer!" he said with amazement. "I've heard so much about you, I feel like I know you!"

"You've heard—"

"Grace talks about you all the time! My God, her wild college days at Smith, you and Nicolas at Dartmouth, how you'd all zip down for weekends to the place in Manhattan and talk and talk all night long. She's going to be so glad to see you! And she needs that right now, actually. Cheering up, I mean. But look, we're going to be late if we don't hurry. So why don't you leave your wheels here and we'll go in my jalopy . . . don't worry about locking up. Anybody climbs over the wall and gets past the broken glass, the neighborhood patrol will fucking shoot 'em!"

Lorenzo was a lot to take in all at once. It was like looking directly at the sun, you needed to turn away. Howie stepped out of his car and followed Lorenzo to the Bentley, which wasn't his idea of a jalopy. It was a vintage Bentley, mid-1950s, perfectly restored, English Racing Green, a color as rich as money.

"Nice car," Howie managed as he slipped into the creamy leather passenger seat.

"Oh, this old thing? I picked it up cheap back in '08 from a hedge fund trader who'd lost everything in the crash. Poor guy, even his wife left him. They're ecological, you know."

"Wives?"

Lorenzo laughed. "No, no—these old Bentleys. They run forever. Something goes wrong, they'll send a guy from England with the part to wherever you are in the world. That's what they claim, anyway. I've never had to try it."

Howie took a deep breath and wished he was home with his cat.

"So, Grace has a new book out?" he asked when Lorenzo stopped talking for a fraction of a second.

"Grace? A new book? No, what gives you that idea?"

"You said something about a book party. I assumed—"

"Oh, no, it's not *her* book." He lowered his voice to a stage whisper. "She has writer's block, but don't tell anyone. She hasn't written a sentence in months. Not a word! I keep telling her, 'Don't push against the river, babe. We'll take a trip to Mexico, or something. It'll come back to you sooner or later, just you wait and see.' But she won't listen. She wants to stay here and stare at her screen and suffer."

"So, the book signing—"

"No, this shindig is for the old man. Her father. It's his book."

"Senator Stanton has written a book?"

"Yup. *The Right Way*, that's what he calls it. It's part memoir and part bitching at all the things he hates that are happening in America. How we can make everything right if we'll only listen to him."

"So, what kind of work do you do, Lorenzo?" Howie asked in order to change the subject.

"Work?" Lorenzo laughed merrily at the thought. "If I may be politically incorrect, my father worked so I don't need to. Not that I'm a wastrel. I'm an attractive ornament on life's Christmas tree. I support the arts, I always pick up the check in restaurants, I'm decent company, and I've never harmed a soul."

Howie forced a smile.

"You know something, Howie?" Lorenzo continued. "It's actually very opportune that you showed up today. Serendipitous, I'd say. Grace has been in a dumpy mood the last few weeks. You're just what she needs to be herself again."

"Well, I don't know about that. I knew Grace a long time ago."

"Seriously, Moon Deer, she's going to eat you up!"

That's what Howie was afraid of.

***

Like many cities, Santa Fe had once possessed bookstores. Borders, Barnes and Noble, all sorts of places where people roamed and browsed and plucked books from actual shelves.

But that was in another universe, far away and long ago.

Today in Santa Fe, Howie knew only one small independent store that still sold new books, and several that dealt with books that were used. Salvation Army was always good if you were looking for a tattered copy of Reader's Digest or a thriller that was a decade old. So Howie couldn't imagine where Senator Stanton's signing for *The Right Way* was going to be held. He was surprised when Lorenzo approached the main entrance of the La Fonda Hotel on the downtown Plaza.

"The signing is at the La Fonda?"

"In one of the banquet rooms. Uh-oh, look over there!"

Lorenzo nodded toward the Plaza across the street where a dozen protesters were holding signs on wooden sticks, bobbing them up and down for maximum visibility. PROTECT A WOMAN'S RIGHT TO CHOOSE! said one sign. EQUAL RIGHTS FOR WOMEN, proclaimed another. In his twelve years as a New Mexico senator, Harlan Stanton had been a vocal anti-abortion crusader and had often spoken in opposition to the Equal Rights Amendment.

The protesters were of various ages, from young to elderly. A mad-looking woman with long grey hair, in a jacket covered with political slogans, waved a sign that said THE MEEK ARE READY FOR THEIR INHERITANCE! Jesus would have been pleased, except for the fact that she didn't look even slightly meek. She looked angry as hell.

"I was hoping the book party would get by under the radar," Lorenzo said thoughtfully looking at the gathering. "You'd think they'd leave him alone after the drubbing he got in the last election. Well, the old bastard deserves it, I suppose. Want a snort?"

Lorenzo produced a small silver vial from his coat pocket. "Time to put on our happy-happy party faces, don't you think?"

"Not for me," Howie told him. "I'll leave my happy-happy face for another occasion."

He watched as Lorenzo bent over below the dashboard and deftly used a tiny silver spoon to sniff cocaine from the vial, one snort to each nostril. He was barely finished when the valet parking attendant appeared at the Bentley's window to take the car. Lorenzo's behavior seemed risky to Howie, even in a trendy place like Santa Fe. But he was certainly happy. He stepped from the car with a new bounce to his step, a man with movie star good looks in the best of all possible worlds. Howie followed feeling drab and dowdy.

The La Fonda was a historic hotel that gave visitors the full Southwest treatment, a multistory adobe hacienda with round viga stumps protruding from the walls. You could buy turquoise jewelry in the lobby, sip a Margarita at the bar, eat an enchilada in the restaurant, and know with certainty that you were in the Land of Enchantment.

The book party was in full swing in the La Terraza Room when Howie and Lorenzo arrived. There were at least a hundred people mingling, nearly everyone with a glass of wine. No one refuses free wine at a book signing. Free wine is what art openings and book signings are all about. Food, too, if you can get it. Waitresses in white blouses and black skirts circulated with trays of canapés, fluffy little things that were difficult to eat politely. Two television crews from Albuquerque stations were roaming around capturing the event for the evening news.

Lorenzo headed off to the bar while Howie remained near the door searching the room for Grace. He spotted the Senator seated at a table at the far end of the room signing copies of his book with the help of several aides. There was a long queue of people waiting for his autograph. Harlan Stanton was a Republican of the old-fashioned variety, a patrician rather than a populist. Since losing the last election, he had become a vocal critic of the new Republican party as well as the Democrats, who he loathed even more. He was a curmudgeon who succeeded in pissing off just about everybody, right and left. Nevertheless, he was a New Mexico celebrity which was why people were here.

Howie spotted Grace in the crowd not far from where her father was signing books. She wore a sleeveless white dress that managed to look simple, elegant, and expensive. Her long dark blonde hair was pulled into a bun in back that showed the aristocratic line of her neck. She was as beautiful as he remembered. Statuesque, poised, glamorous—and now, as a best-selling author, nearly as famous as her father. She stood in a circle of people, men and women who were hoping for a moment of her time.

Howie moved her way warily, not certain she would recognize him after all this time. He came up to the edge of the circle that had gathered around her, a few feet from her left profile, and waited to see how he might edge closer. She was speaking with one of her adoring fans, an elderly woman.

"Oh, I just loved the part in *The Girl Who Ran Away* when Amelia finds the Samurai sword that killed her husband in the koi pond by the old Buddhist temple!" the woman gushed. "Good lord, how do you come up with things like that?"

"Well, you use your imagination," Grace replied with a quiet smile.

"Who is going to play Amelia in the movie?"

"The studio has somebody in mind, but I can't really talk about it," Grace demurred. "She hasn't been signed yet."

"*You* should play Amelia!" the woman cried.

"I'm not much of an actress."

Howie noticed that her eyes had small crinkle lines at the edges that hadn't been there before. She looked older. But age suited her.

Something drew her attention and she turned his way with the vague half-smile that she held on her face like a mask. Howie held his breath as her gaze swept past him and returned without recognition to the woman who was addressing her.

Howie let out his breath.

But then, as though she had received an electric shock, her head turned back his way. Her eyes widened, her mouth opened.

"Howie!" she cried. "Oh, Howie!"

She excused herself from the gushy woman and broke through the circle of people to where Howie was standing.

"Oh, Howie, is that really you?"

"More or less," he told her.

She hugged him fiercely. For Howie, having her in his arms after all this time was both strange and familiar. He had lost his virginity to Grace Stanton when he was 19-years-old and his body remembered the feel of her.

To his surprise, he felt warm tears on his neck as she held him.

For all her fame and fortune, it appeared the beautiful Grace Stanton wasn't a happy camper.

***

She pulled him off to a far corner of the room near a huge cactus that rose in prickly splendor from a painted pot.

"My God, Howie! What are you doing here?" She wiped away the tears from her cheeks with the back of her hand.

"Your, uh, friend brought me. I stopped by your house to see you and he swept me along."

"Lorenzo?" she asked, giving Howie a searching look. "He's lots of fun, isn't he?"

Howie didn't know what to say about Lorenzo, so he only smiled.

"But, Howie, where have you been all these years?" she demanded.

"Not far from here, actually. San Geronimo."

"Only an hour and a half away! And you never came to see me?"

"I didn't know you were in Santa Fe, Grace. Anyway, I wasn't sure you'd want to see me."

"You didn't know? Oh, Howie . . . that summer! I look back on it through a mist of time like some . . . like some paradise lost that I'll never find again! We were so young!"

She held both his hands and gazed at him intensely. Her eyes were fervently blue. A bit too fervent, he worried.

"Oh, I'm so glad you're here! My life's such a mess! I can't sleep, I can't write, everything's topsy-turvy. But look at me! I'm talking too much! Tell me about *you*. I want to hear everything you've been doing!"

Howie sensed it was time to work Claire into the conversation.

"I'm doing fine. I have an interesting job and a great girlfriend. I'll have to introduce you to Claire," he told her.

"Yes, you must!"

"She's in L.A. now. Claire plays cello with the L.A. String Quartet but we see each other nearly every weekend. They're a big deal, the Quartet. They fill Disney Hall. Either I fly to L.A. or she flies to me—"

"Howie, tell me the truth," Grace interrupted. "Did you read my last book?"

"Your last, er . . . let's see, that was *The Girl Who—"*

"*Flew Into the Sun.* It's the one about the girl who runs off to Mexico with a psychopathic gambler who owes half a million dollars to the mob."

"I must have missed that one. I think I read the one before—"

"They've gone downhill. I don't know why, but I just don't feel the passion anymore. Somehow the magic's gone. Each book is worse than the last, total trash. You should have seen my last review in *Kirkus*! They absolutely murdered me!"

Howie smiled. "You look very much alive, Grace. But listen, the reason I'm here is Nick came to see me last night. He asked me to give you a message."

"Nick?" Her eyes lost their fervency. "You've seen Nick?"

"He showed up at my house out of nowhere. I hadn't seen him for years. He needs money, Grace. He's desperate. He wants you to talk to your father about releasing his part of your grandfather's trust fund. He wrote a letter he asked me to give you."

"Nick!" she repeated, stunned. She shook her head. "I don't know if I can help him, Howie. Daddy would kill me!"

"Grace, he needs help. Those two security guards were an accident—you know that? It was a terrible thing, but he was full of misguided idealism, how he was going to save the world from ecological mayhem. He was young and irresponsible. He didn't consider how setting a fire could get people killed. But it's ten years later, he's still Nick, and we need to consider how to help him."

She was shaking her head. "I don't know if I can, Howie. It's all so painful! And Daddy . . . we're not even allowed to mention Nick's name in front of him!"

"Why don't I give you his letter and you can think about it. You were very close at one time, you and Nick. I don't know what's in the letter—I haven't read it. But I imagine he's included some way you can get in touch with him."

He had taken the envelope from the satchel he carried over his shoulder, but she refused to accept it.

"Howie, I just don't know! It's all so . . . complicated."

"Oh, there you are!" said a woman, coming over to where Howie and Grace were standing by the cactus. "Your father is asking for you, Grace. He's going to give a short talk and he wants you to introduce him."

Howie turned to see a tall woman, fiftyish, with a square jaw and a determined expression. She gave Howie a smile cold enough to freeze a polar bear.

"Well, well, it's Howard Moon Deer, isn't it? What a nice surprise!"

Howie was surprised she remembered him. He knew who she was. She was Summer Newsome, who had been the Senator's chief of staff in his Washington office, a formidable woman. He had met her only once, years ago.

"Good to see you again, Ms. Newsome," he said politely.

"Actually, my last name is Stanton these days," she informed him.

"Howie, Summer is my stepmother now," Grace told him. "Daddy and Summer tied the knot . . . when was it? Five years ago."

"Three, actually," said Summer.

"Congratulations," Howie said awkwardly, wondering what had happened to the previous Mrs. Stanton—Anne Stanton, Grace's mother. Had she died? It was best not to ask.

The new Mrs. Stanton was giving him a good looking over.

"Well, well . . . Howard Moon Deer!" she said thoughtfully. "I believe I read somewhere that you're a private detective these days?"

"I am."

"Howie was my big summer romance of long ago," Grace said lightly.

"Yes, I remember," said the second Mrs. Stanton. "Well, come on, Grace—you know how impatient your father is when people keep him waiting. And you come, too, Howard. I'm sure you'll be useful."

Useful for what, he wanted to ask. But Summer had turned her back and was walking away. Grace gave him a helpless look and followed her stepmother toward the table where the Senator was sitting with his stack of books.

Howie was left with Nick's envelope in hand, undelivered. There was nothing to do but follow. He didn't like it, but he was the postman, and the mail must go through.

Chapter Three

"Daddy, look who's here," Grace said to her father as they approached the table where he sat signing copies of his book. "It's Howard Moon Deer. You remember Howie, don't you?"

Daddy looked up from the book he was signing, pen in hand. His eyes narrowed. "How could I ever forget Howard Moon Deer? Our Lakota friend!"

The Senator had an unpleasant manner of speaking from an amused patrician distance.

"It's good to see you again, Senator," Howie answered politely.

"Is it? Is it *good* to see me again, I wonder?"

It wasn't good, as it happened. It was awful. When Howie was a freshman at Dartmouth, Senator Stanton had been friendly enough, happy to show off his *noblesse oblige*, pleased to have an opportunity to exhibit his well-bred tolerance of those who were beneath him. But that continued only as long as Howie was merely his son's college roommate. When Howie had begun an affair with his daughter, Grace, their relationship had gone decidedly south.

Way south.

The Senator had aged considerably in the twelve years since Howie had seen him last. He had become a frail old man with a feathery fluff of white hair. His nose was pinched, his eyes were close together. He looked like a mean old eagle.

The room had become more crowded since Howie had been off in a corner speaking with Grace. It wasn't the book itself that had drawn such a crowd. Few people actually read self-eulogizing memoirs by aging politicians. Harlan Stanton was no longer an important national figure, but his fans who remained loved his curmudgeonly ways. There was a sporting element as they waited to see who he was going to insult next.

Howie was standing a little way off to the side when he felt someone take his arm.

"Howard, I have a chore for you," said Summer Stanton. She wasn't bashful about ordering him about. Gripping his arm so he couldn't escape, she led him toward a middle-aged man who was standing behind the Senator's chair keeping an eye on the proceedings. He had the appearance of an aging, well-educated, white Anglo-Saxon Ivy Leaguer. His wavy brown hair was slightly long, over his ears, touched with gray but still schoolboyish. He wore round glasses that gave him a mild, owlish expression.

"Howie, this is Stephen Halley, our editor from New York. Why don't you help Stephen bring over a few more boxes of books from the table in the back. Grace and I can deal with the sound system."

Somehow, without his consent, Howie had become part of Senator Stanton's entourage. It was the sort of thing you had to watch out for when you, a nobody, were in the presence of a famous personality.

"You don't mind, do you, Howie?" Grace asked belatedly.

"I'm fine," he replied.

And in fact, he didn't mind, not really. It gave him something to do.

He and the New York editor walked to the edge of the room where several cardboard boxes of hardbound copies of *The Right Way* were stacked on the floor, 26 books to a box. Howie lugged one box while Stephen Halley carried another.

"So, you're a book editor?" Howie asked as they carried their boxes.

"I am," said the owlish man. "I have my own imprint at Peckham & Peale."

Howie was impressed. Peckham & Peale was a venerable old publishing house, long associated with top-of-the-line authors.

Summer had set a microphone on the desk in front of the Senator while Grace fiddled with an amplifier on a nearby table. In a few minutes everything was ready. Grace chimed a spoon against a wine glass to call for silence. She gave a brief introduction to the two-term Senator, New Mexico's favorite son . . . and now the author of a fabulous new memoir that laid bare the intrigues of Washington. It was a sales pitch, but the crowd applauded approvingly.

The Senator spoke through the microphone from his chair.

"Good afternoon, friends, neighbors, New Mexicans. You'll forgive me if I don't stand to address you. It's not that I'm unwilling to rise to the occasion, but I've reached the age where I don't much give a damn what people think!"

It was a sour start. A few chuckled but nobody really laughed.

"I'm here today to speak about political correctness. You all know what political correctness is, I assume?"

This hit the right note. There were cheers and whistles.

"Political correctness means you're not allowed to speak the simple truth. You're not allowed to say what your mind knows and your eyes see. Truth isn't fashionable, you see. Today everybody lies. Republicans are liars and Democrats are even worse. But I'm going to tell you the truth because the citizens of this fine state have voted me out of office, and frankly, I no longer have any need to toady myself to public opinion!"

There was some cautious laughter that wasn't entirely comfortable.

"Now, let me talk about the second chapter of my memoir. Chapter Two, you'll be pleased to know, is about my father, Adam Stanton, who was a great and honest man. As many of you know, my father was the Commissioner of Indian Affairs from 1957 to 1971. He did a great deal for the Native American tribes of this country, though you wouldn't know it from what people say about him today. Political Correctness, you see, likes to pretend that native people living in wigwams and trailers aren't in need of improvement. Leave 'em just the way they are, they say—leave them in ignorance and squalor. Leave them in their savagery! Their culture is just as valid as ours. That's what they say . . . and I say, it's nonsense! Their culture is not the equal of ours. Where are their Beethovens, their Shakespeares and Einsteins?"

The room had gone very quiet because this was not an acceptable way to speak about Indians in New Mexico, even for people who considered themselves conservative. New Mexico was an Indian-friendly state. Tourism relied on it.

"I'm going to tell this to you straight. My father—Adam Stanton—worked hard to educate Indian children and integrate them into civilized American society. No, he didn't create the BIA boarding school policy from scratch. That began in 1879 with Lieutenant Richard Henry Pratt, a Civil War hero. But my father, during his time as Commissioner, fine-tuned the boarding school policy and gave Native American children a chance to become doctors, engineers, businessmen . . . even politicians, God help him! He gave Indians a chance to move up in the world and become productive citizens. And here's an example."

To Howie's horror, Senator Stanton turned toward Howie. "I want you to meet Howard Moon Deer, a Lakota boy who grew up on the Rosebud reservation in South Dakota, one of the poorest, most dysfunctional places in the country. But with the good will of American taxpayers and universities that offered scholarships, he graduated from Dartmouth College and later became a post-graduate student at Princeton. That's the kind of opportunity my father wanted for Indian children everywhere!"

Howie stood flushed with embarrassment and anger. He'd had no idea he would end up as fodder for the Senator's misguided notions of history. His experience at East Coast universities had nothing in common with Indian children who were forcibly separated from their parents and forbidden to speak their own language.

He was about to speak up and offer a few opinions of his own when there was a commotion from the back of the room. A group of protestors from the Plaza had managed to enter carrying signs and chanting loudly: "Two, four, six, eight, who do we want to exterminate? . . . Stanton! Stanton! Voice of hate!"

Standing at the front of the group was the woman with a pinched face and long gray hair that he had noticed earlier outside the hotel. She was no longer carrying her sign, but she seemed even angrier than before. Howie judged her to be in her seventies, a granny with a grudge. Her face was red from shouting.

"Goon!" she screamed at Senator Stanton. "Fascist goon!"

Howie hoped she wasn't about to have a stroke.

As he watched, she picked up an entire cake, plate and all, from a table that was crowded with hors d'oeuvres and deserts, the various nibbles that had been set out for the crowd. Howie saw what she was planning to do. The cake was covered with gooey lemon frosting. Holding it with one hand above her head, she rushed toward the Senator's table with the intention of throwing it into his face.

Howie acted quickly. He was a dozen feet away. He didn't have enough time to put himself between the old woman and the Senator to stop her. He leapt across the room and did his best to make a flying tackle. He landed on his stomach with an *oof* of pain, his arms outstretched just far enough to grab the woman's ankles. This stopped the lower part of her body, while the upper part continued its forward trajectory.

The cake flew from her hands in an arc and landed with a gushy smack on the table where the Senator still sat with a pen in hand. The cake splattered all over the stack of books he had been about to sign. A bit of lemon frosting dangled from his nose.

"Goddamnit, Moon Deer! Look what you've done!" he roared at Howie as he was rising to his feet. "How can you be so clumsy?"

***

Two security men in blue blazers appeared from the crowd to help the cake-throwing old lady to her feet. Luckily, she didn't appear to be hurt. Howie didn't want to find himself charged with assault. She was still in good form, shouting her head off.

"Goon!" she cried, glaring at Howie—for he was the enemy now, the oppressor of the people.

"Madam, I am not a goon," he told her as he rose to his feet. He would have added that her First Amendment rights did not include throwing cakes at people whose politics differed from her own, but he was out of breath and the security team was already hauling her away.

"I bet you didn't expect a book signing to be so exciting," said a voice at Howie's side. It was Grace's friend, Lorenzo, who he hadn't seen since they had arrived at the La Fonda. Lorenzo smiled merrily, showing his perfect white teeth. He seemed to find the melee a great joke. "Are you all right?"

Howie could only sigh.

"Come on, you two," Summer Stanton said, appearing out of the chaos to take charge. "We need to get the Senator away from here. You two can guard the back door long enough for us to escape."

Howie had been hoping to sneak away, but he did what she told him. He and Lorenzo worked together, using their male bulk to form a human barrier that kept the crowd from spilling through the side door where the Stanton family had fled. Within minutes, a large squad of hotel security staff arrived to help restore order, and Howie and Lorenzo were able to slip through the door themselves into the hallway where the family was waiting at a rear exit for the Senator's car to pull up.

Howie managed to make his way to Grace. He wasn't going to let her go without giving her the envelope that her brother Nick had asked him to deliver. Once that was done, he could put this family behind him. Forever, he hoped.

"Don't forget this," he said, attempting to put the envelope in her hand.

"Not now, Howie. Let's get out of here first. Where's your car?"

"I left it at your house. I came with Lorenzo."

"Then come with me. I'll drive you back to your car and it'll give us a chance to talk."

"Grace, why don't I just call Uber? You probably want to make sure your dad's all right."

"He's fine," said Grace, taking hold of his arm. "Let's go before the paparazzi figure out there's a rear door."

***

Howie was glad Grace didn't have a Bentley. Two Bentleys in one day would have been more than a poor boy could handle. She had a two-seater Jaguar convertible, sunshine yellow. A splashy car, conspicuous consumption run amuck, but at least it wasn't red.

The day was fading quickly into an early autumn night. Grace was an aggressive driver, weaving in and out of the evening traffic. She seemed intent on getting the better of all the other drivers on the road, winning the race—whatever that race was. It was a cold night, so she had the top raised with the heater purring. The space age lights on the instrument panel made the interior of the Jaguar feel like a rocket ship on a jaunt to Mars.

"So, what did you think of Lorenzo?"

Howie was surprised by the question. "He's very . . . entertaining."

She laughed.

"Yes, I thought so at first. "We met in London. At the Tate Modern, actually. We were looking at the same picture, a Lucien Freud, and he made a comment. Normally, I avoid people who speak to me in museums, but he was clever and amusing so I spoke back. One thing led to another and he ended up taking me to all the fashionable restaurants and clubs. He's very rich, you know. Lorenzo Stein. One of the Hamburg Steins. Do you know them?"

Howie pretended to think. "Hamburg, Iowa?" he asked.

"Howie, honestly! Hamburg, Germany. They're a huge financial powerhouse in London and New York. It wasn't until he came to live with me in Santa Fe that I realized how boring he was. You take someone like that out of their milieu and they just dry up. Like a desiccated cactus!"

Howie managed a smile. She was describing a world he had glimpsed from time to time, international people jetting around, but it had never attracted him enough to want to join it.

"I was on the rebound, Howie. I had just ended a long-term relationship that was going nowhere and I needed cheering up. He's very funny, actually, and quite sweet. But we're not boyfriend/girlfriend, in case you're wondering." She flashed him a complicated look. "Sexually, he's kind of a neuter. But I wasn't looking for that. I was feeling down, that's all. I only wanted someone to make me laugh."

He studied her from time to time as she drove. She was still beautiful, but her features had hardened. As long as he had known her, Grace had been unhappy about one thing or another. At nineteen, that had seemed romantic to him and sexy. But now that she was in her mid-thirties, it wasn't so attractive anymore. It seemed empty and neurotic.

"So how about you?" she asked. "Are you seeing anyone?"

"Yes, I told you," he replied, not surprised that she hadn't been listening. "Her name is Claire."

"Oh, right," she said vaguely. "She plays the harp."

"The cello. Look, if it's okay, let's talk about Nick."

"Nick!" She shook her head and sighed with exasperation. "We were so close when we were young! I loved him to death, I really did. My talented, screwed-up, charming little brother! But then he disappeared on me and it felt like such a betrayal. I'm not sure I even know him anymore. Or want to, for that matter. And you know the worst part about it, don't you?"

Howie saw he had to answer. "What is that?"

"What he did, it wasn't because he was some wonderful idealist. He was getting back at his family, that's all! He wanted to hurt us!"

Howie had to think about this. It was an interesting take on eco-terrorism, that it was about getting back at your family. But Howie didn't entirely buy it.

They had arrived at her home and were sitting in the driveway next to his battered Subaru. His car was missing two hubcaps and the front bumper was bent. Alongside Grace's Jaguar, his Outback looked like a worn-out old shoe. She turned off the ignition and they sat in the darkness, neither of them making a move to leave the car.

"I'm sorry you've been depressed," he said. "But maybe Nick being back will help. He's reaching out to you, Grace. You can be friends again."

She was shaking her head even before he stopped speaking.

"I can't, Howie, I just can't. Daddy would have a stroke if he found out!"

She opened the door abruptly and stepped out of the car. Howie got out from his side and walked around the hood to where she was standing. The early stars were shining overhead and the desert air was sharp and cold.

He handed her the envelope with Nick's letter.

"Look, just read it and then you can decide for yourself. Nick asked me to give it to you, and now I have."

She gave him an appraising look.

"I tell you what, Howie, I'll make a deal with you. I'll read the letter and decide what I can do to help Nick if you'll just do one thing for me."

"Grace—"

"Come to the family Thanksgiving next Thursday at Daddy's ranch. I'll send you directions. Everyone's going to be there, the entire clan. It would be a great help to me if you came."

"Grace, I can't, honestly. I have other plans. And besides, your father would have a fit if I showed up."

"Let me handle that part. Come to Thanksgiving and we'll tackle Daddy together. You can tell him about seeing Nick and how he wants enough money to get away. Daddy might like that. You see, Nick has been a thorn in his side, a political liability. It's not good for a conservative politician to have a son who's a terrorist. Daddy's planning to run for governor of New Mexico next year, and he thinks he has a chance. If Nick doesn't screw it up for him, that is. So, can't you get out of whatever your plans are?"

"I'm afraid I can't. There's an older couple I know, Jack and Emma. I have Thanksgiving every year at their house. Jack's a retired cop from San Francisco and he's my boss. They'd be hurt if I didn't show up."

There was another reason to turn down her invitation, but he kept that to himself. Thanksgiving was the opening day of the ski season on

San Geronimo Peak and he wasn't going to miss it. When you were a powder hound, opening day was a ritual.

"Howie, please! You see, there's someone who has been causing me some trouble. I don't really want to talk about it, but you're being there . . . you'd be a sort of buffer between me and my family. And if you help me, I'll figure out a way to help Nick. Please! Do this . . . well, for what we once were."

Howie shook his head. He'd been young and innocent that summer long ago. Clueless, was the word that came to mind. He was embarrassed even to think about it. He was sorry that Grace had problems, but he knew it would be a mistake to get sucked into her drama. It was Nick he was worried about. Nick was the one who needed help. But for this, unfortunately, he needed her cooperation.

"I can't promise," he said, "but okay, I'll try. I'll call you later in the week and let you know."

Which is how they left the Thanksgiving invitation.

Dangling.

Meanwhile, he could text her in the next few days and cancel politely if the heavens brought snow. He knew where he wanted to be on Thanksgiving Day, and it wasn't with Senator Harlan Stanton. If the mountain gods allowed, he would be swooping down the white slopes like an eagle, racing into the wind.

Chapter Four

But the snow didn't come. It rained.

On the Monday before Thanksgiving, an unseasonably warm weather front moved in from Southern California and it rained hard at the base of San Geronimo Peak for nearly six hours. The highest parts of the mountain, at nearly 13,000 feet, received more than a foot of snow, but that wasn't much use when the bottom third was virtually washed away. There hadn't been much of a base even before the rain and on Tuesday, the resort released a statement that due to the weather, opening day had been delayed to December 9th.

Groans of disappointment echoed throughout San Geronimo County. Meanwhile, Grace had texted Howie repeatedly to say he must—she wouldn't accept a refusal!—join them for Thanksgiving. Why she wanted him, he didn't know, but he had finally said yes. He figured if he couldn't soar down white slopes like an eagle, he might as well revisit the joys and sorrows of youth. The Stanton clan had played a big part in his college days, he had stayed in their houses, sailed on their yachts, dined at their tables, and in an odd way he felt he owed them something. Now the difficulty he faced was getting out of Thanksgiving at Jack and Emma's.

On Wednesday morning, Howie found Jack Wilder, his boss, brooding at his desk when he arrived mid-morning, late as usual. Jack was an eccentric figure. He was blind and with his eyes hidden behind wraparound dark glasses, and his beard and shaggy white hair, he was starting to look like a cross between Santa Claus and Albert Einstein.

Jack had lost his eyesight in a police operation gone wrong when he was a highly placed cop in California, a commander in the San Francisco Police Department. The rank of commander was only a notch below

Deputy Chief and he wouldn't have been on the street that day during a hostage situation if it weren't for his belief that everything would go haywire without him. It wasn't a wise decision. A bullet had grazed his skull and forced him into early retirement. Running a private investigations agency was a way for Jack to get back into the game, but he had never entirely accepted the loss of his career.

"So, what's the matter, Jack" Howie asked, settling into the client chair.

"Nothing's the matter," Jack barked. "I'm bored, that's all. I'm sick to death of damn insurance cases!"

"They pay well," Howie reminded.

"Yes, but who cares?"

Howie cared. He was paying off the bank loan on his land. Like most detective agencies, the bread and butter of Wilder & Associate was insurance cases that were referred to them by lawyers. Their last case was quite a big deal—a multimillion dollar medical insurance scam that had been set up by a crooked doctor. But it wasn't interesting, it wasn't an adventure. Nevertheless, they had done a good solid investigation and Howie was satisfied that in a small way, justice had prevailed.

"Are you sleeping okay?" he asked, knowing that Jack suffered from chronic insomnia.

"No, I'm not sleeping okay!" Jack replied grumpily. "Wait until you're my age, you'll see! Maybe you get an hour or two. Don't get old, Howie—that's my advice to you!"

"Great advice, Jack. I'll keep that in mind the next time somebody takes a shot at me. Anyway, you're only seventy-four. That's not so old these days. Seventy-four . . . I mean, hey, that's the new seventy-three!"

"Ha, ha, Howie! Thank you very much!"

"What do you say I send out for some bear claws from down the street? Judging from the way things are going here, I'd say it's time for a mid-morning sugar rush."

Jack frowned as he considered this. "Okay, but make mine a jelly donut."

"Jack! That's junk food!"

"It's cop food, Howie. I lived on jelly donuts for twenty years in San Francisco, so don't knock it!"

The Wilder & Associate Private Investigations office occupied a two-hundred-year-old adobe building in the historic district of San Geronimo. The building was an authentic relic of the past, which had its pluses and minuses. The office was quaint, visitors often commented on its charm. But the floor was uneven, the windows and doors weren't completely plumb, and the adobe itself was decaying more every year, creating dust that leaked from the cracks and holes in the mud-and-straw walls and kept Howie sneezing for days at a time. Still, they had the entire building to themselves, from Calle Dos Flores at the front to the alley in the back, where there was a rear door and two reserved spaces to park their cars. Parking space in the historic district was a much sought-after luxury.

Jack's office was at the rear of the building, a large comfortable room with a low ceiling of vigas and latillas. The furniture was traditional: trasteros and cabinets of heavy dark wood, like the ceiling. There was a kiva fireplace on one side of the room where Ruth, the agency secretary, had built a small blaze. The floors were also of old dark wood, scoured and uneven with age, with Mexican and Native American carpets covering much of the surface. Katya, Jack's German shepherd guide dog, was stretched out sleeping on a faded Navajo rug in front of the fire. Like Jack, Katya was getting old.

Howie rang the bakery café on Calle Dos Flores, put in the order for the pastries and two double cappuccinos, with a chai for Ruth in the front reception, which would be delivered by one of the young baristas. When he had finished placing the order, he found Jack's dark glasses pointed at him like twin artillery guns.

"I heard the Peak decided to delay the opening," Jack said.

"They had to. They only had a thirteen-inch base, most of it man-made, which would have been enough to open a few runs on the front side. But when the rain came, it washed away whole sections near the bottom."

"Well, cheer up. Emma's bought a huge organic free-range turkey, not an unnatural thing about it anywhere, and we're going to have ourselves an old-fashioned Thanksgiving feast. I'm planning to pull out a few bottles of Bordeaux I've been saving for a special occasion, so we can drown our sorrows. Santo's going to come with his new girlfriend, and your favorite detective is going to be there as well, Dapper Dan."

"You're taking in all the strays, huh?" Dapper Dan was what Jack liked to call Detective Dan Hamm, the youngest, greenest, most unpopular detective at the San Geronimo outpost of the New Mexico State Police.

"Emma's setting dinner for five o'clock. But why don't you hop over about four. If you want to bring something, you can bring a loaf of that cranberry bread Claire taught you to bake."

Howie knew it wasn't going to be easy to tell Jack he wasn't coming this year. In the past, he and Claire—those years when she was in San Geronimo—had a ritual they had followed for years: skiing in the morning and then Jack and Emma's house in the late afternoon for the Thanksgiving meal.

"It sounds great, Jack, really great. But, look—something's come up for me. An old friend showed up unexpectedly and I've had to change my plans—"

"Bring him along!" Jack said. "Emma can set another place."

"It's not that easy . . . you see, he gave me a note to deliver to his sister in Santa Fe, and when I went down there to deliver it . . . well, before I knew it, I sort of accepted *their* Thanksgiving. And, honestly, I feel I ought to go. Her father is Senator Stanton, you see. It's all a little complicated . . ."

Jack raised a rough, old man's hand. "Whoa!" he said. "Slow down! Senator Stanton, you say? You're talking about Harlan Stanton?"

"Exactly. I roomed with his son, Nick, at Dartmouth and we became best friends for a while. His sister, Grace—we were pretty close, too, at one time."

"Grace Stanton? The bestselling author?"

"I dated her for a while. When I was nineteen."

Jack was starting to get the picture. "Wait a minute!" he said, connecting the dots. "You're talking about Senator Harlan Stanton's son, Nicolas Stanton? The terrorist who's on the FBI's most wanted list?"

"Eco-terrorist," Howie said. As though that made it more palatable.

"And he came to see you? A terrorist wanted by the feds for murder! And you ran an errand for him? You delivered a note to his sister? Are you fucking crazy, Howie? You could lose your P.I. license for this!"

"I know it doesn't sound good, Jack, when you say it like that. But I knew this family very well at one time. It just didn't seem like I could say no. And it was harmless, really, taking a letter to his sister."

"Stop right there!" Jack tapped the index finger of his right hand furiously against the desk. "This sister, Grace Stanton, the author—she's good looking, I suppose?"

"Well, she is, Jack. Now that you mention it."

"And she was your girlfriend?"

"Only for a few months. A summer romance, no biggie."

"Right, a summer romance when you were nineteen with a beautiful girl whose father was a U.S. Senator? And you're going to Thanksgiving at her house? What do you think Claire is going to say?"

"A lot of people are going to be there. It's going to be at her father's ranch, some place out in the boonies. Claire won't mind. She knows about Grace, just like I know about Claire's previous relationships. It was over between me and Grace years ago. I don't like her very much, to tell you the truth. She's a spoiled, narcissistic brat. And her books aren't very good, either."

Jack visibly calmed himself with a few deep breaths.

"Why is it, Howie, that I sense you're about to get yourself into one of your usual muddles?"

"I don't know why you say that, Jack. I honestly don't."

"Oh, you don't, huh? Look, you've run an errand for a fugitive wanted for murder—that's aiding and abetting. And now you're getting in deep with his sister, your old girlfriend, Grace Stanton, a famous writer. When Claire hears about this, she's going to hit the roof, my friend!"

Howie made an effort to restrain himself. Recently, Jack had begun to act too much like a disapproving father. They were business partners, that's all, and Howie wanted to keep it that way. He liked Jack, but he wasn't looking for a bossy father figure.

"Jack, I'll be okay. I'm curious, that's all. There are probably going to be interesting people there, it will be an experience. Look, I tell you what. I won't stay there long. I'll stop at the Stantons for an hour or two and then I'll come by your place for dessert. I'll even bring cranberry bread. Okay? You'll see for yourself that I've survived the encounter with my first love."

Howie hadn't meant to say *first love.* That had come out of its own accord.

Jack shook his head. "Howie, somehow you have a knack for getting into trouble. Especially when women are involved. Well, I can't stop you. But I'll be relieved when you arrive tomorrow. Can I tell Emma you'll be at our house by seven?"

"Absolutely, Jack," Howie promised. "Seven o'clock. Bearing cranberry bread. Everything's going to be all right."

***

On Thanksgiving morning, Howie left home in the early afternoon and set off for the Stanton ranch with two loaves of cranberry bread wrapped in aluminum foil riding on the passenger seat. One loaf was for the Stantons and the second for the Wilders, where he planned to arrive later in the day sharply at seven. He had done the baking the previous evening with his cat, Orange, watching sleepily from her spot on the kitchen table.

The day was clear with a cold desert wind blowing and a low horizon of clouds in the northwest. Howie always found the late fall in New Mexico harsh and somehow lonely, once the leaves were gone and before the snow made everything beautiful again. But the roads were empty and the huge vistas of mountains, mesas, brown earth, and sky gave Howie a feeling of freedom as he edged his car to 75 mph on the two-lane highway. With his heater humming, his old Subaru was a cozy bubble. He had Mozart on the CD player, the C Minor Mass, deciding he was in the mood for classical. He had learned a good deal about classical music over the years from Claire, and he found himself retreating into its arcane world more and more, particularly Mozart and Beethoven, who had begun to feel like ballast in a world gone mad.

Howie had spoken to Claire earlier in the morning—early evening, Claire's time in Germany, where she was busy with her ensemble recording the complete Mozart string quartets for Deutsche Grammophon. He had told her that he was going to the Stantons for Thanksgiving, making a funny anecdote about it, how he had been corralled into going.

"This is Grace Stanton? Your first girlfriend?"

"Long, long ago, Claire."

"Well, just be sure to watch yourself, Howie. I don't know how you do it, but women are always trying to get their hooks into you!"

"That doesn't sound like a compliment."

"Oh, you know what I mean. It's just you're, well . . . an unlikely Romeo."

He wasn't sure what he thought about being an unlikely Romeo. He wasn't conventionally handsome, by any means, though Claire always said his face was both intelligent and kind, which were qualities that didn't often go together. In the last few years, she had been prodding him to finish his Ph.D and return to academia where he belonged. He could be Professor Moon Deer instead of a disreputable P.I. In fact, Howie had been working on his dissertation in his free time and he was nearly finished. But he wasn't sure about the Professor Moon Deer part. He liked running around the country as a disreputable P.I.

He and Claire spoke for over an hour and it was good to hear her voice. Comparing Claire to Grace, he was glad he was old enough now to know the difference between love and infatuation. At the age of nineteen, you didn't really know the person you lusted after. Or at least Howie hadn't. It had all been a projection of his own desires and fantasies that had little to do with who Grace actually was.

Fortunately, he was wiser than that now.

Almost middle-aged, he thought to himself with a sigh. Good God, five years from now he would be forty!

Chapter Five

Howie, who had skipped a year in high school, was 17-years-old when he entered Dartmouth College as a Freshman. He had been a bumbling, awestruck kid, foolishly impressed with himself, defensive of his Lakota background, painfully shy.

Dartmouth is one of the oldest colleges in America, founded in 1769 by Eleazar Wheelcock, a Congregational minister, with the express purpose of educating Native Americans in Christian theology and the English way of life. The school's mission, as described in its charter, was "for the education and instruction of Youth of the Indian Tribes in this Land in reading, writing & all parts of Learning which shall appear necessary and expedient for civilizing & Christianizing Children of Pagans as well as in all liberal Arts and Sciences and also of English Youth and any others."

Just what Howie needed. Civilizing!

His childhood in Rosebud, South Dakota, hadn't prepared him for Hanover, New Hampshire. Even the red brick architecture was intimidating. Despite its original charter as an Indian school, Howie found himself in a sea of privileged white faces, all of whom looked as if they had spent their entire wealthy lives preparing for the Ivy League. Everyone except Howie seemed completely at home.

He arrived on opening day by train from New York and found himself assigned to the River dormitory, which was considered the worst place to live on campus because it was far from everything and old. He knew from the letters he had received over the summer that he would be sharing his room with someone named Nicolas Stanton, but who this person was, he had no idea.

Howie arrived first, chose for himself the bed closest to the window, and unpacked his few belongings into one of the wardrobes and chests of drawers. Once he had finished, he stretched out on his bed with a book and nervously awaited the arrival of his new roommate. Outside his window there was a great bustle of parents and students in the grassy quad below, families arriving in station wagons and SUVs full of skis, hockey sticks, guitars, and luggage. All the returning students seemed to know one another. Loud greetings and confident laughter rose up to Howie in his room, where he lay in solitude knowing no one at all.

Because he was nervous and feeling out of place, he posed on his bed reading Hermann Hesse, *Steppenwolf*, determined to show from the start that though he was an Indian kid from South Dakota, he was no dummy. Unfortunately, no one looked in on him so the gesture was wasted and Howie soon fell asleep.

He woke some time later to a clatter of voices and what felt like a herd of elephants coming into the room. In fact, there were only four people: Senator Harlan Stanton, his wife at the time, Anne, Nicolas—his new roommate—and a uniformed chauffeur who was carrying a pair of skis on his shoulder and pulling a large suitcase on wheels into the room.

Much of the noise was due to the chauffeur who wasn't accustomed to carrying skis and dropped them with a loud springy clatter onto the floor. Nicolas picked them up and leaned them against a wall.

"For chrissake, Mom, I can carry my own skis!" he mumbled.

"Nick, you have to be careful of your arm," his mother told him. Her voice was patient but strained.

She turned to Howie who had sat up anxiously on his bed to watch the new arrivals.

"He fell off a horse two months ago and broke his arm," the mother explained. "Can you believe it? He's been riding since he was three and he fell off his horse!"

"He wasn't paying attention," said Senator Stanton. "That's always been Nick's problem. He was fooling around instead of paying attention!"

The dorm room was small and suddenly felt very crowded. It took Howie a moment to focus and sort out who was who.

He recognized Senator Stanton from television and articles in magazines. He hadn't realized when he saw the name of his new college roommate that Nicolas Stanton was *that* Stanton and it came as a shock. Harlan Stanton, from New Mexico, was at that time a highly visible member of the Republican party, the chairman of some important committee that Howie couldn't remember. He was a tall, spry, patrician man with gray hair and a sharp nose.

"Harlan Stanton," he said in a convivial manner, stepping over to shake hands and introduce himself.

"Howard Moon Deer," Howie managed.

"I hope you and Nick will be good friends." He noticed the cover of the book that was open on Howie's bed. "Well, well, look what you're reading! Hermann Hesse. Trash, if you ask me, but Dartmouth will soon set you right. Shakespeare, Keats, Dickens, Ayn Rand—that's the ticket!"

Howie glanced over at Nick. Had he winced? Howie thought so, but it was subtle and his face quickly went blank again.

"And you're a Native American, I see," the Senator continued, undeterred.

"I am, sir," Howie answered politely. He rarely called anyone *sir*, but the Senator seemed to merit the title.

"Very good," said the Senator, nodding his head in approval. "You probably didn't know that my father was Adam Stanton, the Commissioner of Indian Affairs. My family has had a long association with you people."

Howie's polite smile was strained. On the Rosebud reservation, he had friends who used posters with Adam Stanton's face on it for target practice. The Bureau of Indian Affairs wasn't popular at Rosebud. Bureau of Bashing Indians Around was what people generally called the BIA.

"Are you a skier, Howard?"

"No, sir. I've never given it a try."

"Well, you'll soon learn at Dartmouth. You'll have to come visit us some winter. Won't he, Anne?" he said to his wife.

"Yes, he must!"

"Most people don't know that New Mexico has some of the best skiing in the country, which keeps the lift lines short," the Senator continued, touting his state. "We have a ski lodge up in San Geronimo, don't we, Anne."

"We do," she agreed. "And you must come to visit some time with Nicolas once you get your ski legs. We have three hundred inches of snow up there in the winter. Dry powder."

"We keep our powder dry!" quipped the Senator.

It was the first time Howie had heard the name San Geronimo, a town that was destined to be in his future. Meanwhile, the Stanton parents were a difficult act to watch. It was only years later that he realized they were nearly as nervous as he was.

From time to time, Howie glanced at Nicolas who was sitting across the room on his bed looking as though he had retreated into a catatonic trance. He had short blond hair and a slight build. His face was expressionless, empty. Howie didn't see at first that he was handsome. That would only come later, when Nick relaxed and transformed back into himself.

The Stanton parents did their vaudeville act for another twenty minutes while the uniformed chauffeur made two more trips to the limousine below for more of Nicks's stuff. There were duffel bags, tennis rackets, a second pair of skis—cross country skis—and a suit bag full of sports coats and clothes for formal events that Nick would never attend. It was going to be a challenge to fit all these things into the small dorm room.

Eventually the parents left with hearty farewells and handshakes.

Nick let out his breath with a great sigh. "Man, *that* was fucking painful!" he said with relief. "Sorry about that."

"It's okay," Howie told him. "They were trying to be nice. Look, I took the bed by the window because I got here first. But if you want—"

"No, this is fine. So where are you from, Moon Deer?"

"South Dakota."

"So, you're, what?" Nick had to think a moment. "Oglala?"

"Lakota," Howie told him.

Nicolas suddenly smiled. It changed his face entirely. From sullen he now turned radiant. He lit up from inside, he was transformed into the charismatic Nick Stanton who would become Howie's best friend.

"That's genius!" he said to Howie. "You were the guys who killed Custer! Man, you turned that egotistical asshole into a *porcupine*!"

"Well, I didn't have a personal role in that," Howie admitted. "But yes, Little Big Horn. To be honest, it was a feel-good moment, but only for a short time. It didn't work out so well for us in the long run."

Nicks's smile grew brighter and brighter. He almost seemed to burst with sunshine.

"Oh, man, this is so totally cool! I thought I was going to be stuck with some preppy idiot from Choate! Look, Moon Deer, before we go any further, you gotta tell me—what music do you like?"

"Music? Well, I like a lot of stuff. I'm mostly into folk music right now."

"Dylan?"

"Dylan's okay. Some of it I like a lot. But I like John Prine better."

"Really? Why is that?"

This was to prove a typical Nick remark. When you gave an opinion, he expected you to back it up.

"Dylan is a put-down artist," Howie explained. "I mean, he's brilliant, but his sarcasm can be pretty nasty. For me, John Prine has heart and I like that. He has compassion for the human condition."

Nick gave Howie a closer look. "You're kidding? The human condition?"

"Well, sure. Some of Prine's lines totally tear me apart. 'There's a hole in daddy's arm where all the money goes'—for me, lyrics like that go a whole lot deeper than Dylan's self-righteous narcissism."

Nick threw back his head and laughed. "What about jazz? Do you like Miles Davis?"

Howie had to admit he knew nothing about jazz. He had heard of Miles, but that was it.

"I'll have to play you *Kind of Blue*," Nick promised. "You'll like it. So, what other music are you into?"

"Jerry Garcia, I guess. Tom Waits. Pink Floyd. Frank Zappa—"

"Frank Zappa!" Nick cried ecstatically. "The Mothers of Invention! Oh, this is good! We're going to have a great year! Look, Moon Deer, I've got some dynamite weed. How about we slip outside and get high? What do you say?"

At this point in his life, Howie had never smoked anything, neither tobacco nor cannabis. But Nick was about to open doors for him that he had never imagined, so he said what he would almost always say to the Stantons.

He said, yes.

***

Such was the start of a friendship that was to deepen over the course of five years, until it came to an end and they went their separate ways.

Howie had been pretty much a loner up to this time. He'd had friends, but never what might be called a best friend. Nick changed that. He was the best friend Howie ever had. They were inseparable.

Nick taught Howie to ski and they often went for weekends to Vermont, to Mad River Glen, Stowe, Mt. Snow, Sugarbush, sleeping rough in a huge old 1979 Buick Nick bought so they could get around.

They went together to music concerts all over the East Coast, often arriving back at Dartmouth just in time for Monday morning classes, exhausted with hilarity.

They tripped down to New York City for plays and movies and more music still. They ate and drank wine and talked for hours into the night: politics, Buddhism, art, girls, philosophy, the meaning of life, everything and nothing.

It was the perfect college friendship at a time before life got serious, before responsibilities set in. Somehow they managed to keep their grades up. Nick was the sort who did well in school without making any apparent effort, writing term papers at the last minute, scoring high on tests. "You need to know how to bullshit," was his motto. For Howie, it was more of an effort. He worked hard, knowing he couldn't afford to lose his scholarship. With the crazy weekends—skiing, music—he often went with very little sleep in order to get work done on time.

Money was a problem for Howie due to the fact that he didn't have any. Nick kept trying to give him handfuls of cash, but this was one area in which Howie said no. "Come on, man, what's money?" Nick would say. "I've got enough for both of us." But Howie wanted to be a friend, not a retainer, and he had an instinctive aversion to placing himself in debt.

He let Nick pay for restaurants, music tickets, ski tickets, and such—things that Nick wanted to do and Howie never would have managed on his own, and which at first he tried to bow out from. But he guarded his independence and always kept a part-time job in order to pay his own bottom line expenses. He worked as a dishwasher in an off-campus restaurant, then a waiter, until late Sophomore year his favorite anthropology professor hired him to research a book he was writing on the diet of early American settlers, what they ate and how this affected their culture and their lives. Howie found he liked doing research, which was a skill that would prove useful in his future life as a private detective.

Dartmouth had been co-ed since the early 1970s and Nick, with his charm and good looks, attracted girls like bees to flowers. Howie didn't try to compete. He was shy with women, and those he was attracted to tended to be shy in return, so nothing happened. Nick thought this was very funny and gave him many suggestions, opening lines, once even pages of written dialogue that he assured Howie would bring a certain young woman to his bed. But Howie froze up and couldn't get started. In any case, he didn't have enough money to take girls out on dates, and he told himself this was a blessing in disguise. He was at college to work hard and do well. Unlike Nick, he didn't have a wealthy family to fall back on.

Such was the state of Howie's love life until Spring Break Freshman year when Nick invited him to stay in New York, where he met Nick's sister, Grace.

***

New York can be cold in April, but this particular April was magic. The sun shone, a fragrant breeze loosened the last remnants of winter, the first buds were on the trees, and people with happy faces filled the busy streets.

The Stantons kept a townhouse on East 74th Street between Madison and Fifth Avenue. It was a very good address, though the house itself was narrow and dark, four stories high with no elevator, pressed in on both sides by grander buildings. The Stanton's called it, modestly, their Manhattan *pied-à-terre.* None of the family actually lived in New York, but it was a convenient stopping place for whoever was passing through.

Howie had never heard of a *pied-à-terre,* a casual foot-on-the-ground sort of place for rich people who owned more houses than they could occupy at any one time. Frankly, he was impressed. With Howie's family, one house was all you got, and it was generally an old trailer with a few chickens pecking outside.

Howie and Nick had spent time here before on weekend trips from Dartmouth, but this was the first time he had met Nick's older sister.

Grace was in the kitchen on the ground floor when they arrived, making herself a sandwich with a phone cradled against her ear, talking and spreading mayonnaise at the same time. A French door was open behind her leading to a small garden at the rear of building.

"Nicolas!" she cried when she saw her brother. "Talk to you later," she said into the receiver, hanging up, putting down the knife, flinging herself into Nick's arms.

"I didn't expect to see you here," he told her.

"Well, I had to get away. I couldn't take Northampton another minute. All the dramas this idiot I've been seeing has put me through . . . God, am I glad to be rid of that pompous jerk! I'll tell you all about it tonight. Are you free for dinner? I was thinking of Chinatown, I'm absolutely *dying* for some really good Chinese food!"

It was an avalanche of energy and words. Howie stood to the side momentarily forgotten, watching every gesture she made, taking in every nuance of every word. She was the most beautiful creature he had ever seen. He was mesmerized by her.

"Grace, this is my roommate, Howie," Nick said at last. "Howie Moon Deer."

She turned to look at him, granting Howie the briefest flash of her attention. "Moon Deer," she said. "What an unusual name!"

"I'm . . ." Howie couldn't finish the sentence. For the moment, he didn't know what he was.

"He's the man in the moon," Nick said on Howie's behalf.

"Is he? Let's see his profile . . . turn to the side, Moon Deer. No, sorry, your chin doesn't jut out and your nose isn't sharp enough."

"He's Lakota," Nick said. "Isn't that genius?"

"Daddy will like that," she said. "Daddy believes he's an expert on Indians just because he lives in New Mexico. He isn't, of course. He's an idiot."

"Dad doesn't know his ass from a hole in the ground," Nick said merrily.

Grace was two years older than Nick and she was a Junior at Smith in Northampton, Massachusetts, a college she satirized without mercy. She was very good at satirizing people and institutions she disliked. Both Grace and Nick detested their oldest brother, Justin, who had graduated from Yale two years earlier and now was studying at Harvard Business School. Justin was apparently the most boring, uptight, ridiculous person on the planet. Grace and Nick fell into peals of laughter as they described him.

They had dinner that evening in Chinatown with two of Grace's friends and, for the rest of the week that followed, Howie found himself swept along, a background figure of no importance. In fact, Howie didn't mind being in the background. All he wanted was to simply be near Grace and breathe in her magic.

He was in love, of course. It was a version of love ungrounded in reality—he would understand this soon enough. But for Howie, who was not yet eighteen, still a virgin, it was the most thrilling thing that had ever happened to him. Her beauty dazzled him, her poise, her sophistication. He wanted to write sonnets about her, songs, a symphony if possible. He knew there was no chance of anything coming of his infatuation. Not only was she two years older than him, she was rich, beautiful, sexy, she existed in a different realm.

"You're not falling for Grace, are you?" Nick asked on the train ride back to New Hampshire.

"Well . . . she's really something!" Howie managed.

"Sure, she is. She's also selfish and conceited, and she doesn't worry about the hearts she breaks. I mean it, Howie. Don't get burned."

"I won't. Anyway, she barely looked at me the entire time we were there. Which is fine."

Nick turned and looked at him. "You sure it's fine?"

"Honestly," Howie lied.

They returned to Dartmouth and, though he and Nick rarely spoke about Grace, Howie kept the image of her locked in his dreams. He dated other women in a mild way. There was even a bit of making out here and there, though nothing serious. But Grace was always at the back of his mind.

He saw her several more times over the course of the next year and she was friendly to Howie in a casual way. At dinner one night, when he and Nick had driven down to Northampton for a visit, Grace confided that she had discovered that "Daddy," as she called him, was having an affair with Summer Newsome, a woman twenty years his junior who was the Senator's chief of staff in Washington. She had walked in on them in his office, *in flagrante delicto* on the couch.

"It's such a cliché!" Grace complained. "That's what I hate most about it! A rich old fart getting it off with his secretary. It's so . . . ordinary! And what a hypocrite! Daddy got elected preaching 'family values!'"

"Come on, Grace!" Nick said. "This is the epitome of right-wing family values. The little woman stays at home while hubby is off on business junkets with strippers on his lap. Are you going to tell Mom?"

"You bet I am! She has the right to know. Their marriage is a total lie. What do you think, Howie?"

Both Nick and Grace turned to await his opinion. Howie felt on the spot. His knowledge of wealthy couples and their infidelities came only from books.

"Maybe you should let them work it out on their own," he suggested. "It's their drama, not yours."

Grace glared at him. "Really? Daddy's marriage is a fraud and our mother doesn't have a clue what's going on. Do you think that's fair?"

"Fair? No, I suppose not. I just don't know. Every situation is different."

"Really? So, when you get married, are you planning to have a little nookie on the side?"

He blushed slightly and hoped it didn't show.

"When I find the right girl, I'm going to be true forever."

She laughed at his old-fashioned naiveté.

"When you find the right *woman*," she corrected. "Not *girl*."

"Exactly," he agreed, meeting her eyes. "The right woman."

It wasn't exactly flirting. But it was something, he supposed. It was a start.

Chapter Six

Nick's political radicalization wasn't apparent at first, but it grew over the years until it became a problem.

Toward the end of Freshman year, Nick began saying things like, "You know, Howie, the world's really fucked up. I think we need to tear everything down, destroy the system and start all over again. We've got to point history in the right direction. We've got to fight like hell to make this planet beautiful again!"

Howie liked the idea of making the planet beautiful again, but he was wary about tearing everything down.

"Howie, you gotta break eggs to make an omelette," Nick insisted, using the cliché with self-conscious mockery.

Howie shook his head. "I don't know. Once Humpty Dumpty gets cracked, I'm not sure you'll ever put him together again," he clichéd in return. "Violence doesn't change things. You only end up with another thug in charge. Look at the Russian Revolution."

It was the sort of late night dorm room conversation they often had, and this particular subject—violence versus non-violence—was never resolved between them. Howie wasn't entirely a pacifist, but he was doubtful if revolutionaries who storm the barricades ever came up with anything better than what they had destroyed. It was more a gut feeling than an intellectual conclusion.

By Sophomore year, Nick began attending meetings of various left-wing student groups—the Campus Antiwar Network, the Student Marxist Committee, Students for Socialism, and others, trying out different ideologies. It wasn't long before he turned his focus to environmental activism.

"Capitalism is destroying this planet, Howie," he lectured. "The oceans are warming, the coral reefs are dying, nearly two thousand species go extinct every year. We've got to stop it while there's still something left!"

Nick began taking Howie to meetings of the campus chapter of Greenpeace, and one secretive meeting of a group that called itself EFB, Earth Fights Back, that was held in a dorm room. It wasn't that Howie didn't care about the environment. He did. He agreed with much of what was said at these various meetings, but his sense of the ridiculous always got in the way. Where Nick saw Great Causes, Howie saw poseurs, wannabe demagogues, and guys who just wanted to get laid. Some of the left-wing girls, in fact, were very pretty and free-spirited when it came to sex. Sex was one of the great draws of radicalism.

These differences of opinion kept their friendship going rather than pulling it apart. It gave them more fodder for their endless conversation. It wasn't until halfway through Junior year that Howie began seriously to worry about his roommate.

He should have seen the signs earlier. Despite his charm, there had always been a manic quality to Nick's behavior. He alternated between periods of wild exuberance followed by deep depression where for days he would retreat into himself and say nothing at all.

He lacked balance, he had no boundaries. He was like a bottle of champagne that had been shaken too hard. At first, Howie put it down to the fact that they were smoking too much weed. He only realized gradually that his roommate exhibited classic signs of bipolar disorder.

Nick began to spend more time with his friends from Earth Fights Back, and Junior year he began committing "environmental actions," as he called them. One night, he and his group put sugar in the gas tank of a bulldozer that had been leveling a meadow to build a new strip mall at the edge of town. Another time, he dumped a can of pink paint over a

Hanover police car while the officer was drinking coffee inside a diner. The pranks became steadily more serious. He took a chain saw to the exposed wood framing of a house that was being built overlooking a golf course. He put a dead rat in the mailbox of a county commissioner who was notably pro-development.

Howie refused to go along on these escapades. He could only shake his head and warn Nick that he was going to get caught and find himself in a lot of trouble.

Then one night Nick returned to the room, his eyes blazing, full of wild laughter. "You'll never guess what I did!" he cried.

Howie didn't want to guess, he didn't want to know. But Nick told him anyway.

"I robbed the pharmacy on Main Street! Goddamn, it was fun! I got away with $784 from the till!"

Howie had been sitting at his desk working on a term paper. His mouth fell open. "Nick! For chrissake, pharmacies have cameras all over!"

"I wore a ski mask. I kept one hand in my coat pocket and pretended I had a gun. It was so damn easy! The guy behind the counter was terrified."

"But, Nick! Why? Don't you realize he could have had a real gun? He could have shot you. And for what? You don't even need the money!"

"You don't understand, it was a total lark, that's all. And do you know what I did with the money? I drove to the homeless camp by the river and gave it to two drunks, every penny. You should have seen the look on their faces when they saw how much it was! I felt like I was Robin Hood!"

Howie could only shake his head in despair. He told Nick he was going to get arrested and prison would put a serious end to the hilarity.

But his roommate only smiled. For weeks afterwards, Howie expected the police to show up at their room but they never did. Somehow Nick got away with it.

As Howie foresaw, Nick fell into a depression soon enough. "I don't know what comes over me sometimes, Howie. Jesus, I can't believe I actually robbed that store!"

"Okay, you got away with it this time," Howie told him. "But you have to stop this stuff, Nick. You really do. I think you should go to the student health service and talk to one of the shrinks."

"Oh, come on, Howie! Those guys don't know anything."

"Nick, listen to me. You're bipolar, that's what this is all about. Lots of people suffer from this. You can get help."

"No. I mean, you're right about bipolar. But I can deal with that on my own. What I need to do is stop smoking weed for a while. That's what exacerbates everything."

"Good idea," said Howie, who wasn't smoking very much cannabis himself by then. Just the occasional puff, because there was a lot of grass getting smoked at Dartmouth and it was almost impossible to avoid.

Final exams were coming up at the end of the school year and Howie needed to study. To his relief, Nick appeared to settle down and hit the books as well. There were no more episodes of playing Robin Hood.

And then, to his surprise, he invited Howie to spend the summer with him at the family beach house on Cape Cod. Howie tried to say no. He was planning to stay in Hanover and continue doing research for the professor who was writing a book. It would be a way to save money for next year. But Nick kept badgering him.

"Grace is going to be there," Nick promised.

"No, Nick—thanks but no thanks. Grace is the last thing I need."

"You should see her in a bikini, Howie. It's not a sight you want to miss. And look, we have Internet at the beach—you can keep doing research for your professor."

Howie and Nick had gone through a rough patch for a time during "the crazy period," as Nick was now calling his "adventures." But he was behaving in a steadier fashion and they were close again. They had both worked hard and had passed all their courses—Nick with straight A's, Howie with only a single B, in math, his worst subject.

"Please, Howie—I need you there, bro, I really do. When I'm around my family, I get seriously weirded out. You'll keep me out of trouble. And, hey, we got a nice little sailboat. We'll zip over to Martha's Vineyard, we'll get tan and healthy and have a lot of fun . . . Grace likes to sail, too, incidentally."

"Yeah, sure," said Howie with a sigh. "In her bikini, I bet."

"Topless sometimes," Nick mentioned. "She hates tan lines."

What could Howie say?

And so he set forth on his personal Summer of Love. A few decades later than the rest of the world.

***

The vacation house on Cape Cod was a classic white two-story clapboard with blue trim on North Truro Beach. It was a bit run down, both inside and out, but that was part of its patrician charm.

New Mexico families didn't often have beach houses on Cape Cod, but the Stanton men had graduated from Yale for four generations, and the women always went to either Smith or Vassar, so they were a western clan with an East Coast tilt. Nick had been the odd Stanton out, choosing Dartmouth over Yale, which had caused some consternation.

Howie and Nick had the beach house to themselves for the first few weeks in June before the rest of the family arrived and life became more complicated. The "nice little sailboat" Nick had spoken about was a 40 foot Catalina with a luxurious cabin and it didn't seem so small to Howie. It was called *Seas The Day,* which Nick thought an atrocious pun. It was docked at the Provincetown Marina which was a fifteen minute drive from the house.

Howie soon learned the basics of sailing—hoisting sails, tacking, reading charts, radio protocol, navigation, understanding tides and currents, mixing cocktails in gale force winds. The weather was mostly fine, and they spent nearly every day on the water and often slept aboard at night, either anchored in some pretty cove or moored at the marina where there was always a party in progress on somebody's boat, no invitation required. *Seas The Day* had two staterooms, a fully equipped kitchen, a dining area, and a stereo system that could blast a battleship out of the water.

When they weren't on the boat, they were off exploring Provincetown. P-Town, as Howie learned to call it, was an arty, bohemian community with plenty of bars and restaurants and a free wheeling late-night scene. Both Nick and Howie were underage, but Nick managed to get them fake IDs and they were soon enjoying a pleasantly dissolute summer existence of salt and sun, gin and tequila, and not much sleep.

And then Grace arrived. She showed up in a bright yellow two-seater Alfa Romeo, top down, huge sunglasses, blonde hair blowing in the wind, and from that moment on Howie only had eyes for her.

She arrived in a funk, unhappy with life, and spent her time slouching around the house, reading *Buddenbrooks,* and taking long walks on the beach by herself. According to Nick, she had just broken off an affair with her English Lit professor at Smith.

"She's always had a thing for older men," Nick told him. Which Howie didn't take as good news, being nearly three years younger.

Looking back from the future—older, at least somewhat wiser—Howie couldn't say exactly what it had been about Grace Stanton that fascinated him so much. Yes, she was physically beautiful, and that was huge when you were nineteen years old and your hormones were just barely under control. But she was also sullen and spoiled and out of reach. Objectively put, she was a real pain in the ass.

So why did he mistake her for some magical golden girl? Was it the summer itself that he was in love with? Or maybe it was the aura of the Stanton family, their wealth, though he was embarrassed to admit it—the lure of old money and sophistication for a kid from the rez who had read too many books but didn't have a clear idea yet as to what the world was about. For Howie, the blue ocean, the sun, the summer, the magic of youth—it all conspired together to create an overwhelming intoxication.

Whatever it was, Howie found he could think of little else but Grace that June. Sadly, his obsession wasn't returned.

Nick occasionally asked Grace to come sailing with them, but she shrugged and said she wasn't in the mood. Howie in fact saw very little of her until the end of the month when Justin showed up—the boring, conservative older brother—and soon after that their father and mother arrived from Washington with the Senator's chief of staff, Summer Newsome. This was awkward. Howie didn't know if Anne was aware that her husband was having an affair with Summer, but Nick and Grace knew and they didn't like it. The atmosphere in the house was poisonous and Grace decided that getting out on the ocean with Nick and Howie wasn't such a bad idea after all.

Howie was thrilled, though she remained even more remote than ever. She did little to help with the work of sailing and spent most of her time stretched out on the small forward deck with *Buddenbrooks* propped up on her lap. Howie's one attempt at conversation—"have you read *The Magic Mountain*?"—received barely a grunt in reply.

So it came as a surprise on July 4th when she plopped down next to him on the sand around the bonfire they had made on the beach, sitting close enough that their shoulders touched.

She had a bottle of champagne in her hand which she passed his way. There had been a barbecue on the beach at sunset followed by elaborate fireworks. Sparks from the fire flew and scattered into the night. The surf broke and hissed up the sand in the near distance.

Howie raised the bottle by the neck and took a drink. It was very good champagne, Veuve Clicquot, but it wasn't cold. He didn't mind that. It was enough that his lips touched the bottle where her lips had been. He imagined that this was as close to a kiss as he was ever going to get.

"So, are you having a fabulous summer?" she asked sarcastically, as though only an idiot could have a good time on Cape Cod.

"Well, yes, actually it's been wonderful," he admitted. "I love the ocean. Where I come from, South Dakota, we have the Black Hills, which are beautiful—the center of the Earth, as any Sioux will tell you. But we don't have the Atlantic."

"And you'll be going back there when you're done with school?"

"Sure. Though I'm hoping to travel first. As much as I can. To Europe, Asia, and especially Australia. I want to get to know the aboriginal people."

She seemed far away, not really listening.

"I'm worried about Nick," she said, taking back the bottle. "He seems so . . ."

She was unable to finish the sentence and Howie didn't help her.

"Extreme," she decided after a long pause.

Howie knew that Nick was off in the sand dunes with a local P-Town girl named Carol. At a college-age party at night on the beach, sex is never far away.

Grace took a long swig from the bottle and handed it back to him.

"You're Nick's best friend, so tell me—what's going on with him?"

"That's a hard question," he replied. "He seemed a little crazy for a while. But he's doing better, especially here at the beach."

Howie ended up telling her about the pranks Nick had done at Dartmouth, and the time he had robbed a pharmacy and given the money to two homeless men. He didn't want to be disloyal to Nick, but this was his sister and he thought she should know.

"Did you go along with these pranks?" she asked.

"Well, no." He hesitated. "I'm on a scholarship. I'm a poor kid. I have to toe-the-line, so I don't get kicked out. I don't have the luxury of risky behavior."

"Risky behavior!" she repeated thoughtfully. "I guess I'm that way, too." She took a long swig of the champagne and finished the bottle. "Here's what you need to understand about us, Moon Deer. We're the wrong end of the Stanton line. The end of the line. That's why we're so awful. We're the ones who are paying the price."

"The price for what?"

"A hundred and fifty years of bad karma. My great-great grandfather, Jeremiah Stanton, was an army captain in the 1848 war with Mexico. He was from Pennsylvania, but the lawlessness of the Southwest appealed to his predatory instincts, and when the war was over, he stayed and managed to steal himself a big chunk of land. A couple of hundred thousand acres in what is now Lincoln County. He just took what he wanted. The Mexicans had lost the war and he shot anybody who gave him trouble. That's what it was like back then. Jeremiah was a real son of a bitch.

"And that was only the start of it. Jeremiah had two sons and a daughter. One of the sons became a cattle baron, the other a banker, and the daughter went to Washington and became the mistress of Ulysses S. Grant. There weren't many rules back in the Territorial days to stop ambitious white men doing whatever they wanted, and what rules there were, my family broke. You see where this is going, I hope?"

"Not really," Howie admitted. "Jeremiah and his children lived a long time ago. I don't see what this has to do with you and Nick."

"It's bad juju, Moon Deer. The sins of the father. By the time Adam Stanton came along, my grandfather, we'd had a hundred years of greed and thievery behind us, and all the arrogance of thinking we were better than other people. These things don't go away. They leave a mark."

Howie shook his head. "You and Nick don't need to pay for the sins of your ancestors, Grace. You make your own choices as to who you are. You don't have to be like them."

"You think so? I'm not so sure."

She disappeared again into one of her sulky silences, staring into the fire. Howie didn't disturb her. He believed she was thinking profound thoughts. It wasn't until years later that he realized she wasn't thinking much at all. She was simply seized, like a child, by self-indulgent moodiness.

"You know something, Howard Moon Deer? I've underestimated you," she said turning to him. Her face glowed in the firelight. "Come on, let's take a walk. I'm restless."

She stood abruptly. Howie followed her into the darkness away from the bonfire toward the hard wet sand by the edge of the surf. He had never been alone with Grace before and his heart was thumping.

"*Ow-uuu*!" she cried, a coyote howl, as she took off running along the surf. She laughed when a wave caught her, foaming around her ankles. She was fast and Howie had to hurry to keep up. Howie had never seen her like this before and he was fascinated. She was in a wild mood, unleashed.

Looking back from the future, the older Howie—the one who was driving to the Stanton Ranch for Thanksgiving—remembered this moment and said aloud to himself, "Don't do it, Howie, stop—don't run after her! Stop the frame right there!"

But, of course, the man in the future can't speak backward in time to the fool in the past.

And so he ran after her along the surf, caught up in her mood, laughing and full of champagne and desire, until a wave caught them, as waves will.

The water surged nearly to Howie's waist. When the wave hissed back across the sand, he found his pants were sopping wet.

She stopped running and turned to face him. Her eyes glittered in the moonlight. She stepped closer.

"Kiss me," she said, point blank.

"Well, uh—"

"I'd say if ever you're going to kiss me, you'd better do it now, Moon Deer! Or forever hold your lips!"

Put it that way, there wasn't much left for Howie to do except seize the moment. And the kiss.

When their lips touched, he could barely believe how soft and delicious she was. But it was embarrassing because he became instantly aroused and there wasn't much that was separating them. The kiss lingered until the surging tide threatened to pull them off their feet.

"Come on," she said, breaking free. She took his hand and led him toward the sand dunes. "Let's get you out of those wet pants . . ."

Chapter Seven

The Stanton Ranch was located at the foot of mountains that rose to the west an hour's drive from town. It sat in regal isolation on a wide grassy plateau at an altitude of 8000 feet. Though it was closer to Santa Fe than San Geronimo, it was—just barely, officially—in San Geronimo County.

Howie came to an impressive gate that stood by itself in the middle of nowhere, two stone pillars with a heavy wooden beam stretched out across the top. A sign dangled from the beam with an old-fashioned coat of arms that had a lion on it and a pair of crossed arrows, very impressive. The dirt road that began at this point was called, according to Google Maps, Camino de la Vieja Escuela. Old School Road. Howie wasn't certain if old school referred to the fact that Senator Stanton was a political dinosaur of the pre-populist Republican Party, or whether there had at one time been an actual school here.

The gate was open and Howie drove on through. Camino de la Vieja Escuela appeared to go for miles, not a building in sight. At last he came over a hill and saw in the distance a large main house with a peaked roof that was built in the Territorial style. There were a number of barns, outbuildings, horse corrals, pastures with horses grazing, and an old adobe church. It was quite a spread.

Howie knew about the ranch from Grace, though he had never been here himself until today. Senator Stanton had inherited the property in the 1980s from his father, Adam, the Indian Affairs Commissioner. The Senator had done a good deal of remodeling of the main building and had added a swimming pool. For all the money that had gone into the place, Grace had told him that her father spent maybe three or four weeks here in the summer when he wasn't in Cape Cod, New York City, or Santa Fe. When you owned so many houses, it was probably a challenge to decide where to go.

Howie parked by the main building next to a Land Rover and the vintage Bentley that belonged to Grace's house guest, the colorful Lorenzo Stein.

Howie took a very deep breath. In fact, he took several deep breaths. Then he went inside.

***

Howie was met at the front door by an elderly Native American woman with high cheek bones and white hair who gave him a good looking-over, one Indian to another. She seemed to be saying, "What the hell are you doing here, boy, are you crazy?" He found out later that her name was Ramona and that she had been a retainer of the Stanton family for many years.

Ramona led him into a large living room that was full of people standing and comfortably gathered on sofas and armchairs, talking in a murmur of voices.

The room was rustic with leather sofas and a stone fireplace at one end where two huge logs were burning on the hearth. The side tables and walls were crowded with Southwest objects of art—pottery, kachina dolls, sand paintings, sculpture, R.G. Gorman prints, Navajo weavings, all of obvious museum quality. Several large windows looked out across the valley to distant mountains whose high bald reaches were white with snow. Not enough snow, sadly, for the sport Howie wished he were enjoying today.

Grace came his way and kissed him on both cheeks. She was dressed in jeans, cowboy boots, and a flannel shirt. Western chic.

"You made it, Howie! I'm so glad!" She held both his hands as though she were afraid he might get away. "Can I get you a drink? A glass of champagne?"

"Maybe I'll wait," he told her, not wanting to get started with alcohol too early in the day. He couldn't help remembering the long-ago bottle of champagne on Truro Beach that had led them into the sand dunes.

Howie recognized most of the people present, though not everyone. The first person he noticed was Grace's friend, Lorenzo, who was on a sofa in an animated conversation with Stephen Halley, the editor from New York, who was likewise dressed in jeans and a flannel shirt. Lorenzo wore a light blue denim shirt with pearl buttons. When in the Wild West, these were people who liked to dress the part.

"I'd better take you over to say hello to Daddy," Grace told Howie, still clutching onto one hand. "He likes to observe the rituals."

Daddy was on the far side of the room standing by the fireplace with a glass of wine in his hand. He was talking to his oldest son, Justin, who had gained a good deal of weight and looked much older than when Howie had seen him last.

"Well, well, it's Howard!" the Senator said in his deep senatorial voice. "I see you survived our tussle last week with the rabble."

"Rabble?" Howie wondered.

"Those cretins who stormed the La Fonda. Do you know the problem with democracy, Howard? It's allowing the uneducated mob to have a say in government."

"That's our Constitution," Howie replied. "Everyone has a vote. Even cretins."

"Nonsense!" said the Senator. "The Founding Fathers didn't intend for us to have a democracy. We're a republic, which is quite different. In the early days of our country, only males with a certain amount of money were allowed to vote. I often think we would be better off if we had kept to our original intention."

Howie knew he was being baited. In America's early years, only wealthy white males were allowed to vote. No blacks, no women, and certainly no Indians.

"Life moves on, Senator," Howie replied mildly. "Times change."

"Do they? But, you see, I wonder if they change for the better. Has our Grace gotten you something to drink? Has she seen to your needs?"

Our Grace? Howie managed a smile.

"I'm fine, sir. Just fine."

"And you remember Justin, I presume?"

Howie turned to the older brother. It was hard to imagine Nick and Justin were from the same family. Justin looked as though he belonged to a different generation, a different tribe. He wore brown corduroy pants and a dark blue sweater that might have been cashmere. His light brown hair was combed to one side in a style Howie thought of as more 1940s than today. His face was pudgy and his eyes were small. Howie had never had much to do with him.

"So how have you been keeping yourself, Moon Deer?" Justin asked. Like his father, he spoke in an amused, patronizing tone.

"I've been keeping well," Howie replied, hoping that didn't make him sound like a cask of wine in the cellar.

He met Justin's wife, Belinda—a thin blonde woman with a sharp, fox-like face—and Justin pointed out two boys in their early teens on the floor playing Monopoly. "The offspring," he said dismissively. He didn't mention their names, but Howie was willing to bet one of them would be Justin Junior.

"You'd better say hello to my mother," Grace said, coming to his rescue, leading him away.

Howie was surprised Grace would refer to Summer as her mother, and then was even more surprised to discover that it *was* her mother, Wife #1, Anne Stanton, who was standing across the room watching them with an inscrutable expression on her face. She was a gray-haired woman in her 70s but still elegant, unruffled by age. Two wives at one Thanksgiving seemed excessive. But what did Howie know? He was just a poor boy.

"You're looking very spry, Howard," she said. "I'm surprised to see you here, to be honest. After all these years."

Howie didn't mention that he was surprised to see her. "Where are you living these days, Mrs. Stanton?" he asked politely. "Are you here in New Mexico?"

"Oh, God, no! I hate this state, always have! It was one of the main things that drove Harlan and me apart. There's no water. For my sanity, I have to be near the ocean. I'm in Florida now. Palm Beach."

"We have the Rio Grande, mother," said Grace.

"Hmm!" said Anne. "Frankly, that river has never looked so grand to me."

Grace parked Howie with her mother and then left, which he found awkward. He had never felt comfortable with Anne Stanton and wasn't sure how to keep a conversation going. His mind was a blank. Fortunately, Anne took charge.

"I wouldn't be here now, actually, but Harlan insisted. He said we needed to talk."

"Really?"

"About his will, I suppose. He's one of those old misers who's always talking about his will, who he's cutting out, who's currently in line to get the loot. It's really quite despicable. But I came because I was curious to see how he's getting along with that woman he married. And, of course, I wanted to see the children. What do you think of our Grace?"

There it was again, *our Grace!* Howie wanted to say, she's not *my* Grace.

"Becoming a bestselling author, I mean," Anne clarified. "You know, I never would have suspected she had it in her. She never showed the slightest interest in writing when she was young."

"I'm impressed," Howie told her. "I understand it's very difficult to get published these days."

"Have you tried reading one of her books? Too much sex in them, I say. And bad language! Whenever I find a four-letter word in a book, I simply close it and throw it in the trash!."

Howie was wondering how to reply to this when Summer Stanton, Wife #2, appeared at that moment and saved him.

"Excuse me, Anne," she said pleasantly to her predecessor, "but I need to have a word with Moon Deer. Do you mind, Howard? Let's step into my office for a few minutes, shall we?"

Howie was given no opportunity to say no. It was a command, not a request. That was the Stanton family for you. It wasn't so much *noblesse oblige* as *droit du seigneur*.

They were an arrogant clan, every last one of them. So arrogant they didn't even know they were arrogant. They accepted their right to order people around as simply the natural order of things.

Nevertheless, he followed Summer Stanton into her study, curious what she had to say to him.

***

Summer Stanton's home office was a snug den with a low ceiling of heavy beams in the rear of the house.

The decor was a continuation of über-Wild West. The walls were paneled with rustic wood and there was a Frederic Remington painting above the fireplace of a cowboy dressed in chaps and spurs sitting on a horse and peering out onto a wide valley deep in contemplation of his free-spirited cowboy life. He looked like he was about to break into a chorus of "Home on the Range."

Outside the den window, a large white horse was cantering back and forth in a nearby corral, tossing his head and looking frisky.

"That's Grace's horse, Valkyrie," Summer mentioned, following his gaze.

Howie remembered Grace's love of Wagner. She liked power music. The Ride of the Valkyries was just her thing.

"Do you ride, too, Mrs. Stanton?"

"Please, call me Summer. No, not often. I'm a city girl, from San Francisco. But I do love it here. The sky, the open space . . . that feeling that nobody's going to fence you in. Have a seat, Howard. I want to show you something."

Howie settled into a large wooden rocking chair facing Summer, who was seated behind her desk. Despite the frontier folksiness of the room, there was a no-nonsense desktop Mac on a side table and a FAX machine. She handed him a manila folder.

"Have a look," she said. "Harlan has been receiving these over the course of the last month.

Inside the folder were three white envelopes that had been mailed to Senator Harlan Stanton at his home in Santa Fe. The address had been typed by a computer printer. The cancelled stamps showed that they had been mailed from Albuquerque. There were no return addresses in the upper left-hand corner.

Howie opened the envelopes one by one. Each contained a sheet of white A8 paper folded neatly into thirds, each with a single sentence typed in capital letters in the middle of the page.

The first letter read: DIE INDIAN KILLER DIE.

The second: A KNIFE TO YOUR THROAT.

The third: A SCALP TAKEN.

Brief but unpleasant.

"What do you think?" she asked.

"Looks like your husband has an enemy. Have you shown these to the police?"

She shook her head. "We decided not to. We don't want this kind of publicity. Anyway, when you're in politics, you come to expect hate mail and nasty phone calls. It goes with the territory. Harlan is a Republican in a Blue district. A lot of people don't like him."

"But he retired, what . . . three years ago? It's hard to imagine anyone still cares enough about his politics to send letters like this."

"He didn't retire, Howard. He lost. There's a difference. These threats are obviously a reaction to the chapter in his book about his father. 'Die Indian killer die' and the reference to scalping. I'd say these came from some kind of self-styled Indian activist."

"Perhaps," Howie agreed. "Though you can't say that for certain."

"You know, it really bothers me that people don't understand what Harlan's father was trying to achieve with the Indian School policy. He was hoping to bring Native Americans into the modern world. To give them a chance to be . . . well, not so backward."

Howie's smile had become strained. "Yes, that's what the Senator said at the book signing."

"But you don't agree?"

"Mrs. Stanton . . . Summer. Those schools were terrible places. Many of the children were physically and sexually abused. It's been well documented."

"Yes, I'm sure there were instances of that," she said. "But Howie, they're the exception. The basic idea was sound. These days it's being portrayed as some terrible racist program, almost like something the Nazis might have dreamed up in Germany in the Thirties. That's the impression Harlan is trying to correct with his book. The idea back then was basically . . . well, liberal! Don't you see? It was progressive!"

Howie only smiled.

"Now, Howard, let me get to why I called you in here. I'd like to hire you to discover who wrote these letters. I understand you're excellent at what you do. Plus, I happen to know Jack Wilder from when I lived in San Francisco and I'm aware that he's very good also. Harlan and I have discussed this and we both believe you are the right people to get to the bottom of these letters."

"How do you know Jack?"

"Before I became Harlan's chief of staff, I was a reporter for the *San Francisco Examiner,* back when Jack was often the spokesperson for the SFPD. Jack wasn't terribly cooperative with the press, I'm sorry to say. But I respected his ability as an extremely talented detective. So why don't you tell me how much you charge and I'm sure we can come to an arrangement. We'd like you to start right away."

"I haven't said we'd accept the case. To begin with, I'd have to ask Jack, of course. And then I'm not sure it's appropriate for me to take on a case where I have a . . . well, a personal involvement."

"Because you had an affair with Grace?" she asked bluntly.

"Well, sure," Howie agreed. "Plus, Nick was my friend and roommate."

"But that's exactly why we want to hire you! You're close to the family. You'll know how to be discreet if something . . . well, if something sensitive comes up."

Howie shook his head. "Summer, I appreciate the offer. But I think you and the Senator would do best employing someone who has no personal connection to your family. If you'd like, I can recommend a good detective agency in Albuquerque that I'm sure would be happy to take this on."

"That's very proper of you," Summer agreed. "But I don't see that it's necessary. In a case like this, I'd say your connection to the family is exactly what we need."

Howie shook his head. "Poison pen letters are a nasty business, Summer. The first place Jack and I would look for the culprit would be right here in the heart of the family. And I wouldn't want to do that. It wouldn't be appropriate."

"I disagree. I think it would be very appropriate. Especially if this turns out to be personal, as you put it. I'm not saying it is—I still think it will turn out to be some kind of Indian activist with a grudge."

"Summer, I'm sorry," Howie persisted. "But this isn't something I want to get involved in."

"Even to help Grace?"

"I bet Grace knows a lot of people who would tie themselves up in knots to help her," Howie said. "But I'm not one of them."

Summer stared at him without saying a word. She picked up a pen from her desk and slapped it rhythmically against the palm of her hand. She looked at him some more. Howie knew this was designed to make him squirm and he didn't like it. He said nothing in return and stared back.

"Okay, let's get real," she said at last. "Let's say someone close to the family wrote these letters. That would be unpleasant for us if it came out. Like most families, the Stantons have a few skeletons in the closet, things we wouldn't like an outsider to find out. But you're a part of the family yourself. If you came across one of our secrets . . . well, you see, we know your secrets, too, so you'd have to keep your mouth shut about what you find. I call that parity, wouldn't you?"

Howie laughed incredulously. "Are you trying to blackmail me, Summer?"

"Not at all. I'm just putting my cards on the table."

"Then let's back up for a moment. First of all, I'm not part of the family. I had a romance with Grace when I was nineteen, that's all. It was long ago and it's certainly not a secret."

She smiled slightly, but it wasn't a pleasant smile. Howie could imagine she'd been very effective in Washington as the Senator's chief of staff.

"You don't know, do you?" she said.

"Know what?"

"She didn't tell you! Imagine that!"

Howie stood up. "Mrs. Stanton, I came today because Grace asked me. But I'm not really interested in playing games."

"Oh, this isn't a game. Shall I tell you something you don't know?"

"Please, stop."

"You got Grace pregnant all those years ago, that summer when you were lovers."

"No, that's not true. She used birth control."

"She used a diaphragm, Howie. But she was nearly as young as you were and even more impulsive. She didn't always put it in." Summer smiled coyly. "See how much I know about you? The way I heard it, you two often had sex three or four times a day."

Howie was so surprised he sat back down. What Summer said was true. They were young and they had been on fire. But he couldn't imagine how Summer knew these intimate details.

"You're telling me Grace had an abortion?"

She shook her head. "I'm not telling you that in the least. I'm saying you have a daughter. You're a father, Howard. Congratulations!"

Howie's mouth fell open. "I don't believe you!"

"Then you'd better ask Grace. She'll deny it at first, but keep at her and she'll come clean. Then come back to me and I'll tell you how you can find your child. That is, *after* you discover who's writing those notes and make certain they never happen again."

Her smile was triumphant.

"How do you know where this child is?" he asked. "If she even exists."

"I know because I was the one who took care of the problem. Grace went to Daddy, as she always does in the end. And Daddy came to me. I was his fixer for everything. I did the dirty work. I found that unwanted baby a home."

Howie had a sickening feeling that she might be speaking the truth.

"You know something, Mrs. Stanton? You are a very unpleasant woman."

She laughed. "Aren't I, though? And you'd better remember that, Moon Deer!"

Chapter Eight

It wasn't a happy Thanksgiving gathering. But at least the turkey was good and there was plenty of it. Nobody was going to leave the table hungry.

There was corn bread stuffing, mashed potatoes, gravy, green beans with slivered almonds, cranberry sauce, corn pudding, creamed spinach, stuffed mushrooms, three different kinds of salad, on and on. It was about as traditional a Thanksgiving as you could find this side of Plymouth Rock. Ramona, the expressionless Native American servant, appeared from the kitchen every few minutes with a new platter. For dessert, there was pumpkin pie with vanilla ice cream, pecan pie, several different kinds of homemade cookies, and cranberry bread—Howie's modest contribution.

Howie considered himself a "food person"—he avoided the term "foodie" as infantile. But on this occasion, he barely noticed the platters as they came and went. He was upset and angry. The anger grew on him as he sat picking at his dinner. It started out small, like an ember, and quickly grew to a forest fire.

"Is it true?" he kept asking himself. "I have a daughter?"

He didn't believe it.

Yet, on the other hand, he did believe it. Summer Stanton was a nasty piece of work, he didn't like her. But he couldn't imagine she would make up a thing like that.

"Have some wine, Howie," Lorenzo urged. He was seated on his right with a bottle of a very good pinot noir in hand. He had just topped off his own glass and was now refilling Howie's.

Howie didn't say yes to the wine, but he didn't say no. He watched numbly as his glass was filled. If he had a daughter, he was thinking, she would be, what . . . fourteen? No, fifteen.

And Grace didn't tell me? How the hell could she not tell me?

"Have you ever skied St. Moritz, Moon Deer?" Lorenzo was asking.

They had been discussing skiing, the Alps versus the Rockies, though Howie was barely conscious of what he had said.

"St. Moritz? Switzerland?"

"Exactly, Switzerland. Are you okay, Howie? You look a little out of it."

"I'm fine," he said, putting on a smile. "I was just thinking about something."

"Sad thoughts?"

"Not entirely happy ones," he admitted.

"Look, Howie, I tell you what. I have a small chalet in St. Moritz and I was thinking of taking Grace there for a few weeks in February. Why don't you join us? We'll drink up a storm, eat our brains out, and ski. We'll have a fabulous time!"

"Sounds wonderful," Howie lied.

The ranch dining room was large enough for a hoedown. Howie sat part way down a long table made of thick planks of dark wood that looked like they had been hewn from a giant oak. Rural chic. The guests, seated on either side, were lined up facing each other like opposing football teams.

Senator Stanton was seated at the head of the table and Summer Stanton, Wife #2, occupied the foot. Between them, nine places had been set for Howie and the extended family.

Grace sat almost directly across from Howie, studiously avoiding his eye. She was lovely but distant. Her golden hair glowed in the candlelight, but it didn't glow for him.

Anne Stanton, Wife #1, prim and aristocratic, was on Grace's left with an inscrutable smile on her face. Howie was still trying to figure out what in the world she was doing here.

Justin, on Grace's right, was speaking about investment opportunities to his father at the head of the table as he gobbled up a second helping of turkey and stuffing. The Senator, who was pecking at his food, had a pessimistic view of the current stock market and was saying, loudly enough for the entire table to hear, that there was going to be a major correction. Personally, he was putting his money offshore in the Cayman Islands. For a flag-waving patriot, this didn't sound very patriotic to Howie, but who was he to say? He had no money to invest anywhere, offshore or on.

Next to Justin sat his wife, Belinda, a sharp-faced blond who might have been pretty except that her face lacked any sign of joy or humor. Probably she had looked good at the age of 18, before marriage and disillusionment had caught up with her.

Stephen Halley, the owlish middle-aged editor from New York, was on Howie's left, while Lorenzo, on his right, was enjoying an entirely liquid Thanksgiving. Justin and Belinda's two teenage sons—Chris, 16, and Bo, 13—completed the table. Howie had been wrong in supposing that one of them would be named Junior. The two boys sat without saying much, obviously wishing they were with their friends, occasionally sneaking yearning glances at their phones. From across the table, their mother had to tell them twice that they shouldn't have filled up on breakfast cereal earlier in the day, and they weren't going to get dessert if they didn't finish their meals.

Howie had been at Stanton family gatherings before, but never without Nick. His absence today cast a shadow, a ghost hovering in the air. No one mentioned Nick. Nobody said his name. Yet Howie felt his presence everywhere.

Howie, who barely touched his food, made an effort to put Grace out of mind and converse with his two immediate dinner partners. He spoke to the editor about the state of American publishing, which apparently was as gloomy as everything else in America at the moment. Amazon was the villain, of course. Amazon had destroyed traditional publishing and had all but nuked brick-and-mortar bookstores across the country.

"Thank God for women writers!" said Stephen. "They're the bright spot on our list. But male writers, forget it! The Norman Mailers, the Hemingways—they're historical relics, dinosaurs. Men don't read anymore. They're watching football and drinking beer. It's women who read books, and they want to read about themselves—books for women, written by women."

"Writers like Grace," Howie mentioned, glancing across the table.

"Exactly. Our Grace is one of our most reliable authors at pee-pee."

"I'm sorry? Pee-pee?"

"Peckham & Peale. She has a huge following."

"And you've been her publisher since the start of her career?"

"You bet! We discovered her. She's our girl. Six books so far, and we're not going to let her go!"

Grace had heard her name and turned from her mother with a curious glance at Howie and Stephen across the table.

"Then you'd better up the advance for the next installment," she said with a hard smile.

"Ah, yes, the next thrilling thriller!" said Stephen. "Damsels in distress! But let's talk about money another time, don't you think?"

"Good idea, Stephen," Grace answered, "why don't we?"

It was a subtly poisonous exchange. Howie looked back and forth from one to the other as they spoke, wondering about the undercurrents.

Grace pointedly turned her attention back to her mother. Stephen grimaced and took a long drink of wine.

"Authors!" he muttered.

"So how about political memoirs?" Howie asked. "How are *they* selling?"

"That depends. They can make a mint if the politician in question is embroiled in the seamy scandal *du jour*. Otherwise, forget it. Who wants to read a lot of blather?"

"Do you expect to do well with the Senator's book?"

Stephen Halley shrugged. "Naturally," he said vaguely. "Or we wouldn't be publishing it." But he didn't sound convincing.

Howie had run out of conversational book talk. He sat with his glass of wine wondering when he was going to get an opportunity to get Grace alone and have a serious talk. At the end of the table, Justin was telling his father about a survivalist boot camp he had attended that summer, a ten-day course in the use of weaponry for millionaires who were readying themselves for the day when the meek decided their moment had come. The course had been held at a remote property in Montana and had included instruction in stun grenades and fully automatic assault rifles.

"You should have seen it, Dad! All these overweight hedge fund managers and bankers and CEOs in fatigues crawling around on the ground with rifles! They're getting their escape hatch ready, how they're going to get out to the country when the mobs show up at their door. Most of them have overseas houses as well, all ready for them with their money socked away. Switzerland, Canada, Argentina, Panama, all the fun places. Seriously, Dad, there's going to be bloodshed. I hope you're making preparations."

Senator Stanton took a long, thoughtful breath. "There's *not* going to be a revolution, Justin," he said decisively.

"Dad—"

"No, you don't understand. The rabble are asleep. We've bought them off with a modest portion of comfortable living and digital toys. No, son, there's no reason to fear the opiated masses."

"I'm not so sure about that, Dad. There are rumblings. There are lefties everywhere."

As if on cue, they both turned to Howie.

"Then let's take a small survey since we happen to have a socialist among us," said the Senator. "Moon Deer tell us, is there going to be a revolution?"

Howie should have smiled and passed off the question with a laugh. There was no way for him to win a debate with Senator Stanton on his home turf. But he was reeling from his conversation with Summer, worked up. Frankly, he'd had about all he was willing to take from the Stanton family.

"First, I'm not a socialist, Senator. I'm a plain ordinary American—"

"Oh, come on, Moon Deer! You're neither plain nor ordinary! And I'm not sure how American you are!"

"How American *I* am?" Howie cried with incredulity. "I'm an Indian!"

"Don't swear at me, boy!"

"I'm not swearing. I'm just saying I'm American through and through. I believe in life, liberty, and the pursuit of happiness. I believe in the Statue of Liberty. Give me your tired, your hungry, your poor. That isn't socialism. It's democracy."

"Oh, come, come! When you talk about the hungry and the poor, you're promoting socialism. All you want are hand-outs!"

"No, I don't want hand-outs. I want schools, I want health care that's affordable, and I want air you can breathe!" Howie had become more heated than he had intended. "I want every kid in America to have a chance. And I want the rich to pay their fair share. They wouldn't *be* rich if it weren't for the society they live in. They haven't made their money in a vacuum and they owe something back."

It was a pointless conversation. Howie wasn't going to change his mind, nor was Senator Stanton. But they were wound up and they kept at it.

"Do you know, young man, the word school is never mentioned in the Constitution," said the Senator. "Or health care, for that matter. Not once. This is all Marxist nonsense!"

"Public schools are Marxist? You must be kidding!" Howie cried. "American democracy comes from Christianity, if anything. And I mean real Christianity, not your narrow-minded intolerance. To love your neighbor and treat everyone with respect. To share rather than hoard everything for yourself. You need to read your Bible, Senator."

By this point, both Howie and Senator Stanton were speaking in loud voices and the entire table had stopped to listen.

"Read *my* Bible!" cried the Senator. "Why, you lousy upstart! I bet you don't even know the Ten Commandments!"

"Oh, but I do!" Howie countered. "Enough to know that you've broken just about every one of them!"

This was where Howie made his big mistake. He turned to Summer at the far end of the table and gave her a meaningful look. It was a not-so-subtle reminder of adultery. He shouldn't have done it.

"How dare you?" cried the Senator. He was so overwrought he could hardly get the words out. It would have been hard to say how this would have turned out, but Anne, Wife #1, defused the situation. She stood up and took her ex-husband firmly by the arm.

"Harlan, Harlan, listen to me, it's Thanksgiving, it's not good for you to get so upset. Why don't we move into the living room and have our after dinner drinks there. I'm sure your football game is on. You don't want to miss the kick-off."

Anne knew how to handle him. But Howie was surprised that it was Anne, not Summer, who had come to the Senator's help when he appeared to be coming unglued. He watched as she and Justin led Harlan from the dining room toward the football game in the next room.

As the group walked away, Howie heard the Senator say, "And that damn redskin has the nerve to come pussyfooting around my daughter!"

Howie sat at the table and held onto his wine glass tensely with both hands. Somehow the glass was full and he drained it.

Harlan's departure began a general exodus from the dinner table to the living room and after dinner drinks. Howie was left by himself at the table feeling foolish and very much the odd man out. He knew he should have kept his temper.

He was thinking of driving home, getting the hell away from here, when he saw Grace walking toward the kitchen with an empty platter. He rose from the table and followed her into the kitchen. He stood behind her as she put down the platter on a heavy old wooden table where Ramona was spooning the leftovers into plastic containers.

"Grace, I need to talk with you."

She looked at him reluctantly.

"Not now, Howie. For God's sake, I was hoping to help Nick, but you've gone and ruined it. You just made everything worse by fighting with Daddy!"

"Grace, I wasn't looking for a fight—"

"I know he can be off-putting sometimes—"

"*Off-putting*! Grace, he's crazier than a hoot owl! Now look, I spoke with Summer earlier and she told me that you got pregnant—"

"Howie, no, I'm not going to talk about this now!" She gave Ramona an anxious glance. Ramona was putting away food and pretending not to listen. "I tell you what," she said, turning back to him. "Spend the night.

I'll make sure one of the guest rooms is made up and we'll talk in the morning."

"Grace, I'm not spending the night. I need to talk to you now."

"Howie, not now, tomorrow. When we've both calmed down. Besides, you have to spend the night. You can't drive, you've had too much to drink, they'll arrest you with all the holiday roadblocks that are up. So be reasonable, stay the night and I'll tell you everything you want to know in the morning. Okay?"

It wasn't okay and Howie wasn't feeling reasonable. But he knew she was right about him having too much to drink. He hadn't meant to drink. Raising a wine glass had been something for unhappy hands to do, and the wine had crept up on him.

But he wasn't going to let her go without asking the big question.

"You need to tell me, Grace. Do we have a child?"

The old Indian woman was no longer pretending to put away leftovers. She had stopped her work and was staring at Grace with a consuming interest.

"Goddamnit, not now!" Grace cried as she turned from him and rushed from the kitchen. "We'll talk tomorrow!"

***

And so Howie spent the night at the Stanton ranch. Like it or not he was stuck there.

He'd committed the classic mistake of arguing politics around the Thanksgiving table. Plus, he'd had too much to drink and couldn't drive home. How dumb could he be? It seemed to Howie that everything he'd done was wrong, including coming here in the first place. He collapsed into bed around midnight, unhappy with himself, without finding another chance to speak with Grace.

Howie's guest bedroom was on the ground floor, not far from the kitchen, with a sliding glass door that opened onto a flagstone patio. The bed was comfortable and he fell asleep almost immediately, only to wake an hour later full of worry and regret. It didn't help that his tongue was fuzzy and he felt as though his brain was pickled in pinot noir.

"Damnit!" he cried, sitting up in bed abruptly. He had forgotten to call Jack!

He hadn't thought of Jack and Emma's Thanksgiving until this moment! He'd been too preoccupied, fighting with the Senator and discovering that he might be a father. He had meant to phone to say he wasn't going to make it to Jack's house at seven, as promised, but with everything else going on, it had slipped his mind.

Jack was going to be worried and angry. For Howie, this was one more blunder to add to his Thanksgiving from hell.

In the morning, he was determined to talk with Grace and get to the truth of whether he was a father or not. Meanwhile, the digital numbers on the bedside clock moved slowly. 1:59 . . . 2:00 . . . 2:01, the seconds, the minutes, caught in a time warp of creeping misery.

At 2:48, Howie's breathing gradually slowed and he fell into an uneasy sleep. He dreamed that he was a Lakota warrior at Little Big Horn shooting George Armstrong Custer full of arrows. That had been a good day for his people. In the dream, Custer bore an uncanny resemblance to Senator Harlan Stanton.

It was such a convincing dream that when Howie woke at the height of the battle to the sound of a horse galloping outside his window, he thought at first that he was still at Little Big Horn. But he wasn't in Montana, he was at the Stanton Ranch in New Mexico. He sat up in bed, his mouth dry, his heart pounding.

The digital clock on his bedside table said 3:13. Oddly, he still heard hoofbeats, though the sound was fading.

He threw on a shirt and walked to the sliding glass door. The moon was nearly full, illuminating the meadow outside with a silver glow. He thought he saw something move, but he wasn't sure.

He slid the glass door open and stepped outside barefoot onto the flagstone. The night was frigid and still, in the low twenties. Howie was naked except for his shirt and he hoped there was nobody around to see him.

His eyes swept across the meadow beyond the terrace and he saw what had woken him. There was a horse and rider galloping into the distance. He only saw them for an instant, a dark silhouette in motion against the silver light of the moon. Together, the horse and rider made a strangely beautiful sight. But ominous.

As he watched, the rider galloped over the edge of the meadow and disappeared from view. Howie watched a few minutes more, curious if the rider would reappear, but he didn't.

Howie stepped back into the bedroom and closed the door behind him, belatedly realizing how cold he was.

He got back into bed and huddled beneath the covers to warm himself up.

3:19, said the digital clock, glowing green.

Which was when he heard the scream.

***

It wasn't a scream of pleasure, as screams can sometimes be in the middle of the night. It was a scream of terror.

Howie hurried into his jeans as fast as he could, doing a one-legged jig to keep his balance. At last, pants on, he ran into the hall with his shirt flapping.

The hallway was dark but there was a light coming from an open door. He heard footsteps on the second floor above his head. People in the house were awake, alarmed by the screaming.

Howie ran down the hallway to the open door. The room was a wood-paneled office Howie hadn't seen before. Summer was standing near a desk with her back to him. She was in a bathrobe and Howie noted that her hair was in curlers. Her body was rigid, both her hands were raised to her mouth.

"What's wrong?" he asked.

"He's . . . he's . . ."

She couldn't get beyond that. She was unable to speak.

Howie stepped past her and quickly saw what the matter was. Senator Stanton was on the floor, lying on his back on a Navajo rug in a pool of blood that had spread out around his head.

His throat had been cut.

But that wasn't all.

His hair was missing. The top of his head was fleshy pink and awful.

People were coming into the room behind him with expressions of horror and surprise. He heard someone retching.

The room was cold. Howie looked up from the corpse and saw that, like his guest bedroom, there was a sliding glass door leading outside to the flagstone patio. The glass door was open.

He would have liked to investigate further, but he knew he couldn't. This was going to be a crime scene.

"Let's not touch anything," he said. "We all need to back out of the room and wait for the police to arrive."

Howie found a land line in the living room and phoned 911. He managed to give the bare facts of the situation, leaving the full horror for the responding officers to discover for themselves.

This wasn't your everyday twenty-first century homicide. Senator Stanton had been scalped.

Chapter Nine

Thanksgiving for Jack Wilder had been a depressingly moderate affair.

Moderate was his new catchword at the age of 74 and not in the best of health. But it wasn't fun. Thanksgiving was his favorite holiday of the year. It wasn't emotionally complicated like Christmas. There were no presents to give, no guilt, no regrets, no crippling waves of nostalgia. You simply sat at the table and ate until you burst. As far as Jack was concerned, excess was what Thanksgiving was all about.

But not this year. Jack had consumed a mere two glasses of red wine, a nice Bordeaux that he sipped slowly to make the pleasure last. And that was it. *Nada mas*.

He ate moderately as well: one plate of turkey, a large plate admittedly, but no skin (his favorite part, as crisp as possible). He went easy on the gravy. No extra butter on the mashed potatoes. Stuffing of course, but not so much that he himself was stuffed. Creamed spinach, salad, cranberry sauce . . . well, it had added up, he had to be honest. But he'd added no extra salt. Not a pinch, not a shake. And he'd had only one small piece of Emma's pecan pie. She gave him a searching look from time to time because after so many years of marriage, she knew him very well. This wasn't like Jack at all.

In fact, Jack had a secret. Two weeks ago, he had experienced a spasm of pain that had seized his chest like a cold hand. This was accompanied by a wave of nausea, which he knew was a classic sign that things weren't good.

Fifteen minutes later, he felt okay and for two days afterwards he had done his best to pretend it hadn't happened. Jack was good at denial when it came to his health. But finally he had his secretary, Ruth, drive him to San Geronimo Family Practice, telling her it was a scheduled visit. After an EKG and a CT scan, his physician of many years, Dr. Killinger, told him he'd suffered what was known as a SMI, a Silent Myocardial Infarction.

"God tapped you on the shoulder, Jack," said Dr. Killinger. "You'll live quite a few years yet, but you need to change your eating and drinking habits and your lifestyle. No more stress, Jack. You've got to learn to relax. Otherwise, this is going to happen again. Only a lot more serious next time."

Change his lifestyle?

Relax?

That was a tall order for Jack Wilder. It wasn't simply diet. He was a stress junkie. He thrived on stress. It was what had propelled him forward from street cop to commander in the San Francisco PD.

He hadn't breathed a word of Silent Myocardial Infarction to either Emma or Howie. He didn't want them worrying and fussing over him. But it was more than that. To tell people would make it real. They would regard him differently. He would see his own vulnerability reflected in their eyes.

On Thanksgiving day, Jack kept his worries to himself. Lieutenant Santo Ruben came by with his new girlfriend, Angela Santistevan, who was a San Geronimo County Commissioner. Santo's wife had left him two years before and Jack was happy that Santo had found someone new. Angela was slim and pretty, a few years younger than Santo, but not such an age difference as to be a problem.

Detective Dan Hamm had joined them as well, bringing along a bowl of guacamole and chips—the standard bachelor's contribution to any gathering. Dan had been wounded recently, shot in the leg, but he was recovering nicely, doing desk duty at the station, not ready yet for regular rotation.

To complete the party, Emma had invited her friend, Tina Malkovich, an artist of some renown who was single, without a Thanksgiving dinner of her own to go to. Emma occasionally liked to invite a stray, someone she thought might be lonely during the holidays, and she liked having someone at the table who wasn't a cop.

Only Howie and Claire were missing, and Jack felt their absence. He worried about Howie for a number of reasons, both personal and professional. Claire was in Germany and he doubted she would be happy to know that Howie was spending the day with his old girlfriend, Grace.

And as if this weren't bad enough, Howie had delivered a message to Grace from her brother Nicolas, the eco-terrorist who was on the FBI's most wanted list! If Howie lost his P.I. license over that, Jack knew he would have to close the agency. Howie was his eyes. He couldn't be a blind detective without his help.

And then, to top it off, Howie hadn't showed up for dessert as he had promised!

It hadn't been a late night. The guests were gone by 10 o'clock and Jack helped Emma clean up in the kitchen. Though he was blind, he knew every inch of the kitchen by touch and had no trouble washing dishes.

"You're worried about Howie, aren't you?" Emma asked, standing next to him at the sink.

"To be honest, yes I am! Before everyone left, I slipped into my office and tried to give him a call. But there was no answer."

"Probably he's somewhere without service."

That was always a possibility in New Mexico, where there were huge stretches of the state not covered by phone service.

"You know, Jack, you have to stop worrying so much about Howie," Emma told him. "Sometimes you treat him more like a child than a colleague. He's a big boy and he knows how to take care of himself."

"Does he?"

"Of course, he does. So, you just have to stop worrying. It's not good for you. You need to relax."

She was right, of course. He needed to relax. It's what his doctor had told him. Stop acting like the world will fall apart if you're not watching every moment to keep everybody's life on track.

Jack kissed Emma goodnight in the kitchen, then they each went to their separate bedrooms. When they had reached their 70s, they had decided to forgo a conjugal bed. Emma certainly slept better without all his restless tossing and snoring.

In his bedroom, Jack closed his eyes, settled into his pillows, and prepared for his nightly bout with insomnia. He visualized blue water and palm trees swaying in soft southern breezes. This was the ticket, the happy road to sleep. Beautiful thoughts.

He refused to think of mangled bodies and the children he'd seen who had been raped and murdered.

"Don't count sheep," Dr. Killinger had told him. "Count your breaths. Long, peaceful breaths, in and out . . ."

He tried. He honestly did.

Blue water . . . red sails in the sunset . . . the breath flowing in, flowing out, joining the Big Breath of the Universe. How peaceful it was! Nevertheless, at 3 AM he still wasn't asleep. He *was* worried about Howie. He couldn't pretend he wasn't. Why hadn't Howie come by when he was supposed to? What sort of trouble was he in?

At 4 o'clock, Jack was almost asleep, lightly dozing.

At 4:16, he was truly asleep, out to the world, just as his phone rang.

Jack fumbled for the telephone on his bedside table.

"Goddamnit!" he swore. "Who the bloody hell is it?"

It was Howie.

As Jack listened, he sat up in bed, very much awake.

***

The law enforcement response to Senator Stanton's death was painfully slow due to the Thanksgiving weekend and the isolation of the crime scene.

Since Wednesday night, nearly every available San Geronimo state cop had been employed for a well-publicized DWI blitz—Operation Don't Be A Turkey, as it had been named by an overly creative public relations official in Santa Fe. Family holidays in New Mexico were notorious for alcohol, drug abuse, shoot-outs in the backyard, and deadly traffic accidents. Thursday night, there had been sobriety checkpoints from 8 PM to 3 AM set up on all the major roads in the county.

When Howie made his 911 call at 3:44 Friday morning, the county dispatcher shuttled the call to the San Geronimo State Police station where there were only two people on duty. The sobriety checkpoints had only just been closed down with the exhausted officers sent home to get whatever sleep they could manage. The watch commander, Sgt. Ricky Montoya, dispatched his one available officer, Dirk Henderson, to the Stanton Ranch to check out the situation and see what was needed. Lieutenant Santo Ruben, the station chief, wasn't due in until later Friday afternoon and Montoya didn't want to disturb his boss unless it was absolutely necessary. Fortunately, Jack phoned Santo as soon as he had received Howie's call, which got the response moving faster than it would have otherwise.

Officer Henderson arrived at the Stanton ranch at 4:50 AM to find a distraught household quarreling among themselves and relieved to see someone in a uniform take charge. Henderson stepped into the study, took one look at the gruesome remains of Harlan Stanton, and staggered outside to breath deep gulps of cold air in the front yard. Once he recovered, he radioed the station, and asked for immediate back up.

Alone at the station, Sgt. Montoya began making phone calls, waking people up, as soon as he realized he was dealing with a major incident. Nevertheless, the response was sluggish. It was like setting a large ship in motion, slowly at first, gradually gaining momentum. The Crime Scene Unit had to be summoned from Santa Fe, but they were slow to arrive because of two ongoing incidents that needed to be investigated first—a road rage shootout on St. Francis Boulevard, and a domestic quarrel in Española where two people had been killed.

Santo came by Jack's house to pick up him and Katya at shortly before 5 o'clock. With no traffic and Santo's roof lights blazing, they roared down the highway and reached the Stanton Ranch at just after 5:30, forty minutes after Officer Henderson had arrived, but nearly an hour before the CSU team from Santa Fe would be there.

Dawn was still more than an hour and a half away as Santo took Jack's arm and led him to the front door. The night was clear and bitterly cold, 18 degrees Fahrenheit according to the thermometer in Santo's black State Police SUV. This time of year, the afternoon would warm into the 50s, a wild swing of temperature that was common in the high deserts of New Mexico where the air was thin.

Officer Henderson met them at the door, obviously relieved to see his boss arrive.

"I've gathered everyone in the living room," Henderson explained, "but it's been like trying to herd cats. Everyone keeps going off to the bathroom or to make a cup of coffee. These are people who are used to doing whatever the hell they want."

"I hope you've kept them out of the study where the body is?" Santo asked.

"That was the easy part. It's not a pleasant sight."

Santo introduced Jack. "Dirk, you know Commander Jack Wilder, don't you? He's going to give me a hand here . . . Jack, why don't you and Katya wait in the living room with the others while Dirk shows me the crime scene. Then we'll see if we can get this show on the road."

Jack knew by the way Katya was wagging her tail that Howie was nearby.

"Welcome to the Thanksgiving from hell," Howie said in greeting.

Jack snorted a disapproving laugh. "What's the matter? Didn't you get the wishbone? Well, I want to hear about it. Let's go someplace where we can talk."

***

For Howie, the early hours of Friday had been the bleakest, blackest Black Friday he had ever known.

After his 911 phone call, then a second call to Jack, there had been more than an hour wait before Officer Henderson arrived during which he'd had to cope with the Stanton family and guests by himself. He reminded them that the entire house was now a crime scene and they needed to gather together in one room and stay put.

But who was going to listen to Howie? A nobody, not rich, not even a real cop.

Ramona, the inscrutable Native servant, built a fire in the living room, then disappeared into the kitchen to make coffee. Every now and then, she reappeared with danish pastries, toast and jam, pitchers of orange juice, and hot water and packets of tea for those who didn't drink coffee. Howie managed a raspberry danish, hoping to settle his stomach after all the wine and dramas he'd had yesterday.

There was a palpable tension in the living room where the family was gathered waiting for the police to arrive, a restless mixture of worry and impatience, perhaps even an occasional moment of sorrow that the old ogre was dead.

Anne Stanton, Wife #1, positioned herself in a rocking chair near the fire with a bag of yarn and knitting needles. She sat without expression, without a word, rocking back and forth as her needles clicked away.

Summer Stanton, Wife #2, sat nearby reclining on an armchair, her legs stretched across an ottoman, staring intently into the fire.

"Goddamnit!" she said after a long while, more to herself than to anyone in the room. "This sure screws everything up!"

"Summer, for chrissake!" Grace cried. She had been pacing back and forth, too restless to park herself anywhere for more than two minutes at a time. "This isn't about *you*! This is about Daddy! Don't you get that? Or are you too selfish to care about anything except yourself?"

Grace was dressed in a Japanese kimono over creamy white silk pajamas, and she wore fuzzy slippers that had cute mouse faces with ears. Howie had never imagined her to be the sort who would wear slippers with cute mouse ears, but what did he really know about her? For all their penetrations, she had always remained impenetrable.

"Calm yourself, my girl," Summer answered coolly. "This isn't a good moment to become overwrought."

Grace looked like she was going to say something nasty. But she only sighed and continued her pacing more frenetically than before.

Howie still had questions for Grace. Big questions. But there was no chance to ask them now.

Stephen Halley, the editor, sat in an armchair with a baffled look on his face, shaking his head from time to time. People probably didn't get scalped in New York City.

"Who would do such a terrible thing?" Justin's wife, Belinda, asked in her little girl's voice. "Who would kill Harlan like that?"

"Just about anybody in this room," said Justin. He was at the side table making up a bagel with cream cheese and smoked salmon from a platter that Ramona had brought to the living room. "Face it, the man made enemies."

"Don't say that!" Summer told him sharply. "And by the way, we need to be especially careful what we say when the media comes around."

"Oh, come on, Summer! Honestly!"

"No, I mean it. This is going to be splattered across the front page of every tabloid in America!"

Splattered wasn't a very good word to use, under the circumstances.

Belinda picked up a *People* magazine and started to flip through the pages. Her two teenage boys had curled up on large cushions by the fireplace and fallen asleep.

Lorenzo was in an armchair reading a thick volume of *New Yorker* cartoons that he had pulled off a shelf. Howie settled into an old-fashioned platform rocker and felt himself slip into a stupor. Sleep pulled at him. He wasn't certain how much time had passed when he jerked awake to find Justin coming out of the study where the Senator's body lay.

"You weren't supposed to go in there!" Howie protested, standing and crossing the room to him.

"What business is it of yours, Moon Deer?"

"That's a crime scene! The cops aren't going to be happy when they hear you've been in there."

"Then don't tell them. For chrissake, I was only looking for some papers I left on Dad's desk. They're mine, so back off!"

Grace suddenly appeared by Howie's side, blazing mad. "You were looking for the will, weren't you? You son of a bitch! You total sleaze!"

"I don't give a damn about the will," Justin replied with barely controlled fury. "If you have to know, I was looking for a prospectus I left with Dad for the Enchanted Mesa development. It's only a mock-up and frankly I don't want it to go public yet, okay? It doesn't have anything to do with this . . . this *thing*! Anyway, I didn't find it."

Howie had heard about Justin's Enchanted Mesa golf course development last night at dinner. It was a multimillion-dollar real estate deal that Justin was hoping to pull off, but he was facing stiff opposition from local environmental groups. Water for a golf course was a contentious issue in the high desert.

Grace turned to Howie for support. "Make him turn out his pockets, Howie. Don't let him get away with this!"

Howie wasn't sure what to do. He felt powerless.

"Look, there's an easy way to resolve this," he suggested. "You say you didn't take anything, Justin. So why don't you show her what's in your pockets and that will be the end of it."

It seemed like a reasonable request, and Howie liked to be reasonable. But Justin wasn't about to do anything he said.

"Or the cops can do a strip search when they arrive," Howie added. "They like that. It satisfies the sadistic side of their nature."

Justin sighed and gave way. "Okay, okay, let's not make a big deal out of it. I told you, I didn't take anything and I didn't."

Justin was dressed in a plaid dressing gown with pajamas underneath and there were only two pockets to go through. They were both empty except for a slightly soiled Kleenex.

Justin stomped off, vindicated and self-righteous. He veered toward the drink table at the far end of the room and poured himself a shot of early-morning vodka and orange juice.

Howie turned to Grace. He was about to repeat the big question she hadn't answered last night. This seemed to be the moment. They were off by themselves in a far corner of the huge living room. Did you give birth to our child? The words were on his lips. But then he heard the swish of tires in the driveway outside and the sound of a car door opening and slamming shut, and the question went unasked.

It was Officer Dirk Henderson, the first to arrive. Forty minutes later, Jack, Santo, and Katya pulled up to the house. Howie was ashamed of his relief. He wanted to know if he was a father, but the possible answer scared him to death.

Chapter Ten

Neither Santo nor Jack looked like they'd had much sleep. Santo was dressed in his crisp black State Police uniform, but his eyes were puffy, and he was unshaved. Jack didn't look well either. He was pale and out of breath, though he had only walked a dozen feet from the driveway. He was dressed oddly in baggy green pants and a bright red sweater that clashed. Emma generally helped Jack pick out his wardrobe, but she clearly hadn't been awake for a consultation when Jack left the house.

Santo and Dirk went into the study together to inspect the crime scene, which gave Jack and Howie a few minutes alone.

"I'm always astonished," Jack began, "by your ability to get into a muddle!"

"It's not my fault, Jack."

"No, it never is. Well, let's find somewhere to talk."

Howie led Jack down a hallway to the empty dining room. Jack lowered his voice. "You were the one who found the body?"

"No, Summer found him. I heard her scream and I threw on some clothes and went to see what was wrong."

"And Summer is?"

"Summer Stanton is the Senator's second wife. She used to be his chief of staff in Washington back before he got tossed out of office."

"A trophy wife?"

"Well, she has horns. You could mount her head above a fireplace."

"Sure, Howie. Was she in the room with the body?"

"She was. When I arrived, she was standing over the body screaming her head off. Stanton was spread out on the floor. Not a pleasant sight."

"Let's back up a second. You were in bed when you heard her scream?"

"In a guest room on the ground floor. Just down the hall from the study. I got to Summer first, but Justin was there pretty quickly behind me. Justin is Grace's older brother. A number of people were poking their heads through the door as well, but I didn't really catch who was there. My attention was on the body."

"Did you touch him to see if he was alive?"

"I didn't need to, Jack. He was lying on his back with his throat cut wide open. Plus, he'd been scalped."

Jack shook his head unhappily. "Right, you told me that on the phone. Scalping is, what? A Lakota tradition?"

"Most of the Plains tribes did it. But long, long ago. Personally, I haven't scalped anyone since I sold an extra ticket for a Bruce Springsteen concert at Madison Square Garden."

"Howie, this isn't funny."

"I'm not saying it was. The girl I'd invited to the concert stood me up. My feelings were hurt."

Jack pointed his dark glasses at Howie. "Can we move on now?"

"Absolutely. But I don't like the assumption that just because I'm Lakota, I scalped Senator Stanton."

"Well, you'd better get used to it. Because that's the first thing the cops are going to think. Was there any sign of the murder weapon?"

"Not that I could see. As soon as I realized it was a murder scene, I backed everybody out of the room and told them we had to stay clear until the cops arrived. Not that anyone listened to me. A while later, I was sitting in the living room half-asleep when I saw Justin coming out of the study. He said he'd been looking for a prospectus he had left with his father for a real estate deal he's trying to put together. Grace was furious. She accused him of trying to find the old man's will."

Howie spent a few minutes recounting the incident with Justin, how he and Grace had made the older brother turn out the pockets of his dressing gown to prove he hadn't taken anything.

"Okay, I'm sure Santo will want to go over all of this with you. Was there anything you noticed in the study you think might be important?"

"The sliding glass door was open to the outside. It was freezing in there."

"Really? That will certainly be a factor determining the time of death. Is there anything else you need to tell me?"

"Before I heard Summer's scream, when I was still in bed, I was woken up by the sound of hoofbeats outside my bedroom. I looked outside and saw a horse and rider galloping away across the meadow outside my room."

"You could see this in the dark?"

"There was a half moon and the sky was clear. I couldn't make out who the rider was. I could only see a silvery silhouette. It was sort of spooky, actually. I only saw them for a minute before they disappeared over a rise."

"But you were completely awake? You didn't dream this?"

Howie gave Jack a look that sizzled. He didn't answer.

"Okay," Jack said. "I'll take it that you weren't dreaming. You've got to stop being so sensitive, Howie. These are the sorts of things Santo is going to ask. And Santo's your friend. You think this silvery silhouette was the killer?"

"I'd say so, Jack. Wouldn't you?"

"I'd say let's not jump to conclusions. Right now, we can only say this is somebody we need to talk to. Tell me about Thanksgiving. How'd that go?"

"To be honest, it wasn't what I'd describe as a joyful family gathering. The vibes weren't good."

"Vibes?" Jack repeated distastefully.

"Come on, Jack. Undertones. Over tones. Bad juju in the air. Anne Stanton, the Senator's former wife, was there, I have no idea why. Two wives at one Thanksgiving table is a bit extravagant for my taste. But, of course, I'm just a simple Indian who enjoys scalping people. Anne sat through the feast looking as enigmatic as a prune."

"I'm having trouble visualizing an enigmatic prune, Howie."

"That's because you haven't met Anne Stanton yet. I'm afraid I had a bit of a shouting match with the Senator at the dinner table. About politics."

"Howie, don't you know the rule—never discuss politics at Thanksgiving!"

"Yeah, sure, Jack. But he goaded me. He called me a socialist."

"Aren't you?"

"Jack! I'm an Indian! Tribal is my Bible. Don't get greedy, take care of the Earth, and share with your brothers and sisters. That's the *real* America, and if you don't like it, you should go back to Europe where you came from."

"Okay, okay. But it's not great that you had a shouting match with someone who ended up scalped a few hours later. What else can you tell me about this not-so-jolly Thanksgiving?"

"Well, this is interesting. Before the feast, Summer summoned me into her office and tried to hire me to investigate some threatening letters the Senator has been receiving. One of them mentioned scalping."

"Howie! For chrissake, you should have told me about this at the start!"

"Jack, I'm trying to tell you, but you're not giving me a chance!"

"Okay, tell me now. What's this about someone threatening to scalp Senator Stanton?"

"Hold on, I want to hear this, too," said Santo Ruben, who was walking down the hallway to join them. He shot Howie a piercing look that wasn't entirely friendly. "Let's find somewhere to sit down and have ourselves a proper talk."

***

Howie had always liked Lieutenant Santo Ruben. He was a strong, calm, reassuring presence. A man who made you feel the situation was under control. Even when it wasn't.

Santo was in his mid-50s: dignified, handsome, silver hair, with an intelligent face that was prematurely lined with age. An aging Latin matinee idol, Howie sometimes said, describing Santo for strangers. There was a gaunt, romantic weariness about Santo that made middle-aged women swoon over him and want to cook him dinner.

They had settled into a library on the ground floor that had bookshelves on two walls, floor to ceiling, and comfortable green leather armchairs. Whatever else you had to say about the Stantons, they were well-educated. They read books.

There was an old-fashioned component stereo system along with a shelf full of long-playing vinyl records, mostly classical from what Howie could see. The collection was heavy on the three-Bs—Bach, Beethoven, and Brahms. Howie's girlfriend, Claire, would approve.

Santo and Jack settled into the two armchairs. Katya stretched out on the floor by Jack's feet, her long snout resting on her front paws. She closed her eyes and was soon asleep, breathing deeply, twitching every now and then with a doggie dream. As for Howie, he had the hot seat in the middle of the room, an uncomfortable straight-back wooden chair.

"So, Howie, here you are, right smack in the middle of a murder case!" Santo almost always smiled, and he smiled now. His eyes sparkled. He had a trick of doing that, a friendly man who was on your side, you and he together making fun of things. It was a good mask for a complicated man.

"You have a knack for it, Howie," he added.

"Fools walk in where angels fear to tread," Jack threw in.

"Hey, hold on, you guys!" Howie objected.

"Jack filled me in as we were driving here," Santo continued. "He told me about your old roommate, Nicolas Stanton. And Grace, your old girlfriend. You're in the thick of this, Howie, and I'm not going to be able to show you any special favors. The murder of someone as well-known as Harlan Stanton is going to be examined minutely by lots of people, so everything we do has to be above board and transparent. Are you getting my drift?"

"I am, Santo," Howie told him. "I'm drifting."

"Now, I'm going to need a full statement from you later on. Something you'll sign and that may be used in court eventually. But right now, I'm trying to get an overview of what happened so we'll keep this casual. Let's start from the beginning and you just tell me the story. Jack already mentioned Nicolas showing up at your house and giving you an envelope to deliver to Grace, but I want to hear this in your own words."

Howie took a deep breath and began. He started with his freshman year at Dartmouth and his friendship with Nick and how he'd had a long-ago summer romance with Grace. Jack sat with an obscure expression on his face. Katya, wisely, began to snore.

It took Howie half an hour to cover the bare bones of the story, minus the part about Grace getting pregnant and having a child. That was Howie's own business. Unconfirmed, in fact, which made it something he didn't want to discuss with anybody until he had spoken first to Grace.

As Howie told the story, he heard law enforcement vehicles pulling up into the driveway outside the house. After some minutes of doors opening and closing, Detective Dan Hamm knocked on the library door and poked his head inside.

"Excuse me, Lieutenant, I just wanted to let you know that I'm here. Also, the CSU team just arrived."

"Thanks, Dan. Excuse me a minute," he said to Jack and Howie as he stood from the armchair. "I need to say hello to the team and get them started. I'll be right back."

Jack and Howie sat in a strained silence after Santo left the room. It was Jack who finally spoke.

"Howie, I'm not going to say I told you so. But the fact that you helped your old outlaw roommate is going to come back to kick your butt. You've put Santo in a bad position. I'm not sure he's going to be able to protect you."

"Nick was my friend!" Howie said defensively. "Look, I don't like what happened to those security guards. But I can't turn my back on him. And I sure don't want to see him brought down in some gung-ho hail of gunfire!"

"On my part, Howie, I don't want to see you go to jail for aiding and abetting. I don't want to see you lose your P.I. license. But we're going to have to see how this plays out. Santo is our best hope and we need to keep him on our side."

"Okay, Jack. I get it."

"I'm not sure you do. So you'd better tell me now, what have you left out?"

"What do you mean, what have I left out?"

"From the story you told Santo. After all these years, I know you well enough to know when there's something you're not saying, and if I'm going to help, you need to tell me what it is."

Howie sighed. "Well, okay, there's just one thing I didn't mention, but it's something private."

"Howie, wake up. Nothing is private in a murder investigation. Private matters are what murder is all about. You should know that by now. So you'd better tell me what it is before Santo gets hold of it on his own. Which he will, you know, because Santo is good."

Howie didn't answer immediately. He wasn't by nature a secretive person. But this was difficult.

"It's just, well, Summer tried to blackmail me a bit when I told her I wasn't the person to investigate the letters Harlan had been receiving."

"Summer Stanton was blackmailing you? And you think this is something you could keep to yourself?"

"It wasn't exactly blackmail. Maybe pressure is a better word. She wanted me to find out who was sending the letters so she leaned on me pretty hard. She's a woman who likes to get her way. She hinted that there are Stanton family secrets she wanted to keep under wraps. And if I came across them, I would be discreet because . . . well, she knew my secrets, too."

"Go on," said Jack.

Howie shook his head. He groaned. He did everything except wring his hands.

"Howie?"

"Okay, she told me I got Grace pregnant that summer when we were . . . you know, mating."

"*Mating*? What are you, some sort of naturalist all of a sudden? You were screwing the girl, Howie. So, what happened? She had an abortion?"

"No, that's just the thing. She said Grace went to some place to have the baby and gave it up for adoption. She said I have a daughter and she would tell me where she is if I'd take on her case. To be honest, it was overkill. If she'd asked me nicely, I probably would have given in and done what she wanted. But that's Summer. She has a heavy hand."

"Have you spoken to Grace about this?"

"No, there hasn't been a chance. I tried to talk with her last night, but she put me off. So I don't even know if this is true or not. That's why I didn't want to say anything to Santo."

Jack kept shaking his head. "For chrissake, Howie! I mean, look at this how Santo's going to see it! One member of this family, Summer Stanton, tries to blackmail you. The daughter, Grace, you find out last night that the two of you had a child together and it was kept from you. And the brother, Nicolas, is on the FBI's most wanted list, and you helped him out by running an errand for him. And then, to top it off, you had a shouting match with the victim at dinner. You know, my friend, any minute now you're going be sitting in the back of a patrol car with handcuffs on!"

Howie sighed mournfully. "Makes me wish I was up on the Peak skiing right now!"

"Except there's no snow," Jack reminded. "Are you going to tell Claire about this love child of yours?"

"Of course, I am! Eventually. If I find out it's true."

It was a conversation that might have continued, but Santo came back into the library just then and sat down. He looked from Jack to Howie.

"Is everything all right in here?"

"Sure," Howie told him. "Except for the fact that I'm starting to feel like the designated turkey."

"Okay," said Santo, "the CSU team is in the study, a few of my people are here, everything's finally starting to move. Now look, Howie, I have to tell you, it's not good that you ran an errand for a fugitive who's wanted for murder. I'll see what I can do to keep Santa Fe off your back, but I'm not promising anything."

"Thanks, Santo," Howie said, humbled.

"You're welcome. But it's not over yet. And from now on, any contact you have with Nicolas Stanton, I want to know about it immediately. Do you get that?"

"I do."

"Good, because this is going to be a very public case and you don't want to get behind the eight ball, right?"

"Absolutely, Santo. No eight balls for me. I'll avoid them."

"I'll hold you to that. You can go now, but don't go far. I'm going to want to talk with you later. Jack, if you'll stick around, I want to get statements from the rest of the family before these people get lawyered-up, and I wouldn't mind having you with me. I won't be able to let you ask questions because you don't have any official standing. But I think I can get away with calling you a consulting expert if you keep your mouth shut."

"I'm fine with that, Santo," Jack assured him.

"We'll start with Summer Stanton," Santo decided. "Howie, on your way out, tell Dan to send her in."

***

Howie found Dan Hamm at the edge of the living room talking with Officer Sally Loeb, who had arrived with the second wave of law enforcement. Sally was the newest addition to the San Geronimo State Police and all the men in the department had their eye on her. She was in her early twenties, blonde, pretty, and athletic—she had been a ski instructor before deciding on a more serious career as a cop. Dan was smitten, but he was shy and could barely do more than stare and stutter in her presence. Personally, Howie avoided women with 9mm Glocks riding on their hips, but he had to admit she looked good in her spiffy black State Police uniform.

"What do you want me to do, Detective Hamm?" she was asking when Howie approached. She looked up at Dan with large admiring eyes. "This is my first murder scene and I don't want to make any mistakes."

"Well, uh, er . . . I tell you what, Sally . . . do you have a pencil?"

"A pencil?"

Dan blushed. He was Sally's superior, he should have been able to deal with a uniformed officer, no matter how pretty she was. But he could barely speak.

"You see, we're going to need a diagram of the house. Where the bedrooms are. Where everybody was sleeping last night. I mean, if you feel you can manage that."

"Of course, Detective," she told him. "Whatever you say."

Dan looked positively relieved to see Howie. "What's up, Moon Deer?" he asked eagerly.

"Santo wants you to find Summer Stanton and bring her into the library," Howie said.

"Great! I'll get right on it!"

Sally shook her head after Dan dashed off. "Is he always like that?"

"He's a bit awkward at times," Howie told her. "But he's a very nice guy," he added.

"I guess so," she said thoughtfully, watching Dan as he crossed the living room to where Summer was seated on a sofa.

Howie had a sense this was a love affair in the making, but it might take a long time to get off the ground. He left Sally and returned to the guest room where he had spent the night hoping to stretch out on the bed. He was exhausted, but, after a few minutes with his eyes closed, he found himself too keyed up to sleep. Unsure what to do with himself, he got up, put his shoes back on, and stepped outside onto the flagstone terrace thinking a breath of air would be welcome.

The sun had risen into a moody late-autumn sky. A line of thin, milky clouds was moving in from the northwest. Maybe they were bringing snow, Howie thought. But maybe not.

He studied the meadow where he had seen the horse and rider. This time of year, the meadow was only brown stubble that stretched in a gentle downward curve for perhaps a quarter of a mile before it fell sharply away to a valley he couldn't see.

Off to his right, Howie could see a faded red barn with an attached corral and several horses crowding near the fence. A man in a black cowboy hat was using a pitchfork to throw flakes of alfalfa into their feed trough.

Santo had told him to stick around, but he hadn't said anything about not leaving the house. Howie decided to do a bit of exploring.

Chapter Eleven

The barn was a hundred yards from the house along a rutted dirt road that curved around the edge of a greenhouse. There was a musty smell of hay and horse manure as Howie got closer. It wasn't a bad smell. Hay and horse was about as earthy an aroma as aromas got. It took Howie back to his childhood, to his uncle Richard Sweet Water who kept horses in a corral outside his dilapidated trailer and had taught Howie to ride.

When Howie was young, he had been able to jump onto a horse bareback and ride for hours. But that was a long time ago.

He found the cowboy in the black hat had finished feeding the horses and was now pulling a fifty-pound bag of oats from the back of an old pickup truck into a wheelbarrow on the ground. The truck was an off-road monster on huge wheels and struts that looked like you just about needed a ladder to climb up into the cab.

The cowboy was a slight, dark complexioned man, perhaps Hispanic, but Howie was uncertain of that. His face was weathered from many years in the New Mexico sun, and he was dressed in faded jeans and an old sweater that had strands of hay stuck to it. His eyes, when Howie finally saw them, were blue. There was a toothpick dangling from the side of his mouth, bobbing up and down as he worked. He appeared to be in his late forties, though that was also hard to tell. Though he was short—hardly more than five foot five—he didn't look like someone you'd want to mess with.

"Morning!" Howie said politely.

The cowboy gave him a quick look but kept working. Without a word, he tumbled the bag of oats into the wheelbarrow and wheeled it toward the barn. Howie followed him through the double door into a large open space that was divided into horse stalls with an aisle down the middle.

"I was wondering if I could ask you something," Howie said. "I stayed at the house last night, and I was woken in the night by the sound of hoofbeats. I was curious, so I got out of bed and saw a horse and rider disappearing over the edge of that meadow over there. I was wondering if you have any idea of who might have been riding at that hour."

The cowboy gave him another look, sharper than the first, but still didn't answer.

"I'm Howard Moon Deer," Howie continued, undeterred. "Nick Stanton was my roommate at college and I know Grace, too. Somehow I got myself invited for Thanksgiving. I suppose you've heard what's happened."

The man stopped working. Howie had finally gotten his attention. "You're a friend of Nick's, huh?"

"I am. He was a good friend at one time."

"He was a good kid," said the cowboy. "At one time."

"You've been on this ranch a long time, I'm guessing."

"You're right."

Howie wasn't sure how much he wanted to say about Nick, but he sensed this was someone who had a bullshit meter as finely tuned as a seismograph. Being truthful would be the only way to get him to talk.

"Nick came to my place last week," he said. "I hadn't seen him in years, ever since he went on the run from the law. He asked if I would help him mend fences with his father. That's the reason I'm here."

"He wanted his money," said the cowboy flatly.

"He did."

"Sure, he did! These youngsters think they're high and mighty 'til the money runs out. Then they discover life isn't so easy when you're poor. Well, I'll tell you something. The Senator wasn't going to give Nick a penny, no way!"

"You don't think so?"

"I *know* so."

"It sounds like you know Nick pretty well."

"*Knew* him. Past tense. Those kids were running all over this place at one time like a bunch of puppies. When they were young'uns. I taught 'em about horses. I taught 'em to ride. But then they grew up and they didn't have much to do with me anymore."

The cowboy said this without self-pity. He looked like someone who had seen life's ins and outs.

"So how many horses are here now?" Howie asked.

"Well . . ." He pronounced it more like *wahl*. "*Wahl*, right now, I reckon we have five. Used to be six but Comanche, he died last summer. Twenty-seven years old, that quarter horse. Had to put him down finally. Back in the old days, they used to have sometimes a dozen or so horses, all of 'em thoroughbreds. Back when the Commissioner was still alive. But the Senator, he was never the rider his father was."

"By the Commissioner, you mean Adam Stanton, the Senator's father?"

"Yup."

"I bet you'd be able to tell if any of those five horses had been taken out last night?" Howie said.

"I guess I could," said the cowboy. "But I've learned it doesn't pay to poke your nose into things that don't concern you."

"A good philosophy," Howie agreed, "except when there's a murder investigation going on and all hell is about to break loose. Senator Stanton had his throat cut and he was scalped. This isn't something that's going away."

"Scalped, you say!" The cowboy shook his head. "Holy crap! I hadn't heard that!"

"So, will you tell me if any of the horses have been taken out recently?"

"Why? You some kind of busybody?"

"I'm a licensed private detective. And I'd like to get to the bottom of this as quickly as possible. There isn't going to be any peace around here until we do."

The cowboy gave Howie an appraising look. The toothpick bobbed in the side of his mouth. "Okay," he said at last. He offered his hand. "The name's Tucker. Let's go take a look."

***

Howie followed Tucker back outside to the corral. The five horses ambled over to the fence thinking he was going to give them more food.

"Yup," he said.

"Yup, what?" Howie inquired.

"Look at Valkyrie." He nodded toward a white horse standing by the fence. "You can see the saddle mark. Someone's been riding him hard and they didn't bother to brush him afterwards. Things have been changing 'round here. That would never have happened in the old days."

"When was the last time you brushed Valkyrie?" Howie asked.

"Yesterday afternoon. He's Grace's horse. Her boyfriend took him out in the morning."

"Lorenzo?"

"Yup. He brought him back around ten or so. I walked him to cool him down then gave him a good brushing."

"And nobody took him out later on?"

"Not that I saw."

"Was there anybody else who went riding yesterday?"

"Well, those two boys went off for a few hours in the late morning. Justin's boys. They took Domino and Luigi. I was a little worried, to tell the truth. I don't know how well those damn kids ride. I told 'em to be careful."

"Where do people go when they ride around here?"

"If you want an easy ride, you can just stay on the dirt roads. They go on for miles, wandering up and down the land. If you have the time and feel more adventurous, there's a trail that goes up into the mountains to a nice little lake. In the old days, the family would go camping up there and spend a few days."

Howie looked toward the meadow where he had seen the rider disappear over the rise last night.

"What's that way?" he asked.

"If you keep going, it slopes down to the old cattle pond and the bunkhouse."

"Bunkhouse?"

"It's where the cowhands used to live, back in the old days. But it hasn't been used in years. Just a bunch of spiders in there now."

"Can I walk there?"

"Sure. It'll take you about twenty minutes, nothing much. You'll see it as soon as you get over the rise."

"Thanks, I think I'll go take a look. I can use the exercise."

"Suit yourself. But don't expect to find any sign of your midnight rider down there," Tucker told him.

Howie had started to walk away, but he stopped and turned back.

"Why's that?"

"That wasn't no person you saw. That was the ghost."

"Ghost? You're kidding?"

"Nope. He always shows up this time of year. November's when he was killed, you see. Fifty years ago, but time don't mean nothing when you're dead."

Howie smiled.

"You don't know about the ghost?" Tucker seemed incredulous that anyone could be so ignorant. "Man, I thought everybody around here knew about that old murder. It happened right here at the ranch. It's how old man Stanton picked this place up so cheap. Nobody wanted it after that."

As a modern person, Howie took ghost stories with a grain of salt. But his semi-patronizing smile vanished.

"An old murder here at the ranch?"

"It wasn't always a ranch. It was one of those Indian schools. Until 1970, when the murder happened. One of the kids, a twelve-year-old boy, killed the headmaster. Cut his throat and scalped him. That's the ghost, you see. The old headmaster. He comes wandering this time of year looking for his lost head of hair."

"What happened to the boy who killed him?"

"Nobody knows. He ran off and was never found."

"That's quite a ghost story!" said Howie. It was also more than a co-incidence, a murder from fifty years ago that had been reprised last night.

"Well, I only know it secondhand," Tucker said with a shrug. "But them ghosts, you see, the one's that have been murdered—they don't rest until they have their revenge."

Chapter Twelve

Jack and Santo rose to their feet as Detective Hamm brought Summer Stanton into the study.

"Thank you for your cooperation, Mrs. Stanton," Santo told her. "I'm Lieutenant Santo Ruben and this is Commander Jack Wilder, a special consultant from San Francisco, someone whose expertise we often tap. This will be an informal interview. We'll get your full statement later. I'm hoping we can get to the bottom of this quickly so we can let you all go home."

To Santo's surprise, she turned to Jack. "As a matter of fact, Jack and I are old acquaintances. Though I bet you don't remember me."

"I'm sorry," Jack told her. "I'm afraid I don't."

"My name was Newsome then. Summer Newsome. I was a reporter for the *San Francisco Examiner*. I was the pushy one who asked you all those difficult questions at press briefings."

"Ah, yes, now I remember!" Jack forced a smile. He had hated those news conferences and Summer hadn't made his job easy. "You're living in New Mexico now?"

"Yes, here we are, both of us in the Land of Enchantment. Quite a coincidence."

"I'm very sorry about your husband's death, Mrs. Stanton," Santo told her, putting an end to chit chat. He had a routine in cases like this, and he was good at it. He knew what to say to a bereaved family member whose son/daughter/wife/husband had been killed. It was an act he had perfected over the years, yet it was also sincere. Santo was essentially a kind person.

Once the condolences were out of the way, he got to work.

"Now, Mrs. Stanton, you were the first person to arrive at the crime scene. You found your husband's body. Can you tell me how you happened to be there?"

"Of course. I woke up about 2:30 and found Harlan wasn't on his side of the bed. This didn't concern me greatly. He was often restless. I thought he was either in the bathroom or had gone down to the kitchen to get a snack. I closed my eyes and tried to get back to sleep, but somehow sleep wouldn't come."

"You were worried about something?"

"I wouldn't say that. It's just that once I'm awake, it takes me a while to settle down again. But then I heard voices downstairs coming from Harlan's study and I was curious who he could be talking to at that hour. It wasn't any of my business, of course. With the whole family gathered, there were bound to be late night conversations. I didn't want to get in the way."

"Could you hear who it was he was talking to?"

"No, it was just a murmur of voices. I couldn't catch what they were saying."

"Was it a man or a woman?"

"I couldn't tell. Our bedroom is upstairs in the north corner of the house. Harlan's study is almost directly underneath our bed so voices float up sometimes. But very muffled, of course."

"What did you do next?"

"As I said, I tried to go back to sleep. But the voices were . . . well, I didn't hear the words, but it didn't sound like a pleasant conversation."

"It sounded, what? Like an argument?"

"Not a quarrel, perhaps. But confrontational."

"And you have no idea who it was?" he repeated.

She shook her head. "I honestly don't. And I didn't want to intrude. Particularly if he was having it out with Anne."

"Anne Stanton?"

"My predecessor," Summer said crisply.

"Yet you said you had no idea who Harlan was talking with. Why do you think it might have been Anne?"

"No reason particularly. It's just . . . well, you know how it can be with an ex-wife. She might have had some unresolved issue to discuss."

"But you don't have any actual reason for thinking it was Anne down there?"

"No, it was just a feeling."

Santo was starting not to like Summer Stanton. It was catty to cast suspicion on Harlan's first wife. But he let it go.

"Okay, so you went downstairs eventually," he prodded. "Why?"

"Well, the talking stopped. It was quiet. But when Harlan didn't return to bed, after a while I became concerned. If he'd had a fight with Anne . . . or whoever it was," she added, "I thought he might need me to talk things over with. I've always been his sounding board. Even before we got married. I was his chief of staff in Washington, as you probably know."

"What time did you go downstairs?"

"It must have been three or so, but I didn't look at the clock so I can't be sure. I put on my robe, walked downstairs, looked in the door, saw the body, and screamed."

"The door to the study was open?"

"Yes, and the light was on. Harlan was on the floor. It was horrible. I knew he was dead, of course. There was so much blood."

"Did you touch anything?"

"Did I? I don't know. I was in shock so I suppose I might have. I was only in the room for a moment when Howard appeared. You know Howard Moon Deer, I suppose. It was Grace who invited him for Thanksgiving. They had rather a grand affair one summer on Cape Cod and Harlan wasn't pleased that she had invited him. I believe he was worried that the romance would flare up again."

"The Senator didn't like Howie?"

"It wasn't anything personal. He just didn't think he was the right person for his daughter."

"And why was that? Because he's Native American?"

"No, I'd say it was more that he was poor. He wouldn't be able to take care of Grace in the way she was accustomed to. She's quite a spoiled girl, you know. And of course, he's a socialist and Harlan couldn't stand people like that."

Santo studied her for a moment before speaking. "I have to tell you, Mrs. Stanton, I've known Howard Moon Deer for several years and I've never heard him espouse socialism."

"Well, perhaps he wouldn't, not with you. But Harlan and Moon Deer had rather a loud fight about it yesterday at the dinner table. It was quite a shouting match. Harlan was so upset, Anne had to help him into the living room. We were all afraid Harlan might have a stroke. It was awful!"

"Are you suggesting Moon Deer killed your husband?"

"Oh, no, of course not. But they *did* nearly come to blows at the dinner table. In any case, Howard was the first person in the study behind me. I suppose he heard my scream."

"All right, who else came to the study?"

"Let me try to think. It was all so overwhelming! Justin was there. Yes, Justin. And Anne, too."

"How about Grace?"

"No, I don't remember seeing Grace. I have no idea where she was."

Santo nodded. "Now, Mrs. Stanton, how long had you and the Senator been married?"

"Harlan and I were married three years ago," she answered.

"And before that you worked for him in Washington?"

"That's right."

"Then I imagine you knew him very well, even before your marriage. There wouldn't be many secrets between a senator and his chief of staff."

"No, of course not. We discussed everything. Let me be blunt, Lieutenant. You're curious if Harlan and I were having an affair while he was married to Anne. The answer is yes. We kept it secret, naturally."

"For political reasons? Or personal?"

"Well, his conservative base wouldn't have liked it if it got out. He ran on family values. But then he lost the election and it didn't matter anymore. That's when we decided to come out in the open."

"Here's a question I always hate to ask a woman—can you tell me your age?"

"Fifty-one," she answered without hesitation. "Harlan was seventy-one. There was a twenty-year gap between us but that wasn't important. I'm afraid you won't be able to peg me as the stereotypical younger woman, the floozy in the office, if that's what you're getting at. We were equals, Lieutenant. I was never his floozy."

"Yes, I can see that," Santo told her. In fact, Summer Stanton was a formidable woman, smart and confident, and he imagined her as a formidable chief of staff. "Well, let's jump back to the present. You told Howie that the Senator had been receiving threatening letters."

"Yes, there were three letters. The first arrived six weeks ago. The second came two weeks later. And the last was just two days ago."

"Do you have them with you, by any chance?"

She did. Summer was an efficient, no-nonsense woman. She brought them out from her handbag, each in their generic white envelope, each with a short message printed in capital letters in the middle of the crisply folded page. Santo took out a pair of thin transparent gloves and opened the letters carefully, handling them by the edges. He read them aloud so that Jack could hear them.

"'Die Indian killer die . . . a knife to your throat . . . a scalp taken.'" Santo shook his head. "Not very nice! What did the Senator say when he saw them?"

"He scoffed. You have to understand, when you're in politics you get hate mail all the time. It goes with the job and Harlan wasn't easily intimidated. When the first one came, I remember he said something like, 'I guess I stepped on some damn Indian's toes!'"

"He believed it was an Indian who sent these letters?"

"Naturally. Isn't it obvious?"

"Not entirely," Santo told her. "Did your husband notify the police?"

"No, he didn't. He refused to take them seriously. He presumed they were written by someone who had a grudge against his father. Adam Stanton, as you probably know, was the Bureau of Indian Affairs Commissioner in Washington."

"I see. Tell me, do you have any specific person in mind, an enemy who might have sent these?"

"No, no one specifically. But I imagine it's those AIM people. Or what's left of them."

"The American Indian Movement?"

"Of course. They have to blame somebody for their own failure, so why not take it out on poor old Adam Stanton who's dead and can't defend himself? Look, I'm not saying the Indians didn't get a raw deal in many instances. Treaties were broken, and yes, it's sad. But these things happened a hundred years ago and you have to move on."

"Would you say your husband had many enemies?"

"Of course. He had strong opinions and there were people who disagreed rather violently. But as I said, that's what you have to expect when you're in politics these days. Washington has become a very ugly town, I'm afraid."

Santo decided to press forward to more personal issues. "Tell me, Mrs. Stanton, whose idea was it to invite Anne Stanton for Thanksgiving? Wasn't that awkward, to have her here?"

"No, not really. Anne and I have always had a perfectly good relationship. She was ready to leave Harlan, frankly, at just the moment when I was ready to step in. She and Harlan had been keeping up a façade, but the marriage had died years ago. They separated quite amicably. In fact, it was Harlan who invited her for Thanksgiving."

"Do you know why?"

"I don't. I think it had something to do with the trust fund that Harlan's father set up for his grandchildren. But you'll have to ask Anne about this."

"Why would your husband want to speak to Anne about the trust fund?"

"Harlan didn't discuss it with me. But she's the co-executor of the trust so I suppose they need to talk occasionally about how the money is being invested. You understand, Anne and Harlan were still married when Adam died, and the old fellow was very fond of his daughter-in-law. To tell the truth, I think he trusted Anne's judgement more than he trusted Harlan's. In any case, I've made it a point to stay clear of this whole drama. As I say, you'll have to ask Anne about it."

"I will," Santo told her. "Well, all right—as I said, at present I'm just trying to get the overview of the situation. I'm sure we'll be talking to you again. And of course, at some point I'm going to need a formal statement. But for the moment, thank you so much for your time. You're free to go as long as you don't leave the ranch."

"You're going to keep me here?"

"Just for a short while longer, Mrs. Stanton. I hope you understand. We're not going to allow anybody to leave until we have things a bit more sorted out."

Santo stood politely as Summer Stanton left the room.

"So, what do you think, Jack?" he asked when she was gone.

"She certainly went out of her way to implicate Howie."

"Well, yes. But you know, Jack, we need to find out more about this quarrel Howie and Harlan had at the dinner table. We can't avoid it. I like Howie as much as you do, but this is a murder investigation and we have to be impartial. Those threatening letters the Senator received *do* have an Indian angle."

"Santo, you know and I know that Howie didn't scalp Senator Stanton!"

Santo sighed. "Sure, I do. But this is going to be a big case and I can't let personal friendships influence me. You understand that, don't you?"

"Of course," Jack said grudgingly.

"So, who should we see next? Anne Stanton, I'm thinking."

"That would be my choice, if I were running this show—which I'm not, I'm happy to say. I'd say go for Anne next, then Justin, then Grace, in that order. This trust fund business may turn out to be important. And let's not forget that Nicolas Stanton is somewhere on the loose."

"Let's keep it rolling, then. We have a lot of witnesses to interview and I need to be quick about it before this crowd gets restless and starts demanding their lawyers. I'm thinking you and I can do Anne, Justin, and Grace and I'll get Dan started on statements from the others." Santo read from a list he had made. "Lorenzo Stein, Stephen Halley, Belinda Stanton. And the teenage sons, of course."

"Children often notice more than their parents," Jack agreed.

"They do. And we'll want to talk to the servants, too."

"You think the butler did it?"

"Sure," said Santo. "That would wrap it up just fine. You want a cup of coffee first?"

Before Jack could answer, Sally Loeb knocked on the door.

"Excuse me, Lieutenant, we have a problem," she told him. "The Deputy Commissioner of Public Safety has just arrived."

***

The weather was turning dirty. A cold wind had come up and the sky was steel gray. The sun had vanished and it had turned into a melancholy autumn day.

Howie headed across the brown stubbly meadow from the barn, curious to see the bunkhouse that the stable hand, Tucker, had told him about. He wanted to know if this was where the late-night horse and rider had disappeared to. Howie was starting to get an ugly idea about who the rider might be.

As he hiked across the meadow, he tried to remember everything he could about the 1970 Indian school murder, the young Indian boy who had killed his headmaster. He had only a hazy memory of the details. The case had been famous in Indian country, not only for the gruesome murder committed by a child, but because the subsequent investigation had revealed the prevalence of sexual and physical abuse that went on in these schools. As a result, there had been a complete revamping of the Indian school program. Many of the schools had been closed down, and those that remained today were very different, day schools that emphasized vocational training rather than Christianity.

He realized now why the road to the ranch was called Camino de la Vieja Escuela. It wasn't "old school" as in conservative values. There had been an actual school here and it gave him a creepy feeling to think this was where the murder had happened. Places where bad things had happened left a lingering evil. And it couldn't be a coincidence that fifty years later Senator Harlan Stanton had died in the same manner, in the same place, scalped with his throat cut.

The twelve-year-old killer from 1970 had never been found. Howie remembered that now. At the time, most people believed he had escaped into the desert and died from exposure. But maybe not. He would be sixty-two years old today if he was still alive.

Howie continued over the rise of the meadow to where it began sloping down at a gentle angle. Below him, the hill descended into a sheltered valley where he saw a long shed-like building that stood at the edge of a stream near a grove of aspen trees. There was a dirt road that led to the old bunkhouse, but it was overgrown and it didn't look as though any motorized vehicle had come this way for years.

Howie climbed down from the meadow onto the road. There was a small horse corral by the side of the building with a garden hose that ran, gravity fed, from the stream into a metal trough that was gently overflowing from beneath a thin film of ice. A small mound of horse dung lay not far away and it appeared fresh. Somebody had been here recently.

The bunkhouse was a primitive wooden building with a covered porch along the front and four doors leading to the rooms. The wood was dark with age and everything had fallen into disrepair.

"Hello!" Howie called. "Anybody here?"

There was no answer. Howie started his search on the near end of the building and worked his way down along the porch. None of the doors were locked. The first two rooms had two sets of bunks against the walls to sleep four people. Each room had a simple chest of drawers and a metal rod that would serve as a kind of closet. The Stantons had provided only the most basic accommodations for their ranch hands.

The third door led to a very basic bathroom. A toilet stall, a sink, a grimy mirror, a metal shower stall. The water had been turned off.

It was the fourth door that was interesting.

The room contained the same two bunks, dresser, and place to hang clothes. But there was an inflatable camping pad on the floor, a pillow, and a heavy down sleeping bag that had been unzipped and opened up to make a blanket.

There were two candles on the floor stuck into wine bottles, their wicks burned down to stubs, wax spilled down the sides. A third empty bottle was on the floor by the bed along with two wine glasses that still had a hint of purple residue on the bottom. The bottle had an expensive French label. Chateau Margaux. An old-fashioned oil heater stood not far from the bed.

Howie sensed he had found a low-rent love nest for a couple who had good taste in wine. He imagined Santo's CSU crew would discover their identity quickly enough. Unless the lovers had been careful, there would be prints on the glasses and hairs and DNA samples in the sleeping bag.

Howie stood for several minutes in the doorway surveying the room, careful not to disturb anything.

He went through possible combinations in his mind, which two lovers it might have been. When it came to the women, the possibilities were narrow. Summer Stanton, perhaps. She was in her fifties. It didn't seem likely that a woman of Summer's age and character would be so overwhelmed with passion that she would have braved the cold weather and the night to make her way down here for a romantic tryst. But you couldn't entirely rule her out.

Which left Justin's dull wife, Belinda.

And Grace.

Which would it be?

Boring Belinda who in her mid-thirties was already looking staid and middle-aged? Or the forever enticing Grace?

It wasn't much of a question, was it?

Though of course, he shouldn't jump to conclusions. This was something that Jack had drilled into him again and again. He also needed to consider the possibility that the love tryst hadn't necessarily been between a woman and a man. It could have been two men. Or two women. Lorenzo and Justin? Belinda and Grace? It was hard for Howie to imagine any of these combinations, but without evidence, who could say?

Only one thing seemed clear: two wine-drinking lovers had met here, and, judging from the fresh horse poop in the corral, it had probably been last night.

Howie was pondering the possibilities when his eye fell on the edge of a pouch of Drum rolling tobacco that was half concealed by the sleeping bag. He recognized the dark blue of the pouch immediately because Nick had been smoking Drum when he had come by Howie's house last week.

Howie stared at what he could see of the tobacco pouch for more than a few moments, conflicted as how to proceed. On one hand, he knew he shouldn't enter the room, he shouldn't touch anything. This love nest would be a crucial part of the murder investigation.

He needed to get back to the house and tell Santo what he had found. But before that . . . perhaps he might have just a quick peek.

He took off his shoes and stepped into the room in his socks. He walked carefully in a straight line to the edge of the sleeping bag where the pouch was peeking out. He pulled down the sleeve of his sweater over his right hand to use as a sort of glove and lifted the edge of the sleeping bag so that he could see the Drum packet in its entirety.

The flap of the bag was open. There were only a few strands of tobacco inside. There were no rolling papers, no matches, nothing else. But Howie was virtually certain that it was Nick who had spent the night here. Perhaps several nights.

But with who?

Whom.

Two wine glasses. Two candles. Very cozy. But he hadn't spent the night with Summer, or Belinda. It had to be Grace. She was the only logical person left.

Howie felt foolish for not understanding the situation right away. This wasn't a love nest. It was a meeting place. Grace had read Nick's letter that Howie had delivered and she knew where he was hiding. She had ridden her horse here last night when she believed everybody was asleep, bringing along a bottle of wine in order to have a good brother-to-sister chat.

If he was right, it gave both Nick and Grace an alibi. If they had been down here in the bunkhouse at three in the morning, they hadn't been up at the ranch murdering their father.

But then again, it wasn't clear when the murder had happened. Nick and Grace weren't in the clear yet.

Howie very carefully backed out of the room to the door, where he stepped outside onto the porch and put his shoes back on.

He walked up the hill toward the ranch house. He was tired and the climb was steep enough to take his breath away. But he didn't mind that. What he minded was that Grace and Nick had used him. It stung that these two people, once so important in his life, had manipulated him so callously. But he knew it was his own fault. He shouldn't have gotten involved. He shouldn't have let himself be sucked into the past.

As he approached the house, he saw that a number of official vehicles had arrived in the parking area, their roof lights twinkling. Along with the State Police cruisers, there was an ambulance, a white CSU van, and a fire engine. What the fire engine was doing here, he couldn't imagine.

Howie was almost to the house when he saw Grace standing on the flagstone terrace smoking a cigarette.

He lowered his head and charged like a bull in her direction.

Chapter Thirteen

Grace didn't see Howie until he was almost on top of her. She stood lost in thought, smoking languidly, her back to him, exhaling a ghostly plume of smoke into the autumn air.

Howie had stopped smoking years ago but the sight of her with a cigarette stirred an old longing. A smoke after sex. Après coffee. He remembered how he and Grace used to snuggle naked in his sleeping bag on the sand dunes passing a cigarette back and forth, with the surf breaking in the near distance. She smoked Players, a fancy English cigarette that came in a distinctive flat box with a picture of a sailor on it. He smoked Lucky Strike.

"Grace!" he called.

She turned reluctantly. She was wearing a fluffy turtleneck sweater that was pumpkin colored, a little too autumn perfect for his taste. Her blonde hair was pulled back in a feisty ponytail, but her skin was pale, and she looked tired.

"We need to talk," he said coming closer.

"Not now, Howie. I don't think I can bear any more drama."

"We can't put this off," he told her.

"Oh, Howie, this just isn't the right time. Won't you give me a little space?"

"We'll keep it short, then." He paused and felt like a man standing at the edge of a cliff, deciding whether to jump. "Did you get pregnant that summer? Yes or no? You need to answer me. Do we have a child?"

She gave him a deep, searching, inscrutable look. "No, Howie," she said at last. "*We* don't have a child. I mean, yes, I gave birth, I didn't get an abortion. But she's gone. I had to give her away. I didn't have any choice. Once Daddy found out, he made all the decisions."

"Really? And how did Daddy find out?"

"I told him, Howie. I had to. I was pregnant, I was frightened."

"You could have come to me for help."

Her eyes lit with scorn. "Oh, right! An undergraduate without a penny. You would have been a great help!"

"I was the father," he asserted. Then added, "I assume I was, at least."

She flushed with anger. "What are you saying? There wasn't anyone but you that summer. You know that!"

She took a deep drag on her cigarette and nodded knowingly. "My God, now I get it! it was Summer who told you about the baby, wasn't it? That bitch!"

"She called me into her study yesterday before dinner. To be honest, Grace, I was surprised she knew all the gory details. She used it to try to pressure me into accepting a job that I didn't want. I mean, she knew everything. Like the fact you had a diaphragm you sometimes forgot to put in. And that . . . that we had sex, well, frequently."

Her smile was so faint it was hard to see. "*Frequently*? That's putting it mildly. I remember five times one day! I was so sore afterward I could barely walk, but I didn't mind. It was fun to be young, once upon a time in a different universe."

"Yes, it was," Howie conceded. He avoided her eyes, not sure it was safe to acknowledge these memories. "But how does Summer know this intimate stuff?"

"Daddy broke into my desk and read my diary."

Howie was shocked. "That's awful!"

"Well, I suppose so. But that's the way he was. A patriarch who had the right to order us about and read our diaries. He was the king and we were his subjects. I'm afraid I wrote down all the gory details, as you put it. He must have told Summer."

Howie wasn't pleased that the Senator knew such intimate parts of his life. "For chrissake, Grace! You got pregnant and didn't tell me!"

"Look, I didn't mean to get knocked-up. And as much as I enjoyed our summer romp, I certainly didn't intend to get married. My father sent me away to a place in Scotland. That's why I disappeared so suddenly. It wasn't to have some silly junior year abroad. I had the baby and they found a home for her. I didn't want to know her name because that would have made it harder. I didn't want to know where she was."

"You thought you could just wish it away?"

"That's not fair! It wasn't easy for me to give away my child. But I didn't see any other choice."

"You didn't think I should have had some say in this?"

"No, I didn't," she answered firmly. "This was my decision, not yours. Howie, we were very young. I didn't want the responsibility of being a parent. I wasn't ready. And you weren't ready either. Actually, I did you a favor. You had your fun and you didn't have to pay the price. What more could any horny nineteen-year-old college boy want?"

Howie stared at her, speechless. The carelessness of her words bit deep. He had been a fool, he knew that. But it hadn't been some casual bit of fun. He had believed himself in love.

Grace dropped her half-finished cigarette on the flagstone terrace and crushed it with her shoe. "I need to get back inside."

"Not yet," he said coldly. "Somebody has been sleeping down at the old bunkhouse. There's a sleeping bag, a kerosene heater, candles, an empty bottle of good wine, two glasses. You wouldn't know anything about that, would you?"

Grace shook her head. "I don't."

"Yeah? Well, I was woken up at three this morning by the sound of hoofbeats outside my room. I got up and looked outside the window just in time to see a horse and rider disappear across the meadow toward that bunkhouse. It was your horse, Grace. Valkyrie."

She snorted derisively. "How can you possibly know that?"

"Because Tucker and I had a look in the corral this morning and Valkyrie had saddle marks on his back. Tucker was upset that he hadn't been brushed."

"Well, that wasn't me you saw. Why in the world would I go riding at that hour?"

"Because you knew Nick was down there and you wanted to see him. You brought him food and a bottle of wine."

"Howie, I didn't. I have no idea where Nick is. I haven't seen him."

"Really?"

"I swear to God, Howie."

"You know, the CSU people are going to go through that bunkhouse and if they find your prints or any of your hair samples, you'd be smart to admit it now."

She shook her head. "It wasn't me down there. I don't know anything about this."

Howie stared at her, trying to decide if she was telling the truth. But she was impenetrable. Her beauty had always been a glossy shield he had never passed beyond. For all their romping in the dunes, he hadn't known her any better at the end of the summer than when the summer began. And he didn't know her now.

He still had a dozen questions he wanted to ask but just then, Detective Dan Hamm came out of the house and saw them.

"Oh, there you are, Miss Stanton," he said. "We've been looking for you. Lieutenant Ruben wants everybody to remain inside the house."

"Is he ready for my statement?" she asked.

"Not yet," Dan said. "But I'm sure he'll be ready for you soon."

Grace gave Howie a final look that was beyond Howie's skill to decipher. It was part scorn, part regret, a complicated look from a complicated woman.

She turned to walk away, but Howie stopped her.

"Hey," he said. "Aren't you forgetting something?"

She turned with a questioning look in her eyes. "What?"

He pointed to the half-smoked cigarette butt that she had left on the flagstone.

"Pick up your trash, Grace. Grown-ups don't leave a mess and expect someone else to clean up after them."

Her eyes flared. For a moment he thought she was going to slap him. Then she forced an amused smile, leaned over, and picked up the cigarette butt.

"You used to be nicer," she told him before she turned and walked into the house.

Howie supposed she was right. He did use to be nicer, it was true. Back when he was a whole lot more innocent than he was today.

***

The Department of Public Safety was the government agency in charge of the New Mexico State Police, but they generally ruled from a bureaucratic distance and didn't show up at crime scenes. So when Officer Sally Loeb told Santo that Deputy Chief of Public Safety Henry Wierczek had appeared unexpectedly at the Stanton Ranch, Santo immediately stopped what he was doing and left Jack and Katya in the study to see what he wanted. The boss from Santa Fe couldn't be put off.

Jack waited with Katya's head in his lap, giving her a good pet and a scratch behind her expressively furry ears. He wasn't surprised that one of the big shots had shown up. This was going to be a high-profile case.

He knew from his own experience how irritating it was to have some highly-placed bureaucrat insert himself into your investigation. They almost always got in the way.

Santo returned ten minutes later, and he wasn't happy.

"Dammit, Jack, I'm sorry, but I'm going to have to ask you to wait in the living room with the others. Wierczek doesn't like it that you're here. He gave me a pretty good dressing down for bringing in a civilian."

Jack rose to his feet with the help of Katya, using one hand on her back for balance. She was a very helpful dog.

"It's okay, Santo. I understand."

"Well, it's a pain in the ass to stop everything and deal with this jerk! But I don't have a choice. Look, he wants to see the body before it's taken away, so I'm going to be busy playing tour guide for a few minutes. Maybe you can keep your ears open while you're waiting and I'll get back to you as soon as I can."

"Santo, I don't mind. Do what you need to do and I'll be fine."

Santo took Jack's arm and led him down the hall to the living room and parked him on a sofa with Katya stretched out at his feet.

"That's certainly a very civilized animal," he heard a woman say from the far end of the sofa. Her voice was refined and pleasant.

"She's had years of training," he replied.

"German Shepherds make good guide dogs, I've heard."

"Well, they do. But so do Labradors and a number of other breeds. Dogs like to be useful. They're happier when they're trained to work at something."

"I agree entirely," she told him. "I once saw quite a small dog herding sheep in the south of Spain. It was amazing how he dashed from one side of the group to the other, keeping them all in line."

Jack formed visual pictures of people from their voices, their scent—more subtly, their vibration. He sometimes felt like a bat shooting off signals into the dark to see what bounced back. The refined woman who shared his sofa hadn't introduced herself, but Jack was certain he knew who she was.

"I'm Jack Wilder, by the way," he said. "And you must be Anne Stanton."

"I am! How clever of you to figure that out! But, of course, you're the famous detective and that's what you do, isn't it? Deduction."

"Deduction is the word people use in crime novels. But in real life, *in*duction is what detection is all about, Mrs. Stanton."

"Is it? You know, I always get those two words mixed up. Aren't they somewhat the same?"

Jack smiled. "Actually, they're quite different. Deduction means you begin with a theory and then you go about gathering evidence to support it. That's not a good idea for a cop. Induction is the opposite. With induction, you start with observation, you gather evidence, and *then*, if you can, you come up with a theory."

"Ah yes, I remember now. Theism and deism, that's another of those tricky sets of words I always have trouble with!"

Jack laughed. "I get those mixed up, too. Fortunately, deism and theism don't often come up in my line of work. Tell me, Mrs. Stanton, do you still live here in New Mexico?"

"No, I'm in Florida these days. Palm Beach. I have a condo at The Breakers. I love the ocean and it's convenient for an old person like me to live in a hotel with all the services. Do you know Florida, Mr. Wilder?"

"Not well. But I do know The Breakers, one of America's grand old hotels. As a matter of fact, I arrested a murderer there once."

"Really? How fascinating!"

"It was a rich man from San Francisco who poisoned his much younger wife. She was cheating on him and he wanted to teach her a lesson. He pulled it off in quite a clever way, but I got him in the end. He was off celebrating with his new girlfriend at The Breakers when I caught up with him. We had a gun fight around the swimming pool."

"Did you, really? My God, the swimming pool at The Breakers! Did you . . . I know I shouldn't ask . . ."

"Did I shoot him?" Jack knew he was showing off but once he started talking about the Old Days, it was hard to get him to stop. "Well, yes, I did. He didn't leave me a choice."

"You plugged him, as they say?"

"I wouldn't use that expression, Mrs. Stanton. These days we talk more about 'neutralizing threats.' Fortunately, in this case he recovered well enough to end up in the gas chamber at San Quentin."

"What an interesting career you've had! But don't you ever feel sorry for those people you catch?"

"Well, yes, occasionally I *do* feel sorry for them, especially when they've been victims themselves in one way or another. But in this case—believe me, the guy was contemptible and I was pleased to see him get what he deserved."

"And what do you think of this case? My ex-husband being killed? Do you believe you'll catch the murderer?"

"I'd say the odds are good. A remote setting like this, a Thanksgiving gathering, a ranch in the middle of nowhere . . . there aren't that many suspects and that makes it considerably easier."

Her laugh was more an expression of disbelief than humor. "You're saying it's one of us? One of the family?"

"I'm saying it's most likely someone who was here last night, which narrows down the possibilities. But, of course, somebody could have snuck in from outside. It wouldn't have been that hard."

"So it could be anyone? Not the family at all?"

"It could. But you see, when it comes to murder, families are the first thing you consider. There are a lot of emotions in family groupings, sometimes of the kind that lead to violence. Jealousies, old resentments, that sort of thing."

She laughed, this time more like she meant it.

"You're probing me, aren't you? I'm honored, Mr. Wilder—you're using your detective skills on me, hoping I'll tell you about jealousies and old resentments among the Stantons!"

Jack shrugged. "Don't you want to clear up your ex-husband's murder as quickly as possible?"

"Do I?" She paused. "Well, perhaps not—not if it's someone from the family. In any case, Harlan had plenty of enemies, so I'm sure you will find suspects galore."

"Not me, Mrs. Stanton. This is Lieutenant Ruben's case, I'm only a bystander. But in this instance, opportunity is going to be the prime factor. Who had the opportunity to show up here last night in the Senator's study. You'll have to pardon me, Mrs. Stanton, but you don't seem especially upset by the Senator's death."

"Ah, well, you know, I *will* miss the old scoundrel. When you've known someone most of your life, it leaves an imprint. But, no, I won't mourn him."

Jack was just getting going. He was about to point the conversation to her children, and in particular her son, Nicolas, the eco-terrorist. But he became aware that Howie was approaching. It was the familiar rhythm of Howie's somewhat bumbling walk. And if he needed any more confirmation, he felt Katya's tail wagging energetically against his leg.

"Jack," Howie had dipped his head towards the sofa so he could speak quietly. "Can we step outside for a moment? I'd like to have a word."

***

Howie took Jack's arm and led him outside into the driveway where a dozen law enforcement vehicles were parked in the clearing in front of the house.

"Dammit, Howie, you interrupted me," Jack said. "I hope what you have to tell me is important."

"It is," Howie answered. "This property, the Stanton Ranch, used to be an Indian boarding school. Fifty years ago, a famous homicide happened here. One of the students, a twelve-year-old boy, murdered the headmaster. The kid cut the headmaster's throat. And, get this, he scalped him. It's exactly what happened to Senator Stanton last night. Which puts a whole new face on this case. This is a copycat murder, Jack."

Howie was pleased with himself. He had to admit, it was a pleasure to get the jump on Jack.

"Hmm, fifty years later!" Jack said more cautiously. "Deja vu all over again!"

"Jack, this isn't a joke!"

"I can see that. What happened to the Indian kid?"

"He ran off. As far as I know, he was never caught. And there's more. I found out where the horse and rider I saw last night disappeared to. There's an old bunkhouse down below the far edge of the meadow where I saw them go. It's where the ranch hands used to live back in the day when Adam Stanton was still alive, the old Commissioner. One of the rooms was used recently. I found a sleeping bag, an empty bottle of wine, two glasses . . . I thought it was a love nest at first until I figured out that Nick probably has been staying there. The way I figure it, it was his sister on the horse. Grace. She rode down to see him and they had a pow-wow of some sort."

"Not so fast. Let's back up and start from the beginning. First tell me how you found out about this old murder."

"As I said, it was a famous case. Most Indians know about it because it was a big scandal at the time, and it ended up changing the way Indian boarding schools were run. I just didn't realize the murder had happened here."

Howie was about to tell Jack about his conversation with Tucker when Santo and a tall, cadaverous man in a grey suit came walking out of the house together. When they saw Jack and Howie, the man in the suit changed course and came their way.

"Mr. Wilder—Henry Wierczek, Public Safety," he said to Jack. "I know of your impressive law enforcement past, and I appreciate you coming by this morning. Nevertheless, you are no longer a police officer and I need to ask you to leave. Lieutenant Ruben will arrange for a car to drive you home. As for you, Mr. Moon Deer, you will please wait with the others, and you will be allowed to leave once we have your statement."

Jack nodded patiently. "I understand, Mr. Wierczek. I would have given the same instructions in your place. However, if it's possible, my guide dog and I will wait in Howie's car while he gives his statement. Then he can drive me back to town."

"It's not really necessary for you to wait around, Jack," Santo said. He turned to Wierczek. "Look, I've already spoken with Howie and I've gotten his story, start to finish. So let's allow Jack and Howie to leave together now. If Howie drives Jack home, I won't have to lose an officer, and I'll get Howie's signed statement tomorrow. Meanwhile, I have a bunch of people I need to interview before their lawyers arrive and I'm short-handed. Most of all, I really need to keep this show moving."

The Public Safety man nodded warily. "All right, Lieutenant. You know your job. Just keep me up to date. I want a full report from you once a day."

"You'll get it . . . Jack, I'll give you a call later," Santo said over his shoulder as he walked Wierczek to his car.

"Let's get out of here while we can," Jack said the minute he and Howie were alone.

"Don't you think I need to tell Santo what I found?"

"Later, not now. Right now I want to get you away from here before Santo decides to throw you in the slammer."

"Slammer?" Howie asked. "Isn't that a somewhat antiquated expression?"

"Some things never change. Now, let's go before Santo decides that you're the perfect fall guy."

"*Me*, Jack? What did I do? I was just . . . just . . ."

"Right, bumbling along, getting yourself into a fine pickle . . . come on, I want to get back to the office. We can stop at Maria's for a late breakfast along the way."

Breakfast?

Howie had barely eaten anything yesterday at Thanksgiving, and a mere raspberry danish this morning. Meanwhile, Maria's had possibly the best breakfast burritos in San Geronimo. The only question was whether he'd have red chile or green.

Christmas, he decided. Green on one end, red on the other. The rest of life should be so simple.

"*Vamanos*!" said Howie.

"*Andiamo*!" said Jack, who had grown up in the North Beach section of San Francisco and liked to show off his Italian from time to time.

Chapter Fourteen

Santo Ruben felt his body relax, head to toe, when Henry Wierczek, the Deputy Chief of Public Safety, left the Stanton Ranch and returned to Santa Fe where he belonged.

He stood on the front porch and watched as Wierczek's state vehicle, a white Ford Explorer, drove away on the unpaved road that rose up and down a long series of hills toward the highway, until only a plume of dust was visible in the distance. When the car was gone, he felt he could breathe again.

Santo had a number of immediate problems. The first problem was he was hungover and he didn't feel well, a fact which he had done his best to conceal from Wierczek. Normally, he didn't drink when he was in the middle of a work cycle. He was disciplined, he kept himself in check. But give him a few days off, a chance to release the accumulated stress of his job, and Santo drank like a camel that had just crossed the desert. He was a single malt man, which was one of the things that drew him to Jack. Jack had found himself a steady supply of Laphroaig, not cheap, and on the evenings when it was possible, the two of them often sipped and talked long into the night.

Thanksgiving yesterday at Jack and Emma's had been one of Santo's drinking days and today he was paying the price. His hands weren't entirely steady. He felt insubstantial, not quite real. He hoped Wierczek hadn't noticed the pallor of his skin. He had worked hard to appear bright and on the ball, but now he was wondering if he had overcompensated.

The second problem Santo had to deal with this morning was that the small San Geronimo State Police force, fourteen officers strong, had only two detectives, and on this Black Friday, Santo's lead detective—

Jimmy Trujillo, a gnarly old veteran—was off on compassionate leave in El Paso for the funeral of his father. This left Dan as his one remaining detective. Santo liked Dan, despite his gee-whizz manner. But Dan had been a detective for less than a year, he was young, and he had a long way to go.

Which was why Santo was unhappy that he had been forced to send Jack home. Jack would have been a big help, not only with the interviews but as someone with whom he could bounce ideas back and forth.

I rely on Jack too much! Santo told himself gloomily. He knew he did, and it wasn't right. But it was hard not to. Having Jack around was like a high school football coach finding Joe Montana on the sidelines willing to help call plays.

Once Wierczek was gone, Santo sank into an armchair in the Stanton library and gathered his resolve. *I can deal with this!* he said to himself. *I'm a tough old cop!*

Sometimes you had to give yourself a war cry just to get going.

"Bring me Anne Stanton," he told Dan.

***

Santo could tell that Anne Stanton had been quite a beauty in her youth. She was an imposing woman, tall and aristocratic. She carried herself with a confidence born of privilege.

She was in her mid-sixties and didn't bother to disguise her age. She wore no make-up, not even lipstick. Her hair was white, cut short in a stylish but no-nonsense fashion. She sat perfectly straight in the armchair like someone who had learned female deportment in a different era. She looked like a woman who could balance a book on her head if the occasion arose.

"I want to offer my condolences," Santo told her, rising to his feet as Dan brought her into the library. "I know you and Senator Stanton have been divorced for some years, but it must be a shock nevertheless."

"Yes, it's very shocking," she answered simply.

"Now, Mrs. Stanton—do you still go by that name?"

"I do."

"Mrs. Stanton, please have a seat. I have to admit, I'm surprised to find you here this weekend with your ex-husband and his second wife. Isn't that awkward?"

"Not a bit, Lieutenant," she told him. Her voice was what Santo thought of as mid-Atlantic, not quite British but not entirely American either. "Harlan and I separated very amicably and, of course, I've known Summer for many years. She was his chief of staff. His secretary, really. I often had dealings with her."

"You and Summer are friends?"

"Friends? No, I wouldn't go that far, but we have a pleasant relationship. I wasn't surprised when I discovered that she and Harlan were lovers. To be honest, in those busy Washington years, she saw a great deal more of my husband than I did. She was a much better fit than I ever was, really. She lived for Harlan's success. She was the perfect addition to his team."

Santo smiled. "His *team*? You make it sound more like a staffing arrangement than a romance."

"Well, it was. You see, it's very convenient for busy men to fuck their secretaries. That way they can have all their irons in one fire, so to speak. A quick tumble on the desk before she goes off to set up the next appointment. A mere wife can't compete with such an efficient use of time."

Santo had never heard the word fuck sound so classy. She said it with an aristocratic panache that made it somehow elegant.

"But you haven't really answered my question. Why did you come here for Thanksgiving? That seems a bit chummy for a wife who's been supplanted by the girl from the office."

"Oh, I don't know. If ever I was jealous, that was long ago. In any case, I came because Harlan invited me. And I wanted to see my children."

"Where do you call home these days, Mrs. Stanton?"

"Palm Beach. I flew into Albuquerque and rented a car."

"And you arrived when?"

"Wednesday evening."

"Did the Senator have a chance to tell you why he invited you here?"

"No explanation was necessary, Lieutenant. I'm family, after all. I presumed he wanted to discuss the children's trust fund."

"The money that Adam Stanton left for his grandchildren?"

"Yes. As perhaps you know, Harlan and I are co-executors of the trust. Harlan and I were still married at the time of Adam's death, and, to be honest, he trusted my judgement when it came to financial matters more than he trusted Harlan's."

"So, the way the trust is written, you and Harlan needed to agree to any changes?"

"That's right. As co-executors, we both had to be on board. The trust was set up in such a way that it was up to our discretion as to when the children would receive their money. Adam wanted to make sure his grandchildren were mature enough to handle a large inheritance. Harlan and I were charged with making this judgement call. Of course, for some people, maturity arrives early. For others, it never arrives at all."

Santo's smile expanded into a silent laugh. He liked shrewd women and clearly Anne Stanton was no fool. "So, how has the money been distributed so far?"

"Justin received his share when he was twenty-five. Grace will get hers when she's forty. That's two years from now. As for Nicolas . . . well, with Nicolas, we'll just have to wait and see."

"So, what was it about Justin that made you decide he was mature enough at twenty-five?"

"Lieutenant, my first son, Justin, was born middle-aged. He's never done an ill-considered thing is his life."

Santo studied the cultivated woman who was seated across from him. Her face gave away nothing. "This doesn't sound like a compliment."

"It is what it is," she replied.

"Fair enough. Now tell me about Grace. Why does she have to wait until she's forty?"

"That's easy. She's a woman."

Santo raised an eyebrow. "You're saying women are by nature irresponsible? Isn't that an old-fashioned view?"

"Harlan had conservative views about these things, Lieutenant. And in this case, I agreed with him. Grace is a wonderful girl, but she's impulsive. And of course, there have been too many men in her life, some who have been more suitable than others. Men complicate the picture for a wealthy woman. Hopefully, by the time Grace is forty, these relationships will have sorted themselves out."

"I presume you've put Howard Moon Deer in the unsuitable category?"

"Naturally! Howie is a very nice young man. I have nothing against him. But no, he's not even slightly suitable for a girl like Grace. She needs a rider with a strong whip hand."

Santo stared at Anne Stanton in astonishment. A rider with a strong whip hand didn't sound to him like a good qualification for marriage. But he decided to leave it alone.

"Let's return to the trust fund, Mrs. Stanton. How much money did Adam Stanton leave his grandchildren?"

"When he died, it was a pinch over three million dollars. That doesn't seem like very much now, but it was quite a sum in 1989, and it's grown over the years with the rise in the stock market. There's nearly twelve million dollars in it at the moment, and that's after Justin received his third when he was twenty-five."

"And how much money was that?"

"Justin's share? Three million two hundred thousand and some odd cents. This was nearly fifteen years ago. When Harlan phoned me last week, he suggested we find some time over the weekend to discuss changes in our investment strategy."

Santo nodded encouragingly. "What did Harlan have in mind?"

"At the moment, the money is invested in a conservative mutual fund in New York. It's been earning steady interest over the years but nothing spectacular. Harlan was suggesting we put it into something here in New Mexico with a much better prospect for growth. He suggested a large real estate development company called Enchanted Mesa that's planning a luxury development outside of Santa Fe. A golf course, seventy-five luxury houses, a convention center, quite a big deal. Harlan said we could easily double the trust in five years if we took the money from New York and invested it here."

"But, as you said, you both had to agree? He needed your approval?"

"That's correct."

"Were you going to say yes?"

"Frankly, I wasn't. I was skeptical. But I was willing to hear him out."

"Now that Harlan is dead, are you the sole executor? Or has Summer taken on Harlan's role?"

"No, it's only me. Summer doesn't have any say when it comes to the trust. Though, of course, she had a good deal of influence over Harlan when he was alive."

"Did you have a chance to discuss this new investment proposal with Harlan yesterday?"

"No, there was too much going on. We were planning to get together today to talk it over."

"I see. Now, this real estate development you mentioned, Enchanted Mesa—the golf course, the luxury homes. Who's behind it?" Santo asked. In fact, he was almost certain he knew the answer already.

"Didn't I say? It's Justin, of course. Enchanted Mesa is his brainchild. He's done very well over the years and this will be his largest project yet."

"So why were you going to say no?"

"Why? Because Justin is in debt up to his ears. You think I'd give him all of Grace and Nick's money?" Anne Stanton lowered her voice and glared. "No bloody way!"

"So that's the real reason you came for Thanksgiving? To squash the deal?"

"Exactly," she told him. "To kill it once and for all."

"It doesn't sound like Thanksgiving this year was going to be a happy family occasion."

She laughed. "Oh, the food was wonderful. Ramona always does an excellent job in the kitchen."

"I wasn't talking about the food, Mrs. Stanton."

"Well, the Stantons are like most families, I imagine. There are old wounds and rivalries that tend to come out when people have too much to drink. Grace and Justin have never gotten along, even when they were small. Neither Justin nor Grace are particularly fond of Summer. But all in all, everyone behaved themselves until the big blowout at the end between Harlan and Howie."

"Really? And what blowout was that?"

"You didn't know? It was quite dramatic. Politics, of course. Harlan had the idea that Howie is some kind of wild-eyed socialist revolutionary, and they had a shouting match about it. In fact, as far as I know, Howie isn't political in the least. But he was Nicolas' closest friend and Nicolas, as you know, *did* become quite the revolutionary. In Howie's case, I suppose you can call it socialism by association. Harlan may have been shouting at Howie, but in fact it was Nicolas he was thinking of."

"And how did Howie take this?"

"He took it well, at first. He was admirably restrained, doing his best to avoid a fight. But as it went on, Harlan became abusive. And in the end, Howie was doing his own share of shouting as well. There's a subtext, of course."

"A subtext?" Santo repeated. "And what would that be?"

"Grace. Harlan didn't approve of his daughter's involvement with an Indian boy who had no money."

"But that ended years ago, I understand."

"Well, perhaps. But Harlan wasn't pleased that Grace had invited him for Thanksgiving. He got her pregnant back when they were in college, which Harlan found unforgivable."

"I'm sorry?" Santo was momentarily lost. "Who got who pregnant?"

"Howie got Grace pregnant, of course," Anne said crisply. "In the usual way. Grace wanted to have an abortion, but Harlan wouldn't allow that. He forced her to have the child. He threatened to disinherit her otherwise."

Santo was taken aback. "You're saying that Howie's a father? Does he know?"

"He does now. Summer told him yesterday."

"And where is this child now?"

"Somewhere in Europe, I imagine," Anne answered with a shrug. "Harlan sent Grace to a fancy place in Scotland where she had the baby. The child was put up for adoption. It was all hushed up at the time."

"Well, these things happen," Santo said vaguely, as though it wasn't important. In fact, it was very important, along with Howie's fight with Senator Stanton at the dinner table.

Santo moved on.

"Mrs. Stanton, did you know that your ex-husband received a series of threatening letters shortly before his death?"

"Letters? No, I know nothing about that. I'm not surprised, though. He had a way of making enemies."

"Do you have any enemies in mind?"

"I'd say half of Washington, D.C. But other than that, I really don't know."

Santo smiled and stood up. "Well, that will do for now, Mrs. Stanton. Thank you for your cooperation."

***

Santo's next interview was with Justin Stanton, the eldest son. There was something about Justin that Santo disliked from the start. His face was soft and pudgy and his attitude was dismissive, as though Santo was a small irritation he wanted to deal with as quickly as possible.

"Please have a seat, Mr. Stanton," Santo told him. "I know you'll understand that this is a murder investigation and questions need to be asked."

"Fire away," said Justin as he took a seat in one of the leather armchairs. He crossed his legs imperiously.

"First, I must ask what you were doing in the study where your father's body was lying when you were asked to remain outside?"

Justin snorted unpleasantly. "Oh, come on! Asked to remain outside? Yes, I believe Moon Deer said something to that effect. But who the hell gave him the right to give orders in this house?"

"Howard Moon Deer is a licensed private detective and he's familiar with how crime scene investigations are conducted. You should have listened to him. Surely you must have known it was wrong to go into a room where a murder had been committed. If you disturbed anything there, if you removed something, it will be considered tampering with evidence and we can put you in jail for that. Now, why did you go in there, Mr. Stanton? What were you looking for?"

"Papers, that's all. There are things that need to be arranged."

"You were looking for his will?"

"No, though that wouldn't have been a bad idea. I'd sure like to get my hands on it before Summer does."

"You don't trust your stepmother?"

His laugh had no humor in it. "Trust Summer? You gotta be kidding!"

"If you weren't after the will, what were you hoping to find?"

"A financial prospectus for a deal I'm putting together. I'm a real estate developer, as you probably know. I specialize in shopping malls and hotels. Right now, I'm putting together a golf resort with a conference center and town house on a large parcel I have an option on outside of Santa Fe. I'd given my father a copy of the prospectus, but it's a confidential document and I wanted it back before all sorts of people started poking around in there."

"You didn't want anyone seeing it?"

"Of course not! It was a breakdown of costs and profits and things that weren't meant to be made public."

Santo nodded sympathetically. "So why did you give this confidential document, as you call it, to your father?"

"I wanted his advice, that's all. There are political considerations in a real estate deal this size, and I wanted his thoughts about how to deal with the environmentalists."

"When did you give the prospectus to your father?"

"Yesterday when I arrived for Thanksgiving. He said he'd read it over the weekend, but I don't know if he got around to it."

"Had you discussed your golf course project with him previously?"

"Certainly. We've discussed it several times by phone over the past several months. He's been very encouraging. He was even considering putting some of his own money into it. Dad had a wonderful nose for these kinds of deals."

"I'm sure he did," Santo agreed. "What were the environmental objections?"

"Oh, the usual stuff," Justin answered breezily. "Water issues mostly. Water's always a consideration in New Mexico. We'll need to get an exemption from various regulations and a transfer of water rights. Nothing out of the ordinary. People do it all the time. But there's a group that's been trying to stop us. Anti-growth idiots, people who want to turn back the clock."

"I see," said Santo. "Now, the sort of environmentalists who don't like golf courses—you're talking about people like your younger brother, Nicolas, aren't you?"

"Nick!" he said with a humorless laugh. "Let me tell you something—it's elitist rich kids like Nick who want everything to be pretty as a picture, but don't consider the needs of working men and women."

"Or the needs of wealthy developers, wouldn't you say?"

"Sure, rich developers! Why not? This is America, Lieutenant. Investment opportunities are what Capitalism is all about."

"When's the last time you saw your brother?"

"Oh, it must be ten or eleven years now. Not since he and that crazy group he was involved with burned down that construction site in California and killed the two security guards. Earth Fights Back! What nonsense! Dad didn't want to have anything to do with Nick after that, and neither did I."

"So, you father hadn't seen Nicolas either?"

"You kidding? He refused even to say Nick's name. You have to understand, what Nick did hurt him politically. Dad used to say it's why he lost the last election."

"You don't think that's passing the buck?"

"Well, Nick sure as hell didn't help Dad's campaign. Dad was pretty bitter about that, actually."

"How about your mother? Has she had any contact with Nick over the last decade?"

"I doubt it. If she has, she hasn't told anyone. But she's a bit soft on Nick, you know. He's her youngest."

"And Grace?"

"Would she see Nick? Probably. They were thick as thieves when they were kids. But she doesn't confide in me so you'd have to ask her."

"I will," Santo said. "Now, let's talk about the trust fund your grandfather set up for the three of you. You got your share when you were twenty-five, I understand?"

"That's right. And Grace will get her money when she's forty."

"And Nick won't get anything at all?"

"Probably not. He wouldn't have gotten a cent when Dad was alive, anyway. Now that he's dead, it's hard to say. My mother's in charge of the trust now, and like I say, she has a soft spot for him."

"Your mother told me that your father wanted to take the trust money from a conservative mutual fund and invest it in your real estate deal."

"Well, sure. Why poke around at four or five percent when you can triple your money in a few years. These kinds of golf course developments are sure-fire in New Mexico. People from Chicago and Dallas move here for just that lifestyle. Ski in the winter, golf in the summer, drive your golf cart from your front door onto the green . . . a clubhouse with an Olympic sized pool, a restaurant with a great prime rib Sunday buffet. This is the Good Life we're talking about. The American dream. And I can supply it."

"If you can get the water rights," Santo mentioned. "And if you're not already over your head in debt."

"Who told you I was in debt?"

Santo shrugged. "I've heard it suggested. Of course, we'll be looking into your finances, along with everybody else."

"All right, I'm leveraged," Justin admitted. "So what? That's how these things are done."

"I understand. But tell me this. How badly did you need that money? Would your deal fall apart without it? You'd better tell me the truth, Justin, because I'm going to be checking."

Justin sighed. "Okay, sure, of course I've been counting on it. Dad said he would work on my mother to convince her to go along. Now I'm in a bit of trouble. But look at the silver lining! This certainly lets me off the hook for killing the old man."

"How's that?" Santo asked.

"It's obvious. Dad was going to get me the money. But now that he's dead, that's no longer a sure thing. I don't benefit from Dad's death. In fact, the opposite is true."

Santo had to agree. At least for the moment. Anne Stanton had made it clear that she didn't intend to help Justin out of his financial dilemma. Nevertheless, it was a complicated situation and there was much he didn't know.

"All right, just one more question. Where were you last night from three in the morning to four o'clock?"

Justin snorted derisively. "Oh, come on! I was in bed, of course. With my wife. You can ask her."

"We will."

"Great! So, can I go now? I have to be in Farmington this afternoon for a meeting."

Santo gave his best passive-aggressive smile. "I'm sorry," he said mildly. "That's not possible, I'm afraid. For the time being, you'll need to remain here."

Justin was about to leave the room when Santo threw out one last question. "By the way, do you know anything about threatening letters your father was getting?"

"Nope," he replied brusquely as he went out the door.

Chapter Fifteen

"I want to make sure I'm clear about this," Jack said to Howie as they were sitting in his office. "You had a shouting match with Senator Stanton around the Thanksgiving dinner table, with the entire family looking on. And if that's not bad enough, you'd just found out that you'd gotten Grace pregnant, and her father made her give the kid up for adoption because he didn't like the idea of an Indian knocking up his—"

"Jack—"

"—daughter. Then a few hours later, the Senator is found murdered only a few steps down the hall from your bedroom, scalped in a fashion traditional to the Sioux tribe from which you come, his throat cut. Is that a fair summary of the facts?"

"Yes, I know it looks bad, Jack, when you put it together like that. But it's circumstantial. And you're not taking into account what I told you about the 1970 murder and the sleeping bag and bottle of wine in the old bunkhouse where Nick was hiding out."

Jack raised his dark glasses to the ceiling in frustration.

"Howie, you don't know it was Nick who was using the bunkhouse. You don't know diddly."

"I bet CSU will find Nick's prints there."

"Maybe, maybe not. We're going to have to wait and see since Santo shooed us away before you'd had a chance to tell him about your impromptu investigation. He's not going to be pleased about that either, by the way. He asked you to stay at the house."

"He didn't put it like that, Jack. He said, stay nearby. And I did that. The bunkhouse, the barn—they're on the property."

"Oh, Howie—"

"And what about that horse and rider I saw at three in the morning?"

"Listen to me, Howie. It might just as well have been a pink elephant you saw because you don't have any proof it happened. Nobody else saw that rider but you."

"Tucker, the stable hand, told me that somebody had ridden Valkyrie recently . . . and that's Grace's horse, you'll remember."

"Sure. Somebody went riding, but who can say who or when. Plus, this cowhand has certainly brushed down Valkyrie by now, so Santo's not going to have any evidence. Personally, if I were Santo, I'd put you at the top of the list."

"And which list is that?"

"You know very well which list. Prime suspect, that's you. You're the apple hanging on the low branch. It's a good thing Santo's not a lazy cop. He's going to look deeper. A lot of cops, you'd be in jail right now!'

Howie shook his head. "Right, the slammer. You've mentioned that already."

"And don't forget it, either!"

Howie had rarely seen Jack so worked up. They had driven back from the ranch going over everything Howie had seen and done. Jack wanted to know every word of the dinner table quarrel between Howie and Senator Stanton, and he wanted to hear it twice. They had stopped for breakfast, arrived back at the agency office an hour ago, and they were still going at it, Howie in the client chair, Jack in his big rocker, Katya on the Navajo rug by the kiva fire.

Occasionally Katya snored. Occasionally she farted, as dogs will do. She was getting to be an old dog and Howie was starting to wonder what Jack was going to do when she died.

Jack leaned back in his chair. "Well, we'll just have to get there first," he said.

"Get where first?" Howie was starting to be annoyed by Jack's attitude.

"Where do you think? We need to solve the case ourselves. And figure out who set you up."

"You think I was set up?"

"Like a duck in a shooting gallery!" Jack told him. "Like a sheep going to the slaughter! You were sucker punched!"

"You're mixing metaphors, Jack. And look, it's not as bad as what you're saying. We've got a good lead here—that old Indian school killing, the twelve-year-old who scalped the headmaster. That boy would be in his sixties if he's still alive. An old man, for sure, but not so old that he couldn't commit a murder."

"Sixty isn't that old!" Jack fumed. He exhaled a deep sigh of frustration. "Okay, let's look at your theory. You're saying this is about an old murder from fifty years ago? But why now? Why wait half a century to kill the current owner of the property who had nothing to do with that school?"

"But it's all connected. Harlan's father was the Indian Commissioner back then and it was the BIA that ran those schools. The Stanton family still owns the ranch where the abuse took place. So, call it a case of delayed revenge."

"*Delayed?* By half a century? Come on!"

"Jack, give me a few hours on the Internet and I bet I'll have this figured out by the end of the day. There was a huge amount written about that boarding school murder and a lot of it will be online."

Howie left Jack's office with an optimistic feeling that with some research and a little luck, he might soon have Thanksgiving thankfully behind him.

***

Howie's office in the front of the old adobe building was much smaller than Jack's and more modestly furnished, hardly more than twelve feet across, ten feet deep, with a window looking out on Calle Dos Flores, a narrow street that tourists often wandered down in search of quaintness.

Howie's desk was a scuffed-up wooden table that he had bought from a used furniture store for $35. His chair had been ergonomic at one time, quite expensive when it was new. It had all sorts of knobs that allowed it to be set up, down, forward or back, in any position you liked. But now, in its old age, it lurched uncertainly back and forth without warning, occasionally so wildly that you had to grab hold of the arms to keep from being thrown off. It was like riding a bucking bronco.

He had been planning to buy a new chair for years, but he kept putting it off because he hated shopping. In any case, he liked comfortable old things, even when they weren't so comfortable anymore.

Ruth, the agency secretary, was off today due to the holiday weekend, so Howie was able to blast music on his Bluetooth speaker. Loud music helped him concentrate, which Jack found incomprehensible. His playlist today veered eclectically from Willie Nelson to Chopin with a few tracks of Pink Floyd thrown in for good measure.

The Agency had subscriptions to all the major New Mexico newspapers that included access to their morgues—*The San Geronimo Post, The Santa Fe Reporter, The Albuquerque Journal.* They also subscribed to *The New York Times, The Washington Post,* and several other national publications. Howie began with the *San Geronimo Post*, since the murder had occurred in San Geronimo County, and from here he worked his way outward into the national press. As he had predicted, there had been thousands of words written about the 12-year-old schoolboy who had murdered his headmaster in such a violent manner.

Howie read article after article on the large screen of his desktop Mac with a notebook handy to keep track of information. The school where the murder took place was officially known as the Nuestro Señor de la Misericordia Indian School. Most people called it simply the Misericordia School. And misery it had been. The school closed in 1973, scandal ridden, and the name Misericordia came to represent official abuse and concealment. Adam Stanton, as BIA Commissioner, had used his insider knowledge to buy the abandoned property cheaply, some said not in a manner consistent with the law.

Many of the editorials at the time struggled to understand why a child would commit such a grisly crime, scalping the headmaster, cutting his throat—though Howie imagined a good many schoolboys fantasized such an act. Many of the writers blamed the permissive culture of the late 1960s for both the violence and the sexual abuse. All in all, the press had had themselves a feast and Howie realized he had several days of reading ahead of him.

The articles referred to the boy as Ralph White, though Howie understood that was the American name forced on the boy, not his real name. After several hours of reading, Howie still hadn't been able to discover what his Indian name had been, or even what tribe he was from. The BIA had done everything possible to destroy these children's native past in order to create a new rootless kind of Indian, alienated from his culture. Ralph White, whoever this kid really was, had run off into the vast New Mexico desert and never been found, either dead or alive. The land back then was even more empty than it was today and from the school property, the boy could have easily walked for fifty miles without coming to another building.

Most of the writers agreed that forcing Christianity down the throats of Native American children was not the good thing it had once appeared to be. The country had lost faith, for the moment, with its own cultural imperative. Doubt had snuck in. The Vietnam War was raging in 1970, a time of assassinations and urban riots, and many in America had begun to wonder if the White Man really was the superior creature he pretended to be.

Some even thought, back then, that perhaps it was the Indians who had the better answer.

Emma came by to pick up Jack and Katya at five o'clock. They passed by Howie's office to say goodnight, but he barely noticed. It was nearly half an hour later when Howie struck gold. He wasn't sure it was gold at first, but it turned out to be. An article in the *Albuquerque Journal,* written four days after the murder, said that the State Police, who were running the investigation, were holding a fourteen-year-old girl, a student at the school, who they believed might have been an accomplice to the crime. Her name was being withheld due to the fact that she was a minor.

Howie wanted to know more about this girl. He searched the *Journal* for anything else that might have been written about her, but there was nothing. As the week progressed, media interest began to dwindle. But then Howie picked up her trail once again in an article in the *Santa Fe Reporter* that had been written twelve days after the murder. The piece mentioned that the unnamed fourteen-year-old girl who had been held for questioning was in fact the older sister of Ralph White. She had been released into the care of Adam Stanton, the BIA Commissioner, after it was determined that she'd had nothing to do with her brother's crime. The Commissioner had come to New Mexico from Washington to oversee his agency's own investigation of the case.

Howie was struck by the fact that the girl had been released into the custody of Adam Stanton. This seemed odd to him. Why should the BIA Commissioner take this fourteen-year-old girl into his care? It left a question mark. He scanned through several more weeks of the *Santa Fe*

Reporter but found nothing more about her. She would be sixty-four today, if she was still alive.

Howie would need to look at State Police files from 1970 to get to the bottom of this. He knew that old NMSP files, dating back to the 1930s, were kept in Santa Fe. He had worked with them in the past. Most of the files had been converted into a digital format, though not all. But he would need Santo's help to gain access, and Santo was busy today.

Howie felt he was on to something. But meanwhile he could do nothing more without Santo's help and the computer screen had become blurry in his vision. The last twenty-four hours were catching up with him. He was exhausted, physically and emotionally.

He closed down his computer and decided to call it a day.

***

Small white flecks of frozen fluff floated down from a darkening sky onto his windshield as Howie drove home. It wasn't enough snow to get excited about, but at least it was something.

The weather situation, according to the app on his phone, all depended on whether the jet stream inched south from Colorado, where a winter storm from the northwest was settling in to hit Aspen and Vail. That was fine for Colorado, but if the jet stream didn't move, they would only get wind on San Geronimo Peak—two feet of wind, as the locals liked to call it. It was still a week and a half before the delayed start of the season, but the snow would be welcome.

"Come on jet stream!" Howie prayed fervently, as he pulled into the parking area at the edge of his land. "Go south!"

Howie knew it was shallow of him to be thinking about skiing at a time like this, after his least favorite Senator had been murdered. But he couldn't help it. A man needed relief from the tragedies of life. He was considering the condition of his three pairs of skis as he walked up the forest trail to his pod.

Howie owned a pair of short slalom skis, another pair of much larger powder skis, and some old rock skis for bad conditions. It seemed to him that it might be time to replace his slalom skis this season. He could use a new helmet too, the kind with Bluetooth speakers built in so he could blast music while he tore down the slopes . . .

Orange was pacing back and forth on the landing by his front portal meowing loudly as he climbed up the ladder. Howie understood her perfectly. She was pissed that he had been away so long.

"Hold your horses," he told her as he used the keypad to unlock his door. "I'll open a can of that salmon you like . . ."

Howie stopped as soon as he was inside, sensing something was wrong. There was a different smell in the air. It was subtle: clothes that hadn't been washed, a body that wasn't his own. Somebody had been here in his absence.

He turned on the light and saw a dirty plate in the sink and an empty bottle of Third Eye Stout on the sideboard.

"Nick!" he said with a groan. He didn't have a clue as to how his old roommate had gotten inside, but it had to be Nick. It couldn't be anybody else.

First things first, Howie opened a can of Alaskan salmon for Orange and spooned it into her bowl as she rubbed against his legs. "You'd better like it!" he said sternly. "Alaskan salmon isn't cheap!"

Once he was done feeding Orange, he looked around to see if Nick had left him a message.

His refrigerator had been riffled through and the Trader Joe's dinner he had been planning to eat tonight was missing: Chicken tikka masala with basmati rice. Nick had certainly made himself at home!

Howie found the note in his computer nook and he immediately recognized his old roommate's writing. The message was brief:

Mañana, Saturday, 3 PM: 33.9168° N, 106.8629° W. *Come alone, Sitting Bull, no surprises.*

Howie couldn't help but laugh. There was only one person who had ever called him Sitting Bull. Nick Stanton. It was an old joke between them that went back to a late-night bull session, Howie sitting cross-legged on his bed defending some long-forgotten point. He hadn't thought of it in years.

At the bottom of the note there was an additional scrawl:

You need to update your security. This tin can was a breeze to break into.

Chapter Sixteen

It was snowing on Saturday when Howie set off from his house to find the GPS coordinates that Nick had left for him. But it wasn't pretty snow, big gentle snowflakes falling from the sky onto a winter wonderland. This was snow that blew sideways, hard icy pellets that stung your face and swirled in the air like restless spirits. Nasty stuff. Nothing you'd want to ski on.

According to the GPS device in Howie's Subaru, the coordinates led to a remote spot just south of the Colorado border. Howie set out at noon, allowing three hours for the 72-mile drive. That was more time than he needed, but the weather was uncertain and he didn't want to be late.

He drove carefully because the roads were slick and the visibility bad. The windshield kept icing up even with his defroster on full blast. Sheets of snow blew across the highway making it hard to see the pavement. The Lakota word for snow was *wá*, but this was a word for the good kind of snow that made everything beautiful. Howie knew there was another word for the ugly snow they were having today, the frozen pellets that came at you sideways, but he couldn't remember what it was. It worried him that he was forgetting his language. Maybe he wasn't so different from the Indian children who had been forced to speak English.

He had woken up late thinking about the 14-year-old girl he had read about yesterday, the older sister of Ralph White who Adam Stanton had managed to get released from police custody. Yesterday this had seemed somehow suspicious, a collusion of events. But today he wasn't sure. As BIA Commissioner, Stanton had ultimate authority over the boarding school program, and the children in the schools, so maybe it was a simple case of him looking out for one of his charges.

Or maybe not.

And what had happened to that girl?

Here was an interesting thought: What if the 14-year-old sister had grown up to become Ramona, the stone-faced servant at the Stanton Ranch, which had once been the Nuestro Señor de la Misericordia Indian School? Howie didn't have any reason for believing this, it was only a stray idea. But wouldn't that be an interesting coincidence?

Someone at Thanksgiving—Anne Stanton, Howie remembered—had mentioned that Ramona had been on the ranch for a long time, since the Commissioner's time. Ramona was the right age, in her mid-sixties. It very possibly could be her.

Howie tossed this around for a few miles. As a minor in 1970, the sister's name hadn't been released, so he would need to do some digging to discover if his theory had any truth to it. Hopefully, Santo would help him gain access to the State Police archives in Santa Fe.

There was time to think when you were in a car by yourself on a lonely New Mexico highway in the snow, and Howie's thoughts jumped erratically from the past to the present and back again. Like a compass needle pulled by a magnet, his mind turned to Grace.

Had he really gotten her pregnant that summer? He hadn't had a chance to absorb this yet. At Thanksgiving, he had been too angry to consider the long-term implications. He had been angry first at Summer for her attempted blackmail, then at Grace for not consulting him, leaving him so totally in the dark. Now that he was calmer, what he felt mostly was a kind of dreadful awe that there might be a small Moon Deer out there, a child, a girl, a fragment of himself that had resulted from his youthful infatuation.

For Howie, this was both wonderful and terrifying, and not entirely real. If it was true, he knew that somehow, somewhere, he needed to find her. Meanwhile, the weather was becoming steadily worse and he needed to concentrate on his driving.

From Tres Piedras, he turned north onto Highway 285 and headed toward Colorado. The road cut through a lonely stretch of strangely shaped hills and empty distances.

The snow was coming down harder now, blowing and whirling on the road ahead like white dust devils. Occasionally he met another vehicle, a pickup truck or an RV with out-of-state license plates that looked as though it had taken a wrong turn. They passed one other laboriously, slowly, ships on a white sea.

A sign by the side of the road said GET YOUR BLISS AT BUDS, ANTONITO, COLORADO, 23 MILES AHEAD! Marijuana was legal in Colorado though not in New Mexico, which probably accounted for more than half of the traffic on the road.

Following instructions from his GPS device, Howie turned left across a cattle guard onto a Forest Service road while he was still on the New Mexico side of the border, a few miles short of blissed-out Colorado. The road was unpaved, hard frozen ground that was covered with an inch of snow. Howie slowed to 10 mph, glad that he had good snow tires and all-wheel drive.

The Forest Service road took him along the side of a narrow creek into a long valley with a steep hillside of fir trees on one side, and bare, windswept fields on the other. The coordinates brought him to a spot that was indistinguishable from the other 5.3 miles he had driven since leaving the highway. The only difference was there was a shoulder a few feet wide on his left, not a turnaround exactly, but a flat area where he could get off the road and park against the hill.

Howie kept his engine running while he stepped outside to look around. It was about the bleakest, coldest, least hospitable patch of New Mexico he had ever seen. The wind blew snow into his eyes so it was nearly impossible to see more than a few feet in any direction. Howie didn't like anything about this place.

He slid back into his car and turned up the heater. The digital readout on his dashboard said it was 23 degrees outside. His gas tank was a fraction over half full. He didn't want to turn off his engine and lose the heater but he was worried about his return trip to San Geronimo. He should have topped off with gas before leaving town. It might be best to zip over to Antonito. Like all the border towns, there were several cannabis shops in Antonito, but he wasn't sure about anything as practical as a gas station. He looked at his watch and saw that he was forty-five minutes early. He hoped Nick wouldn't be late.

Howie was startled out of his thoughts by the thump of a fist knocking against his window. He turned and saw a dark, hooded figure standing by the side of the car. He looked more like an abominable snowman than a human. A face appeared in his window. It was Nick. He looked raw and cold. There were icicles in his beard. He too had arrived early.

"Come around the other side!" Howie mouthed through the window.

He reached over to the passenger side and pushed open the door. Nick came around and slid inside the car, letting in a blast of wind and snow.

"Where the hell did you come from? You look like a popsicle!" Howie said when the car door was safely shut.

"It's not exactly Florida out there," Nick admitted. When he smiled, Howie saw that a front tooth was broken off to a jagged point. He hadn't noticed this when he had seen Nick last week.

Nick's smile didn't touch his eyes, which were studying Howie without warmth. Howie didn't see any sign of his vehicle, or any indication of how he had arrived here, but with the limited visibility, it was hard to say. Howie was starting to feel that nothing about this was right.

"What are you doing out here?" he asked again, making an effort to sound confident. "This must be the most forlorn spot on the planet!"

"Oh, I've seen worse. I've become a connoisseur of forlorn places, Howie. Here, have a slug of cognac. It'll warm you."

Nick didn't look like he could afford a bottle of muscatel, much less cognac. He was wearing the same battered, stained dark blue down jacket he'd had on the other night. He looked like someone you didn't really want to meet in the middle of nowhere. Howie wanted to pretend this was his old friend, Nick Stanton, his college roommate. But it wasn't. The years living rough had changed him. This was a stranger.

Nick pulled the hood back from his head and reached into a side pocket, bringing out a silver flask. He took a hit and offered the flask to Howie. Normally Howie didn't drink in the day, but his heart was racing and it didn't seem like a bad idea. He raised the flask and took a swallow. The liquor was smooth and mellow and brought a golden glow to his innards.

"I sense this isn't Christian Brothers," Howie said.

"Rèmy Martin, VSOP."

Howie handed the flask back. "Jesus, Nick! What the hell kind of life are you living?"

"The only life that's available to me. Like the song says, I'm staying alive."

"With a thirty-dollar bottle of cognac?"

Nick shrugged. "When I can get it. If not, I go without. Meanwhile, I follow Seneca. *Eudaemonia*, Howie. That's the key."

Howie laughed reluctantly. *Eudaemonia* was the Greek word for happiness. Like Buddhists, the Stoics taught that happiness lay in equal forbearance of pleasure and pain, living in the moment and refusing to be buffeted by the winds of fortune. He and Nick had discussed these things for hours at a time, long ago in their late-night dormitory conversations.

"So how was Thanksgiving, amigo?" Nick asked. "Did you have a good time with the old folks at home?"

"How do you know I was there?" Howie challenged.

"Oh, I have big ears and they tell me things."

"Sure, you do. I found the bunkhouse at the ranch where you were hiding. Grace rode down there and brought you Thanksgiving dinner and a good bottle of wine, didn't she?"

Nick shrugged. "I'm a fugitive, Howie, so I can't say. I don't want to get anybody in trouble who's helping me."

"Including me?"

"Of course, including you. Now look, I don't have time for chit-chat, so tell me about my father?"

Howie gave Nick a stern looking over. "Haven't you heard? Your father's dead. Somebody killed him. And it wasn't a pleasant murder. His throat was cut and he was scalped."

"Indian style, huh?"

"It was meant to look that way. You don't seem surprised that he's dead."

"I heard the news on the radio. I can't say I wished the old bastard well, but I'm sorry he went in such a messy way."

Nick took another hit and tried to pass the flask back to Howie, but Howie shook his head.

"For chrissake, Nick, this isn't a social call. You got me out here miles from anywhere in a blizzard and I'm going to need to drive out before the snow's too deep. Now, what's going on?"

"I need information, that's what's going on. Did Grace manage to speak to my father before he departed to the Happy Hunting Ground?"

"About the trust?"

"Yes, about the trust, Howie. Money, Dirty lucre. But it's my dirty money and I need it."

Howie shook his head. "For what? So you can sail off to the South Seas and live happily ever after. You know something, Nick—this sounds kind of dodgy to me."

"Well, it sounds great to me! So, tell me what's happening with my money."

Howie was tired of being manipulated by the Stanton family, and he wasn't going to stand for it now.

"I'll tell you what, Nick—as it happens, I'm looking for information, too. So how about you answer my questions, then I'll answer yours?"

"You're serious? Don't try to play me, Howie, that would be a mistake. These last ten years have made me someone you don't want to mess with."

"I can see that. And I don't like to be messed with either. I did what you asked, I took your letter to Grace. But getting me involved in a murder is stretching our old friendship a little thin. So, either you answer my questions, or I'm turning around and getting the hell out of here."

"Whoa, slow down, Moon Deer!" Nick smiled, showing his jagged front tooth. "What do you want to know?"

"I want to know what you can tell me about Ramona, the old Indian woman who works on your father's ranch."

"Ramona? Why in God's name do you care about her?"

"You know the history of your father's ranch, don't you? It was an Indian boarding school before your grandfather bought the property. There was a famous murder at the school in 1970. One of the students, a 12-year-old boy, killed the headmaster and scalped him."

"Sure, I know that. No one talks about it much, but when I was little, I was fascinated by the story. Grace used to say there was a ghost at the ranch. She claimed she saw him once. She was nine or ten at the time and she scared the hell out of me."

"She saw the ghost of the 12-year-old?"

"No, the headmaster. Grace said she saw him wandering around holding his scalp in one hand and big bloody knife in the other, saying in a real spooky voice, 'Revenge! Revenge shall be mine!' She always had a big imagination, of course. And she enjoyed scaring me."

"Was Ramona a boarder at the school?"

"I don't know. Why does it matter?"

"Well, it's just an idea I had. I think she might be the older sister of the kid who was the killer."

Nick shook his head. "That's possible, I guess, but I've never heard anybody mention it."

"Isn't it odd that she's stayed on the ranch all these years?"

"Odd? Well, here's the deal about Ramona. When grandpa died, he left all his money to us grandkids in the trust fund, but he left all his real estate to my father—the ranch, the townhouse in Manhattan, the house on Cape Cod, plus another place in downtown Santa Fe where he stays most of the time. However, there was a codicil in his will that he was required to keep Ramona on, provide her with a place to live and pay her a salary of $5 an hour for the rest of her life."

"Five dollars! That's slavery!"

"You bet. Ramona's always been the family serf, but she doesn't seem to mind. It worked out well for my parents. She's a great cook and she takes good care of things. And since my parents were there only occasionally, she has that ranch to herself most of the year."

"If your grandfather left all his money to you and Grace and Justin, how did your father manage to keep up all those properties?"

"Well, Dad was broke back then. All that real estate, and he barely had a pot to pee in. It's my mother who had the dough. She comes from a rich New England family that left her a bundle."

"Anne?"

"Of course, Anne. I'm certainly not talking about Summer! Anne was the one who put up the money for my father to get into politics, and that's when he started getting rich himself. Once you're in the Senate, you never have to worry about money again. That's democracy, American-style."

"Why do you think your grandfather set up Ramona like that? Giving her a place to live and a job for the rest of her life?"

Nick laughed. "What do you think? Ramona was a good looker when she was young. And Grandpa happened to like pretty young girls, the younger the better. She was his little piece of nookie whenever he wanted a tumble."

Howie was stunned. "They were having an affair?"

"You know, Moon Deer, it's amazing how you've managed to maintain your innocence all these years. He was married, of course, but Grandma was one of those women who looked the other way. She died young, shortly after Grandpa bought the ranch. Suicide, everyone believed. Though my father always denied it. Dad liked to keep up the charade of respectability."

Howie could only shake his head. Suicide, murder, the Stantons certainly had a dark history. Bad juju, Grace had told him long ago.

"Now it's your turn," Nick said. "I need you to help me get my money, amigo. With my father out of the way, my mother will be easier to bend. But Grace is going to need to keep up the pressure so you're going to have to ride her. I'd do it myself, but I can't get near her now there are cops swarming all over the place."

"I'm not going to ride Grace, Nick. That's totally out of the question."

Nick ignored him. "Then there's the problem of how I'm going to receive the money. Obviously, I can't open up a bank account myself, so Grace is going to have to park the money in her own account and then get me the cash. Tell her all I want is a million, she can keep the rest, whatever that is. She can think of it as her commission."

"This is totally crazy," Howie managed. "Just tell me you didn't kill your father!"

"Of course, I didn't kill my father! I didn't like him, he was a jerk, but patricide's not my thing. Look, Howie, once I have the money, you can come with me. You'll like Bora Bora and I'll need a First Mate."

"Sure, on your yacht."

"That's right, Howie. On my yacht. Now, look, we did a lot of sailing back in the day and we can do it again. We'll need to work on your navigation skills, but otherwise we're good to go. That was your only problem, Howie. You tended to get lost."

Howie shook his head sadly. He wasn't entirely immune from the call of palm trees and a beach in the South Seas. But he wasn't going to be sucked in.

"Nick, I'm not going to the South Seas with you. And neither are you. It's a fantasy, start to finish."

"It's not a fantasy. I have a sixty-foot catamaran all picked out. My agent is speaking to the owner now, working out the details. We'll pick it up in Tahiti."

"Sure, we will."

"I'm serious. You're going to like the South Pacific. We'll be pirate adventurers. The girls will love us. All I need is for you to help pry my trust fund loose from my unpleasant family. You have to help me, Howie. After all, you're my blood brother."

Howie had been about to remind Nick of their actual situation, that they were a very long way from Bora Bora, sitting in a car in a blizzard near the Colorado border with the police on Nick's tail. But they were in fact blood brothers, and this made him pause. Late one night their Sophomore year at Dartmouth, more than slightly high, they had cut their fingers and brought them together, mixing their blood. The memory made him look at Nick more closely. For all of Nick's bravado, he saw an exhausted friend who needed help.

Howie took a deep breath. "Well, okay. I don't know if I can do any good, but I'll see—"

He didn't have a chance to finish.

"Down!" Nick cried abruptly. "Get down!"

What happened next was as sudden as it was strange. Seemingly out of nowhere, a boulder came rolling down from the hill on Howie's side of the car. It took a bounce, landed on the hood of the Subaru, and slammed against the windshield. The glass shattered with a loud crunching sound into a milky web of a thousand little breaks. Howie was staring stupidly, trying to see outside to what was going on, when Nick shouted at him again.

"Down, Howie! Get down on the floor!"

Howie managed to squeeze the lower part of himself onto the floor, with his chest pressed against the gear stick. When he looked up, he saw that Nick had a gun in his hand. It was an old-fashioned snub-nosed revolver, the kind cops used to carry in black-and-white TV shows from the 1960s.

"What the hell is happening, Nick?"

"There's somebody out there," Nick said. "We're going to have to make a break for it."

"A break where?" It seemed a reasonable question, considering the cold white emptiness outside. "And who the hell is out there?"

"We'll head out my side, across the stream into the trees on the other side. We're sitting ducks here," Nick said. "I'll go first. Count ten then you follow. Here I go . . . one, two, three!"

"Nick!"

But it was too late to stop him. Nick opened the passenger door and slid outside, landing on his hands and knees on the ground. The sky had darkened, snow was falling hard. Nick picked himself up and ran in a crouch. He leaped over the narrow stream and headed toward the vague outline of trees on the other side. Howie was able to follow his progress for a dozen feet, until his outline faded and he disappeared into the white mist.

A gun shot rang out, the sound muffled in the snow. Then there was another shot, louder than the first, from a more powerful gun. The smaller gun fired again twice, two shots right after another. Then the louder gun fired a burst of three shots from somewhere close by. They made a terrible noise. *BANG . . . BANG . . . BANG!*

And then there was silence. Not a sound. Nothing but the wind and the falling snow.

Chapter Seventeen

Howie wasn't sure what had just happened. He couldn't see much from where he was crouching on the floor of the car. The gunfire had come as a shock, but the silence that followed was worse.

The afternoon grew steadily darker, colder, and more ominous. An early twilight had transformed the trees and hills into ghostly outlines.

"Nick!" he called softly. "Nick!" he called a second time, more loudly. He tried to dispel his rising panic. The wind moaned through the trees, but there was no human answer.

Minutes passed before Howie summoned the nerve to crawl across the gear stick into the passenger seat, open the door, and slip out onto the snow. It was an awkward way to exit a car. He got his arms out first, lowered his knees onto the frozen ground, and kept wiggling until he was on all fours. Staying low, he turned and crawled away from the car. There was an inch or two of snow on the ground and his hands were numb. He could barely see five feet in front of him.

Howie was listening hard when he heard an engine growl into life from some distance away. Instinctively, he flattened himself on the snow. At first it sounded like an ATV, the kind of loud off-road vehicle hunters used. But maybe it was a pickup truck with a rough engine.

He listened as the vehicle, whatever it was, set off down the Forest Service road, heading away from him into the mountains. The sound of the engine grew fainter as it drove away, until there was no sound at all.

Howie rose to his feet. He had been crouching so long it took him a moment to unbend and find his balance. The snow and fog made it hard to know what was up and what was down.

He crossed the stream, stepping into icy water, and climbed up the bank on the other side. He took a dozen uncertain steps and tripped over something that sent him sprawling forward onto the frozen ground. He broke the fall with the palms of his hands which sent shivers of pain up his arms. His back foot dangled over the thing that had tripped him. It wasn't a tree limb, it wasn't a rock. It was a human torso. He recoiled instinctively, pulling his leg free, contracting himself into a ball.

None of this was good. In fact, it was awful. But it had to be faced. Howie managed to turn around so that he could see the body on the ground. It was Nick. His old roommate lay spread-eagled on the snow. He had fallen onto his back, his arms were stretched outward in a kind of crucifixion. He had been shot in two places, as far as Howie could see. His face was bloodless, as pale as the snow. His chest was gooey with blood. His right eye was a gaping hole.

Howie raised his head and howled in anguish, an incoherent cry. "Nick, goddamnit!" he cried. He didn't know what he was saying, but it relieved the unbearable sorrow to bellow.

Nick's left eye was open and there was snow settling on the exposed eyeball. Howie tried to brush the eye closed with his numb right hand, but the eyelid was frozen and wouldn't move.

Half-crazed with shock, it took Howie a few minutes to realize that unless he did something to save himself, he could die here, too. He managed to get himself into a sitting position and, with an effort, he stood up. He couldn't see his car through the snow and mist, but the engine was still running and he let the sound guide him. He staggered back to the road and slipped inside the car, closing the door behind him. The heater was going and it was a relief to be inside. But it wasn't going to be easy to drive out of here. The shattered windshield and side windows were covered with half an inch of snow, making it feel like he was inside an igloo.

The heater gradually warmed him, bringing back feeling to his face and hands. He knew he would process Nick's death later, but right now he had other more immediate problems.

Somehow he needed to get out of here and go for help, and he had to do it soon before any more snow settled on the road. With all-wheel drive and good snow tires, his Subaru could handle an inch or two of snow, but any more than that would be a problem. Meanwhile, this was a crime scene and he knew he shouldn't disturb Nick's body. Yet he couldn't just leave Nick in this wild place to be buried in the snow or be eaten by animals. There were bears and mountain lions in these hills.

Howie debated his choices, all of them bad. It would take more than forty minutes to reach Tres Piedras, the first place he might find phone service. Probably it would be another half hour before law enforcement arrived, maybe longer. By that time Nick's body would be almost impossible to find. It was snowing heavily now, big white flakes.

Howie decided that crime scene or not, he wasn't going to leave Nick behind. He turned on his headlights as well as the inside dome light so that he would be able to find his car again. Then he climbed outside, opened the rear hatch, and made his way back across the stream to where Nick lay, already more than half-covered in a white shroud.

The next part was difficult, emotionally as well as physically. He picked up Nick by his arms and dragged the body back across the stream to the station wagon. The dead weight was awkward and the sound of Nick's feet dragging over the frozen ground filled him with despair. A few feet from the car, Howie's feet slid out from under him and he fell clumsily on top of the body.

It was hard to imagine how things could get any worse, but there was nothing to do but go on. He took a deep breath, wobbled to his feet, and resumed the torturous job of dragging the body to his car. With an effort, he managed to slide Nick into the cargo area, slam the hatch shut, and hurry back inside the car to warm himself.

He sat for a few minutes working up the energy for the next challenge: to turn around on the narrow forest road and somehow get back to the highway before the snow was too deep to drive. He wouldn't be able to see through the windshield, so he would need to drive with his head out the window.

"I can do that!" he said, giving himself a small pep talk.

But there was more bad news. The needle on his fuel gauge said he was seriously low on gas, a notch below a quarter of a tank. It seemed to him that the needle had dipped more suddenly than it should have done, but it was an old car and the gauges weren't accurate.

At least he could get back to the main highway. From there, help might arrive before he froze to death. Or maybe not.

He lowered his window and stuck his head out into the falling snow, but he couldn't see much of the road from this position. To drive anywhere, he would need to open the door and lean outside while holding onto the steering wheel and keeping his foot on the gas pedal. But was that possible? He wasn't made of rubber. Howie shook his head. It couldn't be done!

Unless . . .

An idea came to him. His Outback was fifteen years old but it had cruise control. He rarely used it except for a few experimental times on boring stretches of freeway. He was someone who liked to have his foot on the pedal. He didn't like the idea of giving his car the upper hand. He had almost forgotten he had cruise control and he wondered if it still worked.

If it did, he could set the speed at 15 or 20 miles an hour, then stand up with the door open, peering out into the storm like the night watch on the bow of a ship.

It was the only thing he could think to do, so he gave it a try. Howie put the car into first gear and slowly let the clutch out. The station wagon lurched forward and Howie gave it some gas. Moving quickly, he pressed the cruise control button, which immediately lit up with an amber glow. He pressed "set," took his foot off the gas, and found the car was still going. So far, so good. He opened the door and leaned as far as he could into the storm. His headlights did little to penetrate the falling curtain of snow, so he used the flashlight on his iPhone, holding it like a torch in his outstretched arm. This didn't add much to the visibility, but it raised his spirits. It made him feel like the Statue of Liberty.

Howie had to make a hard U-turn to get going in the right direction. Standing in the open door, holding on to the steering wheel with his right hand so he wouldn't fall out, he could see about ten feet ahead of him. It was touch and go whether he would end up in the stream. It was only a shallow stream, he wasn't going to drown in it. But if he didn't make the turn, it would stop him from going anywhere tonight. Fortunately, the Subaru had a short turning radius.

"Good old girl!" Howie cried, ducking back inside the car to get them pointed in more or less the right direction.

There was no time to linger. The Subaru was moving at a stately 15 mph and there were miles to go before he was safe.

5.3 miles, to be exact.

***

It was like driving a speedboat. The road was blown bare in some places, solid ice in others, and for most of the ride Howie fishtailed and sloshed around in two to three inches of powder hoping he didn't end up in the creek.

The 5.3 miles took Howie more than an hour. Several times he came close to careening off the road and he had to stop, reset the cruise control, and get going again in the right direction.

The worst moment came near the end. He was leaning out the door, half standing—iPhone raised—when he hit a bump that caused him to lose his grip on the steering wheel. He was able to grab hold of the door frame just in time to keep from falling out of the car.

Howie was catching his breath when he saw a strange sight up ahead, a weird lumbering vehicle with a revolving yellow light on top. A snowplow! The Forest Service road was coming to a T, about to meet up with the paved highway. This wasn't entirely good news. The snowplow was on the highway, Howie was on the forest road, and the two of them were about to collide.

He wondered if he could get back inside his car in time to turn off the cruise control, skid to a stop, and avoid the crash. He didn't think so.

Howie screamed as his Subaru rolled out onto the highway with the headlights of the snowplow bearing down upon him.

He crossed the road with inches to spare as the monster plow continued on its ponderous way. The Subaru nosedived into a shallow ditch at the far side of the highway where it came to a stop. The crash sent him flying out the door into the snow, but it was a soft landing and he wasn't hurt. He brushed off the snow, got back into his car, turned off the engine, and sighed deeply.

After a moment, the driver of the snowplow climbed out of his cab and came his way. He was a huge man with a beard in an orange jumpsuit.

"Need help?" he asked.

"Do I ever!" Howie admitted.

Chapter Eighteen

Santo came by Jack's office late Saturday afternoon to collapse and discuss the case. He wasn't in good shape. He had been working nearly nonstop since Friday morning and Jack could gauge his exhaustion by the strain in his voice. He settled into the client chair wearily.

"You know what, Jack?" he said. "I'm off-duty and I sure could use a shot of Leap Frog."

"Laphroaig. You've got to say it with a Scottish brogue. It's in the cabinet. You can pour me one while you're at it."

Jack listened as Santo rose and made his way to the drink cabinet, an old trastero of heavy wood that matched the traditional New Mexican decor of the office.

It was a dark afternoon and Ruth had made a fire in the kiva fireplace. Snow was falling outside the window and the office was warm and snug. Jack waited until Santo handed him his glass and settled with his own drink back in the client chair with his feet up on an ottoman.

"I tried phoning you a few times today," Jack told him. "But I couldn't get past Sally. She kept telling me you were busy interviewing witnesses."

"I was . . . and man, am I tired of self-important people! Sally's been a problem, too, frankly. All the guys go into heat when she's around. Dan especially. I've been thinking of transferring her to Albuquerque where she wouldn't cause such a stir. But you can't do that, you know. Not these days. You can't say, oh, she's too damn good looking, so she has to go. That would be considered sexism!"

Jack smiled dutifully. "The reason I called, Santo—"

"Hold on, Jack, let me go first, while I can still keep my thoughts together. Are you aware that Howie had a knock-down shouting match with Harlan Stanton at the dinner table just hours before he was killed?"

"Yep," Jack admitted. "Howie told me. But it was verbal, nobody got knocked down. Stanton started baiting him about politics, calling him a socialist. Which he isn't, of course. The only politics Howie cares about is the cultural divide between white bread and whole wheat."

"That's not entirely true, Jack. Howie got involved in that pipeline dispute a few years ago. That got pretty nasty."

"That was because the pipeline crossed Indian land," Jack said. "And of course, there was a girl involved."

"Isn't there always?" Santo shook his head. "And speaking of girls, did you know that Howie got Grace Stanton pregnant?"

"That was quite a few years ago, Santo. Back when Howie was in college. Anyway, I don't see how that has anything to do with the Senator getting killed."

"Don't you? Well, apparently the old man wasn't happy that an Indian had knocked up his daughter. He sent Grace off to Europe to have the baby and made her give it up for adoption. Howie only found out at the Thanksgiving gathering. Summer told him. Knowing Howie, I can imagine how upset he was that it had been kept from him."

"Knowing Howie, you know he would never kill someone," Jack said firmly.

"Everyone has their breaking point, Jack. Even you, even me. You only need to be pushed hard enough."

"Santo, Howie did *not* kill Harlan Stanton!"

"Okay, Jack—I'm just saying it's a good thing I'm in charge of the case. I know cops who would have him in jail right now. Fortunately for Howie, I have another good suspect. I'm thinking this is about money, not sex."

"The trust fund?"

"You bet. I had Dan doing some checking this afternoon. It turns out that Justin, the older brother, is seriously over-extended with two balloon payments due next month. He'd been trying to convince his father to take the money out of a mutual fund and invest it in his golf development. He needed it badly to save his ass."

"Yes, but here's the problem. Harlan was inclining to give Justin the money. But now, with his death, the decision goes to Harlan's ex, Anne, and she's more likely to say no. So as far as we know, there's no motive for Justin to kill his dad."

Santo smiled. "I didn't say that Justin is my suspect. It's Nicolas who interests me. He's the one who had a motive. And he's killed before."

Jack was happy to divert suspicion from Howie. "Well, then, Santo, you're going to be happy to hear what I have to tell you. Howie did a bit of wandering around the property yesterday morning while you and I were with Summer."

"Damn it! I told Howie to stay at the house!"

"Yes, he interpreted that loosely to remain on the property. But you're going to be glad Howie got wanderlust. Did you send CSU to the old bunkhouse that's off below the meadow at the rear of the house?"

Santo took a deep swallow of whiskey, finishing the glass. "I didn't know there was a bunkhouse. You'd better tell me about this, Jack."

Jack spent the next ten minutes recounting Howie's walkabout on the Stanton ranch Friday morning while Santo listened in moody silence. At one point, when Jack was describing the fifty-year-old murder at the Indian boarding school, Santo's phone rang, but he took a quick look at the screen and turned it off without answering.

"The headmaster was scalped? Jesus, have mercy! Had his throat cut?"

"That's right. In 1970," Jack said. "It came out later that he had been abusing the children for years, physically and sexually. According to Howie, these Indian schools were terrible places."

"And the kid got away?" Santo asked.

"He was never found. At the time it was thought that he most likely died of exposure in the wilds. But his body was never found, so who knows?"

"What was his name?"

"They called him Ralph White. That wasn't his real name, of course. They gave those kids Anglo names as part of their effort to turn them into good Christians. Howie's been busy checking all the old records and news stories, so I'm sure he'll come up with more about him. But right now, we don't know much."

Santo sat for a minute thinking. "Well, what do you think? Is the Stanton murder some kind of weird copycat killing?"

"It's possible. But why wait fifty years and then kill the present owner of the property who didn't have anything to do with that school. His father did, of course. But that's fairly oblique."

"If you went to Catholic school like I did, Jack, you'd know the sins of the father are often visited upon the son. Well, it's something to think about," Santo said wearily. "I'd better call the station and see why they were trying to reach me. And I need to get CSU down to that bunkhouse before those guys get wrapped up in another case."

Santo found his cell phone and pressed his speed dial for the station.

"Dan, you're still there? Look, do me a favor and call Santa Fe . . . *what*?" he asked abruptly. "Please tell me you're kidding! Howie? Another body? Tres Piedras?"

Santo disconnected and sat for a moment in stunned silence.

"With your eagle ears, you probably heard Dan's news?"

"I did," Jack replied.

"Unbelievable! That partner of yours is a walking disaster! Feel like a trip to Tres Piedras?"

***

The drive across the high desert at night was treacherous in the snow. Santo had four-wheel drive in his State Police SUV, but Jack, in the passenger seat, felt Santo's tension as he drove carefully along the unplowed highway toward Tres Piedras. As for Katya, she sat in the back seat sniffing the air through the crack in the window that Santo left open for her.

"Man, this is some weather!" Santo said after ten minutes of no conversation. "Where are the snowplows when you need them?"

"There's no real hurry, Santo?" Jack said hopefully. He was a nervous passenger at the best of times, which this wasn't. Not with the snow plus the fact that Santo had been drinking. "It will be good for Howie to sit and sweat a little."

Every now and then, Jack heard the windshield wiper take a swipe, scraping the icy glass. It was well below freezing and the snow mostly cleared itself, blown off by the motion of the car, but Jack could tell that the visibility was bad by Santo's concentration.

"At least we can eliminate Nicolas from the suspects," Santo said after a while, almost to himself.

"Maybe. But of course, Nicolas could have killed his father and then he was shot by somebody else."

"Two different killers?"

"That makes it messy, I know. But it's possible."

Another few miles went by in silence before Santo spoke again. It was a slow motion conversation.

"Let's say that Nicolas, who was camping out in the old bunkhouse, snuck up to the ranch house on Thanksgiving night and killed his father. His motive, he wanted dad out of the way so that his mother, who was a softer touch, would release his part of the trust fund. But this left Justin in the lurch. If Nicolas got his money, then Justin was in trouble with his golf course development. He wouldn't be able to pay his creditors. So, he arranges this escapade today on the Forest Service road. With Nicolas dead, the trust fund goes to Justin again."

"Minus Grace's share when she's forty."

"Right," said Santo thoughtfully. "Minus Grace's share . . ."

"I wouldn't think about it now," said Jack, who was hoping Santo would return his concentration to the perils of the road. "Let's wait until we speak with Howie. We only got a second-hand account from the officer who arrived at the scene."

"You know, Jack, I'm sensing this case is going to be a ball breaker. It's funny, I've been thinking about retiring . . . maybe this is just what I need to give me the push."

"Don't get ahead of yourself. The first thing we need to do is have Howie take us to the spot where Nicolas was shot and figure out how it happened. If I understand the story Howie told the officer, a shooting like this in a snowstorm in the middle of nowhere would have been difficult to plan."

"It's supposed to snow all night," Santo said gloomily. "Six to eight inches. By morning, any physical evidence is going to be buried."

"Are there houses out that way?"

"Not many. A few ranches where people graze cattle in the summer. Most of them are left empty during the winter months because the roads are impassable. But you can get around by snowmobile and there are some go-it-alone types who hunker down all year round."

The conversation sputtered into silence as they drove slowly through the storm. Occasionally, Santo tried switching his headlights from high beam to low to see if that gave him better visibility through the falling streaks of white, but it didn't help. At the tiny hamlet of Tres Piedras, Santo took a right turn onto Highway 285 toward the Colorado border. Half an hour later he saw the flashing lights of emergency vehicles up ahead on the road. To Santo, it looked like he was arriving at an outpost on an alien planet. He pulled up behind an ambulance and opened his window as a uniformed officer came his way.

"Relieved to see you, Lieutenant," said the officer, leaning in the window.

"Has the medical examiner arrived?" Santo asked.

"Not yet. We've been waiting for you to get here before we do anything. According to Moon Deer, the actual crime scene is five miles down the forest road. But we're going to need snowmobiles to get in there."

"Then get them. Call dispatch and have them send us two 'moes. I want to get in there as soon as possible."

"It will be easier in the morning, Lieutenant. The visibility—"

"I don't care about visibility. We're going in tonight. And while we're waiting, bring me Howard Moon Deer. That damn idiot and I need to have ourselves a talk!"

Chapter Nineteen

Waiting in the back seat of a State Police cruiser, Howie watched as the windows became covered with snow. It was hypnotic. First the glass spotted with white fluff until, gradually, a woolly blanket of snow covered the entire car. Occasionally, a small finger of snow avalanched down the windshield, leaving a streak of clear night-blackened glass until the falling snow once again filled the empty space.

Howie was numb with exhaustion. He knew he was going to be a suspect, perhaps *the* suspect. It was unavoidable. First the Senator, and now Nick—two murders for which he'd been unfortunately close at hand. He wasn't sure what motive they would dream up for him killing Nick, but he knew they would find multiple reasons that he might kill the Senator.

Howie's brain—what was left of it—circled round and round. Nick, Grace, sex on the sand, his daughter somewhere, Claire in Europe . . . the kaleidoscope of his life that seemed to be falling apart around him.

His head slumped backward against the headrest and he went out like a light. It was nice to sleep. He liked it. He could have slept for weeks, but it seemed only a heartbeat before he felt someone shaking his arm.

It was a cop with a fishy face and freckles. "Okay, Moon Deer, let's go. You're wanted."

"Wanted?" he asked stupidly.

"Come on," said the cop. "Don't give me a hard time or you'll regret it!"

Howie already regretted it. He regretted everything. He stepped out into the falling snow. At least a dozen law enforcement vehicles had arrived and were parked on the right lane of the road with their lights flashing, nearly blocking the highway. Two cops with flashlights stood at each end of the blockage ready to guide traffic—should any traffic appear—through the narrow opening in the southbound lane.

The cop with the fishy face led Howie toward a black Ford Explorer with the familiar New Mexico State Police emblem on the side. Howie knew who was inside even before the cop opened the front passenger door for him.

He slipped inside to find Santo in the driver's seat looking very solemn. Jack and Katya were in the back, and they were solemn, too. Even Katya seemed put-out.

"What a night!" Howie said hopefully. "I'm sure glad to see you guys!"

No one answered.

***

"It's not my fault, Santo," Howie said as soon as he was inside the car, forestalling the criticism he knew he was in for.

"Sure," said Santo. "Let's start at the beginning. What the hell were you doing out here, Howie?"

That was a good question and it took Howie a moment to come up with an answer.

"Do you want the long version or the short?"

"Let's start with short, then we'll back up and get the details."

"Okay, when I got home last night, I found a note on my table from Nick. Somehow he got past my security when I wasn't there. He wrote down two GPS coordinates and told me to meet him there this afternoon at three."

"You saved this supposed note, I hope?"

"I did. And it's not a *supposed* note. I have it at home, Santo. The coordinates turned out to be five point three miles down Forest Road

213. I didn't know what to think, but I was curious so I made the drive, and when I got there he was waiting for me. He got in my car, we talked for maybe ten minutes. Then a boulder came down from the hillside where we were parked and smashed the windshield."

"A boulder?"

"Exactly. Medium sized, but large enough to be a problem. I didn't see where it came from. It bounced once on the hood before it hit the windshield. Nick shouted for me to get down, and I did. When I looked up, I saw he had a gun in his hand. He told me again to stay down, then he slipped out of the car. A few seconds later I heard gunfire. There were two different guns, a loud gun and a softer one. Then there was silence. I couldn't see a thing and I didn't know what had happened. After a few minutes, I climbed out of the car and I found his body a dozen feet away in the snow. That's pretty much it."

"Let's back up a minute," Jack said from the rear. "You say Nick was waiting for you on the road. Did you see his car?"

"No, he just appeared from nowhere and knocked on my window. I have no idea how he got there."

"Was he covered in snow?"

"Not much. But it wasn't snowing as hard then as it is now."

"He must have left a vehicle nearby," Santo said. "We'll need to find it. Now, look, Howie—you got home, you found Nick's note, why the hell didn't you call me like you promised? You were supposed to let me know the moment he made contact. Remember?"

"He told me to come alone, Santo. I know I shouldn't have, but I did."

"It didn't occur to you that us poor idiots who work in law enforcement might want to have a word with this fugitive who's wanted for murder?"

"Well, yes, Santo. Of course, it did."

"Howie, I've been trying to protect you. But this is the second time you've crossed a very serious line."

"I'm sorry, I really am. But you have to understand, he was my best friend, Santo. My blood brother. I couldn't turn him down."

"Being a blood brother is a sacred matter with Native Americans," Jack said on Howie's behalf.

Santo turned toward the back seat. "Jack, let me do the talking." He turned back to Howie. "Now, let's hear the long version, start to finish. I want to know everything."

Howie went through the story, leaving out only a few details. He didn't mention Nick's plan to escape to Bora Bora and buy a sailing yacht with Howie as his first mate. He didn't think that would go over well. And it was only a fantasy, after all.

Santo listened carefully, asking questions from time to time. Finally, he shook his head. "Okay, I'm going to check to see if the snowmobiles have gotten here from Santa Fe. Then we're going to take a ride together. You're going to show me where the shooting took place."

"It's going to be cold out there, Santo," Howie mentioned.

"You think so, huh?"

Santo stepped out of the Explorer, slamming the door behind him hard enough that it shook loose the snow that had gathered on the windshield.

Howie turned around to face the back seat. "So what's Santo so pissed off about?"

"What do you think?" Jack said. "He's pissed about coming out here in a snowstorm from hell and finding you with another body."

"I'm sorry, Jack."

"I know," said Jack.

***

Two State Police snowmobiles arrived on a trailer at the head of Forest Road 213 at midnight. Supposedly three more were on their way from Santa Fe, more than a hundred miles away, but when exactly they would arrive, nobody could say.

Santo wasn't happy. Once again, he found himself in a crime scene that was compromised by its remote location and the slow response of law enforcement. Meanwhile, if two snowmobiles were all he could get, he would use them.

Santo drove the first snowmobile with Howie on the rear, hanging on as best he could. The second one followed with Primo Diaz, the head of the CSU team, along with his assistant, Pamela Herzt, on the back. Primo's machine pulled a sled that had equipment tied down beneath a tarp. CSU would do their best to isolate and protect the crime scene where Nicolas Stanton was shot, if in fact they could find it in the snow.

Santo had a sat-nav device on his snowmobile that he consulted frequently, stopping from time to time to clear off the falling snow so he could read the numbers. It was nearly forty minutes later when he found the coordinates that Howie had given him, the 5.3 mile mark.

"This look like the right spot?" he called to Howie, who was relieved to stop. It had been a rough, cold ride. Though not as rough and cold as when he had come the other way, leaning out of his station wagon, hanging on for his life.

Howie peered into the snowy landscape and wasn't sure. The headlights from the two snowmobiles were streaked with falling arrows of snow and did little to penetrate the night. At least six inches of snow had settled on the ground since Howie had left. The tire marks of his Subaru were gone and nothing looked familiar. He couldn't even see the road.

"I don't know, Santo. If your GPS says we're here, then this must be the place. But I don't see anything I recognize."

Howie felt nearly frozen. He had on a heavy sweater and a Gor-tex shell that kept him dry, but his jeans were frozen and his face was numb. One of the cops had loaned him a ski hat and a pair of gloves. Goggles would have been a welcome addition, plus long underwear and a neck warmer.

"Let's get off and see if we can figure out what happened here," Santo said to the crew.

Howie climbed off the back of the snowmobile and sank into snow almost to his knees. He was glad he hadn't left Nick's body to be buried. Everything had changed in the four hours since Howie had been here. He tried to orient himself but nothing was familiar. It didn't help that the headlights from the snowmobiles illuminated only two small circles in the night.

"I guess this is where I parked, but I can't say for sure," he told Santo.

"Just give it a try, Howie. In the morning we'll have more people and equipment here, but anything you can tell us now will be a big help."

Howie stood in the falling snow and tried to recognize landmarks. There should have been a stream on the right side of the road, but if there was, it was buried beneath the snow. He saw a steep hillside to the left where the boulder might have rolled down, but this was a hilly landscape so even that was uncertain. Hopefully, they could trust the GPS numbers.

"Okay, if this is where I parked, Nick slid out the passenger side and got maybe a dozen feet before the shooting began and he was gunned down . . ."

Howie paced twelve feet and stopped. He continued another few feet, remembering the stream that now was buried. "If I'm right, this is approximately where I tripped over his body. But it's only a guess."

"What do you think, Primo?" Santo asked, turning to the CSU chief.

"We sure as hell aren't going to find anything out here tonight, Santo. I'd say, let's close the road for now, protect the scene the best we can, and get a bunch of guys out here in the morning with shovels."

"But where did Nick come from?" Santo asked, thinking aloud. "And where did the shooter go? There has to be a house somewhere nearby. Or a camp. Damn this snow! It's going to make everything difficult!"

Howie wisely kept his mouth shut. He had never seen Santo in such a bad mood.

"So, you heard a loud shot and then a softer shot?" he said to Howie.

"There were a few of them," Howie answered. "Though I wasn't counting. One went pop-pop. I assumed that was Nick's gun. I only saw it for a second but it was a small revolver. One of those snub-nosed things."

"What they used to call a Saturday Night Special. A thirty-eight?"

"That sounds right."

"Okay, pop-pop. What sound did the other gun make?"

"It was more of a boom-boom."

Santo sighed. "Could it have been a rifle?"

"Maybe."

"Maybe! Well, that's helpful! Did you see where the firing came from?"

"Santo, I was hunkering down on the floorboard hoping not to get shot. I didn't see a thing. When the shooting stopped, I waited a few minutes and when I didn't hear anything, I crawled out onto the snow, got to my feet, and tripped over Nick's body."

"But you heard a vehicle of some kind start up?"

"I did, but I couldn't see it. It sounded like an ATV or maybe a noisy truck."

"And it moved off down the road away from you?"

"That's right. I was out this way once in the summer and if I remember correctly, the road climbs up into the mountains a few miles from here. There's a BLM campground and a small lake that fishermen like in the summer. But it would be hard to get up there now."

Santo shook his head. "Fabulous!" he proclaimed. "Well, we're not doing any good out here freezing our asses off. Let's get back to the base. Primo, why don't you mark off this spot as best you can and we'll return in the morning. I'll see if I can find a BLM map that shows the ranches out this way. Once this damn weather clears, we'll get a chopper."

It was discouraging to abandon a crime scene before a thorough investigation could be done and Santo was frustrated. Howie climbed onto the rear of the snowmobile and they made their way back to the head of the road where the growing encampment of law enforcement vehicles was waiting.

A Triple-A tow truck had arrived and Howie watched as they loaded his Subaru onto the flatbed. Nick's body had been removed some time ago. He told the driver to deliver the car to Glass Plus, an auto glass shop on a back road in San Geronimo. He would need to call them in the morning to explain his situation. He had dealt with Glass Plus before, on another case where his windshield had been broken. Howie sensed his insurance company was going to give him the boot.

The officer with the fishy face led Howie to a black State Police cruiser where Jack and Katya were waiting with the heater on. Santo was planning to stay with the encampment, but he decided to send Jack, Katya, and Howie home with one of the officers.

Jack took the front seat, leaving Howie and Katya in the back. There was a metal screen between the front and back seat, which didn't give Howie a good feeling.

"So, did you find anything out there?" Jack asked.

"Nothing," Howie replied. "Only snow."

"I bet you've been wondering how much they're getting up on the Peak."

Howie sighed deeply. "Jack, Nick was my friend. This hasn't been a great day for me."

They were silent after that. It was nearly three in the morning and it was a long uneventful ride back to San Geronimo. Howie fell asleep wrapped up with his arms around Katya's furry torso. It wasn't like sleeping with his arms around Claire, but on a night like this, it would have to do.

It was nearly dawn when the officer dropped Howie, Jack, and Katya off at the Wilder house in town. Howie accepted Jack's invitation to spend the night in the Wilder guest room. Without wheels, he didn't have any other choice. In the morning he would have to see about a rental car until his Subaru was repaired.

Emma had decorated the guest bedroom with a feminine hand. There were white frilly curtains, a vanity table with a mirror, a simple wooden rocking chair, and a single bed.

It wasn't Howie's sort of room, but he didn't mind. He had never felt so utterly spent in all his life. He was asleep as soon as he closed his eyes.

Chapter Twenty

Howie slept profoundly and when he awoke, he could tell it was late morning by the slant of sunlight coming into Jack and Emma's guest room. The storm was over.

While he was stretching luxuriously, wondering if he dared go back to sleep for an extra hour, he had a sense that there was something important that he had meant to tell Jack, but with one thing and another, he had never gotten around to it.

He had to wake up another few notches before it came to him. He hadn't told Jack about Ramona and his research into the 1970 murder at the Nuestro Señor de la Misericordia Indian School. Jack had left the office on Friday while Howie was still on his computer, and then he had gone home, seen the message from Nick on his kitchen table, and everything had gone crazy after that.

Howie was still considering this when he heard two cars pull up at the curb outside the Wilder house. Several car doors opened and shut and several pairs of feet walked up to the front door. Howie listened as the doorbell rang, Chinese temple bells in four different tones. Emma had bought the doorbell in San Francisco where they liked exotic things.

Without moving from the bed, he listened as Emma answered the door downstairs. There was a murmur of voices, but Howie couldn't make out what they were saying. He wondered why Emma wasn't at work until he remembered that it was Sunday. During the week, she ran the San Geronimo Public Library.

A few minutes later, he heard her climb the stairs and knock on his door.

"Howie, are you awake? Santo is here and he wants to see you."

"I'm waking up," he called. "What time is it?"

"It's twelve-twenty. May I come in?"

He said of course. Emma stepped into the room dressed in jeans and a flannel shirt. She was a good-looking woman, intelligent and spry, with short gray hair. Jack occasionally waxed about how lovely Emma had been when they were young, and he believed it.

"Did Santo say what he wanted?"

Emma gave him a deep look. "I have the impression he's come to take you in."

"Take me in?"

"Arrest you," she said. "It seems there have been some new developments."

Howie sat up in bed, entirely awake now. "Where's Jack?"

"I drove him to the office at ten o'clock. He said he had work to do. I was supposed to drive you there when you got up, but I guess that's not going to be necessary now."

"Arrest me for what?"

"I wish I knew. He's waiting for you downstairs. He's come with another officer. I'm sure it's just a mistake."

Howie sighed. Life was relentless and he was starting to wish he could call timeout.

"Emma, would you call Jack and let him know what's happening? There's something important I forgot to tell him. Tell him that Ramona, the old Indian servant at the Stanton Ranch, was a student at the Indian school, and the police took her into custody at the time of the 1970 murder. I think she may be the older sister of the boy who killed the headmaster, but that's just a guess. Tell Jack that this may be the connection between that old murder and today. And here's something else that's interesting. It was Adam Stanton, the Commissioner, who got Ramona released from custody. You can see how this—"

"Howie!" a voice called loudly from downstairs. It was Santo and he didn't sound like he was in any better a mood than he had been at three in the morning. "I need you to come down here! Now!"

***

Howie found Santo and Dirk Henderson waiting for him in the foyer at the foot of the stairs. He and Dirk had skied together occasionally in past years. They were friends of a sort, though not close. But Dirk refused to look him in the eye and Santo wasn't smiling.

"So, can I get you guys some coffee?" Howie asked optimistically.

Santo shook his head. "This isn't a social call, Howie. I'm afraid you'll need to come with us. We have to detain you for questioning."

"Are you serious? Are you arresting me, Santo?"

"No, you're not under arrest. But we can hold you for twenty-four hours without making a charge and that's what we're going to do. I'm sorry, Howie. I don't like doing this, but I don't have a choice."

"But this is crazy! What's going on?"

"I'm afraid we have some new evidence that implicates you in the death of Senator Stanton. A witness has come forward."

Howie's mouth was hanging open. "A witness? What are you talking about? What witness?"

"You know I can't tell you that, Howie. You'll need to get dressed and come along."

"Santo! For chrissake, you know I didn't kill the old idiot! Come on, what witness has told you some wild tale? I need to know what I'm up against."

Santo shook his head wearily. His shoulders sagged. He looked exhausted. "Okay, if you've got to know it's Grace Stanton. She says she saw you coming out of the Senator's study at three in the morning and there was blood on your hands."

Howie's mouth fell open wider. "Grace? You're kidding? Grace Stanton told you that?"

"She did, Howie."

"But it's a lie! Come on, Santo, you don't believe this do you?"

"As a matter of fact, I don't. But Grace Stanton is a prominent person and I can't ignore her accusation just because we're friends. It's not my decision. Santa Fe is insisting I bring you in."

"Santa Fe?"

"My boss. This is a big case with huge media interest. There's going to be a press conference later in the afternoon and they want to be able to tell the press that we're detaining a possible suspect."

"That's what this is about? A press conference?"

"Howie, there are lots of wheels turning here. Stanton's death is a big deal. Have you listened to the news this morning?"

"Well, no," Howie admitted.

"It's the lead story on every network. Look, we'll get to the bottom of this, I promise. But meanwhile, you need to come with me. Let's not make a big deal out of this. Knowing Jack, he'll have you out in an hour or two . . . if you're innocent, that is," he felt it necessary to add.

Chapter Twenty-One

Sunday was a difficult day for Jack.

Emma phoned him the moment Santo drove off with Howie in the back of a State Police cruiser. She had been very upset. Howie hadn't been in handcuffs, at least, but it was a disturbing development.

As soon as Jack hung up with Emma, he spent the next three hours trying to reach Santo, who had made himself unavailable. This was a statement in itself, of course. Santo was saying, though we're friends—though I'm happy to drink your whiskey!—I'm a cop and you're a civilian, and I'm running the show.

Finally, at nearly five o'clock that afternoon, it was the station's civilian secretary, Maria Chavez, who phoned Jack to say that Santo had given his okay for Jack to visit Howie at the jail.

"About time!" he huffed.

Emma picked him up at the office and drove him to the jail adjacent to the San Geronimo County Courthouse. She waited in the car with Katya while he went inside. A guard brought Howie from a holding cell to a small windowless meeting room that was usually reserved for prisoners and their attorneys.

"I'm not going to say I told you so," Jack said grumpily when they were seated. "But I told you so, didn't I? I said you were cruising for trouble when you headed off to that Thanksgiving with your old girlfriend, and look at you now!"

"Jack, for God's sake, give me a break! You've got to get me out of here. Do you have any idea what they feed you in this joint?"

"Forget food. That's the least of your worries, Howie. Santo has the right to hold you for twenty-four hours—longer if he wants—and it seems he's going to do it."

"Twenty-four hours!"

"What is, is, Howie."

"That's easy for you to say!"

"I'm not the one who got sucker-punched by an old girlfriend. Yes, I know about that. Santo's avoiding me, but Emma told me. Now, why has Grace turned against you?"

"I don't know, Jack, I really don't."

"Did you two have a fight at Thanksgiving?"

Howie had to consider this. "Well, not a fight exactly. But I confronted her Friday morning. About her getting pregnant and giving away the baby without consulting me."

"Was she angry?"

"Grace? No, *I* was the one who was angry. And we were interrupted before anything was resolved. Dan appeared and said that Santo wanted to see her."

"Well, whatever her reasons, she's decided to make you the fall guy. Now, look, we only have half an hour so let's focus. Tell me about what you learned about Ramona and that old murder on the ranch."

Howie did his best to focus. He repeated what he had told Emma earlier in the day and they spent the remaining time discussing what had happened—or might have happened—in 1970.

The half hour went quickly, and, it seemed they were just getting started when one of the guards entered the room to say their time was up.

As Jack was leaving, Howie said, "What we need to do is get access to the police archives and see what they can add to the newspaper accounts. If we can pin down why they were holding Ramona and why they released her to Adam Stanton, I think we're going to be a long way toward learning what this whole thing is about."

"Sure, *if* the two cases are related," Jack cautioned. "But I'll see what I can do."

Jack went home to a meal of Thanksgiving leftovers, which were now in their third reprise, not as exciting as the first day. He had little appetite. He wasn't as optimistic as Howie that they would be able to tie the present deaths to the 1970 murder. It was hard to imagine what the motive might be. Plus, they didn't even know for certain that the elderly Ramona who worked on the Stanton ranch was the same person the police had detained fifty years ago. Jack had worked cold cases, but nothing as old as this, and he wasn't certain how he was going to proceed. Meanwhile, with limited resources, it seemed that the contentious trust fund was what they should be concentrating on.

On Monday morning, Emma dropped him off at the office on her way to the library. Ruth, the agency secretary, came in promptly at 9 o'clock after her four-day weekend, and they spent several hours together sorting through bills, receipts, and requests from various attorneys they had worked with in the past, all of them concerning insurance fraud. Jack didn't like insurance cases, but they were their bread and butter and he needed to dictate a number of polite letters to law firms that he couldn't afford to alienate.

Ruth was a sharp-tongued woman in her seventies, a retired New York City school teacher, who ran the office like a preschool teacher in charge of naughty children.

"I hope you didn't stuff yourself with turkey, Jack," was the first thing she said to him this morning. No hello, no friendly greeting.

"I was very moderate, Ruth, thank you," he told her.

"You need to watch your cholesterol or you know what will happen. Kaput! You'll keel over one day, stone cold dead. I've seen it happen, Jack. Believe me. Someone your age, with all your bad habits—a heart attack could come along any time."

"I'll keep that in mind," he assured her.

Fortunately, Ruth was a terrific secretary and she had Wilder & Associate so organized it felt like a military operation. Neither Howie nor Jack dared to cross her.

Ruth had just returned to her office in the front of the building when Santo, at last, returned Jack's many calls.

"Sorry I couldn't get back to you earlier, Jack," he apologized (breezily, not a real apology), "but these murders have kept me hopping."

"I'm sure they have," said Jack. "Now, when are you going to release Howie? You know he didn't kill anybody, no matter what Grace Stanton said. And frankly, I need him."

"Ah," said Santo. "Well, that's a problem. I'm afraid we're going to keep him another twenty-four hours."

"For chrissake, why? He's told you everything he knows! This is ridiculous, Santo, and you know it."

"No, it's not ridiculous. Everything about this case points to Howie. His shouting match with Harlan at the dinner table, the manner of the death, getting his daughter pregnant. Howie's been all over this case. And now we have Grace saying she saw him coming out of the study that night. I can't ignore the mounting evidence. So, if you want to help Howie, you're just going to have to come up with an alternative suspect who's more plausible."

"I'd be happy to do that, Santo. But I need Howie's help!"

"I'm sorry, but I can't let him go yet. Not with Santa Fe breathing down my neck."

"That's it, huh? Santa Fe?"

"Of course, it is. They're insisting I keep Howie for another day, that's all. We have the legal right to do it. Hopefully we can let him go after that. Now, look, I gotta go. I'm sorry to run, but I have five people who are trying to get my attention. Talk to you soon . . ."

Jack knew that Santo was busy, but it felt like a brush off. Probably he was embarrassed about caving in to Santa Fe. Jack sat rocking furiously in the big wooden rocker behind his desk. He didn't know who he was most angry with—Santo, for keeping Howie another day, or Howie for getting himself in such a jam.

"What a goddamn mess!" he said aloud to Katya. "Damn!"

The big problem, of course, was Grace. Why had she decided to make up her story about Howie coming out of the Senator's study at three in the morning? Was she trying to protect the real killer? That seemed the most likely answer. Or maybe it was Grace who had killed her father. Or her beloved brother Nick. But then, who had shot Nick?

Jack didn't know the answer to any of these questions and, worse, he had no idea how he was going to proceed. He was stymied, physically limited by his blindness. Jack considered himself the brains of the agency, but Howie was the eyes. They needed each other. Without Howie, Jack was severely limited. Simply put, he couldn't get around.

He had faced this problem in the past, of course, when Howie wasn't available. Occasionally, Emma had agreed to be his driver so that he could pursue an investigation. But Emma was busy with her own work and he was reluctant to ask for her help. Detective work could be dangerous and he didn't want to put her in harm's way.

Ruth was another possible person who could get him around, but there were issues here as well. He wasn't sure he could bear listening to her predict that he was about to have a heart attack. Jack was pondering this when Ruth knocked on his office door. He had trained her to do this, though it had taken time. During her first months at the agency, she had simply barged in.

"Yes, come in!" he called in the patient voice he used with her.

"Jack, there's a young man who wants to see you."

"A young man? For chrissake, Ruth—get rid of him! Of all the things I can't stand in life, young men top the list!"

"Sure, Jack. You're a real peach where young people are concerned. That's why they love you so much."

"Ruth, I don't want to have this conversation now. I'm busy thinking."

"I get it. But this young man says he knows you. He says his name is Buzzy."

"Buzzy?" Jack paused. "Buzzy Hurston?"

"Exactly. He's tall and skinny and doesn't look like much. But don't worry, I'll toss him out into the street."

"Hold on, Ruth. Get his phone number. Tell Buzzy I can't see him right now but I'll give him a call as soon as I can."

Jack drummed his fingers on the desk as Ruth began to leave.

"Stop!" he commanded. "I've changed my mind!"

"Well, that's a first!" Ruth remarked.

"Tell Buzzy I want to see him. Send him in."

***

"Hey, Jack," Buzzy said, coming into the office. "How's tricks?"

"Tricks are tricky," Jack replied. He listened as Buzzy settled into the client chair. Jack pictured him in a teenage slouch, but maybe not. Buzzy wasn't a teenager anymore. Adding up the years, Jack realized—to his astonishment—that Buzzy must be twenty.

Howie had first encountered Buzzy in the San Geronimo Big Brother program back when Buzzy was in the fifth grade, a dysfunctional kid who had been busted selling pot to his classmates. Becoming a Big Brother had been Claire's idea. She had been urging Howie for some time to get more involved in the community and this seemed a way to make her happy. Howie hadn't been enthusiastic at first, but he gave it his best shot, and before long he and Buzzy developed a real friendship. It was an unusual match—a nerdy, overeducated Indian (as Jack saw Howie), and a whacky, smart, unstable kid who had grown up in a hippie commune in the desert with an alcoholic, drugged-out mother who changed partners every few weeks.

Howie turned out to be a surprisingly good Big Brother. He took Buzzy camping, skiing, to movies, plays, concerts, once even to New York City because he wanted to expose his Little Brother to the art museums there. In fact, Buzzy was more than smart, he was brilliant, and one of Howie's biggest challenges was to keep Buzzy attending school despite the fact that he was so far beyond his classmates that he was bored half to death.

When Buzzy was in the sixth grade, Howie gave him a second-hand laptop, a Mac, and this proved to be a life changer. Buzzy took to computers with passionate interest and before long he was reprogramming both Howie's and Jack's devices, adding all sorts of extras—some of which were legal, and others not. He completely reworked the agency computer system as well as Nancy, Jack's specialized Mac with Kurzweil software for the blind.

Buzzy was a brilliant, oddball kid, so smart that Howie managed to arrange for him to get a full scholarship to Stanford, where he was admitted to an elite computer science program. This took several years of planning, along with tons of paperwork, and Howie counted it as one of his great life achievements.

"So, Buzzy, how's life in California?" Jack asked.

"Hey, it's cool, Jack. Pretty much."

"Pretty much?"

“Did I tell you I got my diving certificate last summer? I did the test down in Monterrey. Man, it’s totally wild, the things you see in Monterrey Bay! Whales, sharks, rays, old shipwrecks!”

“Whales and sharks are fascinating creatures, Buzzy,” Jack agreed. “But let’s get back to pretty much. How are your studies going?”

“Hey, I’m acing my classes. School’s a breeze.”

“But?” Jack inquired. “Why is it I hear a but in your voice?”

“Well, I got suspended, Jack. That’s why I’m home.”

Jack didn’t say anything for a moment. “You got suspended from Stanford? Even with all those good grades? What did you do, Buzzy?”

“It wasn’t a big deal. They just took it the wrong way.”

“What did you do, Buzzy?”

“Well, okay, I closed down BART for three hours. Just as an experiment, you see. A kind of class exercise.”

BART, Bay Area Rapid Transit, was a vital commuter transport system, built at great expense, that carried 118 million passengers a year through the Transbay Tube back and forth from the East Bay into downtown San Francisco.

“You closed down BART?” Jack asked, stony-faced.

“Only for three hours, Jack. I hacked their system—as a public service, really, to show how vulnerable they were to a cyber attack. But, well, it caused huge traffic problems on the Bay Bridge and the school wasn’t happy when they found out what I did.”

Jack shook his head. “I didn’t hear about this and I follow news from San Francisco. When did it happen?”

“At the end of October. Halloween, actually. BART pretended they closed down for repairs, they didn’t want to admit how crappy their computer system was. Personally, I think they should have given me a medal!”

"For chrissake, Buzzy, Howie's not going to be happy when he hears about this. He worked his ass off to get you into Stanford!"

"I know, I know! And I'm afraid to tell him. Where is Howie, by the way? I drove to his house last night thinking I'd pop in, but he wasn't there."

"Howie's in jail, Buzzy. He's the prime suspect in a murder investigation."

"No kidding? Did he kill somebody?"

"No, of course not. But he's in jail anyway, and I'm trying to figure out a way to get him released." Jack drummed his fingers momentarily on his desk. "How long are you planning to be in San Geronimo?"

"I'm not sure. I'm waiting to hear if Stanford is going to let me back in next semester. And, well . . . I'm not supposed to say anything about this, but some guy from Washington came to see me just before I left California. He asked if I wanted to work for the Pentagon."

Jack laughed. "And what did you tell him?"

"I said maybe, I needed to think about it. And he said maybe, too—he needed check me out some more to see if I was a security risk. I think he's going to come back to me with an offer, but I'm not sure. If Stanford decides to take me back, I'd rather be there."

"So, at the moment you're in limbo?"

"I guess so."

"Do you have a car?"

"Just an old beater. The Honda Civic that Howie got me three years ago. It broke down in Arizona. I had to get a new radiator. It took every cent I had."

Jack smiled. "You're broke, at loose ends . . . congratulations, Buzzy, you're just the guy I need. You're hired!"

***

Jack didn't waste any time giving Buzzy his first assignment.

"Can you get me a cell phone number for Grace Stanton? The author. She lives in Santa Fe."

"Sure, that's a no-brainer. Do you want me to use one of the online services? They charge a dollar or so. Or I can go deep and get it for free."

"Pay the dollar, Buzzy. Ruth will give you the agency credit card. Let's not break the law." *Unless you have to*, Jack added silently. "You can use the computer in Howie's office."

Buzzy had introduced Jack to TOR, the dark side of the web, several years ago, but Jack didn't like going there if he could avoid it. Buzzy returned a few minutes later with the number and waited in the client chair while Jack made the call.

Grace answered on the second ring.

"Yes?" she said abruptly. "Who is this?"

"Hello, Miss Stanton, this is Jack Wilder. We met briefly on Friday. I'm Howard Moon Deer's partner in San Geronimo."

"I know who you are. What do you want?"

It wasn't a friendly response.

"I want to talk to you about Howie. He's being detained by the State Police due to your claim that you saw him at three in the morning leaving your father's study."

"Yes, what about it?"

Jack raised an eyebrow. "What about it? I want to know why you told the police something that isn't true. You know very well that Howie didn't murder your father."

There was a pause from Grace's end of the conversation.

"My attorney has advised me not to speak about this to anyone except the proper authorities," she said after a moment. "Goodbye, Mr. Wilder. Please don't contact me again."

"Don't hang up!" he told her, but it was too late. He lowered his phone with a grunt of displeasure. He shouldn't have tried to speak to her on the phone, giving her the chance to hang up. He should have waited to question her in person. He had allowed his impatience to get the better of him. He had assumed, wrongly, that she might still have feelings for Howie and would be having misgivings about her statement.

Buzzy had overheard the conversation and was waiting for Jack's response.

"Well, if that's the way she wants to play it," Jack said grimly, "then that's how we'll play it, too! Can you break into her computer?"

"Do you know her email address?"

"No, is that a problem?"

"Not really. It'll just take me a few minutes longer. What are you looking for?"

"Most people keep a digital calendar of appointments and such. I want to know her schedule. Where she's going to be, when."

"No problem. Anything else?"

Jack considered this. "Let's get her banking information. In fact, while we're at it, let's take a look at her email. Let's see if we can discover why this damn woman is setting Howie up!"

Chapter Twenty-Two

On Sunday morning, Santo Ruben was feeling stymied and frustrated. His plan for the day had been to return to Forest Road 213 and take a good look in the daylight at the place where Nicolas Stanton had been killed. But while he was still at home eating breakfast, he got a call from Henry Wierczek, the deputy chief of Public Safety, who had other ideas.

On Saturday night, Wierczek had received a phone call from Charles Anderson, the Stanton family attorney, with the bombshell news that Grace had seen Howie coming out of her father's study at three in the morning, Thanksgiving night, with blood on his hands. Anderson and Wierczek were old friends, they played golf together, and Wierczek took the accusation seriously. In his opinion, people like the Stantons didn't lie. Above all, he was pleased that he would be able to hold a press conference in which he could announce a major breakthrough in the case. As usual, there were politics involved. Henry Wierczek was hoping to be named the next head of Public Safety and a speedy conclusion to this case would boost his chances.

On Sunday morning, Wierczek drove to Grace's home to get a formal statement from her. She wasn't home, but Wierczek decided that the word of his friend, Charles Anderson, was good enough so that he was justified in calling Santo with instructions to detain Howie, without charges, for as much time as the law allowed while they searched for further evidence to close the case.

This was Santo's investigation and he wasn't pleased to find himself bypassed, but there wasn't much he could do. After delivering Howie to the San Geronimo County Jail, Wierczek ordered him to drive to Santa Fe and await further instructions. The grisly murder of Senator Harlan

Stanton apparently was too big a deal to be left in the hands of a mere lieutenant without oversight from the top.

"And we'll want you to stick around for the press conference later in the afternoon," Wierczek added. "We may decide to stick you in front of a mic. Are you up for that?"

"Why not?" Santo replied, resigned to the worst.

In Santa Fe, he spent the late morning and early afternoon closeted with Wierczek and Chief Dave Sanchez, the head of the New Mexico State Police. At 1:30, he had a break for two hours before the press conference, and since he was in Santa Fe, he decided this was a good opportunity to pay a call on Grace Stanton to inform her of the death of her brother and use this as an excuse to see if he could shake her story about Howie. But when he went to her house, there was no one at home except an Hispanic maid, a middle-aged woman who said that Grace had left early Saturday morning for a cabin in southern Colorado where she sometimes went to write without interruptions. According to the maid, it was a secluded place where there was no Internet and she could turn off her phone so that nobody could reach her. Santo was disappointed but he supposed it was the sort of thing that a novelist might do. Still, it surprised him that Grace would disappear at a time like this.

Santo treated himself to a late lunch at The Cowgirl, a barbecue café on Guadalupe Street, which in his opinion had the best hamburgers in New Mexico. At 3:30 he returned to the State Capital where he stepped reluctantly in front of a microphone and addressed several dozen print journalists and TV crews. In fact, he was good at handling the press. He kept back as much information as possible, such as the fact that the Senator had been scalped, while at the same time giving the impression of transparency.

It was after 5 o'clock by the time he was finished in Santa Fe, too late to drive to Forest Road 213. Santo didn't like it that he had been forced to waste an entire day, but such was life when you were a public servant.

On Monday morning, he set his alarm for 6AM and arrived at the head of the forest road by 9 o'clock. It had snowed heavily Saturday night, then on and off on Sunday, but Monday had dawned clear and cold. The snow near the Colorado border at 8500 feet was sparkling white against a blue sky in the low morning sun. On Santo's orders, a snowplow had already made four swipes up and down the forest road, which was now a flat white surface with banks of snow on each side rising in some places higher than the roof of his SUV. Santo had 4-wheel drive and snow tires, so he had no problem driving the 5.3 miles to the spot where Howie claimed the shooting had taken place. He pulled up to a dead end and parked behind a small convoy of emergency vehicles, vans and pick-up trucks that had brought the tools and materials to set up a base of operations.

The CSU team had put a tent over the possible crime scene. Two figures in white outfits—it was impossible to say who they were, or even their sex—had cleared snow from a six square foot surface and were now working to retrieve physical evidence. Another tent had been set up a dozen feet away which Santo appropriated for his own headquarters. The tent provided no warmth, there wasn't even a floor, only snow that had been packed flat by all the boots walking in and out. But there was a table with a coffee urn for the workers, a box of donuts, and a satellite telephone.

At noon, Santo met with Ewan McDonald, a tall, rosy-faced man with a bushy mustache who was a ranger with the BLM. McDonald arrived at the camp with a detailed map of the surrounding area all the way to the Colorado border.

"I'm interested in old ranches," Santo told him. "Cabins, any sort of building someone might find shelter in or use as a hide-out. Even old ruins."

McDonald had a skeptical smile. "That's a tall order, Lieutenant. This is mostly public land but there are pockets of private land, people who have old claims that have been grandfathered in. It's a mixed-use area—recreation, grazing, hunting, fishing, all sorts of activities going on. Including marijuana cultivation, which we do our best to discourage."

"Glad to hear it," said Santo.

"Well, I don't mind cannabis particularly. Smoked some myself when I was young. But the growers often pollute the streams and it brings crime into the area. Then there are other folks who come out here with permits to cut firewood. And, of course ,we have the usual survivalists who are getting ready for the end of the world. You can disappear in these mountains if you want to. Summer and fall are the main seasons, but there's snowmobilers and cross-country skiers in the winter. None of the old ranches are occupied this time of year, as far as I know. There's no access. You saw what a hard time you had getting up this road, and this is only the first storm of the season."

"An abandoned barn or cabin is exactly what I'm looking for," Santo told him. "Let's start with where we are and maybe you can tell me what's nearby, say, in a radius of two or three miles."

Santo and the ranger had begun their conversation in the tent but they soon moved into the front seat of Santo's Explorer with the heater on. McDonald had a large map spread out on the dashboard.

"Okay, here we are now," he said pointing to a spot on the forest road. "The closest ranch is the Howard place. That's over here. Let's see . . . one point five miles, I'd say, from where we're sitting. The Howards have been here since the 1890s, but these days there's only a few of them left. They run cattle in the summer, but I doubt if there's anyone there now. They're usually gone by early October."

The ranger had his finger on the map. "You'd need a snowmobile to get in there now," he said. "If you continue up this road for another mile, you'll find a side road that branches out to the right. There's no sign, but if the snow's not too deep, you should be able to see a rickety one-lane bridge that crosses the stream. The Howard place is maybe a half a mile from there."

"What exactly is there now?"

"A barn, an old farmhouse, a horse corral, not much. There's a small lake, but it's mostly meadowland with a few patches of forest."

"Sounds like a perfect hideout."

"Maybe. Someone could break in, no problem. But you'd have to be a tough customer to survive a winter up there."

Santo grunted. He was searching for a tough customer and the old ranch sounded like a good possibility.

"What else is around here?"

"Within two miles? Nothing that I know about. Of course, that's hard to say for sure. Someone who's determined could set up camp under the trees and it would be hard for us to spot them. Now, if you go past your two-mile limit, you get to an old cabin that's about here, I'd say." McDonald pointed to another spot on the map that was farther to the south. "The last time I went there was three summers ago and part of the cabin was falling down, so I'm not sure how much shelter it would provide in a storm like we had the other night. We had a complaint that a few hippies had moved in and set up a kind of commune. But I doubt if they're still there. Most of the back-to-nature types give up pretty quickly once they discover that nature isn't always easy."

"Any other places?"

"No, you'd have to go at least eight miles to Magdalena Lake. There are a few cabins there that fishermen use in the summer."

Santo was glad to have his choices narrowed to two possible sites. He thanked the forest ranger for his help, bundled up in his warmest winter gear and goggles, and set out in a convoy of two snowmobiles to see if he could find any clues to the riddle of Nicolas Stanton's death.

***

Santo rode the lead snowmobile with Dan Hamm following a dozen feet behind, far enough to avoid the spray of snow that was sent flying in Santo's wake.

Dan had Sally on the back of his snowmobile with a Colt M4 carbine slung across her back. Her hands gripped his waist so she wouldn't fall off.

Sally had been included in the expedition because, though she was young, she was the best marksman in the group, the winner of numerous competitions. Santo was coming prepared for danger. He would have brought a larger force, but he still had only two snowmobiles at his disposal despite promises from Santa Fe to send additional machines.

Dan had had very little sleep since Thanksgiving Day, but Sally's hands on his waist gave him a jolt of energy. He was especially aware of her legs touching his legs, her knees pressing forward against the back of his knees. They were dressed for the weather in white snowsuits with gloves, helmets, ski goggles, and neck warmers pulled up above their noses. Nevertheless, it was a challenge for Dan to think about anything except Sally's body so close to his.

Sally had to shout to get his attention. It was nearly impossible to hear over the noise of the two snowmobiles. "Watch out for the low—"

Branch was the word she intended, but it was too late. The low branch whipped against Dan's helmet and sent an explosion of snow falling down on them.

"Sorry!" Dan shouted.

"What?"

"I said sorry! I hope you're okay!"

Dan had been raised in a conservative Texas family, and he was the butt of many jokes at the station due to the fact that he didn't drink or swear. It wasn't just that he was from a different culture, he seemed at times from a different era. He had to stop himself from calling Sally *ma'am*. He avoided the issue by not calling her anything at all.

The snow had erased all natural landmarks. The contours of the road were lost beneath a soft blanket of white. Santo had to stop occasionally to check his GPS device and the Forest Service map Ranger McEwan had given him. Fortunately, the turn-off to the rickety wooden bridge that led to the Howard ranch was still partly showing. The bridge crossed the stream that ran parallel to the road, then climbed a steep hill and down the other side into a copse of aspen trees, whose bare white trunks were almost the same color as the snow. After leaving the main road, they continued for another twenty minutes until they saw an old farmhouse and a barn in a clearing at the edge of a forest. Santo cut his speed and approached cautiously.

The house and barn looked as though nobody had been there for decades. One corner of the barn had disintegrated into a rubble of fallen timbers and the entire structure was leaning precariously to one side. Santo stopped by the ruins of an old windmill that was missing a propeller.

Dan pulled up beside him and allowed Sally to slip off the back before he swung his leg free of the snowmobile and joined Santo. Sally took the carbine from her back and cradled it in her arms.

"So, what do you think, Lieutenant?" Dan asked.

"I'm thinking we're not going to take any chances," he replied. "Sally, you go around the house to the right. Dan, take the left. See if there's a back door. I'll try the front. We'll get into position, but nobody goes in until I give the word. Make sure your walkie-talkies are on but keep the volume down. Let's move out."

Dan's Glock was buried beneath several layers of clothing. He got it out after some fumbling with zippers and began his circumnavigation of the house with the gun in his ungloved right hand. He shivered involuntarily, worried that there might be a sniper inside watching. The snow was deeper here than down on the forest road, coming up above his knees as he post-holed his way around the side of the building. He stopped every few feet and listened but the only sound he heard was the wind whistling through the timbers of the half-ruined barn.

Dan worked his way around to the back door without coming across any signs of life. It was a basic, no nonsense one-story house, no picture windows, no French doors, nothing extra. It looked to him like something from the dustbowl 1930s. There was no smoke rising from the chimney.

He was wondering if he should continue working his way around the house when his walkie-talkie came to life with a squawk. Dan turned the volume down so that the voices were faint.

"What do you see, Sally?" he heard Santo say.

"I'm looking in a window to the kitchen," she answered. "There are no dishes in the sink, nothing on the stove. I don't see any signs that anyone's been here for a long time."

"How about you, Dan?"

Dan had to hold his Glock between his knees while he fumbled with the walkie-talkie to find the transmit button.

"I'm at the back door," he said. "No signs of life either."

"Dan, can you break in that door?"

"Why, sure. It looks half-rotten."

"Get ready! I'm coming in the front door on the count of three. Sally, you stay where you are by the kitchen window and keep an eye out. Here we go. One . . . two . . . three!"

Dan took a running start and crashed his right shoulder against the wooden door. The door shook but didn't open. On his second attempt, the wood around the lock shattered and he tumbled into a pantry with shelves of canned food and an antique ringer washing machine in one corner. He heard Santo smash his way inside from the front.

"This is the police!" Santo called. "If there's anyone here, make yourself known!"

There was no answer. Dan moved cautiously from the pantry into the kitchen, his gun leading the way. He could see Sally looking in at him from outside the window with her rifle pointed his way. He gave her a high-five and continued from the kitchen into a parlor. His eyes scanned the room. There was an old couch, an overstuffed armchair, a coffee table, a floor lamp. Dan had seen parlors like this in West Texas, old rooms from hard times.

He made his way along a short hallway to a small bedroom that was filled almost entirely with a double bed. The covers were pulled back and it looked as though someone had slept here recently. There was a stack of blankets piled on top, including an old bear rug. The head was hanging down over the edge of the bed staring at the floor with glassy eyes.

Dan's gun swept the room. His heart was beating fast. He'd been wounded a year ago, a nasty gun shot to his left leg, and he didn't cherish the thought of getting shot again.

There was a closed door at the far end of the bedroom. It led either to a closet or a bathroom, Dan wasn't sure.

He approached cautiously, raised his right leg, and smashed the door open with a powerful thrust of his foot.

It was a bathroom.

Dan stopped abruptly.

There was a young woman standing in the enamel claw-foot tub. She was fully dressed. She couldn't have been more than seventeen. Being from Texas, Dan took her immediately as undocumented Mexican. She had long black hair and an olive complexion. Her mouth was open like she was about to scream, but she didn't. She didn't say a word.

"*Hola*!" Dan said, trying to appear friendly. That plus the phrase *hasta la vista* was pretty much the only Spanish he knew.

He raised his walkie-talkie and called Santo.

"Lieutenant, you'd better come on through to the bedroom."

Chapter Twenty-Three

A hundred miles away in Santa Fe, at ten minutes to five on Monday afternoon, Jack and Buzzy sat waiting at the curb outside a business that called itself 10,000 Pleasures on Agua Fria Street.

10,000 Pleasures sounded like a whorehouse to Jack, though Buzzy assured him it was a spa, a place where expensive people could soak in pools of hot water and get themselves massaged and tanned and perfectly relaxed. Their website advertised mud baths, yoga, past life repair, and aural cleansing. For women only. Men were probably too crude to enter such a place.

"Self-indulgence for the over-privileged!" Jack said grumpily. "Whatever became of stoicism?"

"Stoicism went out of style about two thousand years ago, Jack."

"You studied philosophy at Stanford, did you, Buzzy?"

"Sure. a little. Marcus Aurelius, Seneca the Younger, the works. Schools like Stanford want you to become a well-rounded individual. Whatever that means."

"It means a ticket into the upper classes," said Jack. "Well-rounded is a luxury the poor can't afford!"

"You're getting kind of radical in your old age, Jack."

Am I? Jack wondered. He supposed it was true. It came from spending years in close proximity to Howie, a kind of osmosis: Howie had grown more conservative, Jack more revolutionary. Meanwhile, he had to admit that Buzzy had become a good deal more sophisticated after two years in Northern California.

Back at the office, Buzzy had tried to tell Jack how much Grace put on her Visa card for her weekly sessions at 10,000 Pleasures, but Jack stopped him.

"Not another word, Buzzy. You're not telling me this."

"But I *am* telling you."

"No, you're not," said Jack. "I have my P.I. license to consider. If I heard about illegal activity, like hacking somebody's credit card account, I'd have to report it."

"So, you want me to keep this to myself?"

"No, Buzzy, I want you to talk. But judiciously. You understand?"

Buzzy sighed. "You know, Jack, I'm starting to. But how do I tell you something without telling you?"

"Very, very carefully. For example, how much would you *guess* somebody like Grace Stanton earned last year? An author with several books on the best seller list?"

"I can tell you exactly, Jack. I looked at her—"

"No, no, no! You're just guessing. You don't know anything for certain. You're a bright kid at one of the best universities in the country, you have no specific information, but you know how things work. So give me an educated guess."

"Okay, I'd guess that someone like Grace Stanton earned $223,197.18 last year."

"Really?" Jack considered the figure. "With two books on the *New York Times* bestseller list and a movie in the works, I would have expected more."

"Well, that's my guess, Jack," Buzzy told him. "And I'm sticking with it."

Buzzy had hacked Grace's computer with frightening ease, and since her iPhone was in sync with her home laptop, he had gained entry to both. Gaining access to her Wells Fargo account had taken fifteen minutes longer. As for email, there were a number of messages back and forth with her New York editor, Stephen Halley, and there appeared to be some delay with her new thriller, *The Girl Who Had Everything*, but there hadn't been time to look into that closely. Jack anticipated taking a deeper look at Grace's correspondence later tonight.

They had driven to Santa Fe in a rented Kia and were positioned outside 10,000 Pleasures waiting for Grace Stanton to emerge from her weekly session at the spa. The Kia was due to the fact that Jack was far too nervous a passenger to ride in Buzzy's beat-up Honda. Ruth had arranged to rent the car for one week, at which point Jack hoped to have the twin murders of Harlan and Nicolas Stanton solved and done with. Sooner, if possible.

At five o'clock, Buzzy stepped out of the car and positioned himself near the front door of the spa. A number of attractive women flowed in and out of the building but Grace didn't appear for another ten minutes. She wore huge dark glasses and was dressed in white sweatpants and a white sweatshirt with a knee length winter overcoat. Buzzy recognized her from the photographs he had studied.

"Grace!" Buzzy said pleasantly, as though they were well-acquainted.

She looked up expectantly, and when she didn't recognize him, she put on her public famous-author face.

"I'm sorry, do I know you?"

"Only indirectly. Howard Moon Deer was my Big Brother when I was a kid in San Geronimo, so I feel I sorta know you secondhand, if you see what I mean."

Grace gave him a stern look. "Did Howie send you?"

"Nope, Howie's in jail. He's not in a position to send anybody anywhere, I'm sorry to say."

"That's too bad, but this is totally inappropriate!" she told him. "Now, if you will excuse me . . ."

She began walking away, but Buzzy took hold of her arm. "Not so fast, babe. Jack Wilder is waiting in a car by the curb and he wants a word with you."

Her face flushed with outrage. It wasn't clear what outraged her more, that Buzzy had called her babe, or Jack was stalking her after she had specifically told him to leave her alone.

Jack was seated in the front seat of the car following the conversation with the window open. He saw it was time to take over.

"Miss Stanton!" he called out the window. "Come here, please. We need to talk."

Grace stormed toward the car. "You have a hell of a nerve! I told you on the phone, we have nothing to say to one another. Now, if you don't leave me alone, I'm going to call the police!"

"I wouldn't do that if I were you, Miss Stanton. The police are going to ask you some hard questions and I'm the only person who can help you. Your prints were found in the old bunkhouse on your father's ranch along with your brother, Nicolas's. This isn't looking good for you, I'm afraid. You've lied to Lieutenant Ruben several times now, and in a murder investigation that could get you prison time. Now get in the car and I'll see what I can do to help."

Jack was lying. No prints had been found in the bunkhouse belonging to either Grace or Nicolas. In fact, Jack wasn't certain CSU had even gotten to the bunkhouse yet. But as bluffs go, it was plausible. Jack waited for Grace to make up her mind.

"Well, I don't know," she said, hesitating.

"Buzzy, help her into the back, please."

Buzzy opened the back door and guided Grace toward the seat. But she balked on the curb when she saw Katya.

"There's a huge dog in there!" she exclaimed.

Jack stepped briskly from the passenger seat to the sidewalk, glad to find that he could still move quickly. With one hand on the car to guide himself, he forced Grace into the back seat and slid in beside her, blocking her exit.

"Katya won't hurt you," he said. "As long as you behave yourself... *go, go*!" he said to Buzzy, who had jumped back into the driver's seat and was pulling out into traffic.

***

"You're kidnapping me!"

"Not a bit," Jack told her. "You'll be free to leave as soon as you answer a few questions."

"But that's outrageous!"

"Those are the rules," he said blandly.

Buzzy bustled them out of town on the highway to Galisteo. He pulled off onto a narrow country road that had weeds growing up through the asphalt. He stopped by a snowy field where two horses were cantering back and forth.

Throughout the drive, Grace appeared to accept her imprisonment with sour good humor, a bad joke that would soon be over. She had obviously concluded that Jack wasn't going to harm her.

"So, are there really ten thousand of them?" Jack asked when they came to a stop.

"I beg your pardon?"

"Pleasures," he said. "Ten thousand pleasures?"

Despite herself, she laughed, though it wasn't a merry laugh. "All right, let's get this over with," she said. "What do you want to know?"

"I'm not letting you get away with this, Miss Stanton. Howie is my partner and friend. He was also your lover not so long ago. In case you've forgotten, you had his child. So, I want to know why you're making trouble for him."

"Oh, honestly! It was only a summer fling!" she said impatiently. "I liked Howie. In fact, I liked him quite a lot. But it wasn't meant to be anything serious. I was trying to get over somebody else, that's all. Howie was . . . well, he was transitional."

Jack shook his head. "In other words, you were using him."

"If you put it that way, I suppose I was," she replied without a hint of remorse.

"Miss Stanton, I repeat—why are you making up this story about Howie?"

"How do you know I'm lying? Perhaps I'm not."

"Because I know Howie. He can be rash, certainly. But he's no killer. You know that as well as I do. Now, who got to you? Who's making you say this?"

"Nobody's making me. It's true!"

"You're lying, Miss Stanton. But we'll leave that for a moment. When did you find out that your brother Nicolas was down at the old bunkhouse?"

He felt her stiffen, but she didn't answer.

"Remember your fingerprints were down there," he pressed, gambling that it was true. "And so were his. So, let's have the truth, please. I want to hear what you were doing Thanksgiving night and early Friday morning. And I'm not letting you out of this car until I'm satisfied you've told me the truth."

"You can't do that! You're a policeman!"

"I *was* a policeman. But I'm not anymore. I can do what I like. So stop playing games and let's get to the bottom of this. How did you know Nick was in the bunkhouse?"

She crossed her arms and gave him the silent treatment.

"Miss Stanton, this is a dangerous situation," he continued sternly. "There are now two deaths in your family. First your father, and now Nick. There's no telling who might be next. It may even be you. So, you need to stop playing the little princess and tell me what you know."

She turned to him, her mouth agape. "*What*?" she demanded. "What did you say about Nick?"

Jack was taken aback. It hadn't occurred to him that she might not know her brother was dead. It was a day and a half since Nick's death and he had assumed that either Santo or one of his officers would have contacted her with the news.

"You haven't heard that Nick was shot?"

"I've been away, I haven't heard a thing. My God, tell me it's not true! . . . I don't believe you!"

Her astonishment seemed real and Jack softened his tone. "I'm sorry, I assumed you would have been told by now. I hate to be the one to bring you the news. It happened late Saturday afternoon on a forest road near the Colorado border."

"No!" she cried.

Jack sat back and allowed her to absorb the news. He thought she might cry, but you never could predict how people would react to news like this. Her reaction was to become angry. "Goddamnit! Goddamnit to hell! You better not be lying to me!"

"I am not, Miss Stanton. I'm sorry. Your brother is dead. Please tell me—where were you this weekend?"

"Where was *I*? You think I killed my brother?"

"No, of course not. I'm just trying to get straight how it is you don't know."

"I was away, up in my cabin outside of Pagosa Springs. My house guest, Lorenzo, left on Friday for Dallas where he has some boring rich friends. I was happy to see the end of him, frankly — I was sick of him, sick of everybody. The place in Colorado is my escape hatch when I'm tired of the human race. So I took off, that's all. I turned off my phone, I didn't listen to the news, I just wanted to be alone and sit in front of the fire and think about Daddy. And now, oh, God, you're saying Nick is dead, too!"

She did cry now. She wasn't the silent type of crier. She blubbered, she gasped, she snorted. Jack waited patiently until she had calmed down. He wasn't particularly surprised that Santo had allowed Lorenzo to leave the state. Santo had gotten his statement and Lorenzo wasn't a suspect. Nevertheless, if it had been Jack's case, he would have kept everyone who had been at the Stanton's Thanksgiving close at hand. It was frustrating not to be in charge.

Grace's tears gradually turned to sniffles. She found a tissue in her bag and blew her nose.

"Oh, Nick, Nick . . . I loved him so much, but he was always getting in trouble, even when we were kids. Goddamn him! Why didn't he take better care of himself?"

"Howie was with Nick when it happened," Jack said, leading the conversation back to where he wanted it to go. "He's very broken up about this, just as you are."

"Howie was there? But how? How did it happen?"

"When Howie got home on Friday night, he found a note that Nick had left for him on his kitchen table. It gave some GPS coordinates and asked Howie to meet him there on Saturday afternoon. The coordinates turned out to be in a remote spot five miles down a forest service road south of Antonito, Colorado."

Jack noted to himself that Antonito wasn't very far from Pagosa Springs where Grace claimed she had spent the weekend. Perhaps an hour away by car. Close enough so that she could have made the drive easily. He spent a few minutes describing the circumstances of her brother's death, how Howie and Nick had been talking in the car when the killer appeared out of the storm, seemingly from nowhere, and began shooting.

Grace sniffled as she listened. "But Howie's okay?"

"Howie's not okay. He's locked up in the San Geronimo jail. Because of what you told the police."

Jack paused, wondering suddenly how she had made her damning statement about Howie if she'd been incommunicado all weekend. "Who did you talk to at the State Police about seeing Howie outside your father's study?" he asked.

"I didn't tell the cops anything. I didn't want to get Howie into trouble. But it was a murder investigation and I kept worrying about holding back something so important. So, on Friday night I phoned my lawyer and told him, and he said he would pass it on to someone he knew at the State Police."

"Who is your lawyer?"

"Charles Anderson, he's in Santa Fe."

Jack made a note to himself to check this out, who told who what. It struck him as strange that the police had detained Howie on such flimsy, secondhand evidence. He proceeded cautiously.

"Let's go back to Thanksgiving, Miss Stanton, and perhaps we can clear this up. How did you know that Nick was in the bunkhouse that night?"

"It was in the note Howie brought to me. He said he'd be down there all day Thursday and all that night. He said he wanted to see me, but I should wait until I could get away without anyone noticing. He asked me to bring him a plate of turkey, if I could. Typical Nick!"

"And did you?"

"I rode down on my horse. It was dark and I didn't want to walk."

"What time was this?"

"Sometime after midnight. I saddled Valkyrie and took a bottle of wine and a plate of food and rode to the bunkhouse. Nick and I used to play there when we were kids."

"So, you weren't surprised Nick was hiding there?"

"No, it was the logical place. Nobody ever goes down there anymore. It hasn't been used for decades."

"But there was a sleeping bag and mattress, an oil heater. Somebody had gone to some trouble to make the room warm and habitable. I don't think that was Nick. People on the run don't carry oil heaters with them. That was you, Miss Stanton. You've known he was coming for some time, even before Howie gave you that letter. It must have taken some time to carry all the stuff down there to make a hideaway for your brother. And you had to do it without anyone finding out. How long have you and Nick been in contact?"

She treated him to a moment's silence.

"Come on, Miss Stanton, let's hear it. You've come this far, now let's hear the rest."

"He's my brother, for chrissake! We were close. We had to keep together to survive our toxic family life. So okay, I've been in touch with him for years. Ever since he went on the run."

"What exactly do you mean, in touch?"

"I sent him money. We wrote email back and forth on fake accounts we'd set up. Sometimes he didn't have access to the Internet so I wouldn't hear from him for months. He was living rough up in the hills of Northern California, no electricity, a very sketchy life. Up in Humboldt."

"How did you send him money?"

"I put it into a joint account we have in St. Croix. How Nick transferred it to California, I don't know. He didn't tell me everything in case we got caught. He did his best to protect me."

"Why did he come to New Mexico for Thanksgiving?"

"You know the answer to that already. He was tired of being on the run. He needed money to buy a passport and set himself up in a safe new life somewhere. He told Howie he had a plan to go to Bora Bora, but that wasn't his real destination."

"He lied to Howie? That doesn't sound like a best friend. So where was he planning to go? . . . you can tell me, Grace. It doesn't matter anymore."

"I suppose not," she said unhappily. "Uruguay. There's a beach town he knew that he thought would be a good place to hide."

"Okay, let's get back to Thanksgiving night. You got to the bunkhouse sometime after midnight. What happened down there?"

"Nothing much. We went through a bottle of wine. He wanted to know the family gossip, how Thanksgiving dinner went, that sort of thing."

"Did you talk about the trust, how you were going to change your father's mind?"

"No, that was pretty much settled."

"Really? Settled how? From what I've been told, your father was a very stubborn man. How were you going to change his mind?"

"With a bit of pressure, that's all."

"Go on."

"Like all families, we have our skeletons. Daddy was hoping to get back into politics and he didn't want old scandals to come out. Nick was threatening to go public with something unless Daddy relented about the trust."

"You're saying Nick was blackmailing your father?"

"It wasn't really blackmail. Only a bit of pressure, like I said. And now that Daddy's dead it's not the sort of thing anybody really needs to know."

"Grace! Listen to me. There have been two murders and secrets are going to come out, whether you like it or not. Lieutenant Ruben isn't going to be happy that you haven't told him about this. Now, I can help you, but you're going to have to trust me and tell me everything you know."

She shook her head. "It wasn't even about my father—it concerned my grandfather. It's very unpleasant, actually. Grandpa was a great man in his way, but he had a rather major flaw. You see, he liked young girls. Very young. He used his position as BIA Commissioner to molest some of the children in the boarding schools. Those kids had nobody they could tell. They were easy targets for someone like Grandpa."

"I'm sorry to hear that. Howie's been telling me for days how these children were abused, and I see he wasn't exaggerating. But this is a crime your grandfather committed, not your father. Why was he worried about it coming out?"

"Because Daddy has known about it for years, and he covered it up to protect the family reputation. Maybe fifty years ago, the public would have accepted that as an excuse. But not today. If this came out now, it would wreck any chances of him getting back into politics. He was planning to run for New Mexico governor next year."

"And Nick was threatening to expose him?"

"Only if he didn't give Nick his money. Was that so wrong? The money *was* Nick's!"

"Right or wrong, I suspect this has a lot to do with why your father was killed. But tell me more about your grandfather. You're aware, I imagine, that the Stanton Ranch was the site of an Indian school fifty years ago where the headmaster was murdered by one of the students?"

"Yes, of course I know that!" She gave an exasperated laugh. "It's another family skeleton!"

"When it happened, one of the girls, a fourteen-year-old student, was detained by the police. We believe she was the older sister of the boy who killed the headmaster, but we don't know that for certain. Whoever she was, the police thought she might have been an accomplice. But then your grandfather showed up and managed to get her released. Do you know why he did that?"

"Isn't it obvious? Grandpa liked her. She was just the right age for him, and she was very pretty."

"How old was your grandfather in 1970?"

"I'm not sure exactly. Late fifties, I'd guess."

"So, a man in his late fifties and a fourteen-year-old child!"

"I told you this wasn't pleasant. It's why my father wanted to keep it hushed up."

"And this Indian girl—she's Ramona, isn't she? The servant at the ranch?"

Grace nodded. Jack was unable to see such a gesture, but he felt it.

"Yes or no?" he insisted.

"Yes, Ramona Montoya. Grandpa was obsessed with her. And you're right—it was her brother who murdered the headmaster. The boys and girls were kept separate, you understand, but sometimes they found ways to meet. I think she may have helped her brother in some way, though she always denied it, and there wasn't any proof. I don't know the details, but Grandpa got her cleared of any charges and brought her to the ranch. After he died, he left the ranch to my father, but there was a codicil in the will that Daddy was required to take care of her for the rest of her life. I suppose Grandpa loved her in his way."

Jack sensed he had arrived at the core of the case, though it still wasn't clear to him exactly what this meant and how it had unfolded.

"How do you know this old history, Miss Stanton? Was it general knowledge in your family?"

"No, of course not!"

"Then I repeat, how do you know?"

"Nick told me. He'd found out somehow."

Jack considered this.

"I see," he said, though he didn't entirely see. "Did Nick tell you how he found out?"

"No. He was a little cagey about it, actually. I was curious, of course. But he only laughed. He said it was better I didn't know."

Jack nodded. "So, this was how Nick was going to blackmail your father into giving him his money? It wasn't only that your grandfather was molesting children. It was more damning than that. Your grandfather helped conceal evidence in a horrendous murder case, and your father knew about this and never said anything."

Grace sighed. "Yes," she said wearily. "It would have been the end of Daddy's political career. Even his new book would have been recalled. Nick was jubilant. He knew he had Daddy in a corner."

"Miss Stanton, did Nick kill your father?"

"No, of course not! He was down in the bunkhouse the entire time. He never went near the main house!"

"As far as you know?"

"Well, sure, as far as I know. I was only with Nick for an hour or so."

"Let's get back to Howie," Jack said. "You didn't really see him outside your father's study that night, did you?"

"No," she said after a pause.

"Good. Now, who told you to make up this damning story about him?"

She didn't answer.

"Grace?"

"All right, if you have to know, it was Justin," she said. "My asshole older brother! Are you happy now?"

Jack wasn't happy. But he was starting to connect the dots.

Chapter Twenty-Four

They dropped off Grace back at 10,000 Pleasures and from there, Jack told Buzzy to go to the Stanton Ranch, which was forty-five minutes away. Buzzy fiddled with his phone to find the directions.

Jack sat in the passenger seat thinking hard about what Grace had told him, trying to fit the pieces together with what he already knew. He kept asking himself who had both the motive and opportunity to kill the Senator and his youngest son, as well as the sheer resolve to carry it out. But his mind was a blank. The afternoon sun was warm through the car window which put him in a pleasant torpor. The absurd part of insomnia, as far as Jack was concerned, was though he couldn't sleep at night, in the daytime, it was struggle to stay awake.

He woke with a start when they left the pavement and began driving over the rutted dirt road that led to the ranch.

"You were snoring, Jack," Buzzy mentioned.

Jack sighed. "Are we there yet?"

"It's just a few minutes ahead . . . *now, what the hell is that*?" he said suddenly. "Jack, there's a plume of dust coming at us from down the road. It's a vehicle of some kind going really fast . . . I can't see it! Oh, there it is. It's a pickup truck. Jesus! It must be going 70! It just came flying over the hill . . ."

"For chrissake, calm down, Buzzy. Tell me what's happening!"

"It's one of those big redneck trucks, a Dodge Ram on huge wheels, and it's coming at us like a bat out of hell . . . hold on, Jack! He's going to run us off the road!"

"Buzzy, slow down!"

The Camino de la Esquela Vieja was not quite wide enough for two cars to pass one another. Buzzy decided not to play chicken, sensing he would lose. He waited as long as he dared and then pulled hard to the right, flying off the road into the sagebrush.

"Christ!" Jack cried as they bounced violently over a rock. He grabbed the dashboard to keep from being thrown through the windshield. Katya squealed from the back. It was a rough few seconds as they careened over the desert to a stop. He heard the whoosh and roar of the pickup rush past in the direction from which they had come.

Jack couldn't speak for a moment He had to catch his breath.

"Who?" he managed. "Who the hell was that?"

"I told you, it was this big V8 asshole truck!"

"Yes," Jack said patiently. "But who was inside?"

"I couldn't see, Jack. It was pulling a lot of dust and I was trying not to crash."

"I'm grateful we're alive, Buzzy. But now think for a moment. You looked at that truck long enough to say it was a Dodge Ram so you must have seen who was driving. Was it a man or a woman?"

"I think it was a man," Buzzy answered. "But maybe it was a woman. I don't know. It was only a shape that I saw for a second."

Jack wondered if it was worth turning around to try and catch the truck. He didn't think so. It was too late, and the Kia was no match against a souped-up truck with a big engine. Plus, he didn't trust Buzzy's driving.

"Get us back on the road, Buzzy. Let's see what's happening at the ranch."

***

They drove for another ten minutes before Buzzy said the ranch was just coming into view.

"Do you see any cop cars out front?"

"The driveway's empty. It doesn't look like there's anybody home."

Buzzy stopped in the parking area in front of the house. They left Katya in the car while Buzzy took Jack's arm and guided him to the front door. Buzzy rang the doorbell, which chimed inside. There was no answer so Buzzy rang again.

"What now?" Buzzy asked after the third try.

"Let's look around."

They returned to the car to let Katya out. Jack put her into her harness, and with Katya on one side, and Buzzy on the other, they walked down the snow packed road toward the horse barn. As they got closer, they heard the sound of a hammer tapping rhythmically against a nail.

"There's a cowboy dude outside the barn shoeing a horse," Buzzy said. "He has the horse tied up to a rail and he's working on one of the front hooves. His back is to us and I don't think he's seen us."

Jack assumed this must be the stable hand that Howie had mentioned. He tried to remember his name. Tucker, he believed. He wasn't sure he had ever heard his last name.

"Hello!" Jack called as they approached. "Sorry to disturb you. I'm looking for Ramona."

The cowhand lowered the horse's leg and turned to face Jack and Buzzy. "She's not here," he said after a long beat. "You must have seen her in the ranch truck as you were driving in."

"That was Ramona in the Dodge?" Jack asked.

"You another cop? You don't look like one."

"I'm a detective," Jack told, leaving it vague what sort of detective he was. "So that was Ramona? In the truck that drove us off the road?"

"Guess so," he said. "Though I don't know nothing about her driving you off the road."

"Why was she leaving here in such a hurry?"

Tucker only shrugged.

"Do you know when she'll be back?"

"Don't know that either."

"Did she say where she was going?"

"Nope."

It was like pulling teeth to get anything from this cowboy.

"So, you must be Tucker," Jack said.

"What's it to you?" he answered.

"Does Ramona have her own cabin on the property or does she live in the main house?"

"Look, mister, I'm busy and I got nothing to say to you."

"That's a pity, Tucker, because two people have been killed and this is serious. If you want, I'll give Lieutenant Ruben a call and we can continue this conversation in his office which would be a lot more inconvenient than talking to me. So, you might want to answer my question."

It took Tucker less than a heartbeat to decide in Jack's favor. "She has a cabin behind the kitchen."

"Thank you. How long have you been working on the ranch, Tucker?"

"Long time. Twenty-six years come January."

"You sure must like it here, then!" Buzzy said, throwing himself into the conversation.

"Buzzy, let me handle this, please." Jack said, turning to him. "So, do you like working at the ranch, Tucker?" he repeated.

"It's okay. I like horses."

"What horse is that you're shoeing?"

"This here's Valkyrie."

"That's Grace Stanton's horse, isn't it?"

"Yep."

"And he threw a shoe?"

"Yep."

"How did he do that?"

"Don't know."

"So, it's just you and Ramona here most of the time?"

"Yep. Just the two of us. The family is only here a few weeks in the summer and at Thanksgiving. Sometimes Christmas."

"With just the two of you, I'm guessing you've gotten to know one another well."

Tucker shrugged. "Nope. Neither one of us are what you'd call talkers."

"Did she ever tell you about her time as a young girl here at the Indian school?"

"Nope, never heard nothing about that."

"She's been here a lot longer than you, hasn't she? Since Adam Stanton's time."

"Yep. Far as I know."

"Did she ever talk about him?"

"Nope."

"And she didn't tell you where she was going today?"

"Nope."

It went on like that for another few minutes with Jack getting nothing from him but yep and nope. Laconic didn't begin to describe Tucker. He was stubborn as a mule.

Jack eventually gave up. He left his card and asked the cowhand to tell Ramona to give him a call when she returned. Probably Tucker would toss the card in the trash as soon as they were gone.

Jack had Buzzy walk him around the main house before they left, asking him to describe what he saw. He didn't know what he was looking for. Atmosphere, he supposed. Anything that would give him a clue about why murder had intruded into the privileged lives of the Stanton family.

At the rear of the house, they came to a cabin that stood next to a fenced kitchen garden. Jack assumed this was where Ramona lived, but the door was locked, the curtains were drawn, and there was no way to see what was inside. Jack considered breaking in but decided that wasn't a good idea. He had nothing on Ramona except knowledge of her tragic past and he didn't want to lose his own P.I. license.

Was it a wasted trip? Not entirely, he thought as they drove away. But he was sorry they had missed Ramona. She would have had a lot to tell him, if he had been able to get her to open up.

But she was gone. And after the way she drove off, as though the hounds of hell were on her heels, he doubted she would be returning any time soon.

Chapter Twenty-Five

Jack had to wait until they were nearly back to San Geronimo to get cell service in the car. He'd been trying to call Santo for the last twenty miles and his frustration had increased with each mile. Jack hated cell phones. But when they didn't work, he hated them even more. It was the dilemma of a grouchy modern man.

"Santo!" he barked, when he finally got through on Santo's private number. "I've got news."

"Jack? That you? . . . You're fading in and out."

"I am *not* fading! I can hear you perfectly! Now, look—I happened to run into Grace Stanton a little while ago—"

"Jack, I'm losing you . . ."

"*Grace*!" he shouted, as if that would get his voice through the spotty service.

"Okay, there you are," said Santo. "What do you mean you were with Grace Stanton? Jack, I told you to back off this case!"

"It was a chance meeting, Santo. I just happened to run into her. I was checking out health spas in Santa Fe and there she was coming out the front door."

"Really? You've never been to a health spa in your life!"

"Exactly, which is why I'm checking them out. I'm turning over a new leaf, getting healthy. Now, listen—"

"Hold on! I'm not buying this story of yours! And if you went down to Santa Fe to bother Grace—"

"Santo, you need to shut up and listen. We had a talk, Grace and I, and now she's saying she didn't see Howie coming out of her father's study after all. She admitted she made the thing up. She didn't see anybody."

Santo was paying attention now. “You’re serious?”

“You bet I’m serious. And guess who put her up to it?”

“Who?”

“Her brother Justin. The one who has always disliked Howie. The one who is eager to throw suspicion away from himself.”

“Justin?” Santo considered this for a moment. “You’re not bullshitting me are you, Jack? I know you want to get Howie off the hook.”

“Check it out. Talk to Grace yourself and she’ll tell you the truth.”

“Justin!” Santo repeated, starting to warm to the idea. “I said it was him from the beginning, didn’t I? It’s all making sense. He’s our guy.”

Jack was starting to have very different ideas about who their guy was. But he left that alone.

“The main thing is, Howie is in the clear,” he said. “You need to let him go.”

Santo took a moment to consider this. It wouldn’t be easy for him to go against the suits in Santa Fe who liked Howie for the crime and wanted to wrap up this case quickly.

“Where are you now, Jack?”

Jack looked over at Buzzy. “About fifteen minutes east of town,” Buzzy whispered.

Jack repeated the information to Santo.

“Okay. Come straight to the station,” Santo told him. “I’ve got news for you, too.”

***

Howie was not enjoying life in the San Geronimo County Jail. It wasn’t like he was in San Quentin or Sing Sing, but it was bad enough. It was boring, bleak, and depressing. Plus, the food was horrible and the company wasn’t the best.

It was an educational experience, he supposed. Howie tried to look on the bright side of bad experiences, and "educational" was often the word he settled on. He discovered, for instance, how easy it was to buy drugs in jail. One of the jail guards, Manny Pacheco, a weasley guy with sad eyes, sold weed, uppers, downers, oxycodone, Xanax, but not heroin—he was firm on this point, saying he was a county employee and he wouldn't cross that particular line. Howie looked to Manny like a potential sale, someone with money, and he was disappointed when Howie assured him that his drug days were over, long ago in his college past.

The jail was in the San Geronimo Civic Center, but it was a different universe from where people voted and paid their property taxes. The men's jail was a single drab room with narrow windows that were placed above eye level so you couldn't see out. There was a line of four cells, each with four hard beds that folded out from the wall. Every cell had a toilet in the corner that offered zero privacy.

Howie shared his cell with two other jailbirds: Donny, a skinny 19-year-old kid with a bad complexion who had beaten-up his girlfriend's father because of some family drama that was too complicated for Howie to follow. And Kelly, an old geezer who had been picked up for lewd behavior, lurching drunkenly in a downtown street shouting obscenities and waving his genitals at any passerby. The San Geronimo Tourist Board discouraged that sort of thing.

Time passes slowly in jail. Howie felt that he had been plucked from the pleasant river of life and parked in a black hole. Sunday crawled by, second by second. Monday lasted even longer.

By evening, Howie had decided he would rather go hungry than eat what passed for dinner at the San Geronimo jail—thin slices of unidentifiable meat in a glutinous brown sauce, green beans from the can, reconstituted mashed potatoes—when Manny, the guard who sold drugs, came for him.

"You need to come with me, Moon Deer. Lieutenant Ruben is here to see you."

Howie followed dutifully and found both Santo and Jack waiting for him in an administrative office at the end of a hallway.

"How's the jailbird?" Santo asked. "I trust you found life in the slammer instructive?"

"I learned a lot," Howie told him. "From now on, I'm going to be on the straight and narrow."

"Sure, you will. Well, we've come to get you out. You'll be glad to know your old girlfriend retracted her story. It seems she didn't see you outside her father's study at three in the morning after all. It was Justin's idea to make you the fall guy and clear the family name. We're definitely planning to have a word with him. Lucky for you, Grace couldn't go through with it. When she heard Nick was dead, she lost her appetite for lies."

Howie shook his head. "Grace!" he said mournfully.

"Don't take it so badly. It seems she still has a soft spot for you in her hard-boiled heart. Now, here's something else you need to know. We found an abandoned ranch out on Forest Road 213 where Nick Stanton was holing up. There was a girl there who's been living with him. A little thing. Underage, I'm betting. Dan believes she's undocumented. I think she knows a lot of what Nick's been up to these last few months, but she won't talk with us, only a few monosyllables. We don't even know her name yet. You speak some Spanish, don't you, Howie?"

"A little," he said.

"Good," said Santo. "I'd like you to try your hand at talking to her."

"Why me?"

"Because you have a much better chance of getting her to trust you than we do. Tell her that you were Nick's friend. Lay it on thick, if you need to. How you were blood brothers and all that. Come on, Howie. We're waiting on you. Let's go."

"Wait a second! You mean, right *now*?"

"You bet now. We're holding her at the station and I need to get her sorted out quickly."

"I don't know, Santo. Frankly, all I want to do is eat a decent meal, take a shower, and get a good night's sleep. Do you have any idea what those jail bunks are like?"

"No time for that, I'm afraid," said Santo. "You can sleep all you want when you're dead."

Chapter Twenty-Six

Howie took a deep sniff of night air. It was clear and cold and wonderful. There was nothing like a couple of days in jail to make you appreciate the huge New Mexican sky. But Santo and Jack hurried him along.

The San Geronimo New Mexico State Police outpost had to be the ugliest building in town: a square, one-story cinderblock structure with few windows and a roof bristling with electronics. The compound was surrounded by a high cyclone fence with rolls of razor wire on top. It was a place Howie avoided whenever possible.

The girl Santo had found in the abandoned ranch was parked in his office with Sally Loeb to watch over her. She hadn't been charged yet with any crime. Probably they could nail her for trespassing, but for the moment Santo was proceeding gently.

Howie found her sitting primly in a straight-back chair, her hands folded in her lap. She was Latina, very young, sixteen or seventeen, more like a pretty doll than a woman. She regarded Howie with large waif-like brown eyes.

She hadn't said a word since she had been picked up, and Santo had been unable to tell Howie anything about her. There was evidence that she and Nick had been camping out together in the abandoned ranch for a number of days, burning furniture in the pot-belly iron stove to stay warm. Santo led Howie into the office and then he and Sally left the room, closing the door behind them. Howie settled behind Santo's desk and faced the girl. Her waifish eyes followed him intently.

Howie's Spanish was far from fluent. But he gave it his best shot.

"Hola," he said. *"No soy policia. Mi nombre es Howie Moon Deer y era amigo de Nick en el universidad. Lo siento mi español no es muy bueno."*

The girl continued to stare at him.

"*Me entiendes?*" he asked.

"I understand you very well," she answered in perfect English. "University is a feminine noun, by the way. *La universidad*, not *el universidad*."

"I struggle with the gender of Spanish nouns," he admitted.

"Nick told me about you. He said if anything happened to him, I could trust you," she said. "Can you get me out of here?"

"I don't know," he answered truthfully. "It depends on what you've done."

"I haven't done anything! I came to New Mexico to be with Nick. Is that against the law?"

"It is if you've been helping to hide a fugitive."

"I didn't know he was a fugitive until I got here. I thought he was just a trippy guy."

"You know he's dead, don't you?"

"Yeah," she said simply, no drama, no tears. "I heard the pigs talking about it."

Pigs? Howie hadn't heard that expression for years. The love generation hadn't always been so loving. He studied the girl more closely, but her face was a mask.

"So, you were Nick's girlfriend, I suppose?"

"*Girl*friend? What century are you from? We hooked-up, that's all. We were hanging out."

"Okay, hanging out," he agreed. "Sounds romantic. When did this hooking up occur?"

She shrugged. "A few months ago. We met in Portland at a protest. The pigs were tear-gassing us and I couldn't breathe. I have asthma. He saw I was struggling and he picked me up and carried me down the street to where the air was good."

Howie had to laugh, imagining Nick in this swashbuckling role. Probably getting tear-gassed together was as good a way to start a modern relationship as you were going to find. Better than flirting in a bar.

"What's your name?" he asked.

"Why?"

"I can't just call you, hey you."

"You don't have to call me anything. But if that bothers you, you can call me Zero."

"Zero? As in nothing?"

"You can look at it that way. I see Zero as freedom. An empty page that you fill. A fresh start."

"Okay, I'll call you Zero. But Lieutenant Ruben is going to want more than that. Like the name your parents gave you when you were born."

She shrugged. "He can want all he likes. What he gets is something else."

"So, you're a revolutionary, huh?"

"Don't you want to change the world? You accept the shit that's going down?"

Howie smiled. "I'm starting to see what drew you and Nick together. How long have you been in Portland?"

"I grew up there. Why does that matter?"

"How about Nick?" he asked. "Was he living there, too?"

"He'd been hanging out in the mountains somewhere. But I don't know for sure. We didn't talk about the past much."

"And you didn't know he was on the run?"

"Not at first, but it wouldn't have mattered. So, look, are you going to help me get out of here, or what? He said you were his blood brother."

Howie was starting to regret that long-ago cutting of fingers. "He was a good friend once," he answered. "Did he tell you we were roommates at college?"

"Yeah, at some snooty white-privilege dump in New Hampshire!"

"Just for the record, Dartmouth started out as an Indian school. And you can get a pretty good education there, no matter the color of your skin."

"Whatever," she said, sizing him up in a new way. There was a speculative glint in her eye that was worrisome. "So, I'm going to need a place to crash when I get out of here. You don't have a spare part of a mattress, do you?"

Howie was stunned by the frankly sexual appraisal she gave him.

"No, I don't," he said firmly. "But I'll do my best to get you back to Portland, where I think you'll be happier than you are here. But you have to help me. I need information. Why did Nick say he was coming to New Mexico?"

She gave him the look again. The frank appraisal. For an androgynous revolutionary street-waif, she knew how to send signals.

"Will you give me money to get back to Portland?"

"I will, I'll help you get home. If I can convince Santo to let you go. But you need to answer my question. Why did Nick say he was coming to New Mexico?"

"To get the trust money his grandfather left him. And to see his sister. He wanted to see you, too."

"How did you get here from Oregon?"

"We drove his car. It's an old Jeep, a real junk heap. But it has four-wheel drive."

"Where is it now?"

"It's in the shed behind the old house where the pigs found me. We drove in before the snow started. I don't think it would make it now."

"How did you find that old ranch? It's in the middle of nowhere."

"His sister knew about it. She sent Nick the directions how to get there."

"Really? He'd been in touch with Grace?"

"I guess. I don't really know."

"Did he see her while he was here?"

"Don't know that either. He was in and out a few times, but he didn't say where he went."

"He left you alone up there in the woods?"

"Yeah. It was kind of a drag, really. But I liked him enough to go along."

"Did you know he came to my house with a note that he wanted me to give to his sister?"

"Sure. He said you'd had a thing with Grace once, and you'd be hot to see her."

Howie shook his head. "I was *not* hot to see her. It wasn't that at all, okay?"

She smiled. "If you say so."

"Did you read the note he wrote?"

"No."

"So, you don't know what was in it?"

"No. Nick was kind of mysterious about everything. But I like mysterious guys. I like Indians, too," she added.

Howie did his best to bat that last comment away. He kept at her for some time, but she didn't appear to know much. According to the girl, she came to New Mexico because she thought Nick was cool and she wanted to be with him. That was the extent of it, she wasn't privy to his plans. Meanwhile, she wasn't the sentimental type. Now that Nick was gone, she was ready to change horses in mid-stream, so to speak.

"One of the things I like about Indians," she said, "is you're part of the oppressed classes."

"You're going to be oppressed, too, if you don't give the cops more than this. We need to figure out who Nick saw while he was here. And who he made angry enough to kill him."

She shrugged.

"Let's go over this again," he said. "You were here with Nick for how many days?"

She had to think about this. She counted on her fingers. "Eleven days," she decided. "We got here on Wednesday, the week before Thanksgiving."

"Okay, how many times did Nick go off and leave you alone at that abandoned ranch?"

She had to count on her fingers again. "There was that one time when he went to see you . . . and then that second time . . . three times," she said.

"Coming to see me was the first time?"

"Yeah."

"And the second time?"

"Don't know."

"The third time?"

"Well, that was Thanksgiving. He said he was going to see his family. He left on Wednesday and got back late Friday. He seemed upset but he didn't say why. When I asked too many questions, he got mad at me."

Howie considered this information. Assuming it was true, the first time he left Zero on her own, Nick had come to see him. How he had discovered where Howie lived, he didn't know. Most likely, he had tracked him down on the Internet.

On the Wednesday before Thanksgiving, Nick had gone to the Stanton ranch where he stayed two nights. On Friday he had returned late to their hideout in the woods, which left him with enough time to drop off the note at Howie's pod leaving him the GPS coordinates for their rendezvous on Saturday.

This left Nick's second excursion unexplained.

"The second time he left," Howie said. "When was that?"

Again, the counting on the fingers. "Let's see, we got here Wednesday . . . Wednesday, Thursday, Friday, Saturday, Sunday . . . it was Sunday! Sunday afternoon."

"Do you think he went to see Grace?"

"No, I had the impression it was a man."

"A man? Did he say anything about this man?"

She shook her head. "No, but he made a kind of joke I didn't really get. About seeing a ghost."

"A ghost?" he prodded.

"I remember now. Ghost Ranch, that's what he said. He said he was going to see a ghost at Ghost Ranch."

"A ghost? This is important. Did he say anything else?"

"No, just that. I didn't know what he was talking about. I mean, there's no ranch for ghosts, is there?"

"There is, actually. Ghost Ranch in Abiquiu. It's not far from here. Georgia O'Keefe lived there before she died, but it's owned now by the Presbyterian church. They use the place for workshops."

"Who's Georgia O'Keefe?" Zero asked.

"An artist," Howie told her. "A very good artist, as a matter of fact."

"Art is bourgeois decadence," she informed him.

Howie let that go. He was thinking hard about Nick's so-called joke, that he was going to see a ghost at Ghost Ranch. There was a caretaker at Ghost Ranch, and, if a workshop had been in session, there would be possible witnesses. With luck, they might discover who this ghost was.

"Look, I'm going to need a place to sleep," she reminded him. "Are you sure you can't put me up?"

"I'll put you in a motel," he told her.

She shook her head sadly, as though Howie didn't know what he was missing. In fact, he could imagine it all too well.

Her eyes hardened. "Will it have an indoor pool?"

Howie sighed. "You have a swimsuit?"

"I'll let you buy me one."

***

By the time Howie got home that night, his mind was a fuzzy mush. It was nearly midnight. He was exhausted, brain dead, beyond caring about anything except getting to bed as quickly as possible.

But first he had to feed his cat. Orange was sitting on the kitchen table giving him a dirty look.

"I was in jail, okay?" he told her, not about to put up with her abuse. "You should have seen the food they gave me there! A bologna sandwich! On white bread! So, don't look at me like that."

I'll look at you any way I want! she told him.

Or maybe she didn't say that. Maybe he was so tired he only imagined it. Nevertheless, he opened a can of albacore tuna hoping to make amends. She turned her back on him while she ate.

Howie was so tired, he almost didn't brush his teeth. "Come on, I can miss one goddamn night!" he told the bathroom mirror.

"No way, dude!" the mirror said back at him. "Miss one night, then you'll miss the next night, and before you know it, your whole life will go down the tubes!"

Mirrors don't lie, so Howie brushed his teeth. Once this was out of the way, he climbed the ladder to his loft and stretched out on his bed with a mighty groan.

After his interview with Zero, the pint-sized groupie revolutionary, he had spent an hour with Santo and Jack, who had appeared at the station driven by Buzzy. Howie told them what he had learned from Zero, including the interesting news that Nick had met someone, a man apparently, at Ghost Ranch on the Sunday afternoon before Thanksgiving. Santo said he would send Dan to Abiquiu first thing in the morning to question the staff there. Ghost Ranch was a busy place, a big tourist draw for Georgia O'Keefe fans, and with luck, there might be CCTV footage showing who Nick had met.

The other interesting news concerned Ramona. Santo had sent Dan to do some checking in the State Police archives, and it was now solidly established that she was Ralph White's older sister and that she had been detained as a possible accomplice in the murder of Matthew Cordell, the headmaster of the Indian School, before Commissioner Adam Stanton had used his position to get her released into his care. Meanwhile, there was no sign of Ramona anywhere. She hadn't returned to the Stanton Ranch and it appeared likely that she was on the run. Santo had already put out an APB to pick her up.

All in all, there was a lot to think about, including why Justin wanted Grace to lie about Howie coming out of Senator Stanton's study at three in the morning, but Howie was beyond caring. After his session with Santo and Jack, he used Jack's rented Kia to drive home. He would need to rent a car of his own tomorrow since his old Subaru would be in the shop for at least a week, but all he wanted now, his entire aim in life, was to sleep.

At least Orange was in a better mood after finishing the can of tuna. She climbed up the ladder to the loft, wrapped herself around Howie's head, and purred loudly. Howie rolled over on his side, gently so he wouldn't disturb her. He moved her front paw from his nose and quickly fell into a deep void.

It was after one in the afternoon when Howie woke to discover a tongue licking his ear. It was an odd sensation. He'd been dreaming about Claire and at first, in his sleep-deprived confusion, he thought she was in bed with him. But it wasn't Claire who woke him. It was Orange.

"Stop that!" he told her. "Stop that right now!"

As soon as he was halfway awake, he turned on his phone to find three voice messages from Jack. The wording in each message differed slightly, but they all said basically the same thing: "Where the hell are you, Howie? Get to the office as soon as you can!"

He dragged himself out of bed, wishing he'd had another hour or two of sleep. He lingered long enough to make a pot of coffee and pour it into a thermos for the forty-minute drive into town.

"How kind of you to drop by," said Jack, his usual acerbic self. "Have you had breakfast yet? We could send out for Eggs Benedict if you like."

"Jack, save it. It's been a rough few days."

"Well, I have some news. We've made progress while you were sleeping. Santo located Ramona. Guess where she ran off to?"

"I can't guess, Jack. So why don't you tell me?"

"The Pine Ridge reservation in South Dakota. She went home."

"*Home*?"

"Exactly. We've unearthed a good deal more about her from the old State Police files. Both Ramona and her brother were originally from Pine Ridge, which makes them Lakota, your people. Santo found her because she used her credit card to buy gas in Chadron, a town that's just south of the reservation. It's on the Nebraska side of the border. Santo has a friend in the highway patrol up there who picked her up at a motel where she was spending the night. Once again, her credit card gave her away."

"That wasn't very smart for somebody on the run."

"Yeah, but that's the problem, you see. She claims she wasn't running. She says she just had an overwhelming desire to get back to her roots. The way she drove away from the ranch, it was like a lifetime of suppressed anger finally burst. Says she was fed up with the white man's evil ways, and she wasn't going to take it anymore."

"I don't blame her," Howie said. "I'm getting sick of the white man's evil ways myself! What else did she have to say for herself?"

"Not much. Dan's flying up there now and hopefully he'll get more out of her."

"Santo's bringing her back to San Geronimo?"

"At the moment, no. He'd have to get an extradition order from Nebraska, and right now he doesn't have probable cause. Whatever else Ramona might have done, I don't figure her for killing Nick. Maybe she offed the Senator, but that seems a stretch, too. If it was a revenge killing of some sort, I still can't imagine why she'd wait fifty years and then off the son of the man who abused her."

"What about the Ghost Ranch meeting that Zero told us about? The one between Nick and the mysterious stranger? Has Santo checked that out yet?"

"He's working on it. He and Sally are at Ghost Ranch as we speak. The good news is that there *are* CCTV cameras at the ranch to protect the old Georgia O'Keefe studio. So, he's optimistic he might discover who the mystery man is."

Howie did his best to suppress a yawn, but it got the better of him. It was a noisy yawn that spanned a few octaves and lasted a while.

"Am I boring you?"

"Not at all, Jack. I'm still tired, that's all."

"Well, good—you'll be able to sleep on the plane."

"Excuse me? What plane?"

"The red eye to Miami with a change to West Palm Beach. I've already made your reservation. I'm afraid there won't be any time for you to bask on the beach. You'll fly back the same night. I can't spare you any longer than that."

Howie groaned. "This doesn't sound like the vacation of my dreams. But why, Jack? Why?"

"I want you to talk to Anne Stanton in person. She has a condo at The Breakers and I want you to find out what she knows about Ramona. Anne married Harlan in 1975 when Adam was still alive, so if anybody can tell us about that old Indian school murder and what happened afterwards, she can. You've known Anne for quite a few years, Howie. You need to get her to open up her box of family secrets."

"That's wishful thinking. Those aristocratic old ladies don't give away secrets easily. And aren't we spending a lot of time and money on a case where we don't even have a client?"

"Howie, let's chalk this one up to curiosity. Don't you want to know who killed your old roommate Nick?"

Howie had to admit that yes, he did.

Chapter Twenty-Seven

Howie had the narrow middle seat on the flight from Albuquerque to Miami, squeezed between a large man with a pudgy face on the aisle and small elderly women by the window. The pudgy man was dressed in shorts and T-shirt, despite the fact that it was late November. Where he had come from, it was impossible to say. Another solar system perhaps. He was reading a magazine called *Guns & Ammo*, breathing heavily over photographs of assault rifles.

As for the elderly woman by the window, she was small and gray with a pinched face and sharp nose, reading a tabloid newspaper spread open on her lap. Howie managed to glance at the open page without appearing to do so. HILLARY GIVES BIRTH TO SATANIC TRIPLETS! proclaimed the banner headline. Howie looked away quickly. It was a challenge these days to set forth into mid-America.

They flew into turbulence somewhere above Alabama that was so severe Howie hoped the wings weren't going to fall off. It didn't help that a baby began screaming two rows back. Nevertheless, he lowered his arm rests to protect his few inches of space, closed his eyes, and managed to drift into a restless half-sleep. It wasn't easy to sleep in the middle seat with the back raised in what the flight attendants called "an upright position." He could only hope he didn't slump forward into a neighbor's lap. Theoretically, he could lower his seat back a notch, but in economy class there was so little room you could crush the person's knees behind you or get a knife in your back.

From Miami, Howie caught a commuter flight to West Palm Beach where he rented a compact car at the airport, a Chevy Nova. He was tempted to get a Mustang convertible at twice the price. He could picture himself with the top down, a la *Miami Vice*, his ponytail flying in the tropical breeze, but Jack was a stickler when it came to expenses.

It was after four in the afternoon Florida time when Howie set off across the inland waterway toward Palm Beach proper. The afternoon was blazing hot, which was a jolt after northern New Mexico. Of course, that's why people came here, escaping cold and discomfort. Howie was a four-season person himself. For him, summer was meaningless without winter. He had never been to Florida before and he didn't think he would move here.

The voice on his iPhone guided him to South Ocean Boulevard where he drove north for several miles with the blue Atlantic on one side and ponderously sleepy mansions on the other. There were plenty of skinny palm trees with shaggy tops swaying in the wind. It was said that Henry Flagler, one of the founders of Standard Oil, had burned down a Negro shantytown here to make room for the white and the wealthy. Howie didn't know if the story was true, but the white and the wealthy had certainly filled the void.

The Breakers was one of America's grand old resort hotels with rooms starting at a thousand dollars a night. Howie had called ahead and Anne Stanton was expecting him. She lived in a luxury condo on the north side of the hotel proper, a spacious, airy residence with sliding glass doors that opened onto the beach. A young woman in a very short tennis skirt met him at the door. She had dark hair, dark eyes, dimples on her cheeks, and a soft Spanish accent.

"Please come this way," she told him. "I'm Esmeralda, Mrs. Stanton's personal assistant. She will see you on the patio."

Esmeralda led him through a living room that had white furniture, white walls, and only an occasional dash of color. They passed through a sliding screen door onto a patio that was shaded by palm trees and lush tropical plants. The ocean was visible beyond a low hedge. The sound of children's voices drifted through the flowery air from the beach.

"Please," said Esmeralda, indicating a wicker armchair with yellow cushions beneath a large yellow sun umbrella. She leaned intimately closer. "May I get you something?" Her voice was almost a whisper. "Perhaps a cold drink?

Howie found the girl frankly unnerving. "I'm . . . well, how about a glass of water," he managed.

"Sparkling or still?" she inquired.

"Just plain old water, please."

She smiled as though they shared a secret. "I'll go see if Mrs. Stanton is ready to see you."

Howie wasn't sure he was ready for Palm Beach. Along with the wealth, there was a disturbing undercurrent of decadence in the air. Anne Stanton appeared a moment later dressed in a loose yellow shift that was the same color as the umbrella and the cushions. He was shocked by her appearance. She looked ten years older than when he had seen her just a week ago at Thanksgiving. Her walk was hesitant and there was a lost look on her face. She had become a frail old woman almost overnight.

He stood to greet her.

"How nice of you to come all this way to see me, Howard," Anne said as she settled into a matching wicker armchair. Her voice was nearly as frail as her body. "You were such a good friend to Nicolas! Please, sit down."

"I'm so sorry about Nick," he told her. "And the Senator, of course. This must be terrible for you. I don't know what to say."

She shook her head and seemed at first unable to answer. He watched as she gathered her energy and made an attempt to be the imperious, patrician woman he had always known.

"Nicolas . . . my sweet Nicolas! Oh, Howard, there's nothing worse—nothing!—than for a mother to lose a child she loves!"

"I'm so sorry," he said again, not knowing what else to say. He couldn't imagine the grief of losing a child. He noticed, however, that her grief didn't appear to extend to her ex-husband.

Esmeralda appeared with a glass of water and a platter of shrimp on ice with a small bowl of red cocktail sauce and toothpicks that had frilly plastic flags of different colors on the ends. The water had a slice of lemon in the glass and ice.

"Are you certain you won't have a real drink?" Anne asked.

"No, thank you, I'm fine. Mrs. Stanton, I was with Nick when he died, and I want you to know that he was in a very good place emotionally. He was full of plans for the future, determined to make a new life for himself."

Anne closed her eyes. "What makes me so sad is that all he wanted from me was money!" she said faintly. "Money, money . . . once my children were grown up, I never saw them except when they needed money. And now my family is being killed off one by one!"

Howie studied her. "You think somebody is deliberately killing off your family?"

She opened her eyes and gave him a shrewd look. "Well, it does seem that way, doesn't it? Do you think the police will be able to stop this person before he does any more killing?"

"They're making good progress. And my boss, Jack Wilder, is giving it his best effort, too. Now, the reason I'm here is because we've become increasingly curious about Ramona, the old Indian woman who works on the ranch. I know this must be difficult for you, but if you're up to answering a few questions, it would be very helpful for the investigation."

"Yes, of course, Howard. Please, I want to help. Ask whatever you like. You wouldn't know it today, but Ramona was very pretty when she was young. She was fifteen when I first saw her. The ranch hands couldn't keep their eyes off her! But why are you interested in Ramona?"

"She took a runner, I'm afraid, which has caused Lieutenant Ruben to take a closer look at her. The police picked her up not far from the Pine Ridge Reservation in South Dakota, which is where she was from originally. We've learned that she and her brother were placed at the Indian school that was located on the property where the Stanton Ranch is now. Ramona's brother was Ralph White, the boy who killed the headmaster of the boarding school. At the time, the police suspected Ramona of being his accomplice, and they held her until your father-in-law, Adam, managed to get her released."

"You've done your homework, Howard. These are old matters, long forgotten."

"Old crimes cast long shadows, Mrs. Stanton. You can still find accounts of the 1970 murder in newspaper archives. And old State Police files, of course. Can you tell me why the Commissioner took such an interest in her?"

"I should think that's obvious. Adam was a horny old goat. And he liked girls who were very young."

"He was a pedophile, in other words."

"Pedophile? Well, perhaps. Of course, Ramona looked much older than her age. She was developed, you might say."

"How did he convince the authorities to release her into his care?"

"That wasn't so hard back then. Adam was an important man in New Mexico, and ultimately, as BIA Commissioner, he was the person who was responsible for those children. You have to understand, Howard—

he was besotted with her. He even made some evidence disappear so he could bring her to the ranch and have her close by."

"Evidence?" She spoke so softly that Howie wanted to make sure he had heard right. "What evidence did he make disappear?"

Her smile had a hard edge. "Dear little Ramona wasn't as innocent as she pretended. She gave her brother the knife that he used to kill the headmaster. You see, the girls at the school worked in the kitchen where they had access to knives. The kitchen supervisor had discovered that one of the knives was missing and he suspected that Ramona had taken it, but Adam paid him a bit of money to keep his mouth shut. He was the ultimate boss and the staff did what he told them. Ramona would certainly have gone to juvenile detention if Adam hadn't helped conceal her part in the crime. He held this over her afterwards, of course. It was at least part of the reason that she complied with his wishes."

"But that's incredible!" Howie said. "Why haven't you told anyone about this before?"

"Why? Because I was a loyal Stanton, loyal to the clan. We kept our family secrets. I'm only talking now because the family is dying off at such an alarming rate. And I'm concerned about Grace, of course."

"Grace does seem to be going through a difficult period," Howie admitted. "She told me she's having a hard time finishing her new book. But Mrs. Stanton, how do you know about Ramona giving her brother the knife? Did she tell you this herself?"

"No, it was Adam who told me. You have to understand, when I married Harlan, I was a young woman myself. And I was rather attractive myself back then, if I'm allowed to say such a thing."

It took Howie a moment to absorb this. "You're saying your father-in-law came on to you?"

"That's putting it mildly. I hardly dared go into the barn to saddle my horse. He used to come up behind me and grab my breasts."

"That's terrible!"

"Well, Howard, there are no rules for the arrogant and Adam did what he liked. Harlan didn't object because he needed his father's money."

"So, Adam actually told you about what he did to help Ramona?"

"Oh, yes, he bragged about it. To me, at least. He wanted to impress me with his power. He was quite a despicable man, really. When he got Ramona pregnant, he made her give the baby away."

"*What*?" Howie interjected. "Ramona had Adam's child?" This was starting to look like a family trait, getting rid of inconvenient children.

"You didn't know that? It was common knowledge in the family, though we all kept quiet about it. Adam sent her away to some place to have the baby. It was a boy."

"Good God, this changes everything!" Howie said.

"Does it?"

"Of course. This child, wherever he is, is Harlan's half-brother!"

"Well, it was cruel for Adam to force her to give the child away. He held that knife business over her head, of course."

"But why did she stay on the ranch all these years after Adam died? Once he was gone, she was free to do what she wanted."

"Well, caged birds sometimes don't fly away when the cage door opens. Ramona had very little education, no skills, and little confidence that she could survive in an outside world she didn't know. So, she accepted her lot. And of course, Adam provided for her in his will, and he left a letter for her to open after his death saying where her child was."

Howie was almost afraid to ask the next question.

"Ramona found her son?"

"Oh, yes. He was in Oklahoma, not that far away. Adam had arranged for the boy to be brought up by a family who were beholden to him in a number of ways. They were Mexican immigrants, hard-working people—Adam set them up in a restaurant in Tulsa that was quite successful. After his death, Ramona brought the boy to live with her at the ranch."

"So, what happened to this boy?" Howie asked. "Where is he now?"

"Don't you know? He's still on the ranch, of course."

"What do you mean? There's nobody on the—"

Howie stopped mid-sentence, because the answer came to him just as Anne Stanton was putting it into words.

"It's Tucker, the man who works with the horses and does odd jobs around the ranch. Not a very pleasant individual, actually. You probably met him when you came for Thanksgiving. Tucker is Ramona's son. Harlan's half-brother."

As well as the uncle of Nick, Grace, and Justin, Howie realized.

One of the family!

***

Seagulls floated on the late afternoon breeze above the blue Atlantic. Children shrieked as they splashed in the surf. The sun was golden. Without really noticing what he was doing, Howie managed to finish off the platter of cocktail shrimp, plucking them up one by one.

They spoke for nearly another forty minutes, but Howie learned nothing new. He had gotten what he had come for—more, in fact, much more—and he was impatient to phone Jack. Finally, Anne Stanton walked him from the patio back inside her light-filled living room.

"I'm going to tell Esmeralda to wrap up a care package for you, Howard," she told him. "There's half a roast chicken sitting in the fridge that needs a home. I wouldn't want you to starve to death."

"Mrs. Stanton, I'm fine . . ."

"Clearly, you're not. You need a woman around to feed you properly. I'll be right back."

Despite his objections, Anne disappeared into another part of her condo to ask her assistant to make up a food package. Not sure what to do with himself, Howie wandered toward a side table crowded with framed photographs of the Stanton family at various ages. He stopped in front of an 8 X 10 black and white photograph of Grace at the age of 18 or so, looking very much the way he remembered her when they first met. It brought back a surge of memory, how lovely she had been, how much he had wanted her.

In the photograph, she was standing in front of a college building with half a dozen other girls and two tweedy looking men. The taller man Howie recognized as Philip Roth, the famous author. The other man, shorter in stature, was familiar also, though Howie couldn't quite place him. Another author, maybe? John Cheever? No, he didn't think so.

He was still studying the framed photograph when Anne returned to the room with half a chicken wrapped up in aluminum foil in a Saks Fifth Avenue bag.

"That's Grace her Sophomore year at Smith," Anne said. "How young she looks! It was taken after some sort of writer's conference with Philip Roth."

"But who's this other fellow?" he asked, pointing to the shorter man.

"You don't recognize him? You sat next to him at Thanksgiving. That's Stephen Halley."

"*Halley*?" Howie studied the photograph more closely and saw it was true. Stephen had gained weight, his face had filled out, but it was him, an earlier version.

"He was her literature professor at Smith. Grace was barely eighteen and she found him terribly romantic. Stephen was only thirty-two then, so it wasn't really such an age gap. She always liked older men. It's the Daddy's girl syndrome, I'm afraid."

"They were . . ."

"Lovers, yes, of course," Anne said when Howie balked at the word. "He had published two novels with small presses, though they only sold a handful of copies and certainly didn't support him. That's why he was teaching. I'm sure she believed he was a genius. They had to keep their affair secret, of course, which added to the allure. But it was a stormy relationship, full of tears and drama. God only knows how many times they broke up and got back together again!"

"Grace was a stormy girl," Howie added.

"Yes, she was. And stormy girls can be very attractive to a certain kind of man. Like you, Howard."

He shook his head. "I plead youth," he told her. "Luckily, I grew up."

Anne nodded approvingly. "That makes you a whole lot smarter than Stephen. He never got over her. Even after she got him fired from Smith."

"Are you serious? She got him fired?"

"After one of their fights. She caught him flirting with one of the girls in the class. So she went to the dean and said he had seduced her. Frankly, I suspect it was the other way around. This was before the Me-Too movement so they let Stephen go quietly. My daughter can be vengeful when she's crossed."

Howie thought back to the first time he had met Grace, when he and Nick had taken off together from Dartmouth for a long weekend in New York. She had mentioned then that she was just getting over a relationship. It must have been Stephen.

"In any case, Stephen survived. He believed he was the next Hemingway, so he went to New York, moved into an apartment in the East

Village, and set about writing the Great American Novel. It was turned down by every publishing house in the city. But one of the editors who refused his book ended up giving him an entry level job as an assistant editor. From there he worked his way up the publishing ladder until he got his own imprint at Peckham & Peale. Of course, it helped that he had taught literature at a prestigious Ivy League college. New York publishers didn't care a hoot that he'd had sex with his students. It only added to his allure."

"But what happened to Stephen and Grace?" he asked. "That wasn't the end of their romance?"

"Not a bit. They were addicted to one another. They couldn't let it alone. Some people need melodrama or they're bored. All their fights, all the breaking up and getting back together—it gave them the zest they needed to feel alive."

"When I saw Grace at the book party in Santa Fe for Harlan, she told me she was just getting over someone. Was that—"

"Stephen? Perhaps, I don't know for certain. We haven't been talking much the last few years. Of course, the whole thing between them had become more complicated now that they had a business relationship as well. As you know, Stephen was her editor at Peckham & Peale."

"Right, and the Senator's editor as well. Isn't that all a bit—"

"A bit too cozy? Oh, I suppose so. And I imagine Stephen is going to lose money on Harlan's book, which won't be good for his career. He's risen in the publishing world, but New York's a jungle—a few flops and you're out."

Howie took his chicken in its Saks Fifth Avenue bag and left. Anne had given him a great deal to think about and he was so distracted that he ended up forgetting the bag on a seat in the airport outside Gate 47.

Unfortunately, what you forget can be more of a problem than what you remember. A bomb squad was called, and an entire wing of the

West Palm Beach airport was closed for twenty minutes while the authorities investigated the possibility of a foul plot to blow up the terminal.

Luckily for Howie, he was in the sky by then, on his way home.

Chapter Twenty-Eight

Howie flew home West Palm Beach to Miami, Miami to Dallas, Dallas to Albuquerque. With the layovers and the three-hour drive to San Geronimo, he didn't get to the office until three the following afternoon.

He found Jack behind his desk and Buzzy in the client's chair, both of them in a celebratory mood. They were just finishing a late lunch, a large pizza. There was a single slice remaining in the flat cardboard box on the edge of Jack's desk. It was pepperoni with no additional toppings, which wasn't Howie's idea of gourmet. Still, he was about to make a grab for it when Jack reached first and put it on a plate on the floor for Katya.

Howie watched sadly as Katya gobbled it up.

"So, let's hear about Florida," Jack urged. "I hope you were having fun in the sun while the rest of us were working our butts off, solving this double murder."

"Jack, except for a few hours on the ground, I've been flying nearly nonstop for the past twenty-four hours. With the time changes, my inner clock is spinning like a roulette wheel. But thank you very much for your concern."

"Did you get the old lady to open up?"

"I did. Do you want to hear what I learned, or do you need to digest that pizza first?"

"Sorry, Howie. You tell us your revelations, then we'll tell you ours."

"Okay, let me start with the biggie. Not only was Ramona Adam Stanton's 14-year-old girlfriend, he got her pregnant and she had his child. He forced her to give the baby away, which is a kind of Stanton trademark. When you're a famous family like that, you have your fun, then you get rid of any evidence of your crimes."

"Go on. I sense there's more."

"Well, it turns out Commissioner Stanton wasn't a totally heartless schmuck after all. When he died, he left a letter for Ramona telling her where the child was. He'd parked the kid with a Mexican family in Oklahoma who were in his debt for one thing or another. He gave them enough money to open a restaurant for their trouble. Ramona found her son and brought him back to live with her at the ranch. Now, would you like to know who this child turned out to be?

Jack was paying close attention now. "Okay, Howie, out with it."

"It's the stable hand, Tucker. He uses the last name of his foster parents, Cordova. Tucker Cordova. But he's a Stanton, all right—Adam's son, Harlan's half-brother. Only while Harlan graduated from Yale and got himself elected to the Senate, Tucker was left cleaning muck from horse stalls. Maybe this gave him some unresolved anger issues. What do you think?"

Jack nodded. "Okay, good work, Howie. This confirms what we've been learning the last two days. Sally went to Ghost Ranch yesterday and got hold of the CCTV tape for the Sunday before Thanksgiving. And guess what, we got a hit. There are three cameras at the ranch going twenty-four/seven and one of them picked up Nick Stanton sitting on a bench outside the O'Keefe studio talking to Tucker. There was no sound, so we don't know what they said to each other, but they were together for nearly forty minutes."

"So, is this it? Is Tucker our guy?"

"Possibly. We still don't know about the poison pen letters, of course, but after what you just told me, I wouldn't be surprised if he wrote them. It wouldn't have been easy over the years for him to watch Grace and Nick and Justin get all the perks, and him get nothing. But we're not done yet. Santo is getting a court order to unseal Adam Stanton's will and any documents that concern the trust. Up to now, we've only heard about these things secondhand. The documents are in a safe with the family's attorney in Santa Fe. Ramona has agreed to return voluntarily to New Mexico and I think that once we get her talking, and we see the papers in that vault, this will be a closed case."

"Wouldn't that be nice?" Howie said. But doubt rumbled through his mind like far off thunder, and he had a premonition it wasn't going to be so easy.

***

Howie returned to his office in the front of the building and tried to analyze what was bothering him. He was tired, jet-lagged, it was hard for him to focus. But he had a sense he'd forgotten something.

It came to him ten minutes later. He had forgotten to tell Jack about the photograph he'd seen in Anne Stanton's living room of Grace at the age of eighteen standing with Philip Roth, one of America's great literary luminaries, and Stephen Halley, a wannabe luminary. Grace's lover.

Howie stood up intending to return to Jack's office to tell him about the photograph. But then he sat down again, deciding to wait. The truth was, the photograph most likely had no particular importance except to Howie.

Grace had been very much the sort of girl who would have an affair with her literature professor, and Stephen was the sort of professor who would have an affair with a student. It was a clichéd situation. Somehow it was always the literature professor that girls had affairs with, never the chemistry teacher.

The chances were, none of this had any relevance to the murders they were trying to solve. Still, he thought he might do a bit of Internet research on Stephen, if only to satisfy his curiosity.

Halley wasn't a celebrity, so there wasn't much about him online. There were perhaps a dozen postings, as well as a Facebook page. The Facebook postings were strictly professional, promoting books he had published on his imprint at Peckham & Peale. Grace Stanton was his biggest star and each of her *Girl* thrillers had been given a large display with snippets of glowing reviews and reproductions of their cover art.

Howie noted that the good reviews—from *Kirkus, Publisher's Weekly, The New York Times* and such—were all for her early novels. The later efforts mostly came with quotes from other authors, most of whom—suspiciously—were Peckham & Peale writers. A clear indication that the series was no longer getting as much attention as it had at the start.

Stephen had other authors as well whose books he touted on his Facebook page. There were mysteries, a few literary novels, and several non-fiction titles that were focused on politics and social issues. But Howie was surprised to see that there was nothing about Senator Stanton's memoir, *The Right Way*.

The other online postings dealt with Halley's career as a New York editor. There was an article in *Publisher's Weekly* about the launch of his imprint at Peckham & Peale, Sirius Books—which struck Howie as an awful pun. Several online blogs had to do with speeches he had given at conferences, books fairs, and such.

Howie was still reading at 5 o'clock when Ruth left the office, and he was still at it when Jack, Katya, and Buzzy left for the day forty minutes later, calling goodbye as they went out the door. Howie liked being alone in the building, the peace and quiet, but he still found nothing of any particular interest about Stephen Halley.

Until he came across an interview from twelve years ago in an industry publication called *Writer's Digest*. Here at last was information of a personal nature, a short biography.

Howie had assumed that Halley came from a well-educated upper middle class background. He had that look about him. But it wasn't the case. To his surprise, Halley was from a rough corner of the working class. His cultured appearance—his accent, the subtleties of New York sophistication—were things he had acquired later in life.

Stephen was from the lake district of Upper Michigan, where his father was a professional hunter and guide who took clients on multi-day safaris deep into the wilds to shoot deer and bear. In the winter, he ran snowmobile tours. Stephen had worked as his father's assistant on these safaris throughout high school, saving enough money to go to the University of Michigan, where he was the first one in his family to get a college education. In the interview, Stephen was quoted as saying he had "a very Hemingway sort of childhood," which had encouraged him to become a writer and editor.

Howie was also the first in his family to go to college, and he was inclined to like people who forged their own way. There was nothing wrong with Stephen Halley's background. But it was interesting that Stephen wasn't the effete literary person Howie had taken him to be. This was someone who had grown up knowing how to use guns, snowmobiles, and ATVs. He had grown up knowing how to find his way in the woods.

Howie sat in front of his computer for a long time, lost in thought. The screen eventually went into its light show mode, and finally went dark.

It was odd, he thought, how in the years he had known Grace, she had never shown the slightest desire to be a writer. None whatsoever. It was Stephen who was the writer.

He remembered sitting next to Stephen at Thanksgiving. What had he said about women writers? That they were the success story these days in publishing. It was women who read books, not men. And they preferred books written by women about women's issues. The macho writers—the Hemingways and Norman Mailers—were dinosaurs from a previous age.

He remembered something else, too—a long ago visit with Nick to Smith College to see Grace. They had been talking about the Senator's affair with Summer when Grace had asked what Howie thought about infidelity.

He had answered, "When I find the right girl, I'm going to be true forever."

And she had laughed at his old-fashioned naiveté.

"When you find the right *woman*," she had corrected. "Not *girl*."

So here was the question: would Grace write books that had *Girl* in the title? Wouldn't they be *The Woman Who Said No*, *The Woman Who Laughed Last, The Woman Who Ran Away*?

Of course, like most people, Grace might simply have become less of a rebel as she grew older.

Nevertheless, a vague idea began stirring in Howie's mind.

Up to now, he had believed that the present murders had to do with a ghost from the past: the terrible crime from 1970 where a Native American boy had scalped and cut the throat of his headmaster.

But what if they were dealing with a ghost of a different sort?

What if Grace hadn't written those successful *Girl* books?

What if she'd had a ghost writer?

Chapter Twenty-Nine

Howie decided that he needed to see Grace. Tonight, if possible. It couldn't be put off. She was the only one who could clear up his questions.

Should he phone Jack first to discuss the situation? He decided to wait. His suspicions were much too flimsy, he could easily be wrong. It would be better to drive to Santa Fe, confront Grace, and speak to Jack tomorrow. If any of his suspicions had legs, they would both go to Santo in the morning.

Howie hadn't had dinner yet, but he was hyped and decided he wasn't hungry. Perhaps after seeing Grace, he would make a small detour to the Coyote Café to see what was cooking . . .

***

The night sky was gray and moody, not a single star anywhere. A sky like this usually heralded snow, though tonight it was too warm. Rain was coming.

Howie had rented a Ford Fiesta at the Albuquerque airport on his way home from Florida and he was getting fond of the little car. It was like something from the Flintstones, a toy bubble. It had all the flashy new things, including a big screen where dashboards used to be. The screen talked and could do pretty much everything. Of course, the Fiesta had only 17,846 miles on it. Howie wondered how it would be holding up when it was as old as his Subaru, 193,247 miles and still going. At least it would be going, if someone hadn't rolled a boulder down a hill onto the hood.

He pulled up to Grace's house to find the gate was open and there was an old Toyota Camry coming down the driveway. It was Grace's Hispanic maid, a pleasant middle-aged woman with a kind face. Howie had met her before.

They rolled down their windows as they met, car to car, in the driveway.

"Grace hasn't come home yet, Mr. Moon Deer," she told him through her open window. Howie was surprised she remembered his name.

"I need to speak to her," Howie said from his car. "Do you know where she is?"

"Well, I shouldn't say, but to tell the truth, I've been worried. She left here at ten this morning saying she was going to the ranch to ride Valkyrie and she'd be back before I left at five. But it's after eight now and I really need to leave. I'm babysitting my sister's kids tonight."

"Did you try calling her?"

"I did. Twice. I wanted her to know I was leaving because she's been worried about security and always wanted one of us to be at the house. But there was no answer."

Howie continued up the driveway to the house and stopped in the turn-around with his engine running. He decided it was time to call Jack. Jack's number rang three times before a recorded message came on to say Jack wasn't available but he could leave a message after the beep.

"Hey, it's me. I'm down in Santa Fe at Grace Stanton's house, but she isn't home. The maid told me she went to the ranch earlier in the morning intending to go riding, but she hasn't returned yet so I'm going to drive out there to investigate. I know it's late but I'm worried. I think we've got this all wrong, Jack. Believe it or not, I think our killer is Stephen Halley, the mild-mannered editor who isn't so mild after all. I know this sounds crazy, but Grace has been having an on-and-off affair with Halley since he was her literature professor at Smith, and I think he was the ghost writer for those books of hers. It's complicated and I don't know all the answers yet, but I'll explain it to you when I see you. But look, I'd better get going. I'll give you a call first thing tomorrow."

Howie ended the call and set off on the winding two-lane highway that went from Santa Fe to the ranch, racing the elfish little engine as fast as he dared.

***

Rain was falling steadily as Howie crossed the cattle guard that marked the start of the Stanton Ranch. The night was dead dark. The windshield wipers slapped back and forth, beating a nervous time. Howie's stomach growled, but it wasn't hunger. He felt a growing dread of what he might find.

He came around a bend and saw the outline of the ranch house less than fifty feet ahead. The house was entirely dark and he came upon it unexpectedly. His headlights swept over the front of the house until the beams hit Grace's yellow Jaguar, parked at a careless angle. Howie didn't like any of this. He was starting to wish he'd brought a gun.

He turned off the ignition, which shut off his headlights as well, and stepped out into the dark. The rain splashed around him, covering all other sounds.

After a few moments, his night vision improved and he was able to pick out the shapes of the buildings and the land. He began walking cautiously on the dirt track that led from the house toward the barn. The wind moaned, a ghostly sound that sent shivers up his spine. He urged himself forward.

He continued another fifty feet until he could see the dark looming shape of the barn. There was something on the road in front of him, but he wasn't sure what it was. As he walked closer, the wind began to moan even louder. It almost sounded human.

Howie stopped and listened more closely.

Ooooooohhh! The tone rose and fell until it formed a single word: "Help!" it cried.

Howie broke into a run and almost stumbled over a large lumpish thing on the road. It was a horse on its side, stretched out on the ground. A dead horse. Howie fumbled in his jacket pocket for his iPhone and turned on the flashlight. He should have thought of this earlier.

Grace was on the muddy ground partially pinned by the dead horse. She was moaning in pain and appeared badly hurt. She could have been lying there trapped beneath the horse for hours. In the circle of light, he saw there was a gun not far from her outstretched hand. A semi-automatic pistol of some kind.

"I'm here, Grace," he told her, kneeling in the mud by her body. "It's Howie."

"Howie? Is that you?" she asked weakly.

"Everything's going to be all right now," he promised rashly. "I'm going to get you out of here."

"I shot him," she said. Speaking didn't seem easy for her. She took a breath. "I shot the bastard!"

"Don't talk, Grace. You can tell me this later."

"No, you need to see if he's alive. He shot Valkyrie out from under me. But I got him when he started coming my way. Bastard didn't know I had a gun! I think I got him . . . he's by the corral somewhere."

"Stephen?"

"Yes, Stephen!" she said emphatically. "Oh, God, this hurts!"

"Let me get you out from under Valkyrie."

"No, find him . . . make sure he's dead. He'll kill us if he can!"

Howie rose to his feet and walked further up the road toward the barn with the flashlight on the iPhone lighting the way. He was pretty sure Halley was either dead or gone, otherwise he would have taken a shot at Howie as he was walking up the road.

Howie found him sprawled on his back in the mud on the road about thirty feet from Grace. He was dead. His eyes stared vacantly into the falling rain. There was a nasty looking pistol by his outstretched right hand.

He jogged back to Grace and knelt by her side. "He won't be bothering you anymore," he told her.

"Howie, oh, God, I'm going to die!"

"Don't say that. I'll get you out of here."

This was easier said than done. Howie took a closer look at the situation and saw that it was going to be difficult to pull her out from under the dead horse. Her left leg was pinned in the stirrup beneath Valkyrie's bulk and Howie presumed it must be fractured in several places. No wonder she had been moaning. It was amazing she could speak at all. Valkyrie must have died almost instantly, collapsing as Grace was sitting in the saddle. She had managed to free her right leg from the stirrup, but it was bent at an awkward angle over the horse's back.

Grace clearly needed help as quickly as possible. The temperature was in the low forties, and though she was dressed for November weather in a good parka and a riding helmet, she didn't look like she could take much more.

Howie wished he could call an ambulance and a truck with a winch to pull the horse off her, but there wasn't time. If he didn't get her inside some place warm, she was going to die.

He spoke as calmly as he could.

"Look, here's the plan, Grace. I'm going to get my car and use it to pull Valkyrie off you. Okay? Then I'm going to bundle you into the back seat and get you to a hospital. You just have to hang on a while longer."

She nodded weakly.

Howie stripped off his own parka and folded it around her body to give her some additional warmth. The parka was Gore-Tex, waterproof, and he put the hood over her face to protect her from the rain.

Once this was done, he ran as fast as he could back to his rental car, praying the small engine and city tires would be up to the job of dragging a two thousand pound horse off his long-ago girlfriend on a muddy road in the soaking rain.

Chapter Thirty

Rental cars didn't come equipped with either chains or rope to drag dead horses off injured women.

Howie was too wet and cold and frightened to think clearly, but he came up with a sort of idea. It wasn't a good idea, but with luck he thought it might work. He drove back to where Grace lay trapped and got out of the car with the engine running and the headlights on.

"I'm back!" he said optimistically.

Grace didn't answer. Her breathing had become shallow and her face was pale as ice. She appeared no longer capable of speech.

He knew there would be lead ropes in the barn, but Howie didn't want to take the time to look for them. Meanwhile, Valkyrie—poor Valkyrie!—didn't need his bridle any longer. Howie got down on his knees and pulled the leather halter over the horse's ears and the metal bit from his mouth. This wasn't easy. He had to pry Valkyrie's mouth open with his fingers to get the bit out.

The reins were good leather and he hoped they were strong. He slipped both reins beneath the cinch that held the saddle, pulled them through all the way, and threaded the ends through the metal bit to close the loop. When this was done, he got back in the car and inched close enough to tie the ends of the reins to the front bumper.

He returned to the driver's seat, put the car in reverse, and backed very slowly. He felt the tension in the leather as the reins pulled tight. He gave the car a little gas. Slowly, he felt the weight of the horse drag his way. What this was doing to Grace's injured leg he couldn't imagine. But he had to get Valkyrie off her, there was no other choice.

To his relief, it worked. He moved the dead weight of the horse nearly two feet before the wheels of the Fiesta began to spin in the mud and he couldn't go any further.

He got out of the car and returned to Grace. His headlights lit her and Valkyrie in bright light and deep shadow. Grace was no longer conscious, and that was probably a blessing. Valkyrie had been pulled nearly clear, but the last few inches of Grace's left boot were still wedged beneath his stomach. Howie grabbed the cinch with both hands and heaved upward with all his strength. The bulk of the dead horse barely moved, but it was enough so that he was able to use his right foot to kick Grace's left foot free.

He collapsed onto the horse's side, out of breath and off-balance.

"Right!" he said to himself. "Keep going!"

He got to his feet, opened the back door of the Fiesta, and returned to where Grace was lying in the road.

"I'm sorry," he told her. "I'm really, really sorry, but I'm doing the best I can."

He picked her up in his arms, carried her to the car, and managed to get her into the back. That done, he was so exhausted he slumped down the side of the car and sat in the mud catching his breath. It was all he could do to force himself to keep moving.

He climbed back into the driver's seat and debated what to do next. The closest hospital was in Española, but that was at least forty minutes away and he wasn't sure Grace would make it. He knew from Thanksgiving that there was no cell service out here, but if he could get inside the house and use the landline, he could call for help. What he needed now was a medical helicopter.

He drove back to the house and was relieved to find the front door unlocked. After finding the lights in the living room, he used the phone on the side table and called 911.

It was a complicated situation and Howie had to repeat himself several times before the operator fully understood his predicament. She instructed him to wait at the ranch. Do not attempt to move the injured woman, she told him. Help would be on its way.

Howie returned to Grace where he had left her in the car. When he opened the back door, he was surprised to find that she was sitting up.

"Oh, good! You're—"

Doing better, was what he meant to say. But his words died in his throat.

Grace was holding the semi-automatic he had last seen in the mud by her outstretched arm. How she had gotten hold of it, he couldn't imagine. She was sitting up with difficulty, he could tell that she was in pain. But the business end of the barrel was pointed at his heart.

"I tried to warn you that the Stantons were a bad lot," she told him. "You should have listened, Moon Deer!"

***

At 10:25 that night, Jack Wilder was in the larger of the two interrogation rooms at the State Police station when his phone vibrated. A pleasant female voice told him that Howard Moon Deer was calling but Jack let the call go to his voice mail. At the moment, he was more interested in the conversation that was unfolding in the interrogation room. He would call Howie back later.

He was seated at a desk with Santo, Dan Hamm, and Ramona Montoya, who had returned voluntarily to New Mexico. Santo had already interviewed her earlier in the evening, but he wasn't sure he believed Ramona's testimony and had sent Dan to pick up Jack at home to get his opinion.

Ramona was an elderly woman who had spent a lifetime keeping personal matters to herself, and it wasn't easy to get her talking now. Santo had been forced to lean on her hard, using her son Tucker as a bargaining chip. Two of his officers had picked up Tucker at the Stanton Ranch yesterday afternoon and they were holding him in the cell that Howie had recently occupied. Santo was threatening to charge Tucker with the murders of Harlan and Nick Stanton, unless Ramona could offer a better explanation of what had happened.

Jack began his own interrogation with facts from fifty years ago that he already knew. Ramona admitted that Ralph White, the boy who had murdered the headmaster, was her younger brother. His birth name, she said, was Terence Little Eagle.

"And did you help your brother plan the murder of Matthew Cordell?" Jack asked.

She shook her head.

"Unfortunately, I'm blind," he told her. "You'll have to speak up."

"There was no plan. It wasn't nothing like that. Little Eagle had enough, that's all. He was bullied and abused and he couldn't take any more. He'd been reading those IOAT things. I guess that's what gave him the gumption to fight back."

"IOAT things?"

"Indians of All Tribes. Those folks who took over Alcatraz. They had a brochure about it."

Jack remembered the group of Indians and activists who had occupied Alcatraz Island in the late 1960s. It had been a very big deal in San Francisco at the time.

"Did you give him that brochure, Ramona?"

"Of course not! It was some Navajo fellow who worked in the kitchen. I wish he hadn't. We were kids, there was no way we could fight the white man. It only caused us trouble."

"Did you see much of your brother at the school?"

"Not much. The boys and girls were kept apart. Sometimes I was able to have a word with him in passing, that's all. I got him that knife because he said he needed some way to protect himself from all the bullies. I worked in the kitchen, you see. But I sure didn't know he was going to kill anyone, the way the cops said later."

"They detained you?"

"They put me in jail," she said wearily.

"Right. Until Adam Stanton arrived from Washington and he got you off. Tell me about that, please."

Ramona told the story in a flat voice without emotion, how the Indian Commissioner had convinced the authorities to release her into his care, and the price she paid, having sex with him at the age of fourteen, then giving birth to a baby which he forced her to give up.

Unlike her brother, Ramona had accepted her lot. If she had any anger about what Adam had done to her, she had suppressed it long ago. In return, she was given a life of docile security. She did her job, she went along. As for her brother, Little Eagle, she claimed she had never seen him again. She assumed that he had died in the wilds of thirst and exposure. That's what happened to Indian children who ran away.

Meanwhile, life on the ranch was okay. It was a peaceful existence in a pretty place, and though it was very isolated, she didn't mind that. When Adam died, he rewarded her years of service by leaving her a letter saying where her child was, and—with Harlan's help—she was able to find the boy and bring him to the ranch. Harlan knew the story of his father's sexual liaison with the girl and he made it clear that the one thing she must never do was tell anyone what Adam had done to her. Silence was the price for her secure existence. There would be no family scandal. As for Tucker, he was never told the true story of his birth, only that he was illegitimate and that his mother had given in to the desires of some unknown man.

Jack spent some time establishing things he already knew before he worked his way to the present.

"Now, Ramona, you knew of the trust fund that Adam set up before he died. Did it surprise you that he bypassed Harlan, his son, in favor of his grandchildren?"

"Naw. He didn't like Harlan so much. Used to say he was a namby-pamby. Anyway, he left the Senator the ranch and the other houses around the country. He said if that wasn't enough, it was too damn bad."

"But he didn't leave you or your son anything either. That must have made you angry."

"He left me five thousand dollars," she said. "That was okay. I didn't expect more than that."

"Really? He left millions to Justin, Nick, and Grace, but only five grand to you. That doesn't seem fair somehow. After all, to all practical purposes you were Adam's second wife."

"I wasn't any kind of second wife," she said without rancor. "I was his whore."

Jack was startled by her description of herself as Adam Stanton's whore.

"But he left me alone pretty much by the time I was twenty," she added. "He liked 'em young."

Jack frowned. "I see. Now, I understand that in the past few weeks Justin had been trying to convince his dad to invest the trust fund money in his real estate project. Did you know about that?"

"Oh, sure. I know pretty much everything that goes on with that family. Nick wanted the money, too, I guess. That's what I heard, anyways. But Grace, she was the worst. She kept calling every day or two saying it's my money and oh, please, Daddy, I need it now, I'm so broke."

"Really? Grace said she was broke? But she makes a ton of money with her books, doesn't she?"

"I'm just telling you what I heard. I guess she spends a lot. Grace was always the spoiled one. The funny thing was, here are these three kids crowding round like a bunch of vultures, all of them wanting money, and the money was gone."

Jack raised an eyebrow. "What do you mean the money was gone?"

"It was gone, that's all. The Senator had been looting that trust fund for years. First it was for his campaign, that last election he lost. And then there was keeping up the ranch and all the different houses. Every time he had to repair something or pay taxes, he hit the trust a little more. Justin, I guess he got his share when he was twenty-five. But Nick and Grace, when it came around to their turn, they were going to find the well was dry."

"But how is that possible? His ex-wife, Anne, is co-executor of the trust. He couldn't get money out without her consent."

"Sure, he could. That family, they're all cheats. He fiddled it. He made me help him."

"How did you help him?"

"I learned to write her signature," Ramona said blandly, apparently unaware that forgery was a crime. "I practiced for weeks to do it right. But I was always good at drawing. Then he would take it to someone he knew in Albuquerque who put a stamp on it making it look like the real thing."

"A notary public?"

"I guess that's what he called it. Senator Harlan was good at fixing things. When you're a Senator, I guess you have lots of friends. All the trust fund papers came to him and he fiddled them, too. The numbers, I mean. The copies he sent to Mrs. Anne were full of lies. Mrs. Anne found out, though, and, I tell you, she was hopping mad!"

"Really? And when was it that Anne discovered that Harlan was stealing their children's money?"

"Just before Thanksgiving. That's why she came, I guess. To have it out with him."

Jack was speechless. It would take a subpoena to get the mutual fund company in New York to open their books in order to corroborate Ramona's accusations, but that wouldn't be difficult to arrange.

Jack turned to Santo. "What do you say we take a break for fifteen minutes. Perhaps Ramona would like coffee and a sandwich? I know I would."

Dan helped guide Jack into the hall where he checked his phone messages while Santo ordered food.

Jack listened to Howie's voice mail with growing concern.

"I think we're going to need to skip the refreshments," he said as Santo joined him in the hall. "I just got a message from Howie. It seems Grace went off to ride her horse this morning and she hasn't returned. Howie's on his way to the ranch to see what happened. Meanwhile, it looks like Grace may not have written those bestsellers of hers after all. Howie believes she had a ghost writer. Stephen Halley. I tried to phone Howie back just now but there's no answer."

"Howie's in trouble again, is he?"

"Santo, I think we need to get to that ranch as fast as we can."

Chapter Thirty-One

Grace kept her gun pointed at Howie as he leaned in the open car door looking down at her. Her hand wasn't steady, her eyes were dull with pain. But the gun was real and it made Howie pause.

She was lying stretched out on the back seat, propped up against the closed door on the far side, lit only by the single dome light overhead, which wasn't flattering.

The Ford Fiesta wasn't Grace's sort of automobile and she didn't look comfortable. A memory flitted through his mind, the fancy yellow convertible two-seater sports car she drove the summer of their romance, an Alfa Romeo. That was Grace's kind of car, not a Ford. She had always been a fancy girl, despite her flirtation with bohemianism in her college years. Rich girls often went through a boho phase, though they got over it quickly enough.

"Put the gun down, Grace," he said calmly. "It's over. The only thing left is to get you to a hospital."

"You think they'll be able to help me?" she asked with the ghost of a laugh. "Well, who cares anymore? I don't!"

Howie watched as she lowered the gun to her side and let it fall from her fingers to the car floor. He reached down and picked it up.

She closed her eyes and her breath flowed out in a long sigh. "I had to do it, Howie! You understand, don't you? None of this has been my fault!"

"Look, you don't have to talk. I called 911 and help is on the way. What you need to do is save your energy until they get here."

"I'm going to die!"

"Grace, you're going to be okay. You just have to hang on for maybe twenty minutes. I'm going to turn on the heat so you'll be more comfortable. It won't be long now."

Howie stepped around to the driver's seat, turned the ignition, and put the heat on its highest setting.

"I didn't even write those books!" she said from the rear. Her voice was stronger now, angry.

"I figured that out. But we can talk later."

Howie wasn't sure he could take another death. He wanted her to rest until the medics came. But she was worked up and she just kept going.

"Howie, I've got to make you understand! Stephen came to me. He said he had a brilliant idea. He would write the books and I would be the front person. I looked good, my father was a Senator, I'd be able to get on all the TV shows. We would split seventy-five percent for him and twenty-five for me. I should have demanded fifty-fifty, but he said he was the one doing the hard work so he should get more. He used me, the bastard! And I went along . . . I've always been too trusting, Howie . . . and people always let me down . . ."

"Shh," he said, hoping to quiet her. "It's just a few more minutes, Grace, and then you'll be safe."

But she wouldn't stop.

"He abused me!" she cried excitedly. "As far back as I can remember. The bastard! Fucking bastard!"

"Stephen abused you?" Howie asked. His curiosity got the better of him.

"No, I was just a little girl! Not Stephen. What are you talking about? Grandpa! He'd sit me on his lap and put his finger inside of me. Then he'd unzip his pants and make me jerk him off. That's why all my life I've had so much trouble with men."

Grace managed a kind of strangled laugh. "I told my father about it, but he wouldn't listen. He said if I didn't keep my mouth shut, he'd put me in an institution! Can you believe that, Howie? Everyone in the family knew what grandpa did to children. But we had to cover it up because Daddy was in politics!"

"That's awful," he told her, and it was. "But you don't need to talk about it now."

"I knew you'd understand, Howie. You're the only one who ever loved me completely. My God, you worshipped me! I was such a fool to leave you! We should have been together!"

Howie sighed. He scanned the sky for any sign of a helicopter, but there was nothing but darkness and rain.

"It was Nick's idea to kill Daddy," she continued bitterly. "Nick dreamed up the whole thing, it wasn't me! He was the one who told me to invite you for Thanksgiving. He knew Daddy would pick a fight with you and it would be easy to set you up. You were the perfect fall guy!"

Howie tried to absorb this, but it wasn't easy.

"And then I had to kill Nick . . . you understand, don't you? I didn't have a choice!"

"No, I don't understand," Howie told her sharply. "I don't understand at all!"

"Money," she said.

"Money?"

"Money!" she repeated, more firmly. "I couldn't wait until I was forty, Howie! I needed that damn money now!"

"But you *have* money," he objected.

"No, I don't. It's always been Daddy's money. He gave me an allowance, but it was never my money, it was always his. That's why I fell for Stephen's scam. And it was perfect for a few years until he left me high and dry, Howie . . . high and dry. I couldn't write a word without him, and if I didn't finish the book, I'd have to give back the advance. Two hundred thousand dollars, Howie! I didn't have it, everything was running out, everything was gone!"

"Grace, I'm trying to understand. But, my God, you killed your father! Then Nick and Stephen. I just don't get it!"

"It wasn't me who killed Daddy. It was Nick. We planned it together, sure. But he did the actual killing."

Howie felt like a balloon with the air hissing out. This was the final disillusionment. He had meant to let her rest, conserve her energy, but he couldn't let this go.

"Not Nick!" he said wearily. Yet part of him knew it might be true. Nick had always gone to extremes.

"It was his idea that I should invite you for Thanksgiving. We knew you and Daddy would get into a fight about politics. When Summer told you about the baby Daddy made me give away, we decided this was the best chance we would ever have. With Daddy out of the way, Nick would get what he needed to leave the country and I could get my life back from Stephen."

Howie could only shake his head. He was beyond words.

"I couldn't watch!" Grace went on. "I told Daddy I needed to talk with him that night, that it was urgent. Daddy didn't mind the late hour, he'd always been a night owl. But you should have seen his face when Nick showed up with me at his study! Nick didn't give him a chance to speak. He had the knife in his hand, a big hunting knife. He just stepped forward, grabbed Daddy by the hair and cut his throat. Daddy gagged, he couldn't speak. But, oh, God, Howie—the way his eyes glared at me! Then when Daddy was on the floor, Nick . . . well, he did the rest."

"Right. To set me up," Howie managed. "To make it look like I did it."

He didn't want to hear any more, but she wouldn't let up.

"We went up and back to the bunkhouse a few times that night. We cleaned up afterwards down there. That was when you saw one of us on the meadow."

"But why did you shoot Nick, for chrissake? I thought you loved him!"

"I *did* love him! But after he killed Daddy, I was afraid of him. I was terrified. He was so . . . efficient, the way he used that knife. Watching him, I knew he could use it on me. Once he got started, he was like a machine. I knew if I didn't take care of him, he would come after me one day to steal my share."

Howie shook his head.

"I knew where he was staying," she continued, her voice finally starting to give out. "I was the one who found that old abandoned ranch for him. I drove the ranch pickup there. But, you see, I didn't want to kill you, Howie. I hope you know that. That's why I went up on that hill and rolled that loose boulder down on your car. It was to send you both scattering out of the car so I could pick off Nick with my rifle."

Howie heard these things with increasing gloom. He knew it wasn't love that had kept her from killing him. The only reason she didn't shoot him was because she needed him alive to be the fall guy. And with any other cop than Santo, it might have worked.

"But why Stephen?" Howie couldn't stop himself from asking.

"I called him, I told him to meet me here. I said I needed to talk about the series. I needed him to finish the book, just that one book, and then we could let the series die. But he refused. And I couldn't let him do that. You see, don't you?"

"Oh, Grace!"

"We went riding together, for old times sake, I told him. I took Valkyrie, and I gave him Theseus, Daddy's horse which hadn't been ridden in years. I thought he could have an accident out in the desert, but he was a better rider than I expected. So, when we got back to the barn, I tried to shoot him, but I missed. He ducked just in time. That's when I realized he had a gun, too. I was still on Valkyrie. He took a shot at me from the ground as I was riding away, but his shot hit Valkyrie instead, and I went down with him in the saddle and got pinned underneath his body. Stephen thought I was done for, and that's how I got him. I killed him as he was walking toward me. It broke my heart to do it. I loved Stephen. I really did. But he made me do it . . ."

At last there was silence in the back of the Fiesta. And in the distance, Howie heard the *thwap, thwap* of a helicopter coming their way.

He climbed out from behind the wheel and slipped into the back with her. Her eyes were closed but he was glad to hear that she was breathing. Whether he liked it or not, there would always be a connection between them. He had loved her once and they had a child together. Somewhere.

As they waited for the helicopter, he reached out and took her hand.

***

For Howie, it had been a long, sad, terrible conversation, sitting in the Ford Fiesta in the rain, one that he would remember for the rest of his life. In the end, Grace was raving.

Howie blamed himself for being such a fool. He had seen Nick and Grace for what he had wanted them to be, not for who they were. He had been blinded by their glamor and beauty. But people change over time, and sometimes they let the bad seeds in themselves overtake the good. That's how Howie came to see it.

It was all about money, as Grace had said. They claimed to hate the stuff—which was the proper patrician attitude toward money, as long as you had it. Nick, the revolutionary, called it filthy lucre. But he needed it, too. They all needed it, each for their different reasons, and it was there in their grandfather's trust fund, like a golden apple just out of reach.

Howie remembered the line from W.H. Auden: "Lost in a haunted wood, children afraid of the night, who have never been happy or good." That was the Stanton children in a nutshell. They say every great fortune begins with a crime. With the Stantons, the crimes went on and on.

Meanwhile, life had its own wicked sense of humor. It turned out that the trust fund was gone, looted by Harlan to finance his final Senate campaign. There was only a few thousand dollars left to keep the account active. The prize that Nick, Grace, and Justin sought had been a mirage.

And the final joke: Grace spewed forth her rambling confession as she lay propped up in the back seat because she believed she was dying and there was nothing left to lose. But she didn't die.

Her left leg was fractured in three places, but her injuries weren't as bad as they appeared. Exposure had been the gravest danger, the hours she had spent pinned beneath a dead horse in forty-degree weather. But she was strong and she survived.

The girl who had everything would spend the rest of her life in prison.

Chapter Thirty-Two

In mid-March of the following calendar year, Howie flew from Denver to Edinburgh, Scotland—twelve hours in the air, jet lag galore.

His seat in economy wasn't any larger than the one he'd had on his trip to Florida, but at least they gave you a meal on international flights, and you could watch a movie or two. Or three.

He had come to meet Claire who had just finished a three-week engagement as a guest soloist with the Royal Scottish Chamber Orchestra. Plus, he had some business of his own to take care of.

The month of March back home on the Peak had turned out to be the best skiing of the season. The snow had finally come, two feet of it at a time after a skimpy start. Howie had skied less than a dozen times over the course of the season and normally leaving just when the conditions were perfect would have been painful. But this year he was glad to get away. He caught himself thinking too often of Nick and Grace and the dramas of last autumn.

He had seen Claire several times since November, though she was spending most of her time in Europe now because of work. He tried his best to be cheerful when he saw her, but he wasn't his usual self. He was often silent and moody, lost in reflection. Claire gave him space, she didn't push, she knew he had gone through a bad time. But by the spring, Howie had slowly begun to open up and talk about his winter of discontent.

"You just need time, Howie," she told him.

Time? In fact, Grace had already passed from his immediate thoughts, though occasionally—usually late at night—he felt a wave of sorrow thinking about what her life must be like at the New Mexico

Women's Correctional Facility in Grants. Her days of zipping around in expensive sports cars were over.

It was the memory of Nick that filled him with a lasting sorrow. It wasn't only the betrayal of someone he had thought of as his best friend, but the realization of how little he had known Nick. People were like icebergs, he supposed, with ninety percent of them hidden under water. With Nick, beneath the charisma, there had clearly been a vast darkness.

Howie arrived in Edinburgh in time to see Claire's final performance, the Dvorak Cello Concerto, which he had heard her perform a number of times before. It was good to see her so perfectly poised before an orchestra and hear the applause she received. At the end of the concert, while she took her bows and scooped up the bouquets of flowers on the stage, she noticed a humble string-tied bundle of sage from the New Mexico desert. She turned to where she knew Howie was in the fourth row and laughed.

They spent three nights in a hotel in the old part of Edinburgh, not far from the castle, and then Howie rented a car and they drove to Glasgow a few hours away. They planned to spend a week in Glasgow, perhaps longer. Howie had business here and he wasn't certain how long it would take so they were keeping their plans flexible. They hoped to have ten days afterwards to explore the West Scottish coast.

They were lying in bed in their hotel on their first night in Glasgow, wrapped in each other's arms, when Claire brought up "the case," as they had begun to call it in shorthand. She was always curious about his cases, this one in particular since it involved Howie's first girlfriend, and there were still questions he hadn't answered.

"So, who wrote those poison pen letters?" she asked. "Is it all right for me to ask? I'll shut up if you don't want to talk about it."

"No, it's okay. Grace wrote them. She admitted it afterwards when she was awaiting trial. You see, killing her father wasn't an impulsive act. She had thought about it for weeks. Months, probably. She knew about the old Indian school murder and she thought she could use that to throw suspicion away from herself."

Claire propped herself up on one elbow to look at him. "I think it's unforgivable that she tried to make you the fall guy!"

"Well, I didn't like it either. But actually, it was Ramona she was trying to set up. At first, anyway, before I came along and looked like a better prospect. She knew Ramona had been abused by her grandfather and she thought she could work this up into a revenge motive that would make it appear that she had killed the senator. It was pretty half-baked, really. She wasn't thinking clearly."

"She was a cold-blooded killer!"

Howie smiled. Claire liked to pretend she wasn't jealous of Grace, but of course she was. Just a little.

Howie got out of bed and refilled their wine glasses from the bottle by the television set. He returned to the edge of the bed but didn't get under the covers right away.

"I'm not sure cold-blooded is the right word for Grace. She was damaged from her childhood. Sexually abused kids tend to have low self-esteem and she was angry, desperate, and broken. Stephen was the last straw, telling her that he was finished writing those books for her. They'd had a huge fight apparently and he'd finally had it with her. Can you imagine what that was like? For the past few years she had been a big deal in New Mexico—all around the world, really—a best selling author. It gave her status and confidence. And now she would have to admit that she was a fraud. She wouldn't be able to show her face anywhere."

"I suppose so," Claire admitted. "Still, you're talking about someone who grew up with houses in Cape Cod and New Mexico, plus a town house in Manhattan. Then an expensive education at Smith. I'm sorry, but I'm not going to feel sorry for her."

"There are all kinds of deprivations, Claire."

"Howie, *you* are a softie!" she declared. "So, what about that meeting Nick had at Ghost Ranch? That was with Tucker, wasn't it? They caught him on a CCTV tape. What was that about?"

"Nick used to go riding with Tucker back when he was a kid visiting the ranch. Nick was the only one in the family who made an effort to befriend Tucker. Whatever else Nick was, he wasn't a snob. He didn't care that Tucker was a ranch hand, just like he didn't care that I was a poor Indian from the rez. He took people for who they were.'

"But didn't he know that Tucker was actually his uncle?"

"Not then. He only found that out much later, when he was an adult. But there was a bond between Tucker and Nick, even before he found out they were related. Nick set up the meeting at Ghost Ranch because he wanted to know exactly what to expect at Thanksgiving. He was doing his homework, I'm afraid—planning how he was going to kill his father."

"Did Tucker know he was planning a murder?"

"Santo looked into that but decided that Tucker was in the clear."

Howie didn't mind talking about the case with Claire for short amounts of time. But there always came a moment when he felt a constriction in his chest that made it almost impossible even to utter the names, Nick and Grace Stanton, and he felt that come over him now.

"Hey, I haven't told you my big news!" he said, diverting the conversation. "I finished my dissertation."

"*No*!" Grace cried. "Your dissertation! Really?"

"Yup. I had time this winter and I did it. I wasn't in the mood to ski and we had a lull at the agency, so I finished the thing and sent it to my advisor at Princeton."

"Howie, that's incredible news! My God!"

Howie's Ph.D dissertation, "Philosophical Divisions at the Top of the Food Chain," had been dangling for years, so this was a big announcement. There would be more work to do on it. His advisor at Princeton would read his draft and get back to him with suggestions for revisions. Still, Claire was enormously pleased. She had been telling Howie for years that he was not really suited to be a private investigator, he was an intellectual and would be happier in academia. Howie doubted that. He liked investigating the terrible things humans did to one another. It was exciting and adventurous, and occasionally he had the satisfaction of setting things right. He couldn't imagine himself stuck in a classroom. But he was happy to see Claire happy.

When it came to love, the grown-up version was better than youthful infatuation. By far.

In the morning, Howie left Claire sleeping and went by himself to find his daughter.

***

She lived in a semi-detached house on the south side of Glasgow, which was considered a good part of the city: pleasant streets with small stores and cafés, bakeries and vegetable markets, red double-decker busses lumbering by.

The residential streets branched off from larger streets into meandering neighborhoods green with trees and flower beds that people in New Mexico would drool over. This was Scotland and there was plenty of rain.

The street where Howie's daughter lived was lined with nearly identical dark brick houses that had been mostly built before the first World

War. All of them had the date of their construction displayed on their façades: 1907, 1912, 1904.

A "terraced house," Howie had learned, was a long row of 2-story houses that all shared a common wall. "Semi-detached" indicated that only two houses were joined, identical mirror images of each other, with a small strip of land between them and the next two houses. This was the kind of building his daughter lived in, which meant her adoptive parents were middle class but not wealthy. At the top of the food chain, "detached" houses stood alone, generally surrounded by a few yards of garden.

Her name was Georgina Hadley. She was fifteen years old and people called her Georgie. She was a solitary child, a good student who didn't have many friends. Howie had located her with the help of a private investigation agency that had an international presence, with offices in Edinburgh and Glasgow.

The search had lasted all winter and had cost Howie a good deal of money. At the start, he was told his quest was hopeless, he wouldn't find her. Details of adoptions were kept secret. He wasn't even entirely sure she existed.

It was her ethnicity that had led to finding her. Immigration was a divisive political issue in the U.K. with foreigners flooding into the island from the EU and former British colonies, and statistics were kept. Georgina Hadley was listed on the birth records as Native American. There had been no other Indians listed in the records who were born in Scotland during the time frame he gave the detective agency, and so the search was pared down. She still wasn't a sure thing, but she looked possible and—since the American client was footing the bill—a detective with a video camera was sent to find her and investigate her life.

Howie knew from the first second he saw the videos that she was his daughter. She was a few pounds overweight, a chubby girl with a moonish face, black hair, and eyeglasses. Except for the glasses, she was the image of Howie. Grace's genes must have been in her somewhere, but Howie's had prevailed. His heart melted at the sight of her on his laptop screen in far away New Mexico.

The detective agency had given Howie a detailed account of her routines, and he knew she would be walking today from the bus stop at some time between 4:25 and 4:50 on her way home from school. He waited for her in a small bakery café across from her house, sitting by the window where he could look up the block to the bus stop.

She stepped off the bus at 4:33. She was alone, dressed in a blue school uniform with a white blouse and blue sweater that had the school emblem on it. She carried a heavy daypack that appeared overloaded with books.

She didn't look happy. She walked with her eyes on the sidewalk, lugging the pack. Howie had already paid for his coffee, so he was able to get up and leave.

He crossed the street intending to intercept her before she reached home. Howie knew that what he was about to do was unfair. Neither Georgina nor her adoptive parents knew he was here, they didn't know anything about him. Nevertheless, Claire had encouraged him. "Don't speak to her if it doesn't feel right. But honestly, Howie—I think you should see her at least. Or she will always be forever, well a . . ."

Claire paused to consider how to finish her sentence.

"A ghost," Howie said.

"Exactly. She won't quite be real."

As he walked toward her, he had an opening line prepared. He was going to be a lost American tourist, a clueless Yank asking for directions. But as the distance narrowed, he had an attack of shyness and wasn't sure he could go through with it. Maybe it would be best simply to let her pass on by. When she was a few feet away, she looked up from the sidewalk, flashed him a worried glance, then lowered her eyes with the obvious intention to hurry on by.

Howie was in turmoil. Had he come all these thousands of miles to let this moment pass? He had to do it. He forced himself to speak.

"Hi, excuse me, I'm sort of lost," he managed, as she was passing by. Under the circumstances, sort of lost was an understatement. "Can you tell me how to get to West Princes Street?"

She slowed without actually stopping and gave him a closer look.

"I'm American," he said with a helpless smile. "I'm afraid I set out from my hotel a few hours ago, and I have no idea where I am."

"West Princes Street?" She had stopped but was keeping her distance. She looked like she could break into a run at any moment. "That's quite a ways from here. You're a . . ."

"An American Indian," he said quickly. "A long way from home. I'm sorry to bother you, but I keep turning corners thinking I'll see a familiar landmark, and instead I keep getting more and more lost."

"Well, you could take a bus. But you'd have to change at West Nile Street. It might be easier if you found a taxi."

"That's a good idea. Is there a taxi stand near here?"

She pointed over his shoulder. "If you walk two blocks that way, you come to a busy shopping street and you should be able to find a taxi there."

"I'll do that! Thanks!"

Though Howie had seen video footage of Georgina, he hadn't been prepared for seeing her in person. For one, she looked pure Native American. There wasn't a speck of Grace in her. It was a pity she got his looks rather than hers. But otherwise Howie was strangely pleased to find Grace left out of the genetic pot. He loved her Scottish accent, but it came as a shock because she looked the image of the fifteen-year-old girls he remembered from his childhood on the Rosebud reservation.

They had finished their conversation. She had told him how to find a taxi but nevertheless he didn't move, and she didn't either.

"Excuse me, I know this is horribly rude," she said, "But are you by any chance what they call a Plains Indian?"

"Yes, I am!" he answered enthusiastically. "I'm a Lakota Sioux. How did you guess?"

"Well, you see, I'm doing a report on Native Americans for a school project and I've been looking at photographs and reading books."

"Wonderful!" said Howie, grinning foolishly.

He felt so full he thought he might explode. It was all he could do to keep from rushing forward and taking her in his arms. He took a breath.

"But you don't talk the way I imagined an Indian would sound."

He laughed. "I'm a modern Indian, I'm afraid. Today there are more of us in Los Angeles and Chicago than all the reservations combined. And of course, wherever we grow up, we have TV and radio and movies. That's the great equalizer. Many of us go to college, too," he said. "When I was seventeen, I got a scholarship to a university on the East Coast called Dartmouth. I was lucky because it opened up a large world for me. But I haven't been back to Rosebud lately, and I'm starting to feel I should. That's where I grew up. The Rosebud reservation in South Dakota."

Howie expected her to walk away any moment. He knew he was talking too much and he wasn't certain if the look she was giving him was wary or curious. Smart fifteen-year-old schoolgirls didn't speak to strange men on the street. Yet she stayed put, less than ten feet away—ready to run if necessary—inspecting him.

"Rosebud!" she said, letting the name linger.

"You wouldn't want to romanticize it," he told her. "There's a great deal of poverty there. Alcoholism. Drugs. Domestic abuse, the works.

But there are also wonderfully wise people who keep the old ways alive. It's a deep sort of place."

"You know, I think this is what I need for my report! To write about modern Indian life. I mean, anyone can write about American Indians, Sitting Bull, Geronimo, those guys. But to write about how people live today . . . that could be a good slant."

Howie seized the opportunity. "It sounds like you're a serious student. Look, I'm going to be stopping at Rosebud for a month on my way back home to where I live now in New Mexico," he told her, deciding on this change of travel plans on the spot. "I could send you photographs, and maybe get you interviews with some of the elders. I could . . . well, I could help answer some of your questions."

She gave him a skeptical look. She wasn't dumb. Getting a young girl to correspond on the Internet was a classic move of adult predators.

"Think about it, anyway," he said quickly. "I tell you what. I'll leave you my card with my email address on it. For the next two weeks I'll be traveling around Scotland with my girlfriend, but I'll be back in the States after that, and if you want to contact me at Rosebud, you can just shoot out any questions you have. Or thoughts. Whatever. About being an Indian."

Her look deepened. "People say I look like an Indian," she said. "I guess that's why I'm interested in them."

"Actually, you *do* look Native American," he said. "In fact, that's why I decided you might be somebody I could ask for directions."

"I'm adopted, you see. Some kids are mean about it. In the Third Form they started calling me Hiawatha."

"Did they?" Howie felt he would gladly smack the daylights out of any kid who called his daughter Hiawatha. "You should ignore them if you can."

"I do! That's exactly what I do! I ignore them. I have better things to do. I'm working really hard so I can get into university."

"The University of Glasgow?"

"No, Oxford. My parents can't afford it unless I get a bunch of grants, which is why I'm working so hard."

"That's wonderful!" Howie said. "And if I can help you with this report in some way, I would be very pleased. Universities like students who can think and write coherently. I, er . . . I'm just finishing up my Ph.D. in social anthropology. At a university called Princeton."

"I know the university called Princeton," she told him. "I'm grateful for your offer. It's just . . . you see, at school they tell you not to let middle-aged men lure you into having a correspondence online."

Howie wasn't pleased to find himself regarded as a middle-aged man. But of course, he was. In her eyes.

He did his best to look harmless.

"I understand completely," he told her. "And your teachers are absolutely right. To tell the truth, normally I'm not very eager to discuss being an Indian with people I just meet. But you asked an interesting question—what is it like to be an Indian today—and I'd be happy to tell you about my tribe. It's a good story about a noble people who lived in harmony with nature, but are struggling very hard today. I think this is something you should know about," he concluded, perhaps too forcefully for casual conversations.

She gave him a wary look. "Well, thanks again, but I don't think I should bother you."

Howie reached for his wallet and pulled out a card with the Wilder & Associate logo on top. He covered the distance to where she was standing and handed her the card. She reached for it quickly and held it for a moment before adjusting her glasses to give it a better look.

"Howard Moon Deer," she read, "Private Investigations. Gosh! Are you a private eye?"

"I am. Though I'm not working at the moment, of course. I'm on vacation."

"San Geronimo, New Mexico!" she said excitedly, reading the rest of the card. "That sounds like the Wild West!"

"It is," he told her. "It's definitely the Wild West. The 21st century version, at least, with a ski resort and a lot of artists and private jets flying in and out."

"But you said you're working on your Ph.D?"

"Yes, I'm doing that, too. You see, I'm working my way through graduate school. That's quite common in the United States because college is so expensive there. It's taking me longer than I thought, but actually, my job as a private detective has been interesting and I'm not so sure now that I'll go into academia after all."

They talked for a short while longer. By the time he said goodbye, she still hadn't committed one way or the other about emailing him questions. Howie once again mentioned Claire, that he was off with his girlfriend to see the West Scottish coast. He wanted it to be clear that he had a girlfriend and wasn't some kind of weird predator.

He watched her turn and walk away, still holding the card with his email address. Would she contact him? He didn't know. If he didn't hear from her, he would try again. He would have to think carefully about how he would go about it. But he would keep trying.

She took a dozen steps toward her front door, then stopped and turned to give Howie a final curious look.

He couldn't tell what she was thinking. Was she wondering about this strange person who looked so very much like herself? Did she sense the genetic connection between them? Or was she wondering if she should call the police?

He thought she was going to say something. But instead she turned and used her latch key to open the door and disappear inside.

“Oh, Georgie!” he whispered. “May all the gods in heaven keep you safe until we meet again!”

Coming Soon!

WALKING RAIN

A Howard Moon Deer Mystery

Driving home from Utah, Howard Moon Deer is passing through an empty stretch of New Mexico desert when a young Chinese woman staggers onto the highway, seemingly out of nowhere, and collapses before his onrushing car. Howie screeches to a stop and gets her to a hospital, but it is too late. She is dead on arrival.

Who was this woman and where did she come from? When Jack Wilder and Howie are hired by a non-profit organization, The Committee to Abolish Human Trafficking, they are soon embroiled in the most dangerous case of their career: a huge illegal cannabis growing operation on Indian land, financed by Hong Kong money, worked with trafficked labor.

To complicate matters, Howie is making preparations for the visit of his 17-year-old daughter, Georgina, whose existence he only recently discovered. Georgina grew up in Scotland and it's a good thing she's an adventurous girl because she's about to get a real taste of the Wild West.

Inspired by true events, *WALKING RAIN* is a tale of corruption, international crime, and the challenges of parenthood as Howie finds himself an unexpected father to a teenage girl.

Coming Soon!

ROBERT WESTBROOKS'S
An Almost Perfect Ending

The Torch Singer

Book Two

The Torch Singer is a sweeping historical saga that takes the reader from the horrors of Nazi occupied Poland to the glittery excesses of Hollywood in the 1940's and 50's: the rise and fall of Sonya Saint-Amant, a B-singer who schemes her way to fame and brief glory, breaking all the rules.

Book Two opens with the sultry heroine at the height of her career—a glittering, triumphant appearance at Ciro's, the clubhouse for the stars in 1950s Hollywood where everyone wants to claim her as their friend.

But in 1954, popular music is undergoing a revolution in which all but the biggest stars will be cast aside. With her looks and popularity fading, Sonya believes she has come up with the perfect plan to save her career . . . if only she can maneuver a tricky path through the many dangers that beset her, a vortex of politics, sex, blackmail, and murder.

Coming Soon!

MARDI OAKLEY MEDAWAR'S

Murder at Medicine Lodge

A Tay-Bodal Mystery

Book Three

In 1867, the Kiowa travel to Medicine Lodge, Kansas, along with the Comanche, Arapaho, Apache, and Cheyenne to meet with representatives of the U.S. government and to sign peace treaties. But not all of the Kiowa agree that the peace treaty is a good thing, and tensions between them and the U.S. Army ("The Blue Jackets") are running high. So, when the army bugler disappears and White Bear, chief of the Rattle Band, finds his bugle out on the plains, the army command assumes that White Bear has killed the man to steal it. To make matters worse, the bugler's body is later found—murdered—out on the plains. With the army set to try White Bear for murder, and the Kiowa set to declare war if he is not found innocent, Tay-bodal—a healer amongst the Kiowa—is charged by the Principal Chief to investigate and clear White Bear's name. With very little time before an army tribunal is to be held, Tay-bodal must find out the truth about the bugler—a man he doesn't know—and what might have actually happened out there on the plains.

Coming Soon!

STEPHEN STEELE'S

The Cannaster Factor

THE TROUBLE WITH MIRACLES

A MIRACLE CURE FOR VIRUSES
THAT BIG PHARMA WANTS TO KILL...

Book One, *The Cannastar Factor* is a timely and exciting thriller from beginning to end with compelling characters that take untold risks for what they believe in. An alarming issue of today—how money runs the medical world—is vividly brought to life in this riveting story that unfolds with endless surprises and heartwarming relationships. Brilliantly written, its many twists and turns will keep readers turning pages late into the night.

Cyd and Alex are inadvertently drawn together when a close friend and scientist is murdered after developing an organically grown cure for viral disease. The miracle plant is called Cannastar and it threatens to bankrupt a dangerously angry and ever-greedy pharmaceutical industry. Aided by notorious drug dealers, faithful Native Americans and intrepid Iowa farmers, Cyd and Alex find themselves caught up in an epic adventure that ranges from the Montana wilderness, to the political corruption of Washington D.C., to the jungles of Mexico.

On Sale Now!

Sheriff Lansing Mysteries
Books 1 – 9

For more information
visit: www.SpeakingVolumes.us

Made in the USA
Las Vegas, NV
29 November 2023